Macaws of Death

A Robyn Devara Mystery

by Karen Dudley

Karen Dudley

Macaws of Death
copyright © Karen Dudley 2002

Turnstone Press
607-100 Arthur Street
Artspace Building
Winnipeg, MB
R3B 1H3 Canada
www.TurnstonePress.com

All rights reserved. No part of this book may be reproduced or transmitted in any form or by any means—graphic, electronic or mechanical—without the prior written permission of the publisher. Any request to photocopy any part of this book shall be directed in writing to Cancopy (Canadian Copyright Licensing Agency), Toronto.

Turnstone Press gratefully acknowledges the assistance of the Canada Council for the Arts, the Manitoba Arts Council and the Government of Canada through the Book Publishing Industry Development Program and the Government of Manitoba through the Department of Culture, Heritage and Tourism, Arts Branch for our publishing activities.

Canada

Cover design: Doowah Design
Interior design: Sharon Caseburg
Printed and bound in Canada by Friesens for Turnstone Press.

TRA LA LA SONG, by Mark Barkan and Ritchie Adams © 1968, 1969 (Copyrights Renewed) Unichappell Music Inc. & Anihanbar Music Company All Rights Reserved. Used by Permission WARNER BROS. PUBLICATIONS U.S. INC., Miami, FL. 33014

National Library of Canada Cataloguing in Publication Data

Dudley, Karen

Macaws of death

"A Robyn Devara mystery".

ISBN 0-88801-274-8

I. Title

PS8557.U279M32 2002 C813'.54 C2002-910979-5

PR9199.3.D831M32 2002

For Manuela

Acknowledgements

First and foremost, I must thank Nalini Mohan and Andres Barillas Acosta, who convinced me I needed to go to Costa Rica for this book, and helped me when I decided to take their advice. They were right. Costa Rica is an awe-inspiring country. I think everybody should go at least once—after all, when was the last time you came face-to-face with a two-metre boa constrictor before breakfast? Thanks also to Andres' parents, Rodolfo Barillas Fernadez and Aderith Acosta Quesada, for their warm generosity and for washing all my clothes when I finally emerged from the jungle.

I am very grateful to the Manitoba Arts Council for their support in getting to Costa Rica and in writing the book. Also many thanks to the superb staff at Turnstone Press: Todd Besant, Sharon Caseburg, and Paul Nolin. A big thank you to the Whodunit Mystery Writers Group for their encouragement, to Mark Leggott for the botfly story (and for promising to buy numerous copies of the book now that his name appears in it), to Doug Skolrood who still bears a grudge against wiener dogs, and to Scott Gray, who looked after the cats when I went to Costa Rica and who is not at all sure about getting 'killed' in this one.

And finally, thanks to Michael, my spider-hating husband, who accompanied me to Costa Rica. He hiked through boot-devouring mud, tapped cockroaches out of his shoes, hid our soap from the climbing rats, and removed large spiders from our cabin. A brave, supportive soul.

Macaws of Death

The forest is a vast laboratory in which new species are produced, tested, and eliminated if found defective…

Alexander Skutch
A Naturalist in Costa Rica

Chapter 1

My troubles started when he *walked into my office. He was a dark brunette, hair more black than brown, and he came in on a pair of legs that had never heard of quitting time. His peepers were green, big, and innocent-like. The kind of eyes that said he had nothing to hide. I wasn't listening to them. We all have a few skeletons we like to keep stashed behind the hangers. I know a lot about skeletons. My name's Devara. Robyn Devara. I'm a professional bird biologist.*

It's a tough job, but then I'm a tough sort of dame. That's why they pay me the big greenbacks—and I'm not talking about parrots. So when the tall brunette stepped through my door, I knew right away he wasn't here to give me a Swedish massage. More's the pity.

It wasn't the first time he'd sauntered through my door, and it probably wouldn't be the last. His excuses were as thin as a nictitating membrane, but I couldn't afford to ignore him. I never knew when he might sing. The last time he'd made like a canary, it had ruffled more than a few primaries over at headquarters.

From the look of him now, he wasn't fixing on chirping. He had a case for me. And I had a hunch it wouldn't be easy to solve. They never were. . . .

"Earth to Robyn. Come in, Robyn." Kelt waved his hand in front of my face.

I blinked and lowered my book. "Uh . . . what?"

He leaned against my desk and cocked his head to see what I was reading. "*The Long Goodbye*? Hmm. You've been raiding Arif's library again."

"Busted." I grinned at him. "What's up?"

"Phone call for you on line two. I know you're on lunch, but it's somebody from Environment Canada."

"The feds? What do those guys want?" I slipped my bookmark between the pages.

Kelt pushed off the desk and shrugged. "I dunno. Do I look like a leggy secretary? I'm just the mammals biologist."

"Too bad. You'd look pretty cute in one of those skin-tight skirts."

"In your dreams," Kelt smirked as he sashayed to the door.

I ogled his caboose and laughed at him—a little ruefully. As a matter of fact, he did figure rather prominently in my dreams. Not, however, in anything so concealing as a skin-tight skirt.

I heaved a sigh and picked up the phone. "Robyn Devara speaking."

"Hi there, I'm calling from Environment Canada. The name's Ross Anderson. I'm an enforcement officer for CITES."

I perked up at his words. The simple acronym stood for the Convention on International Trade in Endangered Species of Wild Fauna and Flora—quite a mouthful. But the organization had been instrumental in moderating trade in threatened species since the early 1970s. As a conservation biologist, I admired it.

"Hey, Ross," I greeted him. "What can I do for you?"

Ross was, apparently, not one to beat around shrubbery. He came right to the point. "Funny you should put it like that," he said. "I *do* have something you can do for me—at least I hope you can."

"Sure, I'll give it a shot."

"I need your expertise."

"You need a *birder*?" I picked up a pen and started rolling it between my fingers.

"Yeah. You see, a few weeks ago, three suitcases arrived at the Calgary airport. Nobody claimed them, so Customs stepped in. To make a long story short, somebody smelled something bad and opened up the suitcases. That's when I got called in."

"What was in them?"

"Dead birds," Ross answered in the sort of weary tone that said he'd seen this kind of thing all too often. "Scarlet macaws, a couple of great green macaws, a red-lored parrot, a bunch of different parakeets. . . ."

I stopped fiddling with the pen. "The parrot family," I said.

"In a nutshell," Ross agreed. "Bird smuggling—especially parrot smuggling—is a huge problem for us."

"Yeah, I've heard. So, how can I help?"

"With identification."

"ID? Aren't you guys trained in that?"

"And how," he said in a heartfelt tone. "But I tell you, I've got one bird, I can't figure him at all. He's got to be endangered. I've never seen one that looked quite like him before. I tried Fish and Wildlife but they were stumped too. Then I rang up Ella Dolynchuk from the National Museum."

"I was just about to suggest her. She knows more about parrots than anybody I've ever met."

"So I hear. Trouble is, she can't make an ID based on a description. And she's heading out of the country for the next eight months. Some kind of sabbatical thing."

"She recommended me?"

"Yup, said you did your master's thesis on parrots."

"That's right. But I was sequencing macaws, not really describing them—" I paused. "Look, Ross, don't get me wrong. I'm more than happy to have a look at your mystery bird. I just don't want you to get your hopes up. It's quite possible I won't be able to identify it for you."

"I understand, but if you could come down and give it a whirl, I'd be grateful. It beats sending him down to the Forensics lab in Oregon for sequencing—though I might be forced to do that in the end."

I pulled a scrap of paper toward me and picked up the pen again. "Okay, what's your address?"

Ross Anderson was a tall, gangly character with watery blue eyes and the sort of complexion that needed to get out into the sun a little more often.

"It's not a pretty sight," he warned me as we walked down the hall to the freezers. "They were stuffed in PVC pipe. Fourteen birds in one suitcase, eleven in each of the others. They were probably sedated to keep them quiet. Sometimes, you know, they get tequila forced down their throats, other times their eyes are pierced so they won't see the daylight and start singing."

I curled my lip and made a sound of disgust. Ross nodded his agreement.

"So what went wrong?" I asked.

Ross shrugged, his hard expression at odds with the easy gesture. "You mean why did they die?"

"Yeah."

"Believe me, it's not unusual. It's pretty standard to have a mortality rate of nine out of ten."

I sucked in a breath. "That's high."

"I know."

We stopped in front of a gray metal door that was badly in need of a paint job. Ross flipped through a set of keys, found the one he wanted, and jiggled it in the lock. The door opened with a rasping screech.

Thankfully, the confiscated birds had been removed from their PVC coffins and were now stored in a freezer to preserve them. At the very least, it helped keep the smell down. Ross hefted a long, brown cardboard box out of the freezer and slid it onto a stainless steel table in the center of the room.

"Here they are," he said. And he pulled open the flaps.

Even in such an ignominious death, the birds had lost none of their glorious color. Flaming scarlet, rich emerald, a pulsing yellow—they brought a vibrant splash of the tropics into the cold, concrete room.

"Shit," I swore softly as Ross removed the sad bodies and laid them out on the table.

"Here's the one I can't figure out," he said, reaching into the box again. "See what you think."

The bird he placed in front of me was, in a word, spectacular—or at least, it had been when it was alive. It was a macaw, there was no question about that. It must have been close to forty inches long, and it had the large beak and distinct body shape that differentiated macaws from the smaller parrots. But the colors! Snowy white breast, brilliant scarlet chinstrap, and a deep, royal purple back. No macaw I'd ever seen had looked like this. I lifted one of the wings carefully and spread it out. A band of deep yellow decorated the upper wing coverts, accenting the rich purple.

"This is . . . ," I looked up at Ross. He was watching me intently. "This is *astonishing*! I've never seen a macaw this color before. Unless . . . ," I trailed off and examined the bird more closely. That purple and white coloration . . . those gold bands . . . the chinstrap. . . .

"*Son of a bitch!*" I breathed.

Ross wasn't listening. He'd sighed, disappointed. "That's too bad. I was really hoping you could help—"

"No, no. You don't understand!" I interrupted him, rude with excitement. "I've never seen a macaw this color because it's never been described before. At least," I waved my hand around, "at least, not formally. If I'm right, then," I paused and took a deep breath, "then this . . . *this is a completely new species.*"

Chapter 2

"A new species of macaw?" Ben asked, his eyebrows raised skeptically. "Are you sure?"

"Positive," I told him. "I lived, studied, and breathed macaws while I was doing my thesis. The National Museum in Ottawa has the best collection of tropical birds in the country—dead ones, that is. Study skins and mounts. I camped out in their back storeroom for a year."

It wasn't much of an exaggeration. In those last few months, I'd kept a sleeping bag tucked behind a storage cabinet for those all too frequent times when caffeine failed. In fact, if I tallied up my Friday nights, I'd probably discover that more of them had been spent with dead birds than with live men (which was a pretty good reason not to bother counting).

I sipped absently at my coffee, remembering the long nights, the flickering fluorescent lights, and the pervasive smell of mothballs and formaldehyde that had, more often than not, left me smelling like a moldering blanket. Probably went a long way to explaining my uneventful Friday nights.

"I can't believe you're drinking that crap," Ben remarked, indicating my cup and wrinkling his nose in disgust. "It's been sitting there all afternoon."

I looked down at the oily sludge, seeing—and tasting—it only now. "Good point." I pushed it aside.

"A beer would go down much better," he said with admirable nonchalance.

I pursed my lips in mock speculation. "That it would," I agreed.

"Kelt and Ti-Marc are holding a table."

"I see."

"We thought you might want to tell us about what CITES was after."

"Uh huh. And Kaye is . . . ?"

"Out with her niece. Some chick flick at the Plaza."

"Ah," I said, enlightened, then shrugged. "They're your arteries."

Ben rubbed his hands together. "If we hurry, the wings will still be on special. Two for one, you know."

I knew.

I started shoving things in my backpack. "This is me hurrying," I shooed him out of my office. "I'll be ready by the time you turn off the lights."

A couple of months ago, Ben's doctor had instructed him to get more exercise, cut down on coffee, and try not to let the assholes of the world get to him. In addition, she'd inflicted a strict low-fat diet upon him and Ben, perhaps unwisely, told his wife. Woodrow Consultants hadn't been the same since.

Kaye, who is also Ben's business partner, is a pretty shrewd character. So she was always quick to twig whenever Ben tumbled from the wagon, seduced by spicy chicken wings and frothy beer. Ben responded to her disapproval with loudly proclaimed assurances that beer was the healthiest of beverages, and that the cayenne in the barbeque sauce was good for his thickened arteries. And besides, the token bit of celery that accompanied the wings *surely* added enough fiber to counteract the effects of all the fat.

He never convinced anybody—least of all Kaye—but as she told him with a certain amount of acerbity, if he wanted to stuff himself with saturated fats and die young of a heart attack, there wasn't anything she or anybody else could do about it. She just thanked the good Lord that we lived in Canada where health care was free, so at least he wouldn't run up huge hospital bills doing it and she could use the life insurance money to travel around the world, dress in revealing outfits, and have torrid affairs with men much younger than herself.

Ben always ate his celery.

True to my word, I swung out of the office just as the lights flickered off, and Ben and I hopped the Calgary C-Train downtown to Earl's in Banker's Hall. Kelt and Ti-Marc, Woodrow's receptionist, were well into the fun by the time we joined them. Crunching bones, tearing off crispy skin, and licking sticky barbeque sauce off their fingers with loud smacking noises. The whole process was punctuated by thirsty gulping sounds and the occasional ill-concealed burp. Feeding time on the savanna. Ben and I slid into the booth and dug in.

"So, 'ow was your meeting?" Ti-Marc inquired as he dipped his fingers into a bowl of lemon water and wiped them fastidiously on his napkin.

While I waited for my beer to arrive, I told them about the macaw.

"But how do you know it's a *new* macaw?" Kelt asked when I'd finished. "Maybe the museum didn't have that particular species in their collection."

I was already shaking my head before he finished his sentence. "I know it's new because when I wasn't poking and prodding study skins, I was immersing myself in the literature—even the obscure stuff. That's why I recognized the bird and that's how I knew where it came from."

"Costa Rica."

"Yeah. You see, about, oh, ten or fifteen years ago, there was an American guy—Scott Gray—who set up a research station down in Costa Rica. The Danta Biological Field Station—"

"Danta. Isn't that Spanish for tapir?"

"It is," I nodded. "Gray was an expert on tapirs. Studied them for twenty years. That's why he set up the station. I don't think Danta was ever much more than a couple of tin-roofed shacks even when it was operational. It was located down in the Corcovado."

"Corcovado. That is one of the national parks, I think," Ti-Marc said, gathering up all the uneaten celery and offering it thoughtfully to Ben. "I 'ave a friend who went down there last year."

"That's right," I confirmed. "Down in the southwest corner. It's pretty remote. Hard to get to and apparently even harder to hike through, but Gray was determined to study the tapir colonies there. He had a bit of financial backing, so he chopped his way in and set up the station."

With a resigned grimace, Ben started on the pile of celery sticks. "So what happened?" he demanded. "You said the place isn't operating any more. He get his funding pulled?"

I shook my head. "No. There was some kind of accident—I can't remember what exactly, but Gray was killed. Without his influence and energies, the station was abandoned. But there *is* a point to this whole story.

You see, even though Gray was a tapir man, he still kept pretty good field notes on all the other stuff he saw. And he ended up publishing some of it for his local natural history club. I'm not sure why, but the National Museum had copies of these in their archives." I shrugged. "They must have been on the mailing list or something."

"In the good old days when museums and libraries had the money to subscribe to everything," Ben rumbled around his celery.

"Probably," I nodded and continued quickly before Ben could start beating his chest about periodicals funding. "Anyhow, Gray reported seeing a macaw like the one Ross has in his freezer. The purple back, the white front, the scarlet chinstrap—everything. Problem was, he was the only one who ever saw the bird—and even he admitted in his paper that he wasn't much of a bird guy."

"But there must have been other people at the field station," Kelt said.

"Of course. A couple of grad students and probably a few locals, but nobody else clocked the bird. It was thought that the colors probably were not as bright as Gray had described and the bird was written off as some sort of semi-albino blue and gold macaw."

"But you don't agree?"

"No way. That bird I saw today was practically glowing, the colors were so intense. If this was one of Gray's birds—and it certainly looks that way—then it is *not* a semi-albino anything."

Ben crunched his way down another celery stick. "Do they know where the bird was shipped from?"

"Well, the suitcases had tags from San Diego, but apparently, that doesn't mean much."

"The birds are laundered?"

"Yeah," I nodded. "Usually through Mexico, then across the US border. From there, they're shipped around the US, up to Canada, even over to Australia. I'm not sure how the Fish and Wildlife guys tracked this batch, but Ross tells me they think these suitcases started their travels in Costa Rica."

"Which strengthens your hypothesis."

I nodded again and drained my glass. "Ross was pretty interested in what I had to say. With Ella Dolynchuk out of the country, I guess I'm the next best thing to a macaw expert. Our friends at Environment Canada may not be finished with me just yet."

How was I to know this offhand comment would turn out to be right up there with "Houston, we have a problem"? Before we could arrange the next secret beer and wings night, I found myself poked with needles, stuffed with anti-malaria pills, and booked on a plane to San José.

CITES had seconded me.

CHAPTER 3

Every biologist knows extinction can be a natural feature of life. And every schoolchild knows that, in modern times, it often isn't. Over-exploitation, habitat loss, pesticides, and pollution—the list of causes is depressingly familiar. But in the past few years a new kid has muscled into the neighborhood. International trade.

Improvements in transport facilities mean that we can now ship animals and plants to and from anywhere in the world. Not a good thing if you happen to be an endangered species—especially when there are people who will fork out large sums of money to wear you on their backs just *because* you're endangered. Or to keep you imprisoned in a little cage in their home so they can show you off to all their friends. "Look at our new addition. Isn't it beautiful? And very rare, it cost us *quite* a fortune!"

Never mind that the "new addition" is severely endangered. Or that the loss of this one individual might send the whole population spiraling toward extinction.

In 1973, a worldwide system of controls was established on the international trade in endangered species. CITES's objective is not to stop all wildlife trade, but rather to ensure human needs and wildlife conservation objectives are in harmony. Problem is, some people have a pretty broad definition of "need", and when it comes to harmony . . . well, let's just say there are a lot of people singing a lot of different tunes.

These days the illegal wildlife trade is worth an estimated three to five *billion* dollars a year. And that's a conservative estimate. With profit margins comparable to the drug trade, many of the same criminal organizations that deal in drugs and arms are now also involved in wildlife trafficking. The "goods" are transported along the same routes as the drugs and guns, sometimes even in the same shipment. In 1993 hundreds of boa constrictors were seized at the Miami International Airport. Most of them were dead—probably from the eighty pounds of cocaine that had been forced up their cloacae.

Wildlife protection officials caught that shipment, but it makes you wonder how many others go undetected. With the rise of the Internet, wealthy collectors now post want ads on the Web. Or use chat rooms to talk with traffickers. And if you happen to be caught with a backpack full of boa constrictors or a padded vest filled with rare bird eggs? No big deal. All too often, the penalties are about as harsh as a smack on the bum. In the face of all this, CITES seems a poor solution. But it's a hell of a lot better than nothing.

In order for a species to be protected under the convention, a certain amount of scientific information is required. That's where people like me come in. Technically, CITES has its own experts in each country, but establishing the biological parameters of a species is no mean feat. A job like that is best carried out by a team of scientists from several countries and institutions. That way costs are shared and the combined expertise makes for more compelling data.

Along with the CITES scientific authorities in both Costa Rica and Canada, the World Wildlife Fund had taken an interest in the macaw expedition and, more importantly, they were willing to kick in some cash. I had to yank a few strings, meet with countless federal, CITES, and WWF officials, and take an unpaid leave of absence in order to be included on the mystery macaw team. It seemed a small price to pay.

A new species of macaw.

I got a thrill every time I thought about it, which was pretty much every waking minute (and quite a few of the non-waking ones). In an age known more for the disappearance of species, finding an unknown one was sort of like Indiana Jones finding the Lost Ark, except with biology instead of archeology. And (hopefully) no Nazis.

The chocolate sprinkles on the icing were that I'd never been to a tropical rainforest before. And now I wasn't heading to just any tropical land, but to *Costa Rica*, a country with a staggering number of national parks and reserves. A country so peaceful there was no standing army, which (apart from boding well for a lack of Nazis) was practically unheard of in that part of the world. But, above all, Costa Rica, with its incredible diversity of life and its lush, rain-drenched jungles, was a biologist's wet dream. My only regret was that Kelt was not coming along.

Kelt Roberson and I were something more than co-workers, I just wasn't sure what that something was. Friends? Definitely. More than friends? The jury was still waffling. Sometimes I suspected the jury had given the whole thing up as a bad job and gone home. Between him being in the field, then me being in the field, then him in the field again, then him going home to British

Columbia for Christmas, we'd barely been in the same city for more than a few weeks at a time.

Maybe some women wouldn't let a little thing like distance bother them. Maybe some women were so sexy they could vamp a guy from across provincial boundaries. Maybe I'd been reading too many hard-boiled detective novels. But when the New Year brought Kelt back to Calgary and the icy season meant no fieldwork for a while, I'd swayed into his office doing my best Velda impersonation and, with calculated craftiness, asked him to give me cooking lessons.

Oh, I could use a quick tip or two about the kitchen, no doubt about that. I was a bit of a disaster when it came to the culinary arts. But I have to admit I'd been hoping to heat up more than just food—as long as I didn't take the cooking analogy any further or (worse!) put it in terms of country music, in which case Kelt would be facing the rather unpleasant fate of being burned to a crisp and getting chipped off the bottom of my saucepan o' love (this is why I hate country music).

It now appeared, however, that "cooking lessons" would have to wait until I was back. Figures. I hadn't had sex since *Star Trek: Deep Space Nine* had gone off the air, and I was starting to get a little cranky about the whole thing. *Star Trek* I could catch in reruns—heck, I could even rent them from my local video store. Sexual ecstasy is not so easily recalled.

At least Kelt invited me over for dinner the night before I left.

"Did you know that Costa Rica has over eight hundred and fifty species of birds?" Field book in hand, I slouched against his door frame and greeted him with a smile.

Kelt grinned and motioned me inside. "And a hundred

and thirty-five species of snakes, seventeen of which are venomous."

"I'm trying not to think about those guys," I said, making a face.

"I know what you mean. When I went to Belize a few years back, I poked a stick through every piece of undergrowth before I'd walk through it."

I shrugged out of my coat, tossed it over to Kelt, and bent down to take my boots off. "And did you ever see any snakes?"

"Oh, yes. Quite a few, including a bushmaster—the back end of it, fortunately. But it's the ones you *don't* see that keep you awake at night. It's so dark in the rainforest; there might be a snake on the fern right beside you, or coiled under your foot, or even hanging down from a tree like a vine, and you'd never—"

"You know, you could stop talking about this anytime."

Kelt gave me a lopsided smile. "Don't worry," he said, steering me into the kitchen. "After a few days, you won't think about them so much. You *do* get acclimatized."

"But the snakes will still be there."

"Well, yes."

"Hmm."

"You'll be fine," he assured me.

"What about the other stuff, then? I don't know what I ever did to him, but my brother just gave me a book on tropical spiders and scorpions and—"

"Aaah," Kelt waved them off. "Don't worry about *those*."

Easy for him to say.

He laughed at my skeptical look. "Did you even *read* the book?" he asked.

"No time. I just looked at the pictures. Some of those suckers are huge—"

"And none of them are poisonous."

"—and they're . . . none?"

"Not the Costa Rican ones. At least," he amended, "they're not *deadly*. If you get stung or bitten, it might swell up a bit, you'll probably run a fever, but you won't be heading to the big biology lab in the sky."

"Hmm," I said again.

"God, I wish I was going with you," Kelt sighed as he poured the wine.

"Even with all the creepy crawlies?"

He grinned. "Even with them. Do you have any idea how many *bats* there are in Costa Rica?"

I rolled my eyes and folded myself into one of the kitchen chairs. I should have known.

"No, but I'm sure you'll tell me."

"Over a hundred!" His green eyes went wide at the thought.

"No!"

"Oh, yes!"

Kelt had done his master's thesis on bats.

"There are insectivores, carnivores, a couple of blood feeders. And, of course, the frugivores and nectarivores."

"Oh, of course."

"Costa Rica has four species in the genus Pteronotus. *Four!* All of them with amazing echolocation abilities. Do you know they actually combine constant-frequency and frequency-modulated pulses and. . . ."

Now, I was the first to admit that bats were appealing—even fascinating—creatures, but Bat Boy here was perfectly capable of lecturing me about them all night. Quite apart from wanting to be fed, I'd envisioned other, more interesting activities for the evening.

". . . the disk-winged bat even roosts in rolled-up

plantain leaves. And every few days as the leaves unfurl, the bats have to find another roost. . . ."

I made the appropriate noises.

". . . then there are the tent bats. Little, white, furry guys. They scrape their claws along the spine of heliconia leaves so the sides of the leaf collapse and form a tent." He folded his hands together in an inverted 'v' to demonstrate. "Then they spend the whole day huddled up here in the peak of the tent."

"Really?" I asked, intrigued in spite of myself. "Where do those guys live?"

"Osa Peninsula."

"Same area I'm headed to."

Kelt's face fell. "Yeah."

"I'll take some pictures for you," I offered, relenting in the face of his disappointment. "Unroll a few banana leaves. Peek under a couple of leaf tents. Maybe rustle up a few bats."

He lifted one shoulder in a shrug and managed a grin. "Nah. Better not. Tent bats usually have several roosting leaves in one area. Problem is, if the bats aren't under the leaves, you can pretty much bet the wasps will be—and *they're* aggressive bastards."

"I see."

"But if you happen to *stumble* across a colony of bats. . . ."

"I'll fire off a whole roll of film just for you."

"Thanks."

He took some garlicky-smelling breadsticks out of the oven and arranged them in a basket. "I *am* happy for you," he said, trying not to sound too glum. "Envious, but happy. You've never been down to Central America, have you?"

"I've never been *anywhere* tropical," I told him. "Living by yourself and paying off student loans is not exactly conducive to saving for a holiday. The closest I've ever come to a tropical vacation is sitting in a sunbeam in my living room with a tape of ocean sounds on the stereo and a can of tuna under my nose."

"A can of tuna?"

"I was going for the full sensory experience, but Guido the cat made short work of the tuna, so it didn't last long."

Kelt laughed, familiar with my pet and his fish fixation.

"The rainforest is amazing," he told me with a faraway look, "even more than you'd think. Everything is so much . . . more."

"More."

He threw back his arms. "More of *everything*. Plants upon plants upon still more plants. Swarms of insects. All kinds of frogs and lizards. It's darker than you'd think, but even so, the colors are brighter and more vibrant than up here. The humidity is heavier, and sound is different too. You know, you can hear stuff way before you even catch a glimpse of it and—" Kelt broke off. "Hey, speaking of sound, I've got something for you." He ducked into the living room and came back bouncing a cassette tape on his hand.

"Here." He handed it to me. "When you get tired of listening to howler monkeys and macaws, you can slap this in your Walkman."

"You made a tape for me?" Touched, I turned the cassette over to read the sleeve. "Rachmaninoff's *Etudes for Two Pianos*. I don't think I've heard this before."

"It's a pretty rare recording," Kelt said. "I found it at the library when they were clearing out their LPs. It's very beautiful, very relaxing. Quite spiritual. I think you'll love it."

"That's really nice of you," I told him, beaming with pleasure. "Thanks, Kelt."

He smiled back for a moment—a moment which lengthened and stretched outside the space-time continuum. Our eyes had locked together. I don't know what tricks mine were up to, but his seemed to be darkening, the sea-green irises giving way to velvet black pupils. Very sexy. A warm tingling began in my stomach and made a beeline for my groin. I was beyond thought. Beyond breath. My saucepan o' love was ready and waiting on the burner.

Unfortunately, it wasn't the only thing on the stove.

Bzzzzzzzzzzz

I jumped as the oven timer shattered the silence. Kelt spun around to slap it off. Space and time coughed, then fired up again. By the time Kelt turned back, the moment was gone.

Damn. Damn, damn, damn, damn, damn, damn, damn.

"Well . . . the, uh," he faltered, "the other downside to, uh, Central America—besides the snakes—is the music."

Music! Who gave a rat's ass about *music* at a time like this? Certainly not me. But I played along, hoping for another 'moment'. "Um . . . what's . . . wrong with the music?" I managed to ask.

"Not a thing. As long as you like techno and disco."

I wrinkled my nose. "Not my favorite."

"I know. So now you have something else to listen to." He turned abruptly and started putting the finishing touches on dinner.

I'm normally in favor of men feeding me, but at this

point, I couldn't have cared less about dinner. Still, the food *was* delicious. Grilled tomatoes and eggplant on fettuccine with a whole bunch of other stuff mixed in. Tasty. But now there was a definite awkwardness to the evening and, even though I kept crossing my fingers, there were no more spikes on the emotional intense-o-meter.

Instead, conversation revolved around rainforests and field research and moved on to music and hard-boiled detective novels. But our silences were uneasy, and once, when I just happened to brush against him, Kelt flinched and jerked his arm away.

I'd had a half-formed plan even before I arrived, to confront the situation head-on (or, more accurately, lips-on), but the mixed signals he was giving off were confusing me. Every time I opened my mouth to bring up the subject, he started in about something else. I can take a hint as well as the next guy. And maybe it wasn't such a great idea to fire up something like this on the eve of a six-month field season.

So in the end, my last night in Calgary proved a bit of a write-off. Too many expectations, perhaps. When Kelt's sister phoned from BC, asking his advice about universities, I took it as a sign and said my goodbyes. Kelt offered to walk me home, but I told him to stay and talk to his sister. I thanked him for dinner and the tape of Rachmaninoff and for looking after my cat while I was away. Then I slipped out into the wintry night onto the skating rinks that Calgarians laughingly call sidewalks.

Kelt was a real puzzle, I mused as I shuffled and slid my way home. I just couldn't figure the guy out. But one thing seemed clear, he certainly wasn't eager to live up to his name. A kelt is, according to those in the know, a salmon that has spawned.

CHAPTER 4

The flight to Dallas was full. Not a huge problem—except, of course, for the unhappy fact that I'd been seated beside a perfume bunny. Talk about adding your basic insult to injury.

The Injury, of course, had everything to do with Kelt and his mixed signals. Mr. Ambivalent had me tied up in a neat little emotional tangle. I'd be the first to admit I wasn't catch of the year, but I was hardly a month-old calamari, either. Until that morning, I hadn't fully realized how much his indecision rankled. Maybe getting away for a while was for the best.

The only real problem on that front involved my digestive system, which had finally figured out that going to Central America meant getting on a plane—and it wasn't too damn happy about it. All I could do was hope the Dramamine would live up to its ad copy. And now, in the midst of all this turmoil, there was the Insult.

"I'm going to Costa Rica," she announced with an excited wiggle as soon as I settled in. Her blue eyes were heavily made up, and she had one of those high-pitched little-girl voices that makes you want to smack the owner into some semblance of adulthood. Her eau de whatever was an almost visible miasma, and, to top things off, her poor tank top was being tortured by the mammalian version of the rack. I had a hunch she wasn't heading south to go birdwatching.

I blinked, my eyes watering from the noxious fumes, and made a quick bet with myself. "So am I," I told her.

She squealed in delight.

Okay, so it wasn't much of a bet.

"Then you're going on the Bust Out too!" She wriggled again. "Or. . . ." A puzzled frown wrinkled her foundation as she took in my hiking boots and rumpled cargo pants.

"'Fraid not," I told her. "I'm heading down there for work."

This, apparently, was too boring to merit a response so my new very best friend—Brandi with an 'i'—began enthusing about the Bust Out Adventure upon which she was about to embark. I tried to listen politely, but I remembered the Bust Out ads from when I'd been a campus regular. Sun, booze, sex. Woohoo.

I don't like to think of myself as overly judgmental, but really, Brandi-with-an-i was just the sort to go on a Bust Out vacation. Before we'd even left Alberta air space, I'd heard about her ex-boyfriend, how excited she was about going to Costa Rica, how she'd gone out drinking and dancing the night before with Judi and Kelli and Sherri (all, presumably, with i's) and had *so* much fun, and how she was just squeaking through her arts degree and she shouldn't really be going away right now with all the papers she had due but she really needed a break because of the way Kevin (the ex) had dumped her, y'know?

I tried burying myself in my book, but Brandi ignored

the broad hint and kept chattering about all the Fun Things she was going to do on her Adventure and how she hoped the music down there would be half-decent so she could go out dancing, and what did I think about waterproof mascara. I told her I couldn't recall ever having thought about it.

Air rage was rapidly becoming understandable.

Halfway through the flight, I was ready to reach for the barf bag. The perfume cloud was intolerable. What kind of problems would you have to have to make this sort of aromatherapy necessary? I clutched my book like a lifeline and leaned into the aisle. Brandi-with-an-i driveled on.

The sound of quiet laughter floated past my seat. At least somebody was enjoying this flight. I turned and craned my neck to get a glimpse of them. It was a small boy, maybe four or five years old, sitting two rows behind me on the other side of the plane. He'd been whining and fussing a while ago (I could relate) and his mother had looked stressed (I related to that too). But now the boy was chuckling. And when I saw why, I grinned too.

The man sitting next to him had undertaken to cheer the tyke up, despite the fact that he was clearly unrelated to the boy. A few crayons, a little ingenuity, and the man had put together a couple of friendly-looking barf bag puppets.

The child was delighted. His new friends were dressed in snappy outfits with big smiles and squiggly hair. The man was putting on some sort of show with them but I was too far away to hear what he was saying. The boy's eyes shone and, to the relief of the passengers around him, he quieted down to play with his barf bag buddies.

I had the unkind thought that Brandi-with-an-i

wouldn't need crayons to make her own puppet. All she'd have to do was press the bag against her makeup. As she chattered on, I wondered if I could interest her in this activity. I could even help her press.

To my immense relief, the Tim Hortons donut and coffee that I'd sacrificed to the travel gods earlier that morning had been accepted—even appreciated. When we changed planes in Dallas, I got bumped up to first class. Brandi-with-an-i did not. Safely ensconced some fifteen rows behind me, she sat eagerly waiting to bore the ass off somebody else. As for my new travel companion . . . I was now seated beside Mr. Barf Bag. And he was, in a word, a hottie.

"Andres Barillas Acosta." He introduced himself with what was quite obviously the Smile.

When the gods were giving out looks, this fellow had not only been head of the line, he'd clearly gone through twice. His latte-colored skin was complemented by the sensuous lips and smoldering eyes generally found in combination with galloping stallions on the covers of racy romance novels. The Smile was enough to knock my hiking boots askew.

"Robyn Devara," I reciprocated. A bit brusque. And why not? The guy probably had women flinging themselves on his Guccis all the time.

"Robyn Devara?" He did a double take, really looking at me this time. "You are kidding me?"

"And why would I do that?"

"Robyn Devara, from Woodland Consultants?"

I frowned. "It's Woodrow, and how—"

"We're going to be working together!" he exclaimed happily. "I am Andres Barillas Acosta from the Museo Nacional de Costa Rica. I am supposed to meet you in San José tomorrow. What are you doing on this flight?"

"Andres Barillas . . . ?" I echoed.

He flashed the Smile at me again. "Acosta, yes. From TRC."

TRC. The Tropical Research Consortium. This guy was on my field team?

"I . . . uh." I cleared my throat. "I was booked on this flight. I thought you guys knew that. I e-mailed my itinerary."

"Ah! I am afraid that's Costa Rica for you," he said. "We are not great at schedules. I was told you were arriving tomorrow." He shook his head with an apologetic sigh, then brightened. "But, you see, everything worked out okay. You will find it always does somehow." He reached out and patted my hand. His touch was electrifying.

This guy was on my field team?

"This is great!" he said. "We can start getting acquainted right away."

I gave myself a mental shake and smiled back at him. "You going to make me a barf bag puppet too?"

He threw back his head and roared with laughter. A truly breathtaking sight. Whew! With Andres on the team, this job promised to be even more interesting than I'd anticipated—and I'd anticipated quite a bit.

"Only if you cry," he replied, his eyes sparkling.

We were going to get along just fine.

The three-hour flight passed much more quickly than I'd had any right to expect. Like Brandi-with-an-i, Andres was full of stories. But where she talked about Alabama Slammers and Coppertone, he spoke of harlequin frogs and resplendent quetzals. And while her giggling had me verging on insanity, I could've listened to that warm chuckle of his all afternoon.

"We'll be staying for one—well, now two—nights, I guess, at a little house on the edge of San José," he was telling me now. "I know very well the guy who lives there. Rodolfo has been hosting TRC biologists for many years now. He has even built a storage shed and bought some freezers so we have a place to put our stuff. And," Andres gave me a broad grin,"his wife is a very good cook."

"Better and better." I smiled back. "So, how many of us are there? I never got a complete list of the team—another one of your schedule-type slip-ups, no doubt."

"Yes, that is very likely," Andres agreed, then drew his brows together in thought. "We're all coming in at different times, so it's been a little bit confusing to organize everybody. For now there is just you and me and Ernesto. We'll pick up Viviana on our way to the airport."

"The airport?" I was unpleasantly surprised. "I thought we were driving down."

He shook his head. "Oh no, it is much better this way. Driving can take a long time—especially where we are going. Many times, the roadbed gets washed right away because of mudslides. It can be months before they are fixed. Besides, we will not need a vehicle in Corcovado." He shrugged and flashed a lopsided smile. "No roads."

"Ah. So why go to the expense of hiring a Landrover?"

"Yes, exactly. Also, the guy who flies the plane is my niece's husband's brother, so he is giving us a good deal. It will be a little bit less expensive to fly."

"Reason enough," I agreed, though my stomach churned at the thought.

Saving money is a big part of field biology. Scientific research doesn't come cheap—and the competition for those dollars is pretty stiff. Like everybody else in the world, funding agencies like to get the most bang for their buck. They look for multidisciplinary projects, the sexy topics. Stuff like 'are frogs disappearing because of an increase in UV radiation?' You get a project like that going, you'll need biologists, an endocrinologist, a molecular geneticist, and the odd meteorologist or two. Multi-disciplines.

The single-focus projects, like collecting information about a species' basic biology, have to fight a little harder for funding. Our macaw expedition was one of the fortunate few to get money, probably because the search for a 'new' species goes a long way to boosting the sexiness quotient. The funding was generous, as such things go. But generous is a relative term. Saving a few bucks on travel could mean an extra week or two in the field. My stomach might not like it much, but my brain understood it.

"Adelio will be flying us right to Sirena," Andres was saying.

"Sirena. That's where the ranger station is, isn't it?"

"Yes. We'll get there early and take a boat up the Rio Sirena to the start of the trail. It is a few hours to hike to Danta from there. Lizabeth came out to buy more supplies, but she will be waiting at Sirena to go back with us. Oscar and Marco are at the research station. Marco will come to meet us with the boat."

"Back up a sec." I held up my hand. "I know Viviana through the U of Costa Rica. But who are the others?"

"Oscar is our . . . handyman, I think you would say. Mostly he will work on the trails and buildings. He is also in charge of cooking, but we'll all have to take our turns in the kitchen. Marco and Ernesto will be helping us to find the macaw—they are very knowledgeable about the Corcovado. Marco, especially, is an excellent guide. He and Oscar have been down there for many weeks now, trying to get Danta fixed up."

"Fixed up? I didn't think anything was left of it."

"There was not much," Andres confirmed. "Not after so long in the rainforest. Oscar was recruiting some of the Golfito men to help, but there were troubles."

I gave him a sharp look. "Troubles?"

"Nothing for worrying about," he hastened to add. "Just an accident with one of the men. He was not paying attention and he got hurt. Fortunately, Oscar has two cousins who came to replace them. It should work out. They have built one new sleeping cabin—that makes four we have now. There is a big, new dining hall—the old one was rotted to nothing—and an old lab that is not so good. Ernesto and Marco will sleep in the lab until Oscar's cousins can build us more cabins."

I pursed my lips. "Seems like a lot of work for an exploratory project," I said. "Last I heard, we were going to be tenting it."

"We are being optimistic," Andres told me. "If we find this macaw, then we're looking at many years of population surveys and monitoring. I don't know about you, but I would not want to live in a tent for years."

"Point taken," I agreed, recalling a field season during which I'd spent four months living out of a tent. It had been fun for three of them.

"Besides," he continued, "it's not just the macaw. TRC has decided to re-open the station. The Corcovado has the last remaining tracts of lowland wet tropical forest in Central America. There are Baird's tapirs down there and *el tigre*—jaguars. They are very rare, you know. This macaw you found is probably not the only undiscovered species on the Osa Peninsula."

"An ideal spot for a biological research station, then."

Andres beamed at me. "That is exactly what I think. Did you know that we may have some students too?"

"To help with the project?"

Andres shook his head. "No, no. They are wanting to study the rainforest with an American professor, to learn about tropical ecology. I'm not certain if they are coming, but I'll know for sure tomorrow."

"The more the merrier, as they say. But getting back to our field team for a second . . . you still haven't told me who Liz is."

"Ah. Lizabeth Brechtel." Andres' expression, cheerful up until now, suddenly darkened.

I looked closely at him. "Who is Lizabeth Brechtel and what's wrong with her?"

"She is with the International Association of Cryptozoology," he began.

I scrunched my brow in thought. The name was familiar. "IAC. Aren't they the people who rediscover species?"

Andres nodded. "Yes, the animals that everybody thought were extinct. They have found already black lion tamarins in Brazil and thick-billed parrots in Arizona. I even heard they found an ivory-billed woodpecker."

I blinked in surprise. Ivory-billed woodpeckers hadn't been seen since the 1950s. "Interesting work. And appropriate for our project. So what's wrong with Lizabeth?"

Andres pulled his mouth to one side and chewed on his lip. "She is . . . difficult," he said after a long pause.

"Difficult."

"Yes, very angry, always fighting even when there is nothing to fight about."

"A confrontational type?"

"That is a good word for her," he agreed with a nod.

Great. Just what we needed in a small, isolated field camp.

Andres fiddled with the buckle on his seatbelt and slanted me an uneasy glance. "Perhaps I should not have given you a bad opinion of her," he said unhappily. "Just because she and I do not get along doesn't mean that she's like that with everybody."

He lapsed into an uncomfortable silence.

"Hey, I've been on field teams before," I assured him as the silence threatened to drag on. "Sometimes, for no good reason, some personalities just don't seem to click. I'm sure even *I* get up people's noses occasionally—as hard as that is to believe."

Andres' expression relaxed and he chuckled a little.

"Seriously, though," I continued, "I never judge until I see for myself. Don't worry, I'll keep an open mind about Lizabeth."

He smiled gratefully and conversation turned to other, less touchy subjects.

Chapter 5

The noise at San José's airport smacked me upside the head, buzzing across my skull and rattling my teeth. Countless announcements, greetings, goodbyes all melded together into one vast, overwhelming roar. A headache throbbed into existence above my eyes. The Tower of Babel must have sounded like this after the job had gone belly up.

Andres gave the macho thing a whirl and took hold of my elbow to guide me down the stairway to the main floor. I shook off his helping hand with a smile (we *were* going to be working together, after all) and navigated my own way through Customs and baggage claim lineups. The clamor was, if anything, louder on this floor, the crush of people even closer. I was relieved when we finally jumped through all the hoops and were heading out the door. Relieved, that is, until I stepped outside.

"Ye gods!" I exclaimed, shocked into motionlessness.

Andres turned with a questioning look.

"It feels like a *sauna*," I told him.

A grin split his face. "It is nice and warm after winter on your prairies, yes?"

Warm.

Rivulets of sweat were already trickling down my back, and he thought it was *warm*. Slowly I followed Andres out to the parking lot, forcing my lungs to take in deep breaths of the super-heated air. I'd expected Costa Rica to be hot, but the very intensity of the heat, the crushing humidity took my northern-adapted self completely by surprise. I used my sleeve to mop my forehead and sent up a quick prayer to the gods to acclimatize me—fast. Fieldwork in this kind of heat was going to be gross.

Because Costa Rica is so close to the equator, it gets dark early—about six p.m. So all I saw of San José that first night was a confused medley of orange-colored taxis zipping around the airport, countless lights sparkling like fireflies across the hills of the capital city, and several billboards advertizing Salsa Lizano, whatever that was.

I'd read a lot about the friendliness of Costa Ricans—or Ticos, as they liked to call themselves—and Andres had certainly lived up to that reputation. But when we arrived at the TRC house, we were met, not with the wide smile I'd anticipated, but with a forbidding frown.

The man stood under the porch light, arms folded across his chest, his body language understandable in any dialect. He was short and stocky, one of those solid customers who look as if they should be frequenting abandoned warehouses in Gotham City. His set face bespoke a certain hardness of character, and his eyes were flinty and unwelcoming.

"Ernesto!" Andres greeted the man with a friendly wave. "*¿Cómo está?*"

Ernesto's frown deepened and he burst into rapid Spanish. Even after the hours I'd racked up with a Spanish-English phrasebook, I couldn't follow it at all. It didn't matter much. It was clear we were unexpected and unwanted.

Andres' response was equally incomprehensible to me,

but his tone was firm and unapologetic. After what sounded like another tirade, Ernesto turned on his heel and stalked back into the house, leaving the door open behind him.

I gave Andres an inquiring look.

His smile had morphed into a grimace. "TRC messed up again, I think," he told me with an apologetic shrug. "We were not expected until Friday. Rodolfo and Aderith have gone to their house in the mountains. I'm afraid we are here on our own."

"That's okay with me. But," I gestured after Ernesto, "is it okay with him? He seems pretty upset."

Andres opened the trunk and started unloading our gear. "Don't worry about Ernesto. He's a bit—um, how do you say in English—moody sometimes. And anyway, this is not his house so it doesn't matter if he's okay or not."

Moody. Andres was proving to be the master of understatement. I shouldered my dufflebag, slung my backpack over my arm, and followed him thoughtfully up the walk.

The house had a definite air of quiet serenity. Lushly scented flowers lined the porch and decorated the entryway with their deep purple blooms. I left my boots by the front door. The floors were of pale gray tile, cool against my sock feet. A ceiling fan spun gently above the kitchen table. Andres escorted me to a bedroom at the back of the house.

The room appeared to be scrupulously clean, if somewhat poorly lit. It was barely big enough for the single bed, tiny desk, and chest of drawers that had been crammed into it, but it had a ceiling fan and I wasted no time in switching it on.

"There is no food," Ernesto announced as we lugged our bags down the hall. "Nobody expected you, so you will have to eat dinner somewhere else." His manner was belligerent.

"Okay," Andres agreed easily. "There is a good *soda* a few blocks away."

His refusal to acknowledge Ernesto's rudeness clearly irritated the other man.

"Sounds okay to me," I said. "But I need to change into something cooler first, or I'm liable to melt into a puddle on the floor."

Andres chuckled. "You'd better change, then, we don't want you to make a mess. I will have a shower before we go. Can you wait for twenty minutes?"

I nodded and moved past him toward my bedroom, aiming a tentative smile at Ernesto as I did so. He didn't smile back.

I closed the door to my room, kicked off my cargo pants with a relieved sigh, then peeled off my shirt too. With arms outstretched, I stood in my underwear under the ceiling fan and let the breeze cool me off. Even the act of rummaging in my dufflebag for a pair of shorts and a clean shirt was enough to leave me dripping. My grandmother always told me that horses sweated, men perspired, and ladies glowed. Six months of this and they'd be calling me Captain Neutron.

I'd just finished wriggling into my shorts when I heard a low, angry-sounding murmur. Were Andres and Ernesto arguing again? I tiptoed over to the door and pressed my ear against it. I had a momentary qualm about eavesdropping—mostly because it was unlikely I'd be able to understand what they were saying—but Ernesto was part of our field team. If he was going to be a problem, I wanted to know about it.

I listened carefully, but it was soon apparent that only

one voice spoke. I pulled the door open a crack. I could hear the trickling water of a shower. Not Andres, then.

"*Sí, sí. Lo siento.*" Ernesto's voice was an angry hiss. He spat out a few more words, then I heard a loud click. A phone being hung up. And forcefully too.

I eased my bedroom door shut and considered what I'd overheard. The only words I'd recognized were *lo siento*—I'm sorry. What did Ernesto have to be sorry about?

Damn phrasebooks were worse than useless, I grumbled to myself. I may not have understood what Ernesto had been saying, but it was a good bet he wasn't asking 'where is the bus station' or 'how much is the room' or 'how far to the nearest discotheque'.

I stood in my bedroom, undecided, for a long moment, then pulled the door open and made my way to the kitchen. Ernesto was standing by the window.

"*¡Hola!*" I said, taking my Spanish for a test drive. "*Soy* Robyn."

He'd turned at the first sound of my voice. "I speak English," he told me with a thick accent.

I'd sort of figured that out for myself when he'd made his snarky comment about the food situation.

"Oh, okay, then," I said instead. "Hey, Ernesto. I'm Robyn from Canada. I'll be on the field team with you." I held out my hand.

He regarded the proffered hand for a long moment, then took it and pressed quickly. "*¡Hola*, Robyn!"

"I'm sorry we burst in on you like this. I hope it wasn't too much of an inconvenience."

"Inconvenience?" His mouth tried out the word. "What means inconvenience?"

"Um . . . a problem. I hope it wasn't too much of a problem."

He looked at me impassively. "It is no problem."

I'd heard more convincing lies in my time. Hell, I'd *told* more convincing lies in my time.

"Good," I said. "I was afraid we'd troubled you."

"Not at all," he told me. "Now, excuse me, I need to phone my cousin before dinner. There is a nice chair in the living room for sitting, and Rodolfo has many books for reading."

"Uh, thanks." I took the hint and turned to leave.

"Robyn."

I paused and glanced back at him.

He stretched his lips into an insincere smile. "Welcome to Costa Rica."

"So the first step is to see if there is a viable population."

"No," I contradicted him. "The first step is to *find* the macaw."

"Robyn!" Andres chided me. "I am being optimistic!"

"You're just a regular happy face, aren't you?"

He laughed and wagged a finger at me. "But I am not quite so yellow, I hope."

I grinned and assured him he was far from it.

It had been a little jarring at first: the level of integration of North American pop culture into Costa Rican society. Andres' car had been full of plastic Bugs Bunnies and Tasmanian Devils and sunny yellow smiley face stickers. Even here, in the local *soda*, Teletubbies dangled on bright red strings behind the cash register and the waitress sported a faded Mickey Mouse T-shirt. Cultural assimilation through animation. Weird.

Fortunately, there was still a lot about Costa Rica that was unique. The *soda* Andres had chosen was a prime example—no North American establishment would be caught dead in such colors. Orange plastic cloths covered the tables, the chairs were a riot of black, yellow, and royal blue, and the walls, both inside and out, had been painted that pulsing turquoise-green last seen in North America on 1960s kitchen appliances. The *soda* wasn't alone in its flamboyance, either. By the porch light I'd seen that the TRC house was a vivid salmon pink, the homes next to it lime green and sky blue—all carefully designed, as Andres informed me, so the houses would be as attractive as possible for the neighbors to look at. A far cry from the monochromatic subdivisions in Calgary.

Still chuckling at Andres' comment, I glanced over at Ernesto and sobered at his expression. No happy faces here. More like an eat-dirt-and-die face. He was going to be a real bright spot on the field team. I'd been surprised when Ernesto had included himself in our dinner plans. So far he hadn't said much, and as I caught his disapproving eye now, I was abruptly aware that we were excluding him.

I cleared my throat and switched to professional mode. "Okay, once we've found the bird, we'll need to do some kind of census. Find out if the population is viable, and come up with a half-decent estimate on numbers." I held the eye contact with Ernesto and emphasized the word 'we'. "Maybe we can even get an idea of their distribution, and what kind of habitats they like best. Andres tells me you've had a lot of experience with this kind of thing, Ernesto."

Ernesto gave me a small nod. "*Sí*. I have guided many tourists down in the Corcovado. I show them much of the wildlife and where they live. Many, many birds."

"But never one of the macaws we're looking for?"

"No. Never."

Had Ernesto answered a little too quickly?

"Too bad," I said. "That might have made things easier."

Ernesto just looked at me.

I was trying my best to be friendly, but he might as well have been an Easter Island head for all the response I was getting. It was a distinct relief when the waitress brought our supper of *gallo pinto* (lightly spiced beans and rice) and ice-cold *cerveza* (beer). Ernesto put his head down and started shoveling in his food, completely ignoring Andres and me in the process. For that matter, Andres himself became uncommunicative, focusing his entire attention on his plate. I didn't think the airplane lunch had been *that* bad.

"Here," Andres held out a brown bottle to me. "This is Salsa Lizano. You should try some. It's very good on *gallo pinto*."

So this was the famous Salsa Lizano. I sniffed the spicy-smelling sauce and poured a bit over my rice. "This is great!" I exclaimed with delight after the first taste. And so it was. A combination of spice and salty brine that complemented the beans and rice perfectly. I took another enthusiastic mouthful. Maybe lunch *had* pretty much sucked.

Andres grinned at me before turning his attention back to his own food.

Long before I finished scooping up my last bean, Ernesto pushed his plate to one side. "I must go now," he announced. "I promised my cousin to help him with work tonight."

"You'll be back tomorrow to take Robyn around San José?" The question was more statement than query.

Ernesto was silent for a heartbeat. Andres glanced up from his plate and fixed him with a piercing stare. Andres was to be Danta's director and our team's illustrious leader. For the first time since I'd met him, it showed.

Finally Ernesto inclined his head. "Of course," he replied softly, directing a ghost of a smile toward me. And with that, he turned and picked his way past the maze of tables and chairs.

"See you tomorrow, Ernesto," I called after him.

No response. Spine straight and stiff as a rod.

I turned my attention back to Andres, who was mopping up his plate with a tortilla. "What's this about going around San José?" I asked him.

"I have many meetings tomorrow at the museum," he told me, chewing the last bite of his tortilla. "Some last things I must do before we can leave for Corcovado. We also need to pick up a few more supplies. I am hoping you and Ernesto can do that. This way, we can start our trip early the next morning—it sometimes takes all day to get to Danta."

I digested this for a moment. I wasn't overly thrilled about spending an entire day alone with the unfriendly Ernesto, but I'd grown up watching *Sesame Street.* I knew all about cooperation.

"Okay," I replied, putting a bright face on it. "The sooner we can get down to the rainforest, the better."

Andres nodded his approval. "Yes, I'm also eager to start looking for our macaw." He signaled the waitress to bring us more beer. "You must tell me, Robyn, how does a Canadian biologist know so much about tropical parrots?"

Over a couple more condensation-drenched *cervezas*, Andres and I talked shop. I told him about working with the museum's study skins and about environmental consulting. He'd been to Canada only once before and was fascinated by my accounts of fieldwork in the 'frozen north'. Several more beers and we were joking and laughing and regaling each other with the touching tales of which field biologists are so fond. The ticks-in-your-underwear and leeches-on-your-eyeball kinds of stories.

My face grew flushed with the heat of the evening. Gradually and without so much as a sound, a Vaseline-coated lens descended over my vision. Through its soft fuzziness, I began to notice all over again that Andres was an attractive guy. Damn attractive, when it came right down to it. The Smile was appearing more frequently now, and seemed in danger of becoming a permanent fixture on his face. Women of the world, beware.

I snickered at the thought and tried to pull myself up straight. It wasn't easy (or particularly successful).

I blinked and tried to remember why I wasn't trusting anything male in tight pants. Then I pushed my glass carefully to one side.

"Y'know, I think maybe we should go back," I formed the words slowly with just a hint of a slur sneaking through. "I'm really jetlagged and I'm pretty sure I've had enough *cervezas* for one night. I gotta go to bed."

Full of beer and bonhomie, we stumbled back to the house, where I made my unsteady way down the hall and promptly fell into bed. The room spun around me. Nothing alarming, just a nice, gentle rotation.

"Way to go, Robyn," I berated myself. "Your first night in Costa Rica, and you're drunk assa skunk."

Did they even have skunks in Costa Rica? What did Ticos get drunk as if they didn't have skunks? The thought struck me as astoundingly funny, and I had to bury my face in the pillow to smother my whoops of laughter.

Pathetic.

My conscience nudged the word up to the front of my alcohol-befuddled brain. Well, yes, if you were going to be picky about it, I probably wasn't at my best right now. I suppressed a yeasty belch. But, hey, everybody had to cut loose sometime. Brandi-with-an-i would be proud.

With a last dignified hiccup, I told my conscience to get a life and gave myself up to the spiraling room. As I hovered on the threshold of slumber, I saw Andres in my mind's eye. Damn, he was a fine-looking guy! Like one of his *el tigres*. He was flashing that Smile at me again, but in my dream, his black eyes were the color of the sea.

CHAPTER 6

"*¡Buenos días!* I hope you had a good rest."

The wish was accompanied by a wide smile. The weird part was that it was Ernesto, not Andres, who was sitting at the kitchen table and greeting me with such a friendly good morning.

"Uh . . . *Buenos días*, Ernesto. Thanks, I did sleep very well." I smothered a yawn. "I guess I was pretty tired."

Not to mention tanked.

"*Sí*. You needed to *abraso el gorilla*."

"Excuse me?"

He chuckled at my expression. "This is what we say in Costa Rica when we are very tired. It means . . . to embrace the gorilla."

I considered that for a moment. My brain was still a little fuzzy. "Well, I suppose it's no stranger than 'catching some z's'," I conceded.

"Zees? I do not understand."

He still didn't understand even after I tried to explain about z's. I guess some things just don't translate.

Though I was functioning through a lingering haze of jetlag, not enough sleep, and a little too much *cerveza*, it was still clear to me that Ernesto was a very different man today—full of chatty conversation and winning smiles. I would have liked some time to absorb the transformation, to wonder at its cause, but as it turned out, I didn't even have time for breakfast. The first stop on our long list of places to go was the market, and Ernesto was keen to get there early.

"We usually get up around four-thirty in Costa Rica," he told me. "By eight-thirty or nine, it is already halfway through the morning."

I stifled another yawn and glanced at the clock. It was already halfway through the morning. I sifted Ernesto's words for criticism, but, surprisingly enough, found none.

"If we don't get to the *mercado* soon," he was saying, "most of the good things will be gone."

"But—"

"We can get something to eat while we are there," he assured me, reading my mind. "Maybe a nice *café con leche*, yes?"

Coffee. My mouth started watering at the thought.

"Let me go wash my face first," I told him.

San José by daylight was a very different experience. Full of contrasts, it seemed an oddly designed mixture of old butting up against new, of wealthy next door to poor. Several colonial-style buildings were decorated with elaborate metal gates and architectural embellishments. But other structures seemed to have been thrown together out of whatever building materials happened to be on hand. There was clapboard, corrugated metal, cinder blocks, or varying combinations of all three, wildly painted or plain and covered in rust and gunge. The only common denominator was the corrugated tin roofs, which, again, were plain or painted depending on the wealth or ambition of their owners. Building codes appeared to be non-existent here, and many of the houses and shops seemed thrown together with an if-it-sort-of-fits-then-it's-good-enough kind of attitude. The result was a jumble of haphazard structures with little to recommend it in terms of esthetics. Ernesto informed me that even Ticos dislike their capital city.

San José's only saving graces, as far as I could see, were the craggy mountains that surrounded it and the vegetation. Bushes, fruit trees, and a wild profusion of flowering vines glowed in the incandescent sunlight. Plants that you see only as house dwellers in North America were dwarfed here by their lush, tropical cousins. It went a long way to brightening up the city.

The cracked and buckling streets were crammed with pedestrians and cyclists while carts and stands spilled their wares out onto the roadways. And then, of course, there were the drivers. Loud. Maniacal. Seemingly unconcerned with rules of the road (not to mention the pedestrians and cyclists). Even Ernesto, a man on the flip side of fifty, was a madman behind the wheel, disregarding stop signs, leaning heavily on the horn, and weaving crazily in and out of traffic and around cyclists who appeared to think nothing of riding three or four to one bike. Our car spewed a trail of blue, diesel-scented smoke behind us. In fact, most of the vehicles in Costa Rica appeared to run on diesel fuel. I found the acrid odor chokingly pervasive.

I white-knuckled it all the way to the market and several times found myself pressing down hard with my right foot as if there was a brake pedal on the passenger side. If only. By the time we finally stopped, I was feeling a little wild around the eyes. I climbed out of the car with an audible sigh of relief.

The *mercado* was a dizzying assault on the senses.

Colorful fruits and vegetables were displayed on everything from permanent stands to wooden crates to the open backs of pickup trucks. Silvery fish had been laid out in neat rows, their iridescent scales glittering blue and green in the sunlight. Sides of beef dangled from hooks while flies buzzed around them in orgiastic delight. The air was thick with unfamiliar smells, the briny tang of fish, the heavy perfume of overripe fruit, and the smoky scent of roasted coffee beans resting in their wicker measuring baskets. It was light-years away from the coldly civilized aisles of Safeway, and I followed Ernesto into the crush of brightly dressed shoppers with unabashed pleasure.

"I think we go for a *café* first," he called back to me. "And perhaps some *churros*, yes?"

"What are those?"

"Like little fingers of bread and sugar. Very tasty."

"Lead on, Macduff," I told him.

He shot me an uncertain smile, then elbowed his way through the crowds to a small *soda* tucked between a fruit stand and a bakery.

"Look at those mangos!" I stopped and gaped at the fruit stand. "They're *twice* the size of the ones we get in Canada."

Ernesto waded back through the throng. "*¿Cuanto es?*" he asked the vendor.

I dug out a handful of *colones* from my pocket, but Ernesto waved them away.

"It is my pleasure," he said, "to welcome you to my country."

He insisted on treating me to breakfast too. A changed man, indeed.

We perched unsteadily on hard wooden stools set up

around the *soda*'s counter. The coffee was industrial strength, but was served with a pitcher of steaming milk to cut the bitterness. A fine combination. The *churros* proved to be as addictive as Tim Hortons sour cream glazed donuts, and I probably ate more than was strictly good for me. But the mango was the real winner for the day. Succulent, deep golden flesh, dripping with tart juices. My tastebuds almost exploded with the first mouthful. I gobbled down slice after slice, greedily licking the juices that ran down my hand, while Ernesto watched with an indulgent eye.

"That was delicious!" I felt more alert once I'd downed a couple of coffees and eaten my body weight in mango.

"*Pura vida*, yes?"

"*Pura vida*?"

"It means 'great' or 'good life'. All Ticos say this."

"About food?"

"About anything." He spread his arms wide. "When people ask 'How are you?' you say *pura vida*, if they ask 'How was your trip?' . . . *pura vida*. You see?"

I nodded and smiled. "So the mangos are *pura vida*."

Ernesto clapped me on the shoulder as we slid from the stools. "Exactly. Yes! *Pura vida*. You chose a good time to come to Costa Rica, Robyn. The mangos are just starting to be ready now."

"A very good time," I agreed. "Thank you, Ernesto—*muchas gracias*—for breakfast."

"*Con mucho gusto*," he replied.

With much pleasure.

It was a phrase I was to hear many times that morning. Ernesto had been in such a fired-up hurry to get to the market that I assumed we'd sprint through it. I overestimated the Costa Rican sense of urgency.

Adopting a leisurely pace, we sauntered down the narrow alleys, stopping often to examine produce and other food items, picking up some of the things on Andres' list, and haggling with the vendors. Ernesto made sure to introduce me at every opportunity.

"This is Robyn from Canada," he told them in Spanish. "She has never been to Costa Rica before."

Everyone smiled and offered me mangos or ripe papayas or thick slices of sharply fragrant pineapple, all 'with much pleasure'.

"Try some *piña*, it's excellent."

"This is cheese from Monteverde. The best in the country."

"From Canada? *Muy frio*. Very cold there, yes?"

"Welcome! Our country is your country."

I understood now why the guidebooks described Ticos as a warm, friendly people.

"There is the hardware store," Ernest pointed across the street. "Andres needs some ropes and batteries."

"Okay." I stepped out onto the road, but before I could take another step, Ernesto grabbed my shoulder and almost jerked me off my feet.

"Hey!" I protested.

Ernesto released his hold immediately. "Be careful," he admonished and gestured to the car that would have hit me if I'd continued onto the road. "This is not like Canada. The drivers, they will not stop for you here."

I watched the car speed away, narrowly missing two young children. The little girl had to jump out of the way. Not like Canada, indeed. I turned my attention back to Ernesto. "Thanks," I told him. "And thanks for the tip. I'll be more careful now."

"Many *gringos* say that if you want to cross the street,

then you should wait for a Tica with her baby and cross at the same time. It is not really a joke."

We did eventually manage to duck across the street and it was then, in the flush of that minor victory, that I caught sight of my first Costa Rican parrots.

They were sad, bedraggled-looking specimens. Blue-headed parrots. Each confined to a wire cage so tiny, they couldn't even spread their wings. The rusting enclosures had been set out under the burning sun on the pavement in front of a mechanic's shop.

I stopped dead as soon as I saw them. "That's *disgusting!*" I sputtered in fury.

Ernesto looked back at me in surprise and followed my gaze. "Ah," he said in understanding. "They put the birds out to attract customers."

"*To attract customers!* Those birds don't have water. They're filthy. They can't even open their wings! How is that supposed to attract customers?"

He shrugged. "Most people do not see it like this," he said mildly. "They are just birds, after all."

"But—"

"This is what most people think. They are just pretty birds. Put them outside the store or the hotel and you will get more customers. They don't need to spread their wings to look good."

I was speechless.

"Many places do not do this anymore," Ernesto went on. "Now that so many tourists come. *Gringos* don't like to see the birds in cages like that. Things have changed quite a bit."

"Not enough for me," I said, indicating the blue-headed parrots.

All pleasure in our shopping expedition fled with the

sight of those birds. I wanted to confront the owners of the shop, to demand at the very least that they keep the parrots in more humane conditions, but Ernesto convinced me to let it go.

"I know the man who runs this place," he told me. "He will not care what you think. And you'll only make him angry. I'm sorry, Robyn. Blue-headed parrots are not endangered. There is no rule against keeping them."

I hated Ernesto's reasoning, but I couldn't argue with it. I didn't even have the law on my side. And I knew that many countries, Costa Rica included, were getting pretty tired of conservationists telling them what they should be doing. Still, I experienced an almost physical pain as I walked away from those neglected birds, and while we collected the remaining items on our list, I couldn't stop thinking about them.

Parrots are sometimes called 'primates of the sky' because they're so intelligent. They mate for life, live in large flocks, and have a complex social life. Some species live for seventy years. That's a lot of time to spend cooling your talons in a cage, unable to spread your wings, escape from the sun, or interact with your own kind.

And what about the birds that ended up in foreign homes? The most they can look forward to is a life indoors, a limited diet, and, more often than not, a lack of meaningful company. Several months ago, I'd read about a researcher in the States who was trying to develop a Web site for lonely parrots to interact with other parrots.

A Web site.

Were we going to find a new species of macaw only to see it caged or on line?

The captive parrots left a bad taste in my mouth. Maybe that explained the uneasy feeling that shadowed my footsteps for the rest of the day. I went through the motions of shopping and eating and going over last-minute plans for the trip, aware throughout it all that something was not quite right. Like the world had somehow tilted very slightly off kilter in a way I couldn't identify.

We were supposed to leave for the Corcovado by five the next morning. Normally this would mean an early night, but by ten o'clock, it was still way too hot to sleep. So Andres, Ernesto, and I ended up lounging under the ceiling fan above the kitchen table and speculating about the coming field season. I'd half-expected Ernesto to lapse back into frowning disapproval when Andres joined us for dinner, but his change in attitude must have had a good hold, and the evening was surprisingly convivial. It was quite late by the time I finally shut my bedroom door.

I had planned on hitting the sack directly, but one look around my room convinced me otherwise. Earlier that afternoon, I'd taken the opportunity to go over some of my maps and notes again. Now field guides, notebooks, clothes, and sundry other items sprawled in untidy piles on the desk and at the foot of the bed. Being in the field always brings out the slob in me. It must be something about living out of a dufflebag and bathing infrequently.

I contemplated the mess with bleary eyes. If I didn't pack it up now, I'd have to get up at four a.m. just to get myself organized. Incentive enough. I began cramming things into my dufflebag and when that was full, I started in on the daypack. I should have just taken everything out and started from scratch. Somehow what fit before now did not.

"Crap," I muttered, trying to force a water bottle between a plastic bag of toilet paper and a first aid kit. I gave the bottle an almighty shove and the daypack shot off the desk and spun across the room, spewing its contents all over the floor.

I swore under my breath. Why do these things always happen when you're least able to deal with them? With a longing look at the pillow, I got down on my hands and knees. My flashlight had rolled under the bed, and the spare batteries had taken refuge under the desk. I squirmed under the low-slung bed with a gracefulness that Julia Roberts wasn't likely to envy anytime soon. Then I shimmied my hand under the chest of drawers and snagged the batteries. Except. . . .

I'd retrieved more than just batteries.

I stared down in disbelief at the metal objects in my hands. Bullets. Weird-looking ones. Fat, blunt-tipped, shining with a silvery-gold sheen. Not your average hunting ammo. I wasn't exactly up to snuff when it came to heavy artillery, but in my quest for a social life, I'd endured my fair share of Hollywood testosterone flicks. These bullets looked serious. Like they belonged to an Uzi or something.

I pursed my lips in speculation and bounced the bullets on my palm.

What were such nasty bullets doing in such a nice house?

CHAPTER 7

I woke several times during the night, swimming in sweat and hopelessly tangled in the sheets. Should I tell Andres about the bullets? The question kept me awake as much as the heat did.

Before going to bed, I'd rolled the shiny cylinders back under the dresser. But I could imagine them, still gleaming there in the darkness. A strangely discordant note in an otherwise serene atmosphere. Was it legal to have bullets like that? I hadn't the faintest idea. I didn't know the customs or the laws here. For that matter, I didn't know much about bullets, either. I tried to convince myself I was overreacting. The night dragged on.

By the time the sun began climbing into the sky, I had long since given up on beauty sleep. I'd pretty much ruled out fit-for-public-viewing sleep too. The mirror showed me a pair of eyes that looked like two piss holes in a snowbank. I made a face at the reflection, which didn't help my appearance any, but made me feel a little better. Then I pulled the curtain aside and watched the early morning mist spiral up from the asphalt. The world still had that weird edge of unreality to it.

I finally decided not to mention the bullets to anyone—at least not yet. There was probably a perfectly harmless explanation for ammunition under the dresser. I couldn't imagine what it was, but that was my problem. For some reason Costa Rica had me off balance. Culture shock? Maybe. All I knew was that the sooner I got in the field, the better. Familiar work would help settle me down.

Breakfast helped too. In fact, breakfast would have cured much more than a stressful, sleepless night. Ernesto had nipped out to a nearby bakery, and by the time I got to the table, there were two loaves of warm, crusty bread, a bowl of soft cheese, and huge slabs of juicy, sun-yellow pineapple.

"How am I ever going to face Captain Crunch after this?" I wailed.

"Is Captain Crunch your boss?" Ernesto asked politely.

I opened my mouth, then closed it again.

"Your boss is unhappy when you eat breakfast?"

I shook my head. "No, of course not. It's just, uh, Captain Crunch is something we eat for breakfast. Not a person. A kind of cereal."

Ernesto looked puzzled.

"When we say we can't face something . . . it's just an expression," I tried to explain. "A saying. And I don't work for the military."

He nodded his head, but I could tell he thought I needed a coffee.

Andres joined us then and we ate quickly, washing everything down with a couple of mugs of darkly fragrant coffee. Within forty-five minutes, we were on our way to pick up Viviana.

I had high hopes for Viviana Alvaro Morales. She'd studied chestnut-mandibled toucans for her master's degree at the University of Costa Rica, and scarlet macaws and environmental tourism for her PhD at Berkeley. I had a hunch she was a kindred spirit—an unabashed bird nerd like myself.

We pulled up in front of a pumpkin orange house with a royal blue roof. A child was sitting in a chair on the porch. No, not a child, I realized, as the figure jumped up and waved to us. A very small woman. She hoisted a huge dufflebag to her shoulder and strode over.

"*¡Buenas dias!*" she greeted us with a wide grin. "And you are Robyn, of course!" She pumped my hand enthusiastically. "It is so good to meet you in person at last. Welcome to Costa Rica! Are you dying of the heat yet?" Her voice was husky and low. Furry, almost. The sort of voice that comes from smoky blues bars and smooth whisky.

"Hey, Viviana." I smiled back at her. "It's great to finally meet you too. Thanks, and yes, I find it a bit hot."

"I knew it!" She gave a throaty chuckle. "My sister lives in Winnipeg. I went to see her two years ago for Christmas and I thought I would freeze to death." She gave an exaggerated shiver. "Brrr. Not for me, your ice and snow."

"It's not *always* cold," I protested. "Summers can get pretty hot but, I admit, nowhere near as humid as Costa Rica." I fanned my already glowing face. "I'm hoping I'll acclimatize really fast."

"You'll be fine," she assured me as she stowed her gear in the trunk and swung into the back seat beside Ernesto.

Viviana was tiny—maybe five one or two—and as slender as the child I'd mistaken her for. Her skin was pale for a Tica, with a generous smattering of freckles and the slight pinkish blush of sunburn. A few light wrinkles around her eyes were all that betrayed her thirtysomething years. Her hands had gotten smudged with dirt from Andres' car and she wiped them clean on her pants without a second thought. I liked her immediately.

It was a thirty-minute drive to the airport, but conversation proved difficult. Viviana couldn't hear much in the back seat and I was afraid to open my mouth in case I accidentally screamed.

Andres, who had seemed calm enough up till now, careened down the crowded streets at warp ten with photon torpedoes armed and ready. Compared to him, Ernesto was Elmer the Safety Elephant. I clenched my teeth and held on.

We blasted into the airport parking lot in record time. An unnecessary hurry. Our pilot was nowhere in sight.

"It is normal for Costa Rica," Andres assured me. "Ticos are, uh, we like . . . we like to take life the easy way."

"We are laid back," Viviana said.

Andres beamed at her. "*Gracias*. I knew there was a word I was not remembering. We Ticos are very laid back."

"Except when you're driving," I added pointedly.

Andres grinned, unrepentant. "We do not like to drive slowly," he agreed.

Indeed.

"But when it comes to keeping appointments, we are not so quick. I said to Adelio that we were wanting to leave by six-thirty, but. . . ," he trailed off and shrugged. "Perhaps I will go look for him."

"I am going to buy coffee," Ernesto said. "You need some coffee too, Robyn?"

What I needed was a scotch.

"No thanks," I managed a grateful smile. "I'm good."

Ernesto hesitated for a few seconds, then, "Viviana?"

"No, *gracias*." Her tone was a bit clipped. Not exactly brusque but not really friendly, either. Quite a feat for someone with such a sexy-sounding voice.

I slanted them a sidelong glance. Ernesto nodded once, almost as if he'd been expecting her reaction, then, without another word, he sauntered off in search of his coffee. I fiddled with the zipper on my dufflebag, watching Viviana through my eyelashes. She stood for a moment, her eyes following Ernesto, a slight frown marring her forehead. Then she turned to help me with the gear.

We piled everything in an empty corner and settled onto the uncomfortable airport chairs. A bored-looking security guard watched us from across the lounge.

"You must have been very surprised to see that macaw all the way up in Canada," Viviana broke the silence.

"I almost had a heart attack," I agreed.

"And now you are here to try to find them."

"I know! I'm still not sure I believe it. I had to give myself a good hard pinch this morning," I grinned.

"Are you sure that wasn't Andres?"

I shot her a startled look. "Uh—excuse me?"

"Nothing." She waved her hand. "*Lo siento*. Sorry. So you are excited to be here, yes?"

"Big time," I told her with heartfelt enthusiasm. "Do you know, before I came here I'd never seen a parrot outside a zoo."

"Really? This is terrible!"

Andres came up behind us. "What is so terrible?"

Viviana swiveled her head to look at him. "Robyn has only seen parrots in a zoo."

"And dead ones in the museum and at the CITES warehouse," I amended. "But ever since I can remember, I've wanted to see how macaws behave in the wild. To watch a whole flock of them foraging for fruit or gliding above the canopy. You know, I would have jumped at the chance to come down here and study any kind of macaw, but a new species...?" I blew out my breath in a whistle, at a loss for words.

"It's a dream come true," Viviana finished.

"It is that." I smiled.

Andres squeezed my shoulders. "I'm very happy that you are on our team," he said warmly. "Adelio should be here any time now and we can get on our way. The sooner we're down in Corcovado, the sooner we can find a macaw for you."

"For all of us!" Viviana was quick to correct him.

He gave her a tight smile and dropped his hands from my shoulders. "You are right. For everybody."

Uneasy undercurrents.

I shifted uncomfortably in my seat and caught sight of a heavy-set man ambling our way. He was a shady-looking customer with shifty eyes and a thick, drooping mustache. As he drew closer, I could see a row of large red ants marching across the front of his T-shirt with the slogan 'Costa Rican Army' written below them.

Andres didn't notice as the man came up behind him and gave me a long, slow smile. A silver cap on his front tooth lent him a rakish, almost piratical air. Bemused by this apparition, I opened my mouth, but before I could say anything, he brought his finger up to his lips and winked conspiratorially. He raised his arm, stretched it backwards, then....

Whump!

Andres staggered, all the breath in his lungs whooshing out in a startled oof.

"*¿Cómo está, mae?*" the man boomed, his delighted laughter echoing across the deserted lounge.

Our pilot had arrived.

We flew down to the Corcovado in a small, yellow plane that appeared to be held together with duct tape and rosary beads. A faded painting of a serene-looking Christ had been taped above the pilot's seat. I couldn't decide if I should be reassured by its presence or terrified by its necessity. No wonder Andres had gotten us a deal on the fare.

I had to have several quiet words with my feet before they would climb aboard. But as we rose into the clouds, all (well, most) thoughts of safety regulations and air disasters were forgotten. I scrunched my nose against the pitted window and drank in the landscape. *This* was what I had come for!

Mountains. Steep and rugged like the Canadian Rockies, their craggy outlines softened by tropical emerald velvet. Tangles of ivy and vines surrounded towering palm-like trees, which bowed low under the weight of fat, yellow papayas. The brilliant green of the leaves and the achingly bright-colored splashes of fruits and flowers seemed more vivid than reality. Almost technicolor. But as we soared higher, the pulsing oranges, purples, and pinks gradually faded and were lost in the vastness of the verdant landscape.

The plane leveled out and we headed south. I was sitting up front with Adelio, who was flashing his silver tooth and playing tour guide. He'd somehow spotted the fact that I wasn't big on flying, and he was trying to distract me by pointing out the terraces of coffee plantations and the wide expanses of cleared forests where pineapples are grown.

It was interesting, but disturbing, to see first-hand—and with such an encompassing field of vision—the destruction of tropical rainforest. Protected areas were easy to spot from up here. The demarcation between primary forest and cultivated land was a clear one.

At my first glimpse of vast, uncut rainforest, I had the somewhat unromantic impression that we were flying over a landscape of broccoli. Big bunches of broccoli all crammed together in some gigantic produce display. As if the giant of Jack and the Beanstalk fame had had a less celebrated cousin with a penchant for cruciferae.

Costa Rica is not a large country—especially by Canadian standards. The flight took under forty-five minutes. TRC had secured the requisite research and park entry permits, so we flew directly to the Sirena Ranger Station. A small handful of people were playing soccer on the grassy airstrip. Adelio swooped them, but we had to make a second pass before they all cleared off and we were able to land. Our pilot set us down with a jarring thump and another devilish silver grin.

"*Pura vida. ¿Sí?*" He laughed at my audible sigh of relief and slapped my knee companionably.

A real card.

The Sirena Ranger Station was a compact, two-storey lodge with a covered deck that wrapped around the front and side of the structure like an oversized cat's tail. The blue, white, and red of the Costa Rican flag fluttered lethargically in the humid breeze. There were several largish outbuildings, most with sagging ropes of drying clothes in front of them. A large woodcut sign welcomed visitors with a friendly *Bienvenidos.*

The soccer players had retired to the shade. Only one—a tall, blond woman—walked down the cleared airstrip towards the plane.

"*¡Hola!*" Andres called out and waved as he cracked the door open.

The woman waved back without breaking her stride.

"That is Liz Brechtel," Andres murmured as I passed him a backpack.

I handed over another bag and paused to study the woman.

Lizabeth Brechtel was probably quite a few inches taller than me, I guessed. She was wearing khaki shorts and a sleeved shirt rolled up to the elbows. Her legs were long, tanned, and muscular—the kind of legs I always wished the gods had seen fit to bestow upon me. Her dark blond hair was medium length, pulled back tightly into a ponytail. I couldn't see her features clearly yet, but the deep furrow in her brow was visible even at this distance and she marched towards us with a no-nonsense sort of clip. At the very least, a strong personality.

I took the last coil of rope from Viviana and passed it out to Andres, then I hopped down from the plane. Viviana was close on my heels. Liz was just ten or fifteen feet away when Ernesto climbed down from the aircraft. Her response was immediate and unmistakable.

She stopped dead, her ponytail snapping back and forth with the force of it. Her face registered shock, then flushed red in anger. She whipped around to face Andres.

"Andres!" Her voice rang out, clear and strident. "I thought we'd worked this out." She stalked up to him, oblivious to the rest of us in her fury.

"We did," Andres sighed. "Just because you did not like it—"

"I wasn't the only one!"

Andres flicked Viviana a glance so quick I would have missed it if I hadn't been watching so closely.

"Lizabeth," Andres spoke calmly, "TRC had the final approval. We discussed it before. You can always leave if you do not agree."

"You know that's not possible," she said bitterly, "and furthermore—"

"Furthermore, this is Robyn Devara from Woodrow Consultants in Canada." Andres took my arm and propelled me forward.

It had the desired effect of refocusing her attention, but I wasn't thrilled about being thrust into the situation, whatever it was. I disengaged my arm with more force than was strictly necessary . . . and found myself face to face with one of the angriest people I'd ever seen.

Up close, her face was a fascinating study of fury, as if the rancor inside had begun to come out in her features, twisting them, lining them with bitterness and ill will. It was totally at odds with her youthful figure. She couldn't be older than forty. What had happened in her life to make her so angry?

"Lizabeth." I held out my hand. "Glad to meet another team member."

Pale gooseberry eyes raked me over and clearly found me wanting. She seemed the kind of person who would always find fault. Then she held out her hand and stretched away some of her furrows in a brief smile. "Good to meet you."

The smile made a drastic improvement, but it wasn't to last. We stood there awkwardly—at least I felt awkward—until Ernesto broke the tableau by bending over to pick up his bags. He'd remained silent up until now, seemingly neither offended nor insulted by Lizabeth's reaction to him. As her eyes fell on him again, her expression went glacial and her eyebrows scrunched tightly together. She drew a breath as if to say something, then pressed her lips together in a thin line and spun back towards the station.

She didn't offer to help with the gear.

"It looks like we might have to stay here the night," she tossed back over her shoulder as we prepared to follow her. "Something's wrong with the radio at Danta—either that or they're just not paying attention to it. I've been trying to raise them since yesterday to get someone down here with the boat. Then I thought we could use the rangers' boat, but they've had to go out on a rescue. Some incompetent ass who thought he could hike through the jungle." She snorted. "So now we can't go until they come back. I've been asking Dan to give us an ETA. I thought if they hurried things up a little, we could still get out before dark, but he won't commit to a time." Disgust colored her tone.

I glanced at Andres and saw him grimace. His distaste for Lizabeth was evident.

"*¡Hola!*" A friendly voice called out to us.

I dragged my eyes away from our little group and turned my attention to the station. The man who had called out was leaning easily against the deck's railing. As we drew closer, he straightened up and jumped down the steps.

"Hey, you need a hand with that?" he asked Ernesto, who was struggling with two backpacks and a heavy box of supplies. "Sorry, I didn't realize you had so much stuff."

The accent was North American, but the man was dressed in the pale olive shirt and black rubber boots of a Costa Rican forest ranger. He was a wiry character, tanned the color of a Werther's butterscotch, with straight blond hair bleached white on top by the sun.

"*Gracias,*" Ernesto said gratefully.

"*Con mucho gusto,*" the man replied in admirable Spanish. "The name's Dan Elleker," he announced to the rest of us. "Or Dan the Reptile Man, depending on who you talk to." He smiled widely. "So, which one of you is the Canadian?"

"That'd be me," I raised my hand.

"Wonderful!" Dan exclaimed in delight. "I'm from Edmonton, Alberta, originally. Came down here almost twenty years ago on a holiday and never went back."

"Twenty-year vacation, eh? Sounds good to me."

"Ahhh," Dan closed his eyes and sighed happily. "Two decades and a simple 'eh' still says 'home'. Well, don't just stand around in the hot sun, come on in, everybody. We got three cases of Coke in last week. The fridge's acting up so they're kinda warm, but they've still got their fizz."

Chapter 8

"...and you'll be wanting to keep your eyes peeled for *terciopelos*. You usually find them in cultivated fields—you know, making life more exciting for the farmers—but don't be fooled by that, we've got a mess of 'em here in Corcovado."

We were seated on wooden benches around the huge plank table that dominated the ranger station's common room. The soccer players were tourists from Uruguay. They'd offered friendly smiles, shrugged incomprehension at both my English and Spanish, and had gathered in a clump at the far end of the table. Ernesto was settled beside them—as far away from Liz as he could get. He'd fallen back into frowning silence with us, but I noticed he was quick enough to join in the fun and laughter at the other end.

While we inhaled heaping plates of *gallo pinto*, Dan the Reptile Man provided the lunchtime entertainment. His story was a simple one. He'd come down to Costa Rica to see the wildlife and had fallen in love with the frogs and lizards, the lush rainforest, and a lovely Tica, all in that order. Faviola had married him and pestered her father to pull some strings with the local government so Dan could work as a ranger. He'd been living and working in the Corcovado for going on twelve years now and he seemed to know more about snakes than anybody I'd ever met.

For me, this was not necessarily a good thing.

"*Terciopelo* is what we call these snakes in Costa Rica," Viviana told me. "You call them fer-de-lance. And believe me, you don't want to meet one."

"A nasty piece of work, " Dan agreed. "The most dangerous snake in the jungle."

"I thought coral snakes were the worst," I said.

"Depends on your point of view," Dan leaned back and folded his arms against his chest. "Sure, coral snake's got a more toxic venom—and the locals call them the disappearing snakes. Seems odd when you think about it. I mean, they're red, yellow, and black. Hardly what you'd think of as camouflage. But, you know, as soon as they're on the move, all those bright colors blend into each other—like when you spin a color wheel and all the colors turn to brown—and before you know it . . . *zzzip*. They're gone."

"I see." I said. Unenthusiastic.

"Oh, they're lovely," Dan assured me with a misty look in his eye. "Beautiful snakes! You'll be lucky to see one. But those fer-de-lances, they're a whole other story. For starters, they've got longer fangs than coral snakes, so if they bite you, they can go deeper and inject more venom than your basic coral snake could ever dream of. And the venom's pretty bad. A hemotoxin rather than a neurotoxin. It'll dissolve nerve tissue and destroy blood cells. Basically breaks down your arteries. Even if you manage to survive, you'll probably end up short an arm or a leg."

Dan nodded at the horrified look on my face. "Oh, yes. They're nice-looking snakes, but mean buggers, if you catch my drift. And territorial too. The Ticos say they'll actually stalk you."

"Great." I fiddled with my beans and rice. My appetite was on the wane.

"They've even been known to strike at your shadow when you're not in range yet. Impatient little devils. And to make things worse—"

"What, it's not bad enough?"

"You'd think so," Dan agreed. "But, they've also got their bases covered in terms of where they're gonna get you. The juveniles—which, incidentally, are born with fangs and venom—like to hang around in trees, pretending they're vines. The adults are too big for trees, you'll find them on the ground. I say 'them' because wherever there's one fer-de-lance, you can pretty much bet its mate isn't too far away. And—"

"How big?" I interrupted.

"Excuse me?"

"How big do they get to be?"

"Oh, uh . . . eight feet or so. You're not likely to see one quite that large, though. Probably four to five feet is the average."

Four to five feet of deadly snake with an attitude—and a partner. Was there an upside to this? I pushed my plate to one side, wondering what I'd gotten myself into.

Dan lectured us all through lunch, covering everything from *terciopelos* to eyelash vipers to jumping vipers, which were not highly venomous but could be, according to Dan, somewhat startling due to their habit of jumping two to three feet when striking.

Indeed.

The only sour note during the discussion was sounded by Liz.

"I've heard this all before," she interrupted rudely as Dan was describing the life history of a Costa Rican rattlesnake.

He blinked at her in surprise.

"And I still don't see how it's pertinent. The purpose of *our* research is macaws. Birds. Not snakes." Her sneering tone was offensive. "I don't feel this discussion is particularly helpful or relevant to me. I'm going to make sure our supplies are set to go in case your rangers happen to get back anytime soon." She slid off the bench and walked away without a backward glance.

There was an uncomfortable silence.

"I am very sorry," Andres finally said to Dan in an undertone. "She is upset about something else. It has nothing to do with you."

Dan managed a smile, then thumped Andres on the shoulder. "Ah, forget it," he said.

But conversation was slow to start up again.

I cleared my throat. "Well, I, for one, found your discussion extremely relevant," I told Dan. "If something's fixing to put the munch on me, I sure as hell want to know what it is—and how I can avoid it."

"It's only smart," Dan agreed seriously. "We've already lost one out your way. I don't want to lose anybody else."

"Yeah, Liz told us your rangers were out on a rescue."

"They are," Dan nodded. "But they're after a tourist who twisted his ankle. I'm talking about the guy from Danta."

"*What?*" Andres blurted. "What guy from Danta?"

Dan looked back at him in surprise. "Guillermo, of course."

"What happened to Guillermo?"

"You haven't heard?"

"Who's Guillermo?" I asked.

"Are you saying he is *missing?*"

"For days now. Don't your people keep in touch with you?"

"I've been in America. What happened?"

"Who's Guillermo?" I asked again.

Andres turned to me, frowning. "He is a young man—a hiker—who was visiting Danta. Not part of our team. Just a tourist from Alajuela. What happened to him, Dan?"

Dan shook his head with a sober look. "We don't know," he replied. "Seems he left the station one morning and never came back. His gear's still there, his tent, clothes, everything. But no Guillermo."

Andres scrubbed at the sudden furrow in his brow. "What have you done to find him? You *have* searched for him, yes?"

"Of course," Dan nodded. "I've had all my rangers out there as well as Oscar and Marco and a bunch of volunteers from Golfito. Even Liz came out a few times." He shook his head again. "There's just no sign of him."

"How many days has he been missing?" Viviana asked.

"This is the seventh."

Andres frowned and fell silent.

"You think he had an accident in the jungle?" I asked Dan, my mind still on venomous snakes.

Dan seemed reluctant to speculate, but after a moment he nodded. Just once. A short, frustrated gesture. "Yeah. Yeah, I do," he said. "And I think our chances of finding him now are slim to none. I didn't tell you about all the snakes here just so I could have the pleasure of watching your eyes bug out. And I haven't even mentioned the jaguars, the herds of peccaries, and the crocodiles. You're not in Canada anymore, Dorothy. You keep your eyes peeled out there."

Sound advice.

He turned back to Andres. "I'm surprised nobody told you about this. Sorry to spring it on you like that. I thought at least Liz would've mentioned it."

Through the window, I could see Liz sitting by herself out on the station's porch. Andres gave her a black look. "Yes," he said to Dan, "I would have thought so too."

By the time the rangers' boat returned, the station was broiling under the early afternoon sun. A few insects droned by lethargically, but the jungle had quieted and even the small anole lizards sought out the shade. Heat seemed to radiate up from the ground. Frielo and Ricardo, the two rangers who had gone on the rescue mission, emptied the boat of its limping tourist and filled it with our gear. They worked at a speed out of keeping with the drowsy ambience.

"We are trying to get to Danta before night," Andres explained when I remarked on it. "It will take two hours in the boat and then another two or three hours to hike to the station. The path is not very bad now, I think, but it is overgrown. I don't want to get lost in the dark."

"Good point," I said gravely, thinking of the unfortunate Guillermo. I wasn't keen on meeting a fer-de-lance at night—or during the day, for that matter.

Andres and I pitched in, and within twenty minutes Ranger Ricardo was motioning us into the boat. I climbed aboard, settled my back against a pile of duffle-bags, and prepared myself for the journey.

It was scorchingly hot. Sweat ran freely down my back

and between my breasts, soaking my hair, blurring my vision. My eyes stung from the salt, and I had to keep wiping my face with my shirt sleeve. The sun was merciless, searing our heads from above, and burning our faces from below as it danced and reflected off the water around us.

Moist air hung heavily, rippling reality in the midday heat. The river was brown with sediment, as sluggish as the air. The trees pressed closely on either side, drooping right down into the river in some places. A green embrace. I could hear cries and hooting calls from unseen creatures. A couple of caiman were roasting themselves on a sun-heated rock. Dragonflies buzzed lazily up and down the river. At one point, a large insect landed on my knee. It was orange with an emerald head and brilliant turquoise eyes. Before I could get a good look at it, Andres reached over and brushed it off me.

"They give you a nasty bite, those flies," he said. "Not poisonous, but it will hurt like crazy."

"Thanks."

Finely striped tiger herons stood motionless at the river's edge, waiting for an unsuspecting afternoon snack to swim by. A startled Jesus Christ lizard scampered across the water in front of our boat. Turtles paddled leisurely in the shallows, and everywhere floating rafts of water hyacinth drifted up and down the river. By the time we reached our mooring point a couple of hours later, I was in love. The jungle had its dangers, no question about that, but it was heart-stoppingly beautiful.

Ricardo hopped out first, tying the boat securely to a thick tree. The field station's boat bobbed gently beside us. With Ricardo's help, between the six of us, we managed to shoulder all our gear and most of the supplies that Liz had purchased.

Despite Andres' earlier misgivings, the trail seemed quite passable. We set out confidently, though I, for one, was uneasy, half-expecting a young fer-de-lance to launch itself at me in a fit of adolescent pique. I cursed Dan and his snake stories even as I poked through the leaf litter with my walking stick.

I've always considered myself to be fairly skilled at botany, but the sheer wealth of plant life in this forest completely overwhelmed my knowledge. An acre of forest in Canada boasts an average of twelve species of plants. A lowland tropical rainforest has three to four *hundred*. I felt like my brother Jack, whose idea of botanical nomenclature goes something like small-plant-with-white-flowers or big-plant-with-speckly-leaves.

There were plants upon plants upon still more plants, to quote Kelt. It was the shapes I noticed more than anything. There wasn't much variation in color, but the leaf shapes seemed infinite, as did the strategies for shedding moisture in this rain-laden place. Drip tips, waxy coatings, stilt roots. Everywhere I looked, I could see adaptation in progress.

"Ye gods, look at the size of those leaves!" I goggled at a massive plant, each leaf of it at least two to three feet across. "They're *enormous*."

Viviana turned to see where I was pointing. "Yes, those are elephant leaves," she explained. "They are wrinkly like an elephant, so there is more surface for evaporation. We call them poor man's umbrellas. If you get trapped in the rain, all you have to do is stand under a leaf."

Amazing.

There was so much to look at, I didn't want to blink

in case I missed something. There were dragonflies with crimson bodies and black wings, others with turquoise bodies and orange wings. One elegant individual was completely black save for two ruby-red gems on its lacy wings. I watched an anole lizard puff out his yellow dewlap before scampering up a tree trunk. A large spider had the remains of a green tree frog trapped in its wormhole-like funnel web. I didn't even know that spiders ate frogs.

Tiny orchids and other flowers littered the forest floor, along with leaves of uncountable shapes and sizes. We passed a boulder completely covered in bright green moss and studded with hundreds of delicate, tiny, mauve mushrooms. Vines were everywhere, a living web that held the forest together and provided aerial pathways for its inhabitants.

We hiked along a twisted path, stepping over branches and tree roots that wriggled across the trail in front of us. It was difficult to keep an eye out for snakes. Between the roots and the vines, pretty much everything in the rainforest *looked* like a snake.

It was dark too. Much darker than I'd expected even after Kelt's description. As I walked through the heavy, humid gloom, I felt like an intruder, as insubstantial as a wraith. The scent of damp, mold-laced earth was strong in my nostrils and the rusty red volcanic soil was soft underfoot, silencing the sound of our footsteps. I could hear a troop of howler monkeys roaring in a distant part of the forest. In the clearings where giant trees had succumbed to age or disease, searing shafts of sunlight shone down on the forest floor, lighting me into being with their brilliance. I was utterly intoxicated by the wild profusion of life. *Pura vida,* indeed.

I was so caught up in the magic of it all that it took me a while to notice how the dynamics of our little group had expressed themselves in our positions. Liz led the way, stalking through the trees, her back rigid and uncompromising. Since lunchtime, she hadn't said a word beyond what was necessary.

I'd tried to engage her in conversation on the boat, asking about the field station, commenting on the missing hiker. She had dismissed him with a disgusted shrug.

"I don't know why he was there," she'd said. "He shouldn't have been allowed at Danta in the first place." There had been a harshly critical note in her voice, but I couldn't tell whether it was directed at Guillermo or at whoever had given him permission to stay at the station. And when I questioned her further, she'd pursed her lips and refused to say anything more about the man. She responded to my other inquiries in monosyllables and, eventually, I'd given up. Clearly, "plays well with others" had never featured on her report cards.

Andres was second in line now, chatting easily with Ranger Ricardo. Was he really that relaxed? Or was he trying to put on a good face? He had to be concerned about the missing Guillermo, even if the man hadn't been part of our team.

Viviana and I were next, while Ernesto brought up the rear. The far rear. Quite a few paces behind, he plodded along impassively, ignoring the forest around him, talking to no one. A tortoise lost in his own ponderous thoughts.

I stopped to mop my brow.

"You need a drink?" Viviana asked me.

I nodded. "Maybe. I'm not used to this." I slid the daypack off my chest and adjusted the straps on my larger backpack. I'd clipped a bottle handily onto my belt. The water tasted faintly of plastic, but it was still refreshingly cool compared to the rest of me. I took a long slug. Viviana stood to one side and motioned Ernesto to pass us.

As he did, he paused for a moment beside me.

"You must be careful to drink much," he advised. "You lose water very quickly in the jungle. Before you even know it. I have more water if you need some."

"Thanks, Ernesto." I swigged down another large gulp and smiled at him. "I think I'll be okay."

He bobbed his head to Viviana, gave me a small smile, and kept walking.

I took a last generous slurp of water, stoppered up the bottle, and nodded to Viviana that I was ready to continue.

"You are limping a little bit," Viviana noted. "Did you hurt yourself?"

"A while ago," I replied. "I've got a couple of pins in my leg. Normally it doesn't bother me. Just on long, steep hikes."

"It can be very steep around Danta. Will you be okay?"

"I can cope. It doesn't bug me as much as it used to."

The rest of the group was well ahead of us now. That suited my purposes just fine. I wanted to talk to Viviana, but not about my leg.

"Viviana," I began, uncertain how best to proceed. I decided to take the roundabout approach. "What's the scoop on this missing hiker?"

She turned and gave me a long, penetrating look. As if she knew that wasn't the question I really wanted to ask. Then she frowned a little and shook her head. "I did not meet him," she told me. "I didn't even know there was anybody besides us at the station. There are not supposed to be tourists visiting. I'm not sure why he was there."

Same words. A different meaning.

"I asked Liz about him, you know," I told her. "On the boat. She made it sound like he had some unsavory reason for being there."

Viviana made a face. "Liz is . . . ," she began, then stopped and took a deep breath. "Liz is seeing poachers everywhere, I think."

"Poachers?" The word came out in a surprised squeak.

"*Sí*. Because of Ernesto."

"Ernesto?" I was beginning to feel like a parrot. Then I threw all diplomacy to the wind. "What the hell's going on here, Viviana? I'm getting all kinds of weird vibes and I don't understand any of it. I don't think that's fair. We're going to be isolated at Danta. If we've got problems, then I'd really like to know why."

She paused for a moment, then nodded. "You're right," she sighed. "If I was in your position, I would want to know too. I thought Andres would have told you . . . ."

"Well, he didn't, so I'm asking you."

She took a few more steps in silence, organizing her thoughts. "There are several troubles," she said finally. "The first—and the biggest—is Ernesto."

"I gathered that. But he seems nice. A bit moody maybe and—"

"Ernesto is an ex-trafficker."

"He's a *what?*" I stared at her.

"An ex-trafficker. A poacher. He has trapped all kinds of wildlife. Jaguar, ocelot, monkeys, but mostly birds. They were his specialty. He has probably sold more illegal birds than anybody else in Costa Rica."

"And he's on our team?" I was appalled. "What bright spark thought *that* one up?"

"I know." Her already low voice deepened further with suppressed frustration. "I do not agree with this, using these people to help find feeding grounds or new populations. But it seems to be in style right now. In Brazil, you know, they've had a lot of success. When Helmut Sick was searching for the Lear's macaw, he found them because he was talking to the traffickers."

"I know, but still—"

"Here in Costa Rica—at TRC—there are people who believe Ernesto's knowledge is vital. They think he knows more about where the birds are than the biologists do." She shrugged. An angry gesture. "They are probably right, you know. He made so much money from smuggling birds that he would have made it his job to know where they live."

"But how do they—or we—know that he's not going to turn around and trap our macaws?"

"We don't, I guess. Not for sure. Ernesto was arrested five years ago and he spent some time in jail. Supposedly, he had a conversion while he was there. He swears to Jesus Christ that he is not trafficking anymore, but . . . ," she trailed off, letting me draw my own conclusions.

I digested it all for a long moment and decided that it gave me gas. A rare Lear's macaw could fetch forty thousand dollars on the black market; the last Spix's macaw had gone for sixty thousand. The rarer the bird, the more money could be made. It seemed an almost irresistible temptation for an ex-trafficker.

"So that's why Liz was so furious when she saw him," I said.

Viviana nodded. "Yes. I do not like it, either, but she is . . . more vocal."

"Hmm. And she thinks this Guillermo was involved too?"

Viviana shrugged dismissively. "I do not know about that. As I said, I never met him. But if he was a poacher, it seems strange that he would leave without taking his things. And why would he come to stay at Danta? No, I think it is more likely he was just a tourist."

"What do you think happened to him?"

She shook her head. "It's hard to say. If he was not experienced, he could have had an accident. It happens often, you know, people who think they can just walk through the jungle. Even without the animals, there is a strong danger of getting lost. You must be careful, Robyn—at least until you are more used to it."

"I will." I paused to wipe my face again. "You said Ernesto was the first, biggest problem. What's the second?"

"The second is Andres."

"What's wrong with Andres?"

"Nothing really. Except that he shouldn't be the leader of our group."

"Oh?" I prompted.

She didn't need much encouragement. The resentment in her voice was sharp.

"*I* am the one with more seniority. *I* have led many field teams. And *I* know more about macaws than he does. Opening up Danta again was my idea. When I talked to Andres about it, he agreed it was a good idea and we both applied for the funding. What a mistake! I have more experience and more knowledge, but—" she stopped in mid-stride.

I halted beside her, disturbed by her vehemence.

"But I am a woman," she finished bitterly. "And in

many ways that count, Costa Rica is a very traditional country. Do you know, my sisters never even completed school. They are all married and having children. Even my parents don't really understand why I am different. Why don't I get married? Why don't I want a man? Don't I want to have babies?" She threw up her arms. "I tell you, it is so hard sometimes, Robyn. This is why I went to America to study. But my life is here. I look around this forest and I know my life work is here. So," she hitched her pack a little higher on her shoulders, "I am the one who has to live with it. But it makes me furious sometimes."

"I don't blame you," I told her.

And I didn't. It was a common story. Women scientists shunted to the background or passed over in favor of their male colleagues. It's hard to swallow. I am a scientist. Period. That I happen to be a woman seems to me to have little relevance to this. When it comes to science (and most other things, for that matter), I've always thought that what was between a person's ears was more important than what was between their legs. But then, I'm seldom consulted on these things. Oh, attitudes *were* changing, but only those who measured time geologically believed they were changing quickly.

"And that is the trouble with Andres," Viviana said after a few more steps. "But I guess it is really my trouble. So now, you see, I am just another biologist and Andres is the leader because—"

"—he has a penis," I finished.

Viviana looked back at me in surprise, then she gave a throaty chuckle. "That is a good way of putting it. I have the brains and he has the penis." Her smile widened. "Ha! I like this!"

We walked on, the mood lighter now.

"To be fair, he has done a lot of conservation work in Monteverde," she said after a while. "He has never led a field team before, but I guess everybody must have a first time."

"He seems like a friendly enough guy," I said cautiously. "I mean, he isn't coming across like a macho asshole."

"Oh, he is not so bad," she agreed. "He is a bit too much in love with women, I think. But that is typical. You haven't been in our country for very long, so you may not have noticed this yet. If you are a single woman and walking down the street, the men are always hissing at you to show their appreciation."

"What, no wolf whistles?"

"No. No whistles, only hissing. We have a saying that there are thousands of snakes in Costa Rica, but only some of them are in the jungle."

We were still laughing as we walked around a bend in the trail and saw Andres and Ernesto waiting for us.

"What's so funny?" Andres asked.

Viviana and I looked at each other. Her eyes were dancing.

"Nothing at all," I told him, suppressing a smile.

We hiked the last mile as a group. It effectively put an end to my conversation with Viviana, but I didn't mind too much. She'd given me a lot to think about.

For the first time, I felt a pang of uneasiness about the project. An ex-trafficker who may or may not have reformed, a missing hiker, a leadership dispute, and one of the most difficult personalities I'd ever met. All cozied up together in an isolated field station. Rarely a good combination.

X-Originating-IP: [199.137.52.16]

From: "Robyn Devara"
<macaw1@woodrowconsultants.com>
To: "Kelt Roberson" <batnerd@tnc.com>
Subject: The macaw has landed
Date: Fri 29 Mar 15:15:47-0600

Hey, Kelt,

Sorry I haven't responded to your e-mail, but I just managed to download my messages today. The satellite phone is giving us some grief, so our Internet access is sporadic at best.

I can't tell you how good it was to hear news from home (though I am very sorry about your plants—Guido the cat doesn't usually go after plants. I will, of course, replace them all when I get back).

The rainforest is everything you told me it would be and more! I'm not sure I've blinked once since I came. The hummingbirds are like flying jewels, though they're so common here that everybody seems kind of blasé about them. Hard to believe. The hummers, as I discovered early on, adore my red backpack. They dive-bombed (dove-bombed?) me so much that I've had to borrow an old green pack from Andres. Poor buggers must have thought they'd hit the flower jackpot.

I had an interesting experience the other day. I was out with Viviana and Liz when we heard a loud bird call. I was convinced it was a macaw (it was REALLY loud) and practically wet my pants with excitement. You see, we've got a sort of unofficial competition going on: who can find the macaw first? In true field biologist fashion, a six-pack goes to the winner. So you can imagine my excitement. I went tearing off, slipping and sliding through muck and across tree roots . . . only to discover this humongous call was coming from a peentsy little wren! Viviana and Liz were almost peeing themselves laughing. Turns out the vegetation on the forest floor is so thick and shiny with moisture that it tends to amplify sounds. Sigh. That's me, spreading joy and laughter wherever I go. :)

Apart from the wren, my bird experiences have been incredible! Toucans, trogons, and motmots. Wow. The oropendulas, especially, are spectacular and their call sounds like water gurgling down the drain. Remind me again why I have to come back to Canada!

Okay, okay, I'll stop with the bird porn. On to more serious matters . . . we have not, as yet, seen a single macaw, mystery or otherwise (though there're supposed to be scarlet macaws all around here). Danta is little more than a small clearing with a few (very rustic) cabins, an astonishing array of beetles, and a network of extremely overgrown paths. At least, Marco tells me they're paths. I don't think I would have recognized them as such myself. He and Oscar have been here for a couple of months clearing the trails. The amount of growth over a mere ten years is amazing and provides a small amount of hope for those deforested bits we saw on the way down here.

Anyhow, all this means the jungle is thick and pretty difficult to get through. We've decided on a two-fold approach to our search—by treetop and by water. Each day, three groups will set out. One gets into the boat and checks the river and stream banks. The other two groups get to go up into the canopy. We've already scoped out a few climbing trees. I can hardly wait to spend a day in the treetops.

Lemme see, what else? Well, the heat is still gross, but after almost two weeks I think I'm finally starting to acclimatize. The insects are bearable (sort of). I think they must party with DEET for all the good it seems to do in keeping them away. They say that in the Corcovado there are 100 species of mammals, 367 of birds, 117 of reptiles, and 6,000 species of insects. I believe it! But quite frankly, I'd put up with a lot worse than warm temperatures and a bunch of bugs just to be down here. There's just so much to learn.

A case in point . . . I've been noticing quite a few largish brown and yellow millipedes on the forest floor. Yesterday Viviana scooped one up and starting blowing on its stomach (much to my surprise). Then she held it up to my nose and told me to take a whiff. I did, and it smelled exactly like Amaretto! Certainly one of the more interesting defense mechanisms. It does, however, sort of make you wonder who was weird enough to discover this in the first place. If I saw a big millipede, the last thing I'd think to do is flip it over and blow on its tummy.

So, life is generally great—though I think we'd all be a lot happier if we caught a glimpse of the macaw. There are some tensions within the group that are a bit troubling. And there was a bit of upset when we first arrived at Sirena. Apparently, some tourist—a guy named Guillermo—ended up at Danta during his travels but has since disappeared without a trace (he'd been missing for a week by the time I got here). We're all supposed to keep an eye out for him, but it doesn't seem as though anybody's holding their breath about finding him. Viviana thinks he probably got lost (an obviously dangerous thing to do around here). Needless to say, I'm being very careful. Liz keeps hinting that the guy had some kind of ulterior motive for being at Danta, but I don't put a lot of stock into anything she says. Liz is the cause of most of those troubling tensions I mentioned before. A difficult personality. You know what it's like to be part of an isolated field team—everything becomes exaggerated. Likes, dislikes, personality clashes. Hope we can all stay professional about this or it's going to be a long six months.

Okay, this is me going to bed now. Say hi to everyone at work, give Guido a kiss for me and take care.

Cheers,
Robyn

Among the scenes which are deeply impressed on my mind, none exceed in sublimity the primeval forests undefaced by the hand of man . . . no one can stand in these solitudes unmoved, and not feel that there is more in man than the mere breath of his body.

Charles Darwin
Voyage of the Beagle

Chapter 9

Climbing a tree isn't like riding a bike—just another one of those things they don't tell you in field biology school.

Marco and I were trying out a climbing technique popular among penny-pinching grad students and other impecunious researchers. Using what is essentially a modified bow and arrow, the goal is to shoot a round lead weight up into the tree and neatly over a sturdy branch. One person shoots the ball up, the other holds onto the reel of fishing line that's attached to the weight. Once you've got the fishing line over and back down, the next step is to tie it onto a thin black pilot line, which, in turn, goes up, over, and back down. The pilot line serves as a guide to bring up your thirty-odd pounds of climbing rope. But first you have to get the fishing line in place.

Sounds simple, right? Ha. Vines continually trapped my line, snarling it past hope of untangling. Branches turned out to be much higher than I'd estimated. And sometimes the lead ball broke free from the line, flying off into the jungle like a fat metal bird. Robyn Hood, it appeared, I was not.

A couple of times, everything worked like a dream, but when we tried to slide the fishing line snugly into the crotch of the tree—which was sturdier than the limb and therefore safer—the line would catch on something and refuse to budge, no matter how much we pulled and coaxed. In a different situation, our conversation would have raised a few eyebrows.

"Hey, there's a good-looking crotch."

"Yes, nice and big. But what about that one?"

"Oh, you're right, that one's bigger."

"The ball should go right in with no problems."

Good thing my mother couldn't hear me.

After numerous failed attempts on my part, Marco offered to try shooting the weight up, but it had become personal by then and I waved off his helping hand. I cursed, taking care to do so under my breath. I'd uttered a harmless little 'shit' after the third failed shot and Marco had been quite visibly shocked. One of those cultural things again. Sourly, I wondered if swearing in general was taboo, or if it was just because I was a woman and supposedly too delicate for such words.

Like *that* was ever a problem.

We were all working in different parts of the forest—each of the three groups, that is. Until we actually spotted our bird, the more area we could cover, the better. In another environment, we could have gone out on our own, surveyed a larger chunk of the park. But in the jungle, a twisted ankle, a bad fall, or a confused sense of direction could spell disaster—the still-missing Guillermo was testament to that. So each morning we set out with a field buddy.

I'd been teamed up with Marco. He was a boyish, curly-mopped character, probably in his late twenties, with a fair dose of swaggering machismo and a decidedly skeptical slant to his eyes whenever he looked at me. It was obvious he thought women were for cooking *gallo pinto* and making *bambinos*. He seemed perplexed by this Canadian woman who slogged through knee-deep mud, swore like a man, and clambered over fallen trees all by her big, strong self.

It wasn't that I didn't appreciate his offers of help, I just didn't want him to treat me differently because of my gender. He wouldn't have offered to help Andres over a tree root or to carry *his* backpack. Over the past couple of days, Marco and I had reached an unspoken understanding. I knocked cockroaches out of my boots, picked leeches off my legs, and generally got on with the business of fieldwork. And he waited for me to go all squeamish and girlie.

I may not have made the last cut for the band of Merry Men, but by the end of the morning, I did get better at shooting that miserable lead weight. Finally, just before noon, I managed to get the line over a good solid crotch some ninety to a hundred feet above our heads.

"Would you like to go up first?" Marco asked politely once we'd rigged the tree for climbing.

I could tell from the twinkle in his dark eyes that he didn't think I would.

Ah, another thrown glove.

"Great!" I said with enthusiasm. And had the pleasure of seeing the surprise on his face.

I jammed a helmet on my head, stepped into my harness, and got Marco to check the straps. Then, with an air of cool confidence, I casually clipped my Jumar ascenders onto the rope and up I went.

Well, that was the general idea.

"Aaaugh!" I shrieked. A girlie scream if I ever heard one.

Ten feet up, I flailed about, finding myself upside

down and completely twisted around. This was harder than it looked! I moved again and the world spun alarmingly. I clamped my mouth shut on another cry and fought to center my body weight. It seemed to work. At least I was right side up again. With a resigned grimace, I looked down.

Below me, Marco had collapsed on the ground, holding his stomach and roaring with laughter. I swung gently above him. Back and forth. Like a large, overripe fruit.

"You . . . you look like a big *piñata!*" he hooted.

I made a face at him. "You know, that really isn't very helpful."

"Perhaps I should get a stick!"

"Perhaps I should cut the rope and fall on you."

He cracked up again. Then I started chuckling too. Together we snickered and snuffled until I was afraid I'd pee my pants. So much for being cool.

All this hilarity, however, was not exactly conducive to climbing the damn tree. I wiped the laugh tears from my eyes and got myself under control. Then I settled down to the business of ratcheting, or jugging, up the tree. Ten jugs, rest, ten jugs, rest. It got easier as I got the hang of it. Maybe it *was* like riding a bicycle. By the time I'd ascended to about forty feet, I was feeling pretty impressed with myself. Maybe I'd be tapped for the next *Mission Impossible* flick.

Although much of my concentration was on the climb, I kept getting distracted by the myriad forms of life on this single tree. Fern mats the size of sleeping bags tumbled from branch to branch like waterfalls of green Shredded Wheat. Epiphytes, those hitchhikers of the rainforest, were astonishing in their numbers and variety. Taking their sustenance from rain and settled detritus, they blanketed the tree, colonizing every available space. Bromeliads sprang up like explosions of green, clinging to the trunk, wrapping around the vines and lianas. Think of the top of a pineapple and you've got your basic bromeliad. The central whorl of their leaves acts like a water tank, providing drinking water and habitat for many creatures—some of which never descend to the forest floor.

As I jugged up the tree, I strained to peek into each bromeliad I passed. Scientific inquiry, after all, begins with curiosity.

"Be careful, Robyn," Marco called up.

His warning brought me back to the task at hand. The operative word being *hand*. Preoccupied with bromeliads, I was reaching out to steady myself on a mossy branch when suddenly I saw the moss move.

"*Son of a bitch!*" I yelped, snatching my hand away and biting back a scream.

The rope jerked, swinging me away from the tree like a pendulum. Desperately, I stuck out my legs to brace myself against the trunk, but my boot slid on a slick bit of moss. With a muffled *whump*, my torso smacked into the side of the tree. The tree was thick enough to absorb the impact, but the vibrations thrummed down the branches.

The snake's head shot up into strike position. It flicked its tongue, tasting my scent, the smell of my fear. I froze. The world shrunk to the few feet between me and the snake.

It was a small snake, only about two feet long. But its head was wide and I saw with horror the characteristic horny scales above the eye. I knew this snake. It was an eyelash viper.

It seemed to consider me for an eternity, regarding me with flat, reptilian eyes. I held my breath. I could feel the sweat trickling down my face, the only movement in my world besides the snake's flickering tongue.

Just when I thought I'd burst with tension, the snake lowered its head and began uncoiling. I was so close, I could hear the dry rasp of scales scraping against each other. It looped a few coils over smaller branches to give itself better purchase and then, with a last derisive flick of its tongue, it undulated away down the length of the limb.

Time resumed its normal course, and my world expanded once again. The breath exploded out of me as I became aware of my surroundings.

Heat. Sound. Noise.

Marco.

"Robyn! *Robyn!* Are you okay?" He was shouting, his voice thick with worry.

I clung onto the rope, taking deep breaths. Aware now of the erratic pounding of my heart.

"Yeah," I managed to call down, my voice sounding tight and strained. "There's—" I sucked in another breath. "There's an eyelash viper up here. I didn't see it till the last minute."

"*You didn't see—?*" He was incredulous, then he paused and nodded in understanding. "Ah, a green one."

Eyelash vipers come in two color phases: a bright, golden yellow, and a greenish olive speckled with black. One was hard to miss. Both were deadly.

"It was a green one," I agreed shakily. "Damn thing looked like a clump of moss."

"You must be careful," Marco urged.

"No shit, Sherlock," I muttered. But I said it quietly to myself.

I filled my lungs with air, then let it out slowly. My hands were slippery with sweat and my heart still thought it was a member of a drum and bass group. After a few minutes, I started ratcheting up the tree again. I kept my nose out of bromeliads and there were no more nasty surprises. I finished the climb without any more girlie screams.

A hundred feet up in the canopy, the tree enveloped me in its leafy embrace. Thick foliage blocked the dizzying view, providing the illusion of a safety net. The ground, so far below, was no longer visible.

The tree had been an excellent choice, I realized, with a fine, clear view of the surrounding canopy and a fruiting fig twenty yards to our right. Macaws were supposed to like figs. I settled on a thick branch and waited for Marco to join me.

There was more Shredded Wheat moss up here, which sort of got me thinking about breakfast. Which naturally led to thoughts of lunch. I pulled off my daypack and rummaged around in it till I found a package of cold empanadas.

"Y'know, this is really a great spot," I called down to Marco, my mouth full of cheese empanada.

"You are eating lunch already?" The question floated up on a waft of disbelief.

"I'm hungry."

"You are *always* hungry."

"I can't help it. It's hard work."

"You are not eating *my* lunch, are you?"

"Would I do that?"

"You did on Thursday."

"One little mistake . . . I *said* I was sorry. And I let you have the whole mango."

Marco grunted and jugged up the last few feet. I waited till he'd settled himself on a branch, then I handed him his share of the lunch.

"You know," I mumbled, scarfing down another empanada, "we could build a platform up here. Look, we could use that branch . . . and these two over here." I pointed them out while I spoke. "Mount a platform and rig it up with a blind."

"It would work very well," Marco agreed as he unwrapped his lunch. "The macaws, they would not see us this way. But first we must see *them*."

I grinned sheepishly. "Point taken."

We started scanning the trees with our binoculars.

Until the past two decades, the rainforest canopy had been an unknown, inaccessible world. Biologists of the past could only guess at what was up here. Their conjectures were based on observations from the ground and studies of whatever plopped down on them from the treetops. I was tasting an environment that Charles Darwin would have given his left nut to experience. It was exhilarating.

Marco and I split a juicy mango for dessert, and watched a strawberry poison dart frog dunk itself into a large, silvery-green bromeliad. Off to our left, a troop of capuchin monkeys swept across the aerial highway of vines and branches, calling to each other and dropping half-eaten fruits to the forest floor. A wispy, bright green vine snake quickly slithered out of their way.

We saw a small flock of toucans with buttercup yellow bibs and sky blue legs. Their bi-colored bills were huge, which shouldn't have astonished me but somehow did. You'd think I'd eaten enough Froot Loops in my lifetime not to be surprised by their appearance. They seemed so comical, hopping awkwardly from one branch to another, almost unbalanced by their enormous bills, and yet, I had never seen anything so achingly beautiful. I watched, utterly entranced, as they *yo-yip a-yip a-yip*ped to each other in their search for ripe fruits. Seeds helicoptered down around us.

There were bananaquits and tanagers and brief flashes of gem-colored hummingbirds. But no macaws. I kept thinking that the gods sort of owed me after the whole viper thing. I guess they didn't figure it the same way.

We stayed up there for the rest of the afternoon, immersed in life in the canopy. Talking birds, scribbling notes, and huddling through a brief but heavy rain shower with our binoculars stored in plastic baggies to keep them dry. We sat up there until our bums were numb. Still no macaws.

"Maybe next time," I shrugged as we prepared to descend.

"*Sí*. That would be nice," Marco replied.

It had been a slow day, not a wasted one. Never that. But things got a little faster on the hike back to Danta—though not in any way I would have expected or wanted.

"*Por favor,* just a moment, Robyn." Marco held up his hand.

I stopped obligingly and took the opportunity to mop off my face again.

"What's up?" I asked, looking around the forest to see what had caught his attention.

He turned to me, his brow scrunched together in a furrow. "I am not sure. . . ."

"There's something wrong?"

Marco rubbed the back of his neck. "Nooo . . . ," he answered, hesitating. Then he nodded. "Yes. Yes, I think there is something not right. Look up ahead. What do you see?"

I hitched the climbing rope higher on my shoulder and peered into the gloom. "What am I looking for? I see the trail. I see the orange marker on that strangler fig. And I see what looks like another trail heading off to the east."

"Yes!" He nodded vigorously. "That is what I see too." He strode over to the second trail, mumbling to himself and scanning up and down the trees.

"Look," he called out. "This vine has been cut not long ago. And this fern, it was chopped off. Not eaten by an animal."

Puzzled, I followed him. "I don't get it. Why is this a problem?"

He didn't answer me right away. When he finally turned to face me, his expression was troubled. "Robyn," he said, "Oscar and I did not cut this trail."

CHAPTER 10

"Poachers?" Andres' tone was sharp with dismay.

"Maybe *oreros*." Marco shrugged.

"Gold miners?" Liz curled her lip in a sneer. "And how likely is *that?*"

Marco lifted his shoulders again, uncomfortable under her scrutiny.

We were sitting in Danta's dining hall—a largish wooden structure with a corrugated tin roof and wide, unscreened windows, which let in the late afternoon sun. At one end, there was a rudimentary kitchen behind a high counter. A plank table and a row of splintery — benches filled the rest of the room. Mesh bags heavy with vegetables and other foodstuffs depended from the rafters. At night, kerosene lamps glowed softly from their hooks on the moisture-stained beams.

The dining hall had become the center of our project—an informal meeting place where we could gather after work to discuss our progress and map out strategies for the following day. We usually hung out there after dinner too, adding to our field notes, reading, or expounding on the meaning of life. I had a hunch there would be no friendly philosophizing tonight.

Liz had made herself thoroughly disliked during the

past week and a half. Officious, highly critical of others, she'd pretty much alienated everybody on the team—even the easygoing Oscar. I found it interesting that she never tangled with Viviana or me. Either she subscribed to some fellowship-in-sisterhood thing or we simply hadn't ticked her off enough yet. In some ways, she reminded me of one of Dan's snakes. Cold and menacing. Something you wouldn't want to piss off. But no snake I knew was quite this shrill.

When Marco finally answered her, he turned towards me as if I'd asked the question. "It is possible," he said. "The *oreros* still come to Corcovado. The rangers are good about chasing them away, but they come back and—"

Liz dismissed his explanation with a rude snort. "Uh huh. It's pretty obvious to me what we're dealing with—and we don't have to invent stories about gold miners." She gave Ernesto a steady, icy glare.

Ernesto met her stare without expression. "I do not do these things anymore," he said softly.

"Maybe you need to practice that line in front of a mirror, pal, because you're sure not convincing me," she snapped back. "If you're not 'doing' these things anymore, then why are we getting poachers all of a sudden? Ten years of nothing, but as soon as Ernesto gets wind of a new species, we start having problems."

"I—"

"How many of your former 'friends' have you told about this project?"

"I have not—"

"Did you bring anybody here before we arrived? And how is it that Guillermo—"

"Enough, Lizabeth!" Andres slammed his hand on the plank table, rattling the cups and interrupting her tirade.

I flicked a glance at Viviana and raised my eyebrows.

Andres took a deep breath, steadying himself. "It could be *oreros,*" he said finally. "It could be poachers. Okay? We don't know anything for sure right now and there is not enough information either way. We are a team. We should not be fighting like this. It doesn't solve anything."

His tone was gentle, but I could hear the granite behind it. So could Liz. She broke off the staring contest with Ernesto and trained her gooseberry eyes on Andres.

It had been coming for days now, but that didn't stop the rest of us from squirming both at Liz's vituperative attack and at Andres' uncharacteristic show of anger. Given Ernesto's background, I didn't much care for his inclusion on our team, either, but what happened to giving someone the benefit of the doubt? Liz had been hounding the man ever since she'd clapped eyes on him.

Still, Andres would have been better to talk to her in private.

"Any chance the path was cut by that missing hiker?" I asked, as their silent battle stretched on. "Maybe trying to find his way back to Danta?"

Liz dropped her eyes rebelliously. The activity in the room stuttered and came back to life. Viviana murmured something to Andres, and Oscar came over to the table with a basket of tortillas.

Marco shook his head in answer to my question. "Guillermo did not take his equipment with him."

"*Any* of it?"

"No. Oscar and I, we came back from working and he was gone. Everything was here. Even his machete is still in the lab."

"So I guess that leaves us with gold miners or

poachers." I chewed my lip thoughtfully, disliking both possibilities. "How dangerous are these *oreros?*"

It was Oscar who answered my question. "You have to be cautious," he said slowly. "It is illegal for them to be here. Marco is right, the rangers have been very good about chasing them away. A few years ago, it was not so good."

"Are they armed?"

"*Sí*. That is one of the reasons to be careful. Not to make them mad."

I saw Viviana slide Liz a sidelong look.

"Okay, then, what about the poachers?" I asked. "How serious are they?"

Oscar gave a nonchalant shrug. "Not very," he said. "The Corcovado has never been a popular place—"

"Until now," Liz retorted.

He inclined his head.

"But how serious a threat are they?" I was insistent.

Oscar just shrugged again, so I looked to Andres. He drew in a breath and started to answer, but Ernesto beat him to it.

"I will answer if it is okay," he said with an apologetic look toward him.

"Oh, please do," Liz muttered sarcastically.

Andres frowned at her and nodded for Ernesto to continue.

"They can be very serious," he began. "It depends who it is. You know the bird trade is worth much money. But the habitat is disappearing, and the parrots, they do not reproduce quickly. They are getting more rare, and so the trappers are getting more desperate. Sometimes they have machine guns. Also, the rangers are better now at catching us—them." He colored a little at the stumble. "So you see. . . ." He held his hands out as if to say I should draw my own conclusions.

"Stay frosty," I finished flatly.

Ernesto frowned. "Frosty?"

"Sorry. It means stay alert and try not to pi—uh, make anybody mad."

He nodded. "Yes. That would be best."

"How far did you follow this trail?" Andres asked Marco.

"Not far. To a little stream, but you could see that it kept going on the other side."

"We'll have to follow it," I said.

Six pairs of eyes looked at me.

"We don't have much choice," I told them. "I hate to be the one to suggest this, but they might have found what we're looking for. We have to see where that trail goes."

Slowly, Andres nodded his agreement, but his dark eyes were troubled.

That night as we headed toward our shared cabin, neither Viviana nor I could get the mysterious trail out of our minds. I think we both knew deep down that it was a trapper's trail. As Ernesto had reminded me, much of the Corcovado wildlife was rare. That meant it was popular with collectors. And the rangers lacked the manpower to police the park effectively. That meant it was popular with poachers.

"Do *you* think Ernesto is still trafficking?" I asked Viviana as we prepared to turn in for the night.

The kerosene lamp bathed our small cabin in a dusky, orange glow. Pretty, but not bright enough to see if anything nasty had crawled into your sleeping bag during the day. I took my bag off the wooden bed frame, unzipped it, and shook vigorously. A single, large cockroach plopped to the floor and skittered off into a dark corner. It had happened every night so far without fail. Clearly a bug under the misapprehension my sleeping bag was a time-share.

Viviana shook out her own sleeping bag, crawled into it, and arranged the mosquito netting around her before she considered my question. She lay down with her head propped up against her arm.

"I am not certain," she answered finally. "I do not know what to think yet."

"But you've been teamed up with him for over a week now, haven't you gotten some vibes?"

"Vibes?" she smiled, her teeth white in the semi-darkness. "No. No vibes. He is very knowledgeable about the jungle, I will say that for him. And he has good eyes for finding birds."

"Not surprising, given his past."

"Mmm." Viviana nodded her agreement. "I don't know what to tell you, Robyn. He is quiet, but he knows I don't like him very much because of what he has done. We don't spend time with chatting."

"Well, at least Andres didn't try to team him up with Liz."

Viviana gave a mock shudder. "I am glad *I* was not teamed up with her. I don't think I have ever met anybody so unfriendly."

"I know what you mean."

"I guess he had no choice but to team himself with her. Poor Andres."

"So you can spare some pity for him, can you?"

Viviana smiled over at me. "A very little bit," she admitted, her eyes dancing. "Although I can say to you that a tiny part of me is laughing."

We snickered guiltily.

"What do you think about this missing tourist?" I asked after we'd quieted down.

"What about him?"

"Don't you think it's strange that he disappeared like that? Without even taking a daypack or a machete with him."

"Not really. Perhaps he thought he was only going out for a short while. It's easy to be distracted in the jungle, Robyn. And easy to get lost too. It doesn't happen all the time, but it happens more than you think."

I was reminded uncomfortably of my own distraction with bromeliads. And about what had almost happened because of it.

Viviana turned the lamp off and I scooched myself down in my sleeping bag. For the first night this week, it wasn't raining. Torrential rain on a corrugated tin roof effectively drowns out any other noises, even conversation is difficult. But tonight the jungle was alive with sound. The rasping buzz of cicadas, the rustle of nocturnal mammals, the scuttling of lizards. Transparent glass frogs sang of love from the undersides of leaves, and the *tink* of the imaginatively named Tink frog sounded just outside our screened window. A rainforest lullaby.

"I am angry at this news of poachers," Viviana murmured after a long while. Her voice was so low, I almost didn't catch it.

I opened my eyes and peered over at her in the darkness. Waiting.

She was quiet for a long time.

"For years, there has been very little poaching in this part of Corcovado," she said finally. "It has always been difficult to get here. And now we find a trail."

Another pause, longer this time.

"It doesn't feel good, Robyn. It feels now like we are racing, instead of carrying out a scientific study."

I was silent for a moment. The leaves whispered their song of life. The Tink frog called out again. A single voice in the rare and precious rainforest symphony.

"It was always a race, Viviana," I said softly.

CHAPTER 11

Montezuma took his revenge that night. He must have been some pissed off. Viviana spent more time in the outhouse than she did in bed. By morning, her face was pale and beaded with perspiration.

"I think I will stay here today," she said wanly as I was getting dressed.

I finished buttoning up my shirt. "Good idea," I agreed. "You look awful. Can I get you anything? A juice? Cup of coffee?"

She made a face and shook her head. "No, thank you. I'm going to try to sleep some more."

"Okay, then. I'll get Oscar to look in on you a little later."

"*Gracias.*"

I stepped out into a gloriously fresh day. Leaves sparkled with the morning dew, fat drops of moisture hanging from their drip tips like Christmas lights, flashing through all the colors of the spectrum, depending on the way the sunlight caught them. The smell of fecund earth was heavy in the air. Every morning, just before breakfast, a single green honeycreeper came to sing in the avocado tree between our cabin and Liz's. I paused on the step and listened.

Tsup tsup tsup. There he was, right on schedule.

I headed to the dining hall, stepping over the skeleton of a new cabin on my way. That Oscar was a busy guy, I noted. He ruled over the kitchen, maintained the trails and buildings, fought a losing battle with the generator, and always made sure our field gear was stored properly. Now he was cutting trees to build more cabins.

As field stations go, Danta was a bit sparse in terms of housing. Andres had his own spanking new cabin, presumably built by Oscar's cousins. These mysterious cousins had gone off before we'd arrived at the station, but were, Oscar assured us daily, due back "very soon now." Liz too had her own cabin, though it was much older and smaller. Viviana and I shared a similar structure. I'd had the option of having my own space, but the only vacant cabin had a decidedly splintery look to it, a dubious lean, and an extended family of golden orb spiders, all of which seemed prepared to arm-wrestle me for the privilege of staying there. I knew I'd made the right decision when both Ernesto and Marco turned down the place as well. They were ensconced in each of two tiny rooms located in the old lab, a largish building, which eventually (if Oscar's cousins ever returned) would be expanded to include several more rooms and a permanent office. Oscar bunked down in a makeshift room just off the storage shed behind the dining hall.

As a grad student, I'd slept in many a grungy tent, but the American professor and his students were due to arrive the following week, and they had, apparently, been promised cabins. So for the past few days, the buzz of Oscar's chainsaw had mingled with the gurgling calls of oropendulas. I got the impression Oscar was a little peeved with his absent cousins.

Oscar was a huge baritone of a guy, all stomach and luxuriant mustache, who understood beauty in terms of a savory empanada or a steaming bowl of beans and rice with Salsa Lizano on the side. He clucked sympathetically when I told him about Viviana and promised to look in on her. Then he waved me over to a breakfast table that wobbled under the weight of fresh pineapples, deep dishes of beans and rice, a platter of scrambled eggs with melted Monteverde cheese, and a large bowl of sweet, milky porridge. Oscar also understood the degree to which field biologists enjoy being fed.

"Viviana's not well today," I informed the rest of the crew as I loaded up my plate.

"Why? What's wrong with her?"

From anyone else it would have been a polite question. From Liz, it sounded accusing and rude.

"Nothing much," I answered, flaring my nostrils in irritation. "She's just got a bad case of the creeping crud."

"I hope it's not the food," Liz snipped. "That'd be real special."

"Well, you ate enough of it last night, Liz, and you're still here," I pointed out, allowing a hint of disappointment to color my tone.

She stiffened.

"I think the food is very tasty," Marco said.

"Two thumbs up here," I agreed.

He scrunched up his face. "Except for what *you* cooked the other day. That was terrible!"

"Whine, whine, whine," I said. "You ate it, didn't you?"

"Of course," Marco shrugged. "There was nothing else. And besides, *mi mamá* always says I have the stomach of a goat."

"Very funny."

My crunchy beans and mushy rice had been the source of much hilarity. I didn't think it had been *that* awful, but I'd since been demoted to sous chef, trusted only with chopping vegetables and hauling water from the well.

"So, Andres," I turned to him, "you want Ernesto to come with us today?"

Andres paused, his coffee cup halfway to his mouth. "Uh, yes. If it is okay with you."

"Of course," I said affably.

In fact, it wasn't all that okay, but I felt I had to make up for Liz's attitude. I didn't want the Ticos thinking that all North Americans were assholes. Besides, it would give me a chance to get to know Ernesto better, maybe even finesse a few answers out of him. I hadn't forgotten about his odd behavior the first night I'd been in Costa Rica. Or about those bullets I'd found under the desk in the TRC house. Did wildlife traffickers pack Uzis?

Yes, I had a few questions for Ernesto.

Marco and I—and now Ernesto—had been handed the unenviable task of following the mysterious trail. We were armed, but just with machetes—and those only in case the vegetation got too thick. A gun-toting poacher wasn't likely to quiver in his boots at the sight of my machete, but the weight of it swinging from my hip was comforting. Somewhat less comforting was the knowledge that I'd probably whack my own leg off if I tried to use it.

We were doing a routine survey, checking the area out, keeping our eyes peeled for parrot-type shapes (and poacher-type shapes), but mostly looking for good climbing trees. By the end of the morning, we'd found one. Trouble was, someone else had found it first.

"Marco!" I touched his arm and pointed ahead.

He looked and spat out a Spanish word that sounded like a curse.

The tree was one of those rainforest giants. Its branches reached up out of the gloom and into the sunlit canopy; massive buttress roots anchored it in the thin soil. Limbs were covered with the requisite epiphytes and mosses, draped with the requisite vines and lianas. Except a few of those vines were a most unnatural color. Bright yellow, neon orange. Ropes. Climbing ropes.

Ernesto was plowing ahead of us now, flinging ferns out of his way, muttering angrily under his breath. Marco was right behind him. I held back a little, watching Ernesto's reaction with interest.

Still mumbling to himself, he circled the tree once, twice, clearly searching for something. And then with a grunt, he bent down and scooped something up from the forest floor.

"Look!" He held it up. "It is what I thought. Andres is not going to be happy."

I came closer, my attention riveted by the object in his hand. It looked like an arrow. A long, smooth shaft with three feathers at one end. Except where the point should have been on the opposite end, there were two wooden sticks, tied in the center to form the shape of a cross. It was smeared with a black substance.

"Resin," Ernesto said when I reached out to touch the cross. The black stuff was gooey and very sticky.

"Poachers?" I asked, already guessing the answer.

Ernesto nodded once curtly. "*Sí*. They find a perching tree by watching for droppings on the ground," he explained. "When they have found one, they climb into another tree close by and wait. When the birds come—*Foosh!* They shoot an arrow like this."

I sucked in my breath. "But doesn't that hurt the birds?"

"No. The arrow is tied to a thin rope. When it hits the bird, the resin makes it stick."

"So the hunter can pull in the bird without hurting it," I said in understanding.

Ernesto nodded.

I fingered the arrow again. "It's a big arrow."

"*Sí*, the smaller birds are caught in nets. Arrows like this are for larger birds. The parrots and the . . . ," he faltered.

"Macaws."

He bowed his head.

"Hey! *Aquí!*" Marco called out, motioning us over. "Come here!"

He'd been pacing around the tree in ever-widening circles. Now he'd stopped at another tree twenty feet away. I pushed carefully through a clump of ferns to join him. I could see why he'd called us over. Bird poop. Lots of it. On the ground, spattered down the smooth trunk. A perching tree for sure.

"So much for *oreros*," I said glumly.

"What I don't understand," I said a little later, "is how they knew to come here in the first place."

We'd stopped for lunch beside a stream lined with water-smoothed pebbles. Boulders dotted the banks, evidence the small waterway had once been much larger. Warmed by the midday heat, butterflies flickered across the small clearing, settling on tiny, yellow flowers, or soaking up moisture from the damp earth around the stream. Marco and Ernesto were sprawled on rocks in the sun. I'd opted for a shaded boulder.

"I mean, this place is not the most accessible in the country." I rummaged around in my daypack and pulled out a package of empanadas and a large mango. "Ernesto, is your knife handy? Ah, thanks." I started slicing up the mango. "There are plenty of other places to trap birds. Places that are easier to get to. If they wanted scarlet macaws, wouldn't they be better off going somewhere else? Like Manuel Antonio, for example." I named a national park further north, which was known for its scarlet macaws.

"Unless they heard about our macaws," Marco mumbled around his empanada.

I looked down at my own food for a long moment. "Yeah. That's what I'm worried about. But if that's the case, how'd they find out about them?"

"Somebody knew about them before we arrived," Marco pointed out. "Or you would not have found one in Canada."

"I guess," I chewed my lower lip. "But we don't know where that one was taken. Not for sure. The CITES people weren't even positive it came from Costa Rica."

Ernesto had remained silent up till this point, seemingly involved in his lunch. "I know what you are all thinking," he said now. Quiet and defensive.

I held up my hand to stop him. "Hey, relax, nobody's accusing anyone here. It's not like the project's top secret or anything. We're just speculating—guessing—at this point."

"I did not tell anyone." His voice started to rise. "I do not keep in contact with those people. I don't do these things anymore. And I did not know the man that is missing."

Obviously Liz had been at him again.

"Okay, okay." I took his words at face value. "I'm not implying you told anyone. But, you might have some insights, something we wouldn't know. Like, are we dealing with professionals here, or just a couple of local guys trying to make ends meet?"

Ernesto's bushy eyebrows scrunched together. "Ends meet?"

"Sorry. Trying to get a little extra money. You must know the kind of guys I'm talking about. Their fathers and grandfathers caught birds for a living so they think it's okay for them to do it too. I understand that—I don't much like it, but I understand it. So are we dealing with somebody like that? Or are we looking for professionals who come in, get as many birds as they can, and get out?"

"It could be both ways," he answered unhelpfully.

I suppressed a sigh. "All right, then, do you think they're after scarlet macaws or ours?"

He shrugged. "*We* have not even seen our macaw yet."

Which didn't really answer my question.

"I wonder why they left their ropes," Marco said into the lull that followed. "Good ropes like these are expensive. Why leave them?"

"They were either interrupted or they're planning on coming back." I shrugged. "The ropes haven't been here very long, or they would've molded by now. I think whoever left them will be back."

"Yes," Marco nodded. "That is what I think too."

It didn't take long to finish our lunch. None of us felt like lingering. We followed the path for a few more hours, but didn't see any more ropes on trees—or any macaws, for that matter. Marco thought he could hear scarlet macaws, but I wasn't as familiar with their call and I couldn't confirm it. Ernesto denied hearing them at all.

We were a somber group on the way back to Danta late that afternoon. Ernesto had been quiet and sullen for the rest of the day, upset with me for interrogating him. Well, he'd be getting a lot more questions back at the station. I considered Liz's probable reaction to our bad news and found myself almost feeling sorry for him.

I couldn't make up my mind about Ernesto. Was he sincere about his conversion? Or was he using our project to further his own agenda?

I was still mulling it over when we hit the mass of boot-devouring mud just before the main trail to Danta. We'd passed this way earlier in the day, and I'd walked right out of one of my boots, burying my sock foot in the gooey mess. This time, I decided, I'd go around it.

Walking through snake country is a powerful experience. You find yourself hyperaware, noticing every blade of grass, every leaf, every slight movement. After all, it could save your life. Up until now, I had been very aware of my surroundings. Taking note of every rustle in the leaf litter, each squiggly shape on the ground and in the trees. But maybe I was too preoccupied with Ernesto and the poachers. Maybe I was thinking too much about saving my last pair of clean socks.

Whatever the reason, I didn't look closely enough at where I was putting my feet. When I stepped down on a thick patch of dead wood, I felt something squirm and strike at my foot.

"*Son of a bitch!*" I leapt into the air and landed a good three feet away.

Blood pounded so strongly in my ears that all other sounds were momentarily drowned out. And then I saw it. Greenish-brown with darker, pale-edged blotches.

A fer-de-lance.

It whipped itself around, head raised in strike position. I could hear a weird sort of ticking noise. An angry hissing. It started moving towards me, undulating across the uneven ground.

I sucked in a lungful of air and turned to run. But the soupy muck had grabbed my boots in a death grip and I couldn't move. In desperation, I yanked my feet out of my boots and tried to make a run for it in my socks. I slipped and squelched through the slimy mud. Where the hell was Marco?

Out of the corner of my eye, I could see slithering movement. *Oh gods.* It was fast, and it was right behind me. And now I didn't even have the nominal protection of rubber boots.

"*Marco!*" I screamed raggedly.

But it wasn't Marco who came to my rescue. The flash of a machete sliced through the gloom and in a blink I saw Ernesto standing over the snake's severed body.

But . . . I gaped in disbelief. The snake had been cut in two, *but the front end was still coming at me!* It skittered crazily towards me, entrails spilling out behind it.

"*Holy shit!*" I shrieked and tried to move my clay-covered feet.

I'd waited too long. My feet had sunk down into the muck and I couldn't budge. I struggled against it, frenzied with panic. How could the snake still be alive?

A massive heave, and I managed to pull my right foot up out of the mud. But the movement carried through and I lost my balance. I fell with a despairing cry, plunging up to my armpit in sticky mud. My life flew by me in a blinding flash.

Thunk!

Another flash. Not my life this time. A machete. Marco.

The fer-de-lance's severed head lay mere inches away from my leg. I stared at the head. I raised my eyes and stared up at Marco. Then I went and did something unutterably girlie.

A wave of dizziness washed over me and the whole jungle went dark.

Damn.

Chapter 12

By the time reality wavered back into focus, I found myself sitting in the middle of the trail, propped up between Marco and Ernesto. I wasn't in the mud anymore, though my clothes were caked with it. Somebody had retrieved my boots. They were beside my daypack, the worst of the muck scraped from them.

I stirred and felt Ernesto move away. Marco stayed. Probably a good thing. I still felt woozy.

"Ah, hell," I groaned. "Don't tell me I fainted. How stupid."

"Yes, very stupid," Marco agreed.

I scrubbed my face, streaking mud across it, though I didn't realize that till later. Now that the initial shock was over, I was appalled at my stupidity. To step on a snake? And not just any snake, but one of the most deadly, aggressive snakes in the world.

"I—" I began, then stopped, not knowing what to say.

Marco nodded in understanding.

"Thanks," I managed a wobbly smile.

Marco patted my shoulder and helped me to my feet.

Ernesto was standing a few paces away, facing into the jungle.

"*Muchas gracias*, Ernesto," I said. "Thank you for trying."

He turned and regarded me, his expression unreadable. "*Con mucho gusto,*" he replied with a slight bow.

It seemed an oddly polite thing to say.

As we hiked the last few miles to the station, I found myself walking at a sloth's pace, suspicious of every lump of leaf litter, every shadowy depression. My bad leg was starting to ache. When we got back to Danta, I dumped my gear and headed straight for the showers. I needed to wash the mud off, to scrub away the entire incident.

We didn't have hot showers at Danta. Instead, large cisterns caught the rainwater, screens filtered out the worst of the leaves and insects, and hoses snaked down into two, tarp-lined shower stalls. Usually the cold water felt good after a day in the field, soothing insect bites, cooling sunburns. That day, the water left me cleaner, but I was far from soothed. Reaction had started to set in.

Viviana wasn't in our cabin. I hoped she was feeling better—and wished I could say the same thing about myself. I dropped my damp towel on the back of the chair, wrapped myself in my sleeping bag, and shook.

My encounter with the eyelash viper was one thing. This was different. This snake *attacked* me. It went out of its way to come after me. Even after Ernesto cut it in half, it kept coming. What the hell kind of snake was that? What the hell was I doing in a place that *had* snakes like that?

"Wherever there's one fer-de-lance, you can pretty much bet its mate isn't too far away. . . ."

I could still hear Dan's words. Marco had killed one snake this afternoon. One. So . . . where was the other one? And, perhaps more importantly, was it mad?

I was still shivering intermittently when I heard a tap at the door. I looked up, surprised to see the shadows lengthening in the late afternoon sunlight.

"Uh . . . just a second," I called out, shedding the sleeping bag and pulling on some clean clothes.

I opened the door. It was Andres.

"Robyn, are you okay?" Concern was etched across his face.

"Of course," I shrugged, trying to look tough and hard. As if deadly snakes attacked me all the time. As if I was a regular on *Crocodile Hunter*. But Andres kept looking at me with those darkly sympathetic eyes. I gritted my teeth. "Okay, it scared the crap out of me," I admitted.

He put his arm around me and made comforting noises. I let the arm stay there for the time being.

"I thought my number was up," I told him. "I mean, I drive a car at home or sometimes I take the C-train. I know I could be killed in a car crash, or the train might go off the tracks, but. . . ."

"But a snake, it seems much worse."

"Yeah. Yeah, it does."

"But you know, Robyn, there are many, many people living and working in the rainforest and they survive. They are not all bitten by snakes."

"I know, I know." I scrubbed at my face. "And I've been telling myself all afternoon that dead is dead whether it's by snake or car or train."

"This is true. So, you are not going to run away home on us?"

Insulted, I pulled away from him. "What gave you that idea?" I demanded.

"An encounter with a *terciopelo* is always scary—for

anyone. I remember the first time I saw one. It was a juvenile, just a baby. It still had the yellow tip on its tail. I was looking at frogs and when I stood up . . . there she was in the tree, right beside my eye."

I shuddered.

"It's not something you forget too quickly."

"No."

"So, if you are not going home—"

I shot him an angry look.

"—then the best thing to be done is go out right away into the jungle again."

"*What?*"

"So you don't lose your nerves."

I was about to protest, but, on second thought, it was good advice.

Andres pushed himself off the door frame. "Come, I will go with you. We have an hour before it gets dark and there is a wild mango tree not very far."

"Mangos?"

Andres grinned. "Yes, I have noticed you're very fond of them. I will show you where they come from."

I considered that for a moment. I really didn't feel like going back into the forest, but Andres was right. If I didn't get my nerve back, I might as well go home. Besides, I'd never seen a mango tree before.

"Let's go," I told him.

We waved to Marco and Oscar, who were enjoying a smoke in the late day sun. Then we turned and headed back into the jungle. It took some effort to quash my trepidation, but I was determined to do so—and equally resolved not to let on how much it cost me. Tough and hard, I reminded myself, trying not to think of the dead snake's mate.

It was still quite hot—the afternoon hadn't yet relinquished its heat to the cool twilight. The monotonous stridulations of cicadas were the only sounds, a prelude to the evening chorus. Andres pointed out an iguana hanging off a tree, stuck there as if by suction cups, its tail hanging down like a stunted vine. Scarlet-rumped tanagers were flitting across the trail and a single morpho butterfly flashed its azure wings before landing and folding them up to drab brown. I found myself walking with awareness instead of terror and began to appreciate all over again the beauty and complexity of the rainforest.

"Look, Robyn. *Calzoncillo rojo!*"

I turned around. Andres was pointing to a small bird perched on an old stump. It was a lovely little bird, about the size of a warbler, with a blue back, black undersides, and bright red thighs.

"What did you call it?" I asked.

"It's a scarlet-thighed dacnis," Andres replied. "But I like much better its Spanish name. We call it *calzoncillo rojo.* It means 'red underwear'."

I grinned. "*Calzoncillo rojo.*" I tried the word out. A red underwear bird. It was absurd, yet exquisitely appropriate. I laughed out loud, feeling the last tensions of the afternoon slip away.

"And now we are coming to the mango tree," Andres announced, touching my arm lightly to draw attention to where he was gesturing.

"We plant these all along the edge of the Parque Central, you know. When it's mango season, there are so many fruits that you can see them lying on the grass. People will take their buckets and fill them with mangos."

"Sounds lovely. Where's the Parque Central?"

"There's one in almost every town," Andres explained.

"It is a very important place for people to go and hang out. A lot of the young guys go there to look cool and watch girls."

"Are you speaking from personal experience?"

He gave me a boyish smile. "Of course! Standing around looking cool is very important. Watch." He leaned against the tree and assumed an air of studied nonchalance.

"And just how many hours did you spend in front of the mirror to perfect that?" I inquired.

"Robyn! I was born looking this cool."

"And I bet the girls loved you."

"Well . . . except for the time a mango fell on my head."

"You got beaned by a mango?"

"Yes," he admitted ruefully. "Right in front of a girl I liked. She never would go out with me after that."

I was still chuckling when I noticed the intensity of his gaze. Soft expression. Enlarged pupils. Uh oh. Red alert.

I may have had the scare of my life earlier in the day, I may have been without sex for far too long, but I wasn't fooled by that look. A welter of conflicting emotions surged up, chaotic and incoherent.

Excitement. Confusion. Lust. Guilt. And a niggling note of caution.

There are times when I can manage 'attractive'. This wasn't one of them. In all the heat and humidity, I was 'glowing' up a storm. Curls spiraled from my head like auburn fireworks, and my field wardrobe (barely fit for public viewing at the best of times) had wilted visibly in the damp heat. The cargo pants, which had been billed as 'relaxed fit', were now so relaxed as to be practically comatose. I was flattered by Andres' interest. But did I trust it? Not a chance.

I probably should have stayed at Danta, the thought scuttled through my mind. Hung out with everybody in the dining hall until dinnertime. Worked through my nerves with the rest of the team. Avoided temptation.

Temptation? Who knew he'd hit on me now, of all times? Maybe I was misreading the look. It *had* been a while and maybe—

"Did you know the best way to savor a mango is to eat it naked in the bathtub?" His dark eyes glinted enticingly.

Maybe not.

"Uh . . . no. I didn't know that," I said, trying to make it sound like my interest in it was academic.

"With a friend is even better."

Holy Hormones, Batman! The guy was positively oozing sensuous appeal. My sex drive, which had, in recent months, taken off on some long road trip, was now back and revving in the driveway—not that there's anything wrong with this. I'm a young and healthy woman. But, gods, I barely knew the guy! I was just recovering from an encounter with a nasty snake, and here he was talking about getting starkers.

Andres reached up to pick a mango, his arm brushing mine. I felt a tingling sort of shock from breast to groin.

"I'm . . . sure it is." I cleared my throat. "But it's probably safer to eat them with clothes on."

A superhuman effort if I've ever seen one.

"You are sure?" Andres asked in a voice that hinted at his disappointment.

Think of the field team, Robyn, I chanted to myself. *Would it really be that bad?* A love affair in the middle of an isolated field camp was rarely a good idea. *How many years had* Deep Space Nine *been off the air?*

I took a deep breath. "Positive," I said firmly, ignoring the protests of my libido.

He backed off after that, contenting himself with showing me the mangos and all the insect life that depended on them. When I suggested that Oscar would probably have dinner ready, he didn't protest.

Night was falling by the time we got back.

"You go ahead," I told Andres. "I'm going to grab a sweatshirt. I'll meet you in the dining hall."

Under cover of twilight, I watched him cross the clearing and tried not to drool. My steps were dragging as I followed the faint path to the cabin. Would it really have been so bad? Through the screened window, I could see Viviana sprawled on her sleeping bag, reading a novel.

I plopped myself down on the front step and rested my chin in my hand. What the hell was wrong with me? I'd known Andres for all of three weeks and I was *this* close to hopping in a bathtub full of mangos with him (never mind the fact that we only had showers here at Danta). Why? Sexual deprivation was one thing, but I'd learned to live with that long ago. So what was going on?

Was this a side effect of abject terror? The search for life and affirmation after a brush with death? Was that it? I needed the *security?* A disturbing thought. Being a self-sufficient type, I'd never needed to find safety in a man's arms before.

But I was feeling better about my snake encounter now, more at ease in general with the jungle now that I'd faced one of its greater dangers. So, maybe this thing with Andres was real. A natural response to an unnaturally long time with no sex.

I sighed heavily. It didn't really matter if it was real or not. Between the poachers on one hand and Liz and

Ernesto's not-so-quiet war on the other, our little field team had enough troubles without Andres and I making the mammal with two backs. Definitely time to step back.

A pity, though, a slavering little voice piped up through my self-righteousness.

I smacked it back down and rose to go into the cabin. As I pushed the door open, I remembered what Viviana had said about the snakes in Costa Rica.

Three dangerous snakes in two days. It had to be some kind of field record.

Chapter 13

"Oh, that old mango line," Viviana chuckled huskily. "I can't believe he tried that on you!"

"Old as the hills, is it?"

"It has been around for many years," she agreed, still highly amused.

Great. The Costa Rican equivalent of 'what's your sign'. I blew out a sigh, relieved that I hadn't succumbed to temptation. It had almost worked, though, dammit.

I stretched my neck and shook my shoulders out. "What a day!"

Viviana sobered, her amusement fading into sympathetic concern. "I'm very sorry you had such a bad time. Are you all right now?"

I knew she wasn't talking about Andres and his mangos. "Yeah," I nodded. "It was pretty tense at the time, but yeah, I'm okay." I started rummaging in my duffle-bag for a sweatshirt. "Andres thought I was going to high-tail it back to Canada, you know."

"Like a scared woman."

"Maybe. He sure doesn't know me very well."

"He doesn't know *women* very well," Viviana corrected me. "But I am sure he would be very surprised to hear that. We are tough. Much tougher than men. But men don't like to know this. It's a threat to their machismo. Men will do tough things, but all the time they are complaining. Oh, it is so hard. Oh, look at me doing this difficult thing. Women just get on with it."

I chuckled. "Perhaps we should keep that to ourselves."

"Of course," she smiled back. "Men also don't like it when you understand them too well. They like to think they are mysterious."

For the first time in days, I thought about Kelt. He *was* a bit of a mystery to me, no question about that. But I was pretty sure he wouldn't have expected me to go running home after an encounter with a fer-de-lance.

"You know," I said, tugging the sweatshirt over my head, "thinking back on today, the one I feel most sorry for is the poor snake."

"The snake?"

I nodded. "Yeah, here it was curled up, minding its own business, having a nice afternoon snooze, and some big oaf comes along and stomps on it. I know there wasn't much of a choice, but I'm sorry Marco had to kill it. It was really my fault."

"I wonder why Ernesto did not kill it."

Startled, I looked at her. "What do you mean? He tried. How was he to know the damn thing would keep coming?"

"But many people in Costa Rica know this," Viviana protested. "My sisters and I used to scare each other at night with the stories. The half a snake that keeps attacking. It's very common. Everybody knows you shouldn't cut a fer-de-lance all the way through unless you cut it right behind the head."

"Really."

She raised her eyebrows at my tone. "I'm sure it was not on purpose, Robyn. He probably did not get a good angle for chopping."

I winced at her description. "Things *did* happen quickly," I admitted.

Whatever Viviana might have said to this was drowned out in the shout of angry voices.

"What the—?"

I yanked the door open. The voices were coming from the direction of Andres' cabin. I heard a door smack shut and saw two figures facing off in the shadows.

"What the hell kind of conservation project is it when you go around *killing* the animals?" The voice was strident with fury.

Liz. Why was I not surprised?

"*We're* the ones intruding on their territory. Us! How can you condone this?"

"They had no choice," Andres answered quietly. "What were they supposed to do? Let the snake bite her?"

"We've got extractor kits. There's even antivenin at the station. She would have been fine."

"Liz! Be reasonable."

"I am!" she barked.

"You don't know what you are talking about."

"Like hell! I worked at the Serpentario in San José for almost a year. There was no reason to kill that snake. None! I can't believe you don't see that. The only good snake is a dead snake. It seems to be a mantra down here. Is that what this is about?"

"It was about saving a member of our field team—"

"From her own stupidity."

"That is not fair," Andres said mildly, though I could hear the ribbon of anger unwinding beneath the surface.

"You have much more experience in the jungle, I agree, but something like this could happen to anybody—even to someone who has lived here all their life. Why do you think people die each year from *terciopelos?* It's because they are unpredictable and aggressive snakes."

"I still say they didn't have to kill it. Though I shouldn't be surprised that Ernesto had his grubby little paws in it."

Andres made a noise of frustration. "When are you going to stop these attacks on Ernesto? You do not have to work with him. I've made certain of that. You should not get so upset. Come, supper is ready. Calm down."

Andres put his hand on Liz's arm, but she wasn't having any of it. With a strangled sound of rage, she flung his hand off.

"Calm!" She sneered. "So now we're supposed to be *calm* even though there're poachers trapping our birds and we're killing the wildlife. Good advice, Andres." And with that, she whirled and stormed off in the direction of her cabin.

"Lizabeth!" Andres called out, but she kept walking.

I stood motionless at the cabin door, frozen with the guilty knowledge that she was right about the snake. Oh, not about killing it. There had really been no choice about that, regardless of what Liz thought. But I had been careless and the snake had paid the price.

I must have moved inadvertently as Liz stalked by. She stopped in her tracks, whipping her head around to stare at me.

I faced her, not saying anything, waiting for her to make the first move. She stood there. Silent. Forbidding. She didn't need to speak. And I didn't need to see her expression. Even through the veil of shadows, I could feel her eyes piercing me with a venomous glare.

I was on cleanup duty with Oscar that night. I'd just started drying the plates when I noticed an odd texture in the basket of squashes. A jumble of colors that didn't belong. I bent closer and poked at it.

"Holy shit!" I jumped across the kitchen. Away from the basket.

"What is it?" Oscar demanded.

"There's," I pointed a shaky finger towards the squashes, "there's a *snake* in there."

"Yes?" Calmly, Oscar picked up a towel and wiped his hands dry. "Where?"

"In the basket."

He crouched down and had a look. "Ah yes. Look, she's very pretty."

Well, yes. She was. But that didn't mean I wanted her lurking in the squashes. Besides, she'd hissed at me.

"She's just a boa constrictor. Very harmless."

"Oh."

"And young too. Look, she is so small! Very cute."

I came closer and had another look. The snake hissed again snippily. The feeling was mutual.

"She must have come in to get warm," Oscar was saying. "We should really take her back to the forest."

I took a step back and gestured him forward. "Be my guest. I don't think she likes me much."

Oscar started crooning to the snake. Murmuring Spanish endearments, he gently picked her up by the tail with one hand and brought his other hand up to support her body. A regular Steve Irwin. The snake twined herself around his hand and flicked her tongue at his face.

"I will just go and put her in a tree," he told me softly as the snake squeezed his fingers purple. "They are very fond of trees, you know."

"Oh. Sure."

It only took a minute. He returned, massaging the blood back into his fingers. "She has a good grip," he told me with a grin. "But, Robyn, you are not very fond of snakes, I think."

"I'm not that used to them," I admitted. "Especially in the kitchen. And after this morning . . . I guess I'm a bit sensitive right now. Other than that, I like snakes just fine." I picked up another plate and started drying it. "But I like birds a lot better."

Oscar chuckled.

"Tell me about your macaws," he said. "When will you find them?"

I lifted my shoulders in a shrug. "Soon, I hope. But it might be a while. It might be never."

"Never?"

"It's possible, but I doubt it. I think the macaws are here. I just hope we've got a viable population."

"What is 'viable'? I don't know this word."

"It means a healthy population. One that's breeding. If you've got a good mixture of adults and young, then you've probably got a breeding population."

"Ah. So, to have no baby birds is bad?"

"Not a good sign," I agreed. "That's one of the problems with the large parrots like macaws. Not enough babies. So many adults fail to reproduce each year. And we don't really know why. Could be they're sexually immature, or maybe their diet is bad or they're carrying high parasite loads. It could be a lack of nesting sites."

"I have never seen a macaw nest," Oscar said.

"Me either. They're cavity nesters, but almost all the best nest cavities for macaws are produced by only two species of tree."

"This is not much."

"No. And when you get poachers who come in and cut down nesting trees to get at the chicks . . . well, then it's even less." I dried a couple more plates. "That really gets to me, you know. Poachers who cut down the trees. Not only are they destroying nests that could have been used year after year, but they also take the chicks—and kill most of them in the process."

"Why would they do this if they are trying to sell them?"

"Well, they don't do it intentionally," I replied. "But a lot of those chicks still have their pinfeathers—"

"Pinfeathers?"

"Feathers that are just starting to come out of the skin. Pinfeathers are filled with blood because they're growing. So if the poachers are rough when they collect the birds, the chicks bleed to death."

Oscar made a noise deep in his throat. "But I have not heard of trees being cut down here," he said. "There cannot be a strong poaching problem."

I wiped another plate and recalled the resin-covered arrow. "I hope not," I said as I stacked the dish with the others. "I really do."

Later, after I'd gone to bed, I thought about Oscar's reassurances. I hoped he was right, but intuition told me otherwise. I'd read about families who relied on poaching for a living, about children who were sent into the forest with traps and bait. But families like these couldn't possibly afford the kind of expensive climbing ropes we'd found. And if, by some chance, they did have ropes like those, they wouldn't have left them dangling in the forest.

Thoughts of ropes led to thoughts of snakes. I opened my eyes in the dark, thinking about the constrictor in the kitchen. After the fer-de-lance, a boa constrictor hadn't seemed so bad. Startling, of course, but lacking that blood-pounding terror. Oscar's composure had made an impression too. As long as you respected the snakes and didn't go around stamping on them, they were fine. If only Oscar had been around this morning.

Liz hadn't joined us for dinner or the evening's discussion. I'd been grateful for that at the time, but now I wished that she had. That she might have seen how calmly Oscar had handled the young constrictor. How gently he'd carried it outside and set it down in the forest.

It might have made her feel better.

Chapter 14

When Marco and I set out the next day, I was resolved to be more careful, not only because of the snakes, but also because of the climbing ropes we'd found.

"Did you know that tourist who went missing?" I asked him when we stopped for a breather.

"Guillermo?" He looked surprised at the question. "Of course. He was staying at Danta for almost a month."

"A month? Why so long?"

Marco shrugged. "He had been hiking for many days. I guess he needed a rest."

"Long rest."

Marco lifted his shoulders again.

"Was he helping you guys with the paths? You know, around the station?"

"Sometimes. He had not seen a field station before." He unhooked the water bottle from his belt and took a long slug. "Why do you want to know about Guillermo?" he asked curiously, as he wiped his mouth on his shirt sleeve.

I unclipped my own water bottle and took a thoughtful sip. "I'm not sure," I said slowly. "Except that ever since I saw those ropes, I keep wondering if maybe the guy is still out there."

Marco had turned back to the path, preparing to start

chopping again. At my words, he stopped and twisted his neck to look back at me. "You think he is a poacher?" he demanded. Incredulous.

It was my turn to shrug. "I dunno. That's what Liz seems to think."

"Liz!" Marco snorted in disgust and turned to face me. "You should not listen to her. Guillermo, he was not a *poacher*. He asked many questions about the animals and birds, but that doesn't mean he was wanting to capture them. He was a tourist. He had already gone to many national parks: Braulio Carrillo, Manuel Antonio, Rincón de la Vieja. It is not just North Americans and Europeans who enjoy to hike in the rainforest."

"Then why did he stay at the station for so long?"

"Robyn, he was *visiting*," Marco explained patiently. "In Costa Rica, we say 'our home is your home'. It is not just a saying. Here, if someone wants to come and stay, this is great. We are happy to have their company. Guillermo was visiting Danta, but he was also liking our work. Very interesting, he said. This is why he stayed. I think he maybe wanted to study."

"He wanted to be a biologist?"

"*Sí*. Always with him it was *mariposas*—butterflies. Morphos, caligos, glasswings. He was always looking for butterflies. I spent a whole afternoon listening to him while he talked about them. But you know, he never even tried to catch them. He just wanted to watch. He was no poacher."

We started cutting into the foliage again.

"You should not listen to Liz," Marco said again. "She does not understand Ticos."

Half an hour later, we were pushing our way through the thick foliage when Marco stopped short with a gasp.

I lowered my machete. "Are you okay?" I puffed.

He turned back to me. His face was sick.

"What's wrong?" I demanded sharply.

He didn't answer.

"Did you cut yourself?"

"No . . . I . . . Robyn, stay here!"

He disappeared past a large elephant leaf.

"Marco! What's—" I pushed past the leaf.

Oh, shit.

Marco was crouched down on the path, his machete lying on the ground beside him. He was covering his mouth with his shirt sleeve, muffled curses emanating from the fabric. He was looking at a body. Or, at least, what was left of a body.

I swallowed hard and moved beside him, forcing myself to look at the bloated, mottled flesh. Parts of it heaved with insect life and I had to struggle to keep my breakfast down. Marco was still mumbling into his sleeve. His eyes were shocked.

"Guillermo?" I asked softly, knowing what the answer would be.

"*Sí*."

There had been a hatching of butterflies that morning. Several dozen of them fluttered over the corpse, their wings flashing rust-colored spots. Guillermo had found his butterflies. Then I looked more closely. The butterflies were landing on his skin. Proboscises unfurling. They were feeding on his flesh. I swallowed hard and looked away.

Marco swore again. Louder this time. "Look!"

I dragged my eyes back to the decaying body. Marco brushed the butterflies aside, tumbling them into the air. He was pointing to the man's chest.

"Look. There are holes in his shirt. These are not from animals. Robyn, he has been shot!"

X-Originating-IP: [199.137.52.16]

From: "Robyn Devara"
<macaw1@woodrowconsultants.com>
To: "Kelt Roberson" <batnerd@tnc.com>
Subject: grim news
Date: Thur 18 Apr 21:37:22-0900

Kelt,

We found our missing tourist two days ago. He was dead. Shot several times in the chest and left to rot in the jungle. Marco and I found his body. Gods, I don't know what to say. It was horrible. The rangers came yesterday to take away what was left of him. It's been a bad couple of days.

One of the more disturbing things about this is the fact that he'd been shot. I mean, I could understand if he'd wandered off and gotten lost. Or been bitten by a snake, or attacked by peccaries. But . . . shot?? It seems Liz was right and this Guillermo was involved with some kind of trafficking organization. That's the general consensus. It doesn't exactly do wonders for my sense of security. Poisonous snakes and wild pigs are one thing. A falling out—or possibly even some kind of war—between poachers is an entirely different matter. It makes for uneasy times.

Unfortunately, that's not the end of the bad news . . . we discovered this morning that these poachers are a) still in the area; and b) using some of our climbing trees. Yesterday afternoon, Marco and I went climbing. Once we got up about 100 feet, we found a bunch of bare branches. I knew right away we were in a feeding tree (when macaws perch on the branches, they scrape away all the mosses and epiphytes). Sure enough, a little while later, a pair of scarlet macaws glided in. We were hoping that our mystery macaw might join them. That was yesterday, but today

I'm hoping not. You see, this morning when we went up again, we found a bunch of sticky stuff glopped all over the branches. There were a few red feathers stuck in it. I didn't understand right away, but Marco did. Poachers. The way we figure it, those bastards must have snuck in after we'd left for the day and they used our guide ropes to go up and capture macaws.

Andres has been on the radio to Dan, so the rangers are aware of the problem. But with such limited manpower and now with this shooting to investigate, there's just not much they can do about it. Dan's sending a team out tomorrow to see if they can find the poachers' camp. But if they couldn't find Guillermo before, I'm not all that confident they'll be able to track down his associates. Dan thinks they're getting around by boat, so they could be anywhere in the area. There are so many little streams and tributaries and . . . well, you get the picture.

So, this is me crossing my fingers but not holding my breath. From now on, we'll be taking our guide ropes down each night. It's a pain, but what else can we do?

The guy from Berkeley and his grad students arrive tomorrow, and Viviana and I have volunteered to go get them. Not that we have any place to put them. Oscar's cousins, who are supposed to be here building all kinds of stuff (including more cabins), still haven't shown up. Oscar keeps telling Andres that they'll be back any day now. The Americans have been promised cabins and there is one spare. But there're five of them, so Andres has said he'll give up his cabin if they make a stink about it.

It'll be nice to have a few more people here. Maybe with more of us out poking around, our trafficking friends will decide to pack it in. One can only hope.

Anyhow, thanks again for everything. I miss you guys too. I know this e-mail sounds a bit scary, but please, please don't worry about me. I'm being very careful and both Dan and Andres believe the killing was an isolated incident. So give Guido a kiss for me and take care of yourself. I'll write again soon.

Till then,
Robyn

P.S. Thanks for reassuring me about my snake encounter. You never told me that story about the palm viper before I left. It made me feel better about the fer-de-lance. I wish Lizabeth was as forgiving. Even with everything that's happened in the last few days, she's still giving me the frosty shoulder.

P.P.S. Sorry about your sandwich. I never leave ham out on the counter for that reason.

All nature is at war, one organism with another.

Charles Darwin
Journal of the Proceedings of the Linnean Society

CHAPTER 15

Dr. Aleck Tannahill was a professor of tropical ecology at the University of California at Berkeley, the author of one of the foremost books on neotropical ecosystems, and, as it turned out, one of the universe's biggest assholes.

Oh, he'd seemed all right in the beginning—at least for those first few seconds after he stepped off the plane. Friendly. Excited to be here. And he'd invited the rangers to call him Al. A cheery sort of name, Al, the kind of label that conjures up bad jokes and belly laughs. A good times name. Too bad 'Aleck' fit him better.

"Keith, grab those boxes! Pepe, take this end. No, no, you idiot! This end!" The man had clearly never heard of that astonishing literary invention: the word 'please'.

"Keith, I asked you to take those."

"I was just about to—"

"You know, a little initiative might not be amiss here."

I narrowed my eyes and gave him a searching look. You can tell a lot about people from the way they treat others. And you can tell even more about professors from the way they treat their grad students. On the evolutionary tree of academia, grad students are about on par with paramecia. But that doesn't mean they *have* to be treated like single-celled life forms. Unfortunately, someone had neglected to inform Aleck Tannahill of this.

Viviana and I had left the shade of the ranger station's porch to help unload the plane, so we had front row seats for Aleck's little power trip. But before we could introduce ourselves—let alone offer to help with the gear—he waved us off with a disdainful flick of his fingers. Viviana lowered her eyelashes, hiding a brief flash of anger. As one, we stepped back to watch them sweat.

"Candace," Aleck made a sigh out of her name. "Try your very best not to drop this, would you?"

From the tone of his voice, you'd think he was speaking to a child. It offended me and from Viviana's indrawn breath, I could tell she hadn't been much impressed, either. I caught her eye and jerked my head toward the ranger station. I wasn't about to stand around in the hot sun and listen to this. Aleck could damn well come and introduce himself properly when he was ready.

Which he did, eventually, stepping onto the porch as if bestowing on us the honor of his presence. I think he half-expected us to genuflect. Perhaps the name Alexander would suit him best, I thought as I shook his hand. He seemed the sort who would lie awake at night fantasizing about how good his name would look with 'The Great' tacked onto it.

The introductions were made quickly. There were two graduate students, Keith Denham and Candace Young, as well as Keith's partner, Janet Elffers. Another fellow, Pepe Quesada, introduced himself with the ol' 'wink and gun'. He appeared to be a PhD student in search of a dissertation project (or an actor in search of a '70s TV show).

And then, there was Al.

"If I'd known you girls were from Danta, I'd've loaded

you up like camels," he guffawed, trying to explain away his earlier rudeness.

I wasn't laughing.

"I see." Viviana offered him a small smile, though her eyes glinted.

He didn't catch the warning. "Seeing as this station's just starting up, we had to bring a lot of stuff with us. I'm sure glad you girls are here to help because—"

"Excuse me," I broke in politely. "Al. It's been a lot of years since I played with Field Biologist Barbie. I am *not* a girl."

I could almost see Aleck's hackles rise, and there was an audible gasp from somewhere in Candace's vicinity. I held eye contact with him until I saw in his face the unpalatable realization that I was not one of his grad students.

"Oh . . . well," he blustered. "I, uh, certainly didn't mean to imply—"

"That's okay," Viviana interrupted in a sweet voice that I wouldn't have trusted in a dark alley. "Now you know."

Nobody knew quite what to say after this.

"Hey, folks! *Bienvenidos*. Welcome to Sirena." Dan Elleker came to the rescue, poking his head out the station's door. "Why don't you come on in. I know you're itching to get going, so let me check your permits and I can give you the quick 'n dirty orientation. You'll be on your way in no time."

As the last of the Berkeley group filed past us, Dan gave me a solemn wink and let the door smack shut. Viviana and I resumed our places on the deck chairs. Our bottles of Coke were sweating, leaving dark rings of condensation on the aged and graying wood of the table.

It seemed hotter than usual today. Sort of like sitting in a sauna while some happy spark keeps dumping water on the rocks. The icy cola was an unexpected treat, made possible by the ranger station's newly repaired refrigerator. Even at two bucks a bottle, it was a steal.

"Might be a long field season," I remarked after a while.

"Yes," Viviana sighed. "I was hoping that . . . I thought that with new people. . . ."

"Yeah. Me too. We're not the friendliest team, are we?"

"And it has been worse in the last two days. Ever since you and Marco found . . . well. . . ."

"Yeah."

Viviana patted my hand comfortingly. "*Lo siento,* Robyn. I didn't mean to remind you. Don't worry. Things will get better. At least they," she indicated the group in the station, "will be doing their own stuff."

"Hmm." Noncommittal. In my experience, people like Al seldom just did their 'own' stuff.

When Keith and Janet joined us on the porch, they were clutching cold bottles of Coke like a lifeline. Janet was a strong, sinewy type with an angular face and honey-blond hair that was falling out of its loose ponytail. She looked as hot as I felt. Keith too was red-faced and shiny from the heat, but he had a charmingly lopsided smile and his coffee-colored eyes sparkled with mischief. It wasn't hard to imagine the devilish little sprat he had probably been.

"You guys get the snake talk?" I asked them, taking note of their wild expressions.

Janet made a face and nodded.

"Does he do that to everybody?" Keith demanded.

Viviana and I laughed.

"I think so," I told him. "He means well, but. . . ." I shuddered.

"He told us about that poacher you found too," Janet said. Her expression was sympathetic. "That must have been awful!"

I nodded shortly. "It was."

Viviana turned to Janet. "Are you a student as well?" she inquired.

Janet shook her head. "I'm a photographer," she told us, "and not even a wildlife photographer—at least not yet," she amended with a grin. "Weddings and urban environments are more my thing. Problem is, I never get to see this guy here." She thumped Keith on the chest. "You must know what the life of a grad student is like. Always in the lab, or in a seminar, or chained to the computer."

"A stressed-out grad student is a good grad student," I agreed. "And they're never around when you need 'em."

"Exactly! So when Keith told me he was coming down here for a few months, I thought, screw it, I'm going too."

"And maybe now you'll learn to be a wildlife photographer," Viviana added.

Janet smiled at her. "That's the plan."

"So what's your project?" I asked Keith.

"Sweat bees."

"Sweat bees? Huh. I *knew* it was hot here."

"Even the bees are perspiring," Keith agreed with another lopsided grin. "Seriously though, sweat bees are all over the Osa Peninsula. Greenish-black kickass dudes, sort of like Bruce Lee in the Green Hornet."

"Can't say I've noticed any little Katos buzzing around Danta."

"Hmm. That doesn't bode well for my research." He turned to Janet. "Well, honey, guess we'll have to go back."

Janet thumped him again.

"Ow! Hey, that hurt."

"Aah, don't be so gormless," Janet told him heartlessly. "If you lugged around fifty pounds of camera equipment, you could beat up people too."

Keith smiled and kissed her damp cheek. "Gormless? Does this mean I should aspire to a state of gorm?"

Janet chuckled.

"So you're researching sweat bees?" I prompted.

"Somebody's got to," Keith nodded. "Nobody knows anything about their feeding behavior."

"As in what kinds of flowers they like?"

"And how often they visit them and if there's any seasonal variation. Bees are one of the most important pollinators down here. It's astonishing we don't know more about them. Did you know that Brazil nut trees are pollinated by bees?"

"I didn't."

Bee Boy followed this up with a few more fascinating facts. Janet listened to him with the patience of someone who has heard it all before.

"Oropendulas sometimes build their nests close to bee hives," Viviana offered.

Keith raised his eyebrows. "Oro . . . whats?"

"Oropendulas. They are a rainforest bird," Viviana said. "You'll see them all around Danta. They are big and brown with white beaks. Very beautiful."

"Their nests look like a bunch of testicles drooping from the tree, though," I added.

Keith gave me a crooked smile. "I can hardly wait."

I grinned back and glanced down at my watch. The afternoon was getting on. "Speaking of the station, we should probably get going pretty quick. What's taking Aleck so long?"

"He's still pontificating to the snake guy," Janet snorted.

"Janet . . . ," Keith warned her.

"It's true!" She bent her head towards me. "The guy's a jerk," she confided in an undertone.

She didn't have to tell me that.

"You didn't have to tell me that," I said.

The door swung open and we turned guiltily. But it was only Candace. Aleck's voice floated out behind her like an ill wind blowing. It sounded like he was lecturing somebody about tapirs.

I hadn't had a chance to really see Candace before. She'd ducked past me on the deck with her face down, head covered by a Tilley hat. Now she'd taken the hat off and was fanning herself with it. Now I could see what she looked like.

Wheat blond curls framed a face that owed more to Estée Lauder than to Mother Nature. Huge brown eyes were made larger by the application of eyeliner and mascara (probably waterproof). Her khaki-colored shirt covered a pink camisole (was that lace on the edges?) and her matching cargo pants fit a little too snugly for comfort in this heat. Her hat fanned a waft of cologne toward me. My stomach fell as everything clicked into place.

Candace Young was a perfume bunny.

"Hi," she greeted us in a soft, little-girl voice.

My stomach fell even further. Her pink lipstick (Lipstick? In this heat?) had smudged across her front teeth, which made me feel a little better. But still. A perfume bunny? Here?

"*¡Hola,* Candace!" Viviana greeted her.

"Oh," she gave a tinkly little laugh. "Just call me Candi."

"With an 'i'?" I asked before I could stop myself.

She turned and gazed at me with wide eyes. "How did you know?"

I shrugged and managed a sickly smile. "Just a lucky guess."

"Oooo, where did you get those Cokes?" Candi cooed to Keith and Janet. "I so need a cold drink."

"Inside. Just ask Dan's wife, she's in the back room," Keith told her.

As Candi stepped back inside in search of a Coke, Aleck and Pepe came out. For a second, Pepe looked like he was going to follow Candi back into the station. But Aleck was playing big man on campus and Pepe must have decided it would be more politic to stick with him. It was a brief hesitation, but a telling one. Dan came behind them, aiming a friendly wink my way as he rolled his eyes behind Aleck's back. I covered my grin with a cough.

Viviana checked her watch and stood up. "We should get going," she told them. "It will take a while to get back to Danta."

"You folks don't want to be making that trip in the dark," Dan agreed. "Especially not with all the activity we've had around here lately. You'll be careful, right?"

"We've got the satellite phone," I told him. "If we see anything, we'll call for the cavalry."

Just then, Candi strolled out with a drippingly appealing bottle of cold Coke in her hand. Aleck turned to look at her and his eyes narrowed as he spied the bottle. He rummaged in his pocket for a moment and drew out a handful of *colones*.

"Why don't you get me one of those," he said, tossing a few coins at her across the deck table.

Candi blinked and hesitated. I didn't blame her. Aleck's request wasn't unreasonable, but he could have phrased it differently. More politely. And throwing money at her like that was, quite frankly, demeaning. He didn't even wait for a response, either. Instead, he turned his back on her and started talking to Dan.

"We must get going," Viviana interrupted him, her tone noticeably cooler than before.

Aleck looked at her, his eyebrows raised in surprise. "Surely I've got time for a drink. It's going to be a hot trip."

Viviana held his gaze for a long moment. "Drink fast," she said finally.

Aleck made shooing motions to Candi.

Grad students were supposed to be many things—a servant to their advisor was not one of them. But it was clear Candi didn't want to cause a scene. She scooped up the coins and strode off to get Aleck his Coke. I pursed my lips and aimed a hostile stare towards him. He appeared oblivious, both to my glare and to the tensions around him.

Candi returned quickly with another bottle, but when she put Aleck's change on the table, he flashed her a patronizing smile and shook his head a little.

"Why don't you keep that, honey."

I was flabbergasted and I watched in speechless indignation as Candi's cheeks stained with color. Aleck, however, had turned back to Dan. Candi sat down quickly and made a show of rooting around in her backpack for her wallet. The change lay untouched on the table.

I took a deep breath and caught Viviana's eye. She flared her nostrils and mouthed the word 'asshole'. I nodded my agreement. Perfume bunny or not, nobody deserved that—especially somebody young enough to be intimidated by Aleck's position and personality.

"Okay." Viviana clapped her hands together. "We need to start loading the boat now."

I saw her smile to herself as Aleck was forced to chug down his drink.

Yep. It was going to be a long field season.

Chapter 16

"We won't be able to carry all this to Danta today," Viviana insisted.

"But—" Aleck began.

"There are no more buts," she interrupted. "We cannot carry it all, and Danta is too far to make the trip twice today—unless *you* feel like hiking in the night. I would not recommend it, but you are welcome to try."

Aleck snapped his mouth shut, frustrated and angry. We'd been standing at the mooring point for twenty minutes, waiting for Aleck's common sense to kick in. I was beginning to suspect it would turn out to be one of those 'waiting for Godot' things.

"Look," I interjected. "We'll carry what we can today. Make sure you have what you'll need for tonight. Then we can drag the boat up on shore, turn it over, and stow the rest of your gear underneath. It'll be fine till tomorrow. The boat's pretty heavy."

Aleck glared at me, but I just gazed back, mild and calm. Somebody had to be.

"It's very simple," Viviana was saying. "And I am not going to stand here and fight about it any more. We will put your equipment under the boat, or you will sleep here with it tonight. It's your choice. But make your decision fast."

Aleck must have sensed the iron in her voice—it was hard to miss, really—because he stopped arguing with her and started ordering his slaves around.

"Pepe! I guess we'll be pulling the boat up," he sneered unpleasantly. 'We' clearly meant Pepe and Keith.

Aleck, I noticed, *did* lift a finger to help, but only to point out where he wanted the boat. "No, no, don't be a cretin! Not there! Over here."

"Ye gods, he's brought enough stuff to open ten field schools," I murmured in an aside to Viviana.

She nodded darkly. "I think I'll be too busy to help tomorrow."

I watched Aleck berate his students. "Good idea," I said.

When half the gear was stored safely under the boat, Viviana and I began shouldering as many of the remaining packs and bags as we could carry.

"No!" Aleck practically snatched a blue daypack out of my hands.

I blinked at him in surprise.

"I . . . I'll take this one," he told me with a hearty laugh as loud as it was false.

Interesting.

Viviana sidled up to me. "What was that about?" she asked in an undertone.

I shrugged. But I had an inkling. Just before Aleck grabbed the pack, I'd had a chance to feel it. Specifically, the several large, bottle-type shapes that were in it. And when he'd pulled it away from me, I had heard the *clink* of glass hitting glass.

"We are going this way," Viviana said to Pepe, directing his attention to the first orange trail marker.

"Yes, I know," he replied. "I was here before."

Viviana looked surprised.

"Just for a few days," he explained. "You and Andres had not arrived yet. I wanted to see the station before I came to study."

"*Bueno*, then you know the path is overgrown, but it's not so bad."

Pepe nodded.

"Just watch for the orange markers if you fall behind,"Viviana called to the others. "And be careful, there are a few slippery places." She smiled at Keith and Janet, gave an encouraging nod to Candi, then started down the trail without even a backward glance for Aleck. I saw him stiffen, then he hitched his precious pack higher and followed her into the jungle.

I brought up the rear with Candi tripping along in front of me.

Joy.

She was in fair enough shape—didn't even seem overly bothered by the humidity—but it was soon obvious Candi wasn't an experienced rainforest hiker.

"It's so dark!"

"Look at the size of these trees!"

"Oooo! Look at that orchid!"

"Oh! A dormilona!"

She stopped in front of the small fern and bent down to poke its leaves. As soon as she touched them, they seemed to wither and collapse. An interesting defense mechanism. She poked another one and tittered as it cringed away. I urged her on, but she couldn't resist a last poke and giggle. I sighed, feeling a bit like a dormilona myself.

"Oh! A walking palm tree!"

"Oh my god! Leafcutter ants!"

We had to stop again and gawk at the ants.

"They're all over the place at Danta," I relented. "Always in the composter. In some spots, they've actually worn a path about an inch deep in the forest floor."

"Really?" she asked breathlessly. Her brown eyes were wide.

"Yeah. I see them all the time. Last week a whole line of them passed by my cabin, all carrying little yellow flowers." I smiled crookedly, remembering the long line of flowers bobbing along the forest floor.

"You know, they can carry ten times their weight," Candi informed me. "And their anthills are, like, so the size of cars."

So the size of cars?

"They're pretty amazing," I agreed cautiously.

"And they don't actually eat the leaves. They take them all down inside the anthill and grow a special fungus on them. They eat the fungus."

Viviana had told me much the same thing.

"Fascinating," I said.

"I've read so much about them," she twinkled, "but I never knew they wore a path in the forest floor! Sometimes I think I should *so* study ants instead of plants."

"What is your research project?" I asked quickly, trying to head off any more of this perkiness.

"Oooo, plants, of course! Danta is so the perfect place for my study 'cause nobody ever surveyed the plants here. They catalogued the snakes and the mammals—even the scorpions, but nobody was into plants. And you know, all the vegetation around the station is so successional. It was cleared ten years ago when the station was first opened up and it hasn't been disturbed since. That's why there aren't any strangler figs around, 'cause you only find them in primary forest and. . . ."

Candi chattered away about shade-tolerant species and colonizing plants and preliminary data sets. It was weird hearing her little-girl voice rattle off multisyllabic botanical terms. I tried to listen, but I kept getting distracted by the disparity between what she said and how she said it. She even managed to make the word 'cotyledon' sound cute.

"... and so I contacted his old department and they still had his old field notes, which was so a stroke of luck for me."

"Whose old notes?"

"Scott Gray." Candi gave me a wounded look. "You know, the guy who first built Danta?"

"Oh. Right."

"Danta was his whole life. He practically moved down here. And then he got stung by a scorpion and that was it for him—and the station." Her backpack bounced as she shrugged her shoulders prettily. "He had some grad students who tried to take over. But they were so not right for it. They lost their funding and the station was closed and. . . ."

Old news. I already knew the bare bones of Danta's beginnings. I let Candi's chatter flow over me as I considered her first words about the station.

"... but I was *so*—"

"You say you've got the old field notes," I interrupted her.

She stopped and turned at my tone. "Um . . . well, yeah."

"Gray's old notes. About everything they did, and all the stuff they saw around here?"

"Yeah," she said again, mystified by my intensity.

"Have you read them all? Does he say anything about

the macaw?" I tried to keep the excitement out of my voice.

"Oohh," her frown cleared as understanding settled over her like hairspray. "No. Not really." She gave a tinkly little laugh. "I guess that would have so helped you guys."

"So," I agreed through clenched teeth.

She shook her head sorrowfully, as if she felt responsible for my disappointment. "I'm really sorry. I've been through these notes like a hundred times. He wrote about seeing the macaw, but he doesn't say where or anything."

It sounded like the same report I'd seen in the natural history club journal. Too bad. I adjusted my pack straps and prepared to move on.

Candi was still giving me that puppy dog look. And me clean out of Milkbones.

"C'mon," I nodded for her to continue walking. "Let's catch up with the others. It's pretty late and I didn't bring my lights. I don't know about you, but I'd rather get to Danta before night."

Candi squeaked in alarm and scooted ahead on the trail. Hiking faster now. Not even stopping to squeal.

If only I could be confident it would last.

Aleck Tannahill began making enemies and distancing people pretty much as soon as we arrived at Danta. For every story told, he had a better one. For every issue discussed, he had an opinion. And ever since he'd had a little 'rest' in his cabin (which had been, up till that afternoon, Andres' cabin), he seemed even more eager to share his insights with the rest of us.

"A little scorpion like that? Ha! That's nothing. When

I was in Ecuador, I found one holed up in my shorts for the night. Found out the hard way too. The bastard stung me when I put them on. Damn thing was so big, it was practically *wearing* my shorts. Ha, ha, ha."

"That reminds me of the time. . . ."

"I've always known. . . ."

"Well, when *I* first went in the field. . . ."

Jack Daniels. The twenty-first-century philosopher.

Oscar, Andres, and Liz were on dinner duty that night. They'd retreated behind the kitchen counter as soon as politely possible. For the first time in my life, I wished it was my turn to cook.

"Ah, vegetarians are so holier-than-thou," Aleck was saying now.

I wasn't quite sure how we'd landed on this topic, but I knew we should probably change it—and fast. Liz was a vegetarian. But before I could say anything, Aleck bulled ahead.

"They're always so superior because they don't eat meat. Well, I've got news for them. Human beings are omnivores. Take a basic biology class and you know what that means—plant *and* meat eaters. Can't deny your ancestry."

"Oh, but you'll deny your own death," Liz snapped as she slammed a large bowl of beans on the table. Some of the hot liquid spattered on her hand. She didn't seem to notice.

Aleck blinked at her. "What's that, honey?"

I held my breath, convinced she'd rip his face off.

"Eating meat is a way of denying your own death," she informed him icily. "That is part of the philosophy behind vegetarianism. By ingesting the life of another being, you're hoping to extend your own. It's selfish, pure and simple. And as for your 'ancestry' argument . . . traditional hunting/gathering societies actually ate very little meat. Over ninety percent of their diet was plant-derived. So don't go giving me this 'it's in your genes' bullshit!"

Aleck drew breath to contradict her but before he could get any words out, she leaned over the table and pinned him with her gooseberry glare.

"And if you *ever* call me 'honey' again," she said softly, "you'll have to buy yourself a goddamned cattle ranch to deny the death I'll give you."

She spun around and stalked back into the kitchen. Aleck waited till she was out of the room, then he chuckled.

"Well, there's a live wire," he remarked to Keith. Completely unfazed.

Keith didn't say anything.

"What do you think? Must be the wrong time of the—"

"Suppertime," Andres announced brightly, staggering under the weight of a huge platter. "We have fried plantains and beans and even some chicken tonight. Who is hungry?"

Amidst the chorus of 'me's' and the shuffle to get the table set, Aleck's remark was left unfinished. But not forgotten.

As we all settled down to dinner, I found myself picking at my food and watching Aleck through my eyelashes. He related better to men, I realized. He'd trotted out the good old boy act once we'd arrived at the station, asking Marco and Ernesto questions about the fieldwork, clapping Oscar companionably on the shoulder. Still, overall the man seemed more taken with himself. More impressed with his own stories. More tickled by his own jokes. Compared to the towering ego that was Aleck Tannahill, Narcissus wasn't just small potatoes, he was an instant potato flake.

I watched as Aleck stole a quick glance at Liz. When he was certain she was looking at him, he made a show of selecting the largest piece of chicken from the platter. He began tearing at it with his teeth, smacking his greasy lips ostentatiously.

"This is really excellent," he called down the table to Andres. "Much better than the stuff you get at the grocery store."

Andres nodded. "Yes, Dan gets the chickens from a farmer in Golfito. They are always good. Very tender."

"Ha. I knew it," Aleck smacked his lips again. "Nothing beats fresh-killed meat."

Liz flared her nostrils and turned towards Viviana. The conversation surged and splintered into small groups again. Aleck cracked a joke, but I couldn't hear the punchline over the general noise. I saw Keith give him a tight smile. Aleck made another comment. Clearly delighted with his own wit, he threw back his head and shouted with laughter.

I might have to hurt him, I mused as I watched him spray his tablemates with bits of half-chewed food. And if I didn't, I could think of several more people who would gladly assume the responsibility.

As bad as I found him during dinner, Aleck got much worse after the food had been cleared away.

Early evening was one of my favorite times at Danta. Under the soft flicker of kerosene lights, the day's work is discussed, scientific theories are debated, and cutthroat games of dominoes develop like fractals across the dining table.

Keith and Janet were engaged with Marco and Oscar in just such a game. I could hear Marco teasing Keith about the pile of ivory tiles in front of him. "*Una piano completa,*" he laughed.

The rest of us were nursing coffees and discussing the macaw project. A large map was spread out on the table in front of us. Black marker lines indicated the scope of our search.

"Maybe we should cut a trail into here." I pointed to a spot on the map. "The elevation's not bad and look ... there're two little streams running right through it."

Viviana bent closer and peered at the map. "Perhaps you are right."

"I would like to see what's over this way."

"I guess you'll all be a lot happier when you've found your bird," Aleck interrupted. "Then you'll *really* be able to get working."

Like we weren't already?

But Andres nodded. "Oh yes, we are hoping to get some population information. Densities, reproductive rates, this kind of thing. Maybe we can even start to map the habitat."

"So when will you know if you can harvest them?"

"*What?*" Liz and I blurted at the same time.

"Well, that's why you're here, isn't it? To see if sustainable harvesting's feasible."

"Where did you get *that* idea?" Viviana was the first to recover her breath.

Aleck shrugged. "It's just common sense. If this macaw of yours does exist, then it's better to harvest them than to lose them all to traffickers. You've already got a poaching problem—Robyn here found a corpse in the forest to prove it."

I gave him a dirty look, disliking the reminder.

"Your macaw *would* be very desirable," Pepe said. "It combines beauty and rarity. These are very important to collectors. I'm sure there would be many people interested in acquiring a bird like this."

I saw Ernesto open his mouth to say something, but one look at Liz's thunderous expression was enough to make him reconsider.

"You've got to do something," Aleck brought attention back to himself. "Harvesting's your best option."

"The *best option?*" Liz's voice rose an octave.

Janet glanced up from her dominoes with a quizzical look.

"You're kinda jumping the gun here, Aleck," I broke in. "You guys are talking about selective trapping and we don't even know if we've *got* a macaw, let alone what its reproductive capacity is."

"Macaws don't reproduce quickly and their range is restricted," Viviana added. "Also, there are many non-breeding adults in a population. Nobody knows why. These are not promising qualities for harvest."

"We'd need to know its range, its nesting sites, and how adaptable it is." I ticked them off on my fingers as I spoke. "We're years away from that."

"But when you do—"

"When we do," Viviana interrupted, "then we *might* look into sustainable harvesting, but I doubt it. Even the man who proposed this method of conservation is not hopeful for it to be achieved in practice."

Aleck was picking his teeth. He shrugged at Viviana's

words. "It's better than losing the whole species to poachers."

"Is it?" I asked quietly.

He bit down on his toothpick and turned to look at me.

"What happens if sustainable harvesting fails?" I leaned forward, trying to drive my point home. "What if we find, a few years down the line, that we've taken too many birds? That our macaw now exists only in zoos or with private collectors? What then? How is this better than losing the birds to poachers? Would we be able to say the species has survived? No. The birds would have no wild identity. They'd be biologically dead."

I could see from Aleck's patronizing smirk that I wasn't getting through.

"Look," I tried again. "I don't know about you, but I became a biologist because I was fascinated by nature. And I became a *field* biologist because I'd much rather watch nature than experiment with it. Sustainable harvesting sounds great in theory, but in practice?" I shrugged. "It's nothing but a big experiment."

"With the macaws taking all the risks," Viviana said.

But Aleck was shaking his head. "That's idealistic," he told me. "You can't study biology—study nature—apart from man. There's no such thing anymore as pure biology. It's an historical exercise." He pushed his bench back and stood up to leave. "And the sooner you accept that," he added, "the better it'll be for your project."

He retired to his cabin then, leaving behind a bunch of fuming biologists. But it wasn't until I sought my own sleeping bag that I realized what bothered me most about the whole scenario. In a group of conservation biologists, Viviana and I had been the only ones to speak out against

Aleck's inflammatory remarks. Ernesto had been silent, but then, he often was when Liz was around. But Andres hadn't let out a peep and, apart from her initial outburst, neither had Liz.

How uncharacteristic.

CHAPTER 17

"Aaahhh!" The horrified shriek echoed throughout the station.

I looked up from my field notes and caught Viviana's eye.

"Candi?" I asked.

She nodded. "Yes, it sounded like her."

"Should we go check?"

Viviana looked down at her own field book and sighed. "Yes, I suppose so."

As one we closed our notebooks and stood up. It was late afternoon and we'd already put in a long, fruitless day. We were just jotting down some last notes before dinner. The sun was starting to set, the cicadas gearing up to their nighttime serenade.

I stepped out onto the tiny porch and squinted over at the cabin Candi shared with Liz.

"What's that in front of their cabin?" I asked Viviana.

She joined me on the porch. "It looks like . . . a pair of pants?"

"Hmm. That's what I thought too. C'mon."

We went over to their cabin.

"Everything okay in there?" I called.

"There are *termites* in my pants!" Candi wailed from within.

"Termites?"

"Are you okay?" Viviana was asking. "Did you hurt yourself?"

Candi appeared at the door, a towel clutched around her waist. Her complexion was pink with embarrassment.

"No," she assured us. "I mean, I'm okay. It . . . they . . . they just startled me, that's all." She laughed, but it was a nervous sound, and her eyes darted behind me.

I turned around. Aleck was standing on the path, watching us.

"Everything okay here?" he asked.

"Just fine," I told him.

He nodded brusquely and moved off.

Candi's big brown eyes thanked me. In fact, they practically kissed my feet in gratitude. It wasn't hard to figure out why. Much to the disgust of her academic advisor, Candi was not turning out to be the bravest biologist in the rainforest.

After the first eventful evening, life at Danta had quieted down a bit while everybody settled into their work. There had been no sign of poachers for two weeks now. No more mysterious ropes in trees. No more bullet-ridden bodies in the jungle. Having so many people at Danta had clearly made a difference. I was still cautious, but I'd stopped looking over my shoulder every five minutes.

Keith had found his Kato bees and was busily redesigning his research project. Pepe and Aleck were setting up a survey of the birds in the area, though Aleck seemed to be the one directing the research. If Pepe was a PhD student, he wasn't a very serious one. He seemed to spend most of his time talking to Oscar about fast cars—mostly bemoaning the fact that he didn't have enough money to buy one. Each morning he greeted me with his trademark wink 'n gun. My guess was he probably wanted a Camaro.

Janet had quickly found her jungle legs, despite the oppressive heat and her continuing uneasiness about snakes and armed poachers. She'd decided to work up a piece on the Danta Biological Field Station: its history, new beginnings, and hopes for the future. As part of this, she wanted to document our project. She tagged along first with one group, then another, climbing trees, paddling down streams, snapping off pictures, and scribbling notes. Obviously having a blast.

Candi was a different story.

Lady Luck, it appeared, disliked perfume bunnies almost as much as I did. If I had a nickel for every shriek of dismay, every cry of fear, I could've coughed up enough cash for two more field seasons. She was constantly slipping in mud or imagining snakes in every twisting root. She wouldn't go near the kitchen steps where a large tarantula had taken up residence. Mosquitoes feasted on her perfumed flesh, and iguanas seemed to delight in startling her by dropping out of trees like green, scaly bombs. One afternoon, she'd stopped to coo over a troop of howler monkeys. They rewarded her interest by emptying their bladders. She should've known better than to look up with her mouth open.

And then, just the other day, she'd shown us a puzzling bump on her calf.

"It's like a mosquito bite," she said, "but it's so not going away. In fact, it seems to be getting bigger."

"Botfly," Keith informed her.

"What?"

"Does it feel like hot needles sometimes?"

"How did you—"

"It's a botfly larva," Keith told her, a note of excitement creeping into his voice. "The maggot hatched on your skin and burrowed in. It's using you as an incubator—"

"An *incubator?*" Candi's eyes widened in horror.

"Oh man, this is so cool," Keith exclaimed. "You've got to leave it in!"

"What! *Leave it in?*"

"Only for forty or fifty days," Keith told her. "Until the larval fly emerges to pupate. But in the meantime, the maggot will keep growing. Your skin'll stretch and eventually it'll go clear—almost like glass—and you'll actually be able to see the maggot moving around underneath and. . . ."

Candi did not leave the botfly larva in her leg.

"How am I going to get those termites out of my pants?" she asked us now with a helpless gesture.

Viviana looked down at the pants on the ground. They were wiggling ever so slightly. Pale green pants with nobody inside them.

"Well, tossing them outside was probably a good start," I said, rubbing the back of my neck.

"Yes," Viviana agreed. "Just leave them there for the night. The termites will be gone by tomorrow."

"Really?" Candi breathed, her face shining with gratitude.

"You may want to wash them out before you wear them," Viviana warned her.

Candi got a funny look on her face and I braced myself for another cry of dismay. But she got herself under control and nodded in understanding.

"See you at dinner, then," I said, and Viviana and I turned to go back to our cabin.

"Thanks!" she called after us.

"Termites in her pants, eh?" I murmured with a disbelieving shake of my head.

Viviana shrugged. "It could have been worse," she grinned. "It could have been Andres."

I laughed, but it was a thoughtful sort of chuckle.

All the men at Danta were quite taken with Candi—all, that is, *except* Andres. Either he wasn't the mango-loving womanizer I'd been warned about, or his interest in me was genuine.

"The first time I was in the field, my shirt was taken over by ants," Viviana said, interrupting my thoughts. "It happens down here."

"I bet you didn't scream, though."

"No. They were just ants."

"Hmm." And the termites in Candi's pants were just termites. I sighed inwardly.

Candi kept reminding me of why I hate perfume bunnies. Although she appeared utterly incapable of coping with the rainforest creatures at Danta, she was more than coping with the male attention. Every couple of days, her fingernails were a different color, every day she jiggled around the station in a skimpy camisole, and every day she brushed on a pound of (waterproof) mascara before starting her work.

"I wonder how she's getting along with Liz," I mused later that evening as Viviana and I were getting ready for bed.

Viviana snorted inelegantly. "Did you see the shirt she was wearing tonight?"

"Nipple city."

"She has come-and-make-love-to-me-so-I-can-have-many-babies-and-never-fulfill-my-potential written all over her."

"Quite a feat. Given such a tiny tank top."

"She is never going to be taken seriously as a scientist when she dresses and behaves like this. I saw her mending Marco's shirts yesterday. And always she helps with the cooking, even when it's not her turn. What is she trying to prove?"

"Who knows?" I shook my little cockroach friend out of my sleeping bag. "But I don't think she really gives a rat's ass about respect—not as a scientist, at any rate."

"How can she not care?"

"She doesn't strike me as ambitious. She must know she'll never land a prestigious job. I guess she's just happy playing the Barbie doll."

Viviana made a noise of disgust.

"It's not hurting anybody, except herself," I said. "And I imagine Liz is having to bite her tongue on a regular basis."

Viviana snickered.

I folded my arms behind my head and listened to the night. A light rain pattered against the corrugated metal roof, but I could still hear the Tink frogs singing lustily outside the window. I closed my eyes and listened to them, dismissing all thoughts of Candi. So what if she was playing Martha Stewart? She was harmless.

Irritating, definitely, but harmless.

Or was she? The next morning at breakfast, Marco informed me he needed to stay behind and help Oscar with the new cabins.

"You will be able to go with Andres and Liz," he said with a wide-eyed, innocent sort of look.

I wasn't fooled by it.

"Isn't Candi staying at the station today?" I inquired.

"I . . . I do not know." He didn't meet my eyes.

"Hmm. I thought I heard her saying she was going to catalogue some plants."

He colored. "I did not hear that," he mumbled.

Like hell you didn't, I felt like snapping back, but I held my tongue.

It wasn't that I minded going out with Andres and Liz, or even that Oscar needed Marco's help. Andres had been sleeping in a corner of the old lab ever since Aleck had commandeered his cabin. Not the most comfortable of arrangements. I didn't mind that Oscar needed help with new cabins, but if I was losing my field partner because of a perfume bunny? Well, I certainly had a problem with *that*.

"*¡Buenos días*, Robyn!" Oscar greeted me as he brought out a steaming platter of scrambled eggs.

Marco took the opportunity to duck out of the dining room. Coward.

"*Buenos días*, Oscar," I said instead. "I hear you're stealing my field buddy."

Oscar nodded and graced me with a huge smile. "Yes, it is very nice for you to lend him. We will have Andres a proper cabin soon, I hope."

Other station members started filtering in, Keith tossing me a cheerful "Morning, Nanook," which he'd done ever since he found out I was Canadian. Pepe gave me another one of his wink 'n guns, looked around for Candi, then settled beside Oscar when he didn't see her. Aleck came in as he did every morning. Slowly. Carefully. Holding his head as if it was made of glass.

"Robyn, you're with us today. This is great!" Andres plunked his breakfast plate down beside mine. "It will be fun to have a chance to work with you."

The Smile had gotten up early that morning. Maybe a day without Marco wouldn't be such a bad thing.

"Are we going out in the boat?" I asked.

Andres scrunched his nose up and shook his head. "No. We are just not having much luck with that. I think instead we'll try climbing trees."

He reached behind us to snag a map off the shelf. I moved my plate so he could spread it out.

"You and Marco have been surveying this area, yes?"

I nodded, my mouth full of mango.

"And Viviana and Ernesto have been over this way. So I think today we will try this section over here. We'll have to cut our way in, but nobody has even checked here yet. We might get lucky."

"Here's hoping."

"It will be great!" Andres enthused again, then he lowered his voice. "I have to tell you, Robyn, I'm getting very sick of that boat. And it will be good to work with you. It seems like we haven't had much chance for visiting lately." His dark eyes smoldered at me.

"You're with us today?" Liz asked as she seated herself at the table.

I nodded and Andres clapped his hands together, rubbing them gleefully.

"I am feeling very lucky this morning," he told us. "I think maybe we will win those *cervezas*, after all."

Even Liz smiled at that.

Marco had the grace to look ashamed as he waved us off after breakfast. But I noticed he was 'helping Oscar' in full view of Candi's cabin. Silently, I wished him luck with it. Candi might have stitched a few of his shirts, but he wasn't the only male she had all sewn up. I only hoped there wouldn't be any trouble over it. In my experience, flirts like Candi never stopped to consider the consequences of their actions.

Any further thoughts of Candi were effectively banished by the effort of clearing a path through the rainforest. We weren't going very far in—just a little over a mile—but there were no paths and only a few sporadic clearings where towering trees had succumbed to disease. We were aiming for one particular spot, a place slightly higher in elevation than the surrounding area.

"If we can find a good climbing tree here," I had pointed out on the map, "then we'll have a fabulous view."

There was a good climbing tree.

"Be my guest," I offered the bow and arrow to Liz.

She accepted them and took careful aim. The luck that Andres had boasted of at breakfast seemed to have us firmly under its wing. Liz shot the lead weight up and got it right into the crotch the very first time. The line didn't snag once. And when we'd jugged up into the canopy, the very first thing we saw was red. Winging right over our helmets.

RAAAAAAAK RAAAAAAAAK ROWWWWWWKA

I clapped my hands over my ears. The racket was unbelievable!

I saw Andres wince, then heard his cheer above the clamor. The squawks may have been deafening, but the scarlet macaws were exquisite.

My head spun as I tried to count them. One, two . . . five . . . eight. Seventeen.

"Seventeen!" I shouted through the din.

"No, look! Eighteen!" Liz pointed to one I'd missed.

Eighteen scarlet macaws with wingspans as wide as eagles, all dipping and diving against an aquamarine sky. I stared at them in awe, my mouth hanging open at the sight.

"They say that macaws are a feast for the eyes, but an assault on the ears," Liz shouted.

I looked over at her. She was smiling in delight. "They were right," I yelled back.

"Look!" Andres was pointing to the flock.

I'd thought the birds were merely dancing in the late morning sunshine, but I could see now their flight had a purpose. They flew with strong, shallow wingbeats, gradually dropping lower and lower into the forest.

"What are they up to?" Andres mumbled as he focused his binoculars.

I was already peering through my own. "It looks like a clearing. Maybe even a stream. You see the demarcation?"

"Yes!" Andres exclaimed. "Yes, look, they are all going down right in that spot. What have you got there, my friends?" he crooned.

"Over there!" Liz cried.

I turned my head to where she was pointing. Five more scarlet macaws were winging their way over.

"Twenty-three! Are they part of the same flock?"

"No . . . maybe. They are sometimes found in big flocks. But these ones came from another direction."

"Look, they're headed right where the other ones dropped down."

I lowered my binoculars and regarded my teammates. "Fancy a stroll?" I asked.

Andres' grin brightened the air around us. "There is something down there for them, that's for sure."

I prepared to rappel down the tree. "You coming?" I asked Liz.

She shook her head. "You guys go. I'll keep count from up here."

She was back at her binoculars even as we started our descent.

I was ten feet away from the forest floor when I heard her call out.

"Three more from the southeast!"

The ropes above me jerked. "Can't you climb down faster?" Andres demanded.

"I'm going as fast as I . . . okay. I'm down."

Andres was right on my heels (or, more aptly, my shoulders). "Liz!" he shouted up the tree. "We will come back and get you when we find them."

"Two more from the north," she called back in response.

"*C'mon!*" It was my turn to hurry Andres.

"I am . . . but I'm all tangled . . . there, I am coming now."

They were the last words we spoke for a while, saving our breath instead for the physical effort needed to push through primary rainforest. The vegetation was dense, the air heavy and close compared to the cooling breezes of the canopy. Sweat streamed down the side of my face. My arms flexed and burned with the effort of chopping a path through the jungle. Our struggles were silent, punctuated only by grunts and the occasional muffled curse. When I stopped to scrub my face, I could hear the scarlet macaws winging overhead, their raucous squawks muted by the stifling vegetation. Tantalizing us. Urging us on. I lifted my machete again.

When Andres finally stopped, I was so much in the swing of things that I marched right into him. He was lucky I didn't machete him.

"Robyn," his voice was low with suppressed excitement, "look at them!"

I blinked the sweat out of my eyes and stared.

The birds were gathered on the high, southern bank of a small stream. Over the years, the watercourse had cut right into the soil, exposing an outcropping of clay, moon gray against the ruddy, iron-rich soil. There were . . . I collected myself and began to count . . . forty . . . no, forty-one scarlet macaws clinging to the stream bank, their feathers impossibly brilliant in the clear, tropical sunlight.

To this day, I've never figured out how parrots that are so loud in flight can be so silent when they're feeding. And feeding they were, though not on any figs or seeds. They were eating clay.

"A clay lick," I breathed.

As we watched, entranced, five more macaws dropped down like ruby bombs. And then, a quick flash of purple. Purple? Had I imagined it? No! There it was again. Over to the far left.

"Andres!" I hissed, grabbing his arm and pointing.

He turned sharply and I heard him gasp.

"There are two of them!"

"I can't see the front—"

"Look, isn't that a red chinstrap?"

"Yes! But—oh! I see the white breast." Overwhelmed, I sank to my knees, unable to take my eyes off the sight.

We had found our macaw.

I don't know how long we stayed there, drinking in the sight, oblivious to the passage of time. But I snapped back to myself when Andres put his arm around my shoulders and crouched down beside me.

"Robyn! We have found them!"

His smile was snowy against his dark skin. I beamed

back, my attention torn between the macaws and Andres up close and personal.

Really personal.

"We have found them!" he said again.

And then he kissed me.

It was a sweet kiss at first. Chaste. Undemanding. A sort of congratulatory kiss. A woohoo-we've-finally-validated-our-funding sort of kiss. But it didn't stay that way.

He backed me up towards a big fern. I could feel the feather-light touch of a frond tickling the back of my neck. His other arm came up and slid around my waist. His lips grew more insistent, his tongue probing into my mouth, playing footsies with my tongue. His hands moved lower. I was dizzy with the headiness of it.

"I . . . don't think . . . this is a good idea," I mumbled around his lips.

The taste of him was intoxicating. Fresh air and steamy jungles and sweaty men. Yum.

He was fumbling with the buttons on my shirt. "What is not good about it?" he murmured, his voice now as husky as Viviana's.

Then his hands were inside my shirt. Such smooth hands for a man. My nipples tightened and rose to meet them.

But his hands were not the only things to slip inside my shirt.

"*Son of a bitch!*" I yelped as I felt the sharp bite of—

"*Hormigas!*" Andres shouted and he began beating his shirt.

Hormigas? I sprang to my feet, squirming as the fiery stings burned my stomach. "What the hell is a *hormiga?*" I gasped.

"Ants!" Andres grunted, slapping at his pants. "We have come too close to an ant-acacia tree."

Ants? I yanked my shirt out of my pants and slapped the fabric. I could see them now. Tiny, rust-colored bastards scurrying over my skin. Just a few, but their aggressiveness more than made up for their lack of numbers. I smacked at them, trying to brush them off, and jumped again as one nipped my armpit. That hurt, dammit!

We twisted and slapped and hopped around the tiny clearing. The Costa Rican Ant Dance. Your basic mood-killer.

As I finally managed to flick the last couple of ants onto the ground, I noticed an acrid odor in the air. I wrinkled my nose. "Ugh. What's that smell?"

"It's their alarm pheromone," Andres answered breathlessly, still swatting at ants. "We have disturbed the colony."

I tucked my shirt back in and glared over at the big fern—the ant-acacia tree, I corrected myself. Now I could see the hundreds, maybe even thousands, of alarmed red ants swarming out of long, hollow thorns. They covered the fern-like foliage, daring any creature to come near. I should have known better than to let my shirt be unbuttoned in the jungle. In horror movies, a glimpse of breast always means someone's about to be savaged by whichever creature has the starring role. I shuddered, imagining what it would be like to be swarmed by a whole colony of ants. Leninnen versus the Acacia Ants. *I'd* pay to see it.

Andres was still slapping his shirt. I took another big step away from the tree and made careful note of its appearance. I couldn't name even half the tree species I'd seen here, but I wasn't going to mistake an ant-acacia tree again—and I had absolutely no desire to be in the movie.

And then I remembered. The macaws! I spun around and let loose a gusty sigh of relief as I saw them still feeding quietly at the clay lick. Grumbling and burbling to each other, undisturbed by the antics across the stream.

I turned to tell Andres... and almost smacked my nose on his chest. He was right behind me, a mere ant's length away. But I'd had a few minutes to come to my senses—and to rebutton my shirt.

"I don't think it's a good idea," I told him again. Firm this time.

He took it as a cue and smiled, slow and sweet. "What is not good about it? We have no mangos, but. . . ."

I put my hand on his chest to stop him from coming any closer. *It would be so easy to just let my hand slide up and around and...* no.

I drew in a deep breath and let it out slowly, trying to blow off the unrequited lust. "We're too cut off at Danta," I told him.

He paused, a slight frown marring his forehead as the concept tried to compute.

I tried again. "Andres, I can't deny I'm attracted to you. But this is the wrong time and the wrong place. We've got enough problems already."

His expression cleared, the frown smoothing out. "What problems?" he teased, his eyes dark with passion.

Talk about the Thing that Wouldn't Die. You'd think the formic acid from the ant bites would have at least slowed him down some.

"Many problems," I insisted. "Poachers, Liz, Ernesto ... Aleck Tannahill. Take your pick."

My words were reaching his other brain now. The frown was back. Deeper.

"There are too many hostilities in the group already," I told him. "Too much tension. If we start sleeping together, it's going to undermine your authority—and my credibility. And it'll make things awkward for everyone else."

"And if we weren't here at Danta?"

I drew in another breath and looked him directly in the eye. "That," I said, "would be another matter."

"Ah," he smiled and his arms slid around me.

"No!" I had to be forceful about it.

He gave me the Mango Eyes again. "But—"

"No."

"Robyn—"

"No, Andres," I said a third time. Quietly. "I'm going back for Liz." I checked the buttons on my shirt and swung my daypack onto my shoulders.

"For Liz?"

He still didn't get it.

"She'll want to see the lick," I reminded him.

And before I could change my mind, I snatched up my machete and strode down the trail we'd carved out earlier. Andres didn't follow. I'm not sure what I would have done if he had.

I was already having second thoughts.

Chapter 18

"Liz! We've found them!"

"What? The scarlet macaws?"

"And our macaw!"

"Are you *serious?*" Her voice was high with excitement.

I heard crashing somewhere up above me. The ropes started jerking as Liz began her descent.

"That's not even the best part," I called up. "We've found a clay lick."

I heard a muffled *oof.*

"A lick! That's—ouch—amazing! And the macaws were there?"

"A pair of them! Mixed in with a whole flock of scarlet macaws."

"A breeding pair?"

I shrugged, though she couldn't see the gesture. "I'm not sure. They looked identical, but that doesn't necessarily mean anything."

There was little or no sexual dimorphism in Neotropical parrots. In other words, the sexes looked the same.

"But they're sticking pretty close together in that big red flock."

Liz was so thrilled, she almost dropped the last fifteen

feet. The smell of scorched hair tickled my nose as her rappel devices burned the rope. Small curls of smoke trailed behind her.

"A whole *flock* of macaws?" she asked again as her feet touched the ground.

She was breathless, her pale eyes sparkling with exhilaration. The smile she showed me lit her features with delight. It was the only genuine smile I'd ever seen her offer. For the first time since I'd met her, the deep furrows that lined her face lightened and smoothed out, melting years off her appearance. She was quite attractive, I realized, or at least she must have been at one time. Before life had pissed her off.

"And they're all at the lick?"

I grinned back, sharing her excitement. "You ready for this? There are at least *forty* scarlet macaws. Maybe more, but it's hard to tell if we're seeing new ones or if the same birds are coming back to have another go at the clay. But, Liz, those macaws . . . !"

She didn't have to ask which ones I meant.

"What are we waiting for? Let's go!"

I turned and led the way.

We hadn't gone very far when I heard Liz muttering to herself. I turned around.

"A whole flock of macaws," she mused aloud. This time, she didn't sound so thrilled. Her expression was thoughtful and the angry lines were ghosting back.

I pushed past a large fern, checking carefully to make sure it wasn't another acacia tree before I touched it. "You don't sound too happy," I ventured.

She joined me on the other side of the fern. Her brow was scrunched up into its customary frown again. "I'm not," she admitted. "I mean, I'm glad we've found our macaw, but I think I would've been happier if there wasn't a lick."

"But a lick is the best thing about this!" I protested. "Haven't you read about the one in Peru? Every few days, scarlet macaws came back to the lick. The researchers were able to track them from the—"

"Listen to what you're saying! If our macaws come back to the lick every few days, and if those poachers get wind of it. . . ." She didn't have to finish the thought.

"I know," I conceded. "Then it's a damn tempting target for them."

"Too tempting, by far, for my peace of mind! Our trail markers will lead them right to it. They've already shot one of their own. Who knows what they'll do if they follow us to the lick?"

I was trying not to think about that. "So, we'll have to make sure nobody finds out," I said with a certain amount of bravado. "At least until we can get some protective measures in place. This is where Danta's isolation works in our favor."

"And what about Ernesto?" Liz demanded. Her eyes held mine in a challenge, though her voice lacked its usual shrill edge. "Will Andres tell him? Should he be allowed to come with us?"

"Allowed?" I stopped and tucked an errant curl back under my hat. "He is a part of our team," I said slowly.

Liz snorted her bitterness. "So you'll just hand it to him on a silver platter and—"

"No. Listen to me for a second. I know why you don't trust him—and in a lot of ways I can't blame you. But, like it or not, he was hired for this study, same as you and me. Andres seems bent on including him in everything. Even if you make a stink about this, you're not going to change Andres' mind. All you're going to do is make things worse around the station. The gods know we've got enough problems with Aleck Tannahill strutting around impressing himself."

Liz made a sound of disgust.

"At least we can keep an eye on Ernesto," I offered.

I thought she might take my advice—her eyes were lowered as if in thought. But then she looked at me, and her icy gaze raised goosebumps on my arms.

"Keeping an eye on Ernesto won't do a damn thing," she said. "TRC let a so-called tourist come in and look what happened. They knew what Ernesto was, and they still hired him. Andres knows Ernesto is still trafficking, but he ignores it."

"How do you *know* he's still trafficking?" I demanded, a little fed up with her relentlessness. "Viviana told me he had a conversion while he was in prison—"

"A conversion!" Liz scoffed. "Robyn, last year two poachers were arrested over by Golfito. They told the rangers that Ernesto had offered them a thousand dollars each if they brought him scarlet macaws."

Her words silenced me.

"The police seized seventy-three birds. Seventy-three! Macaws, parakeets, parrots, toucans. And this was *after* Ernesto 'saw the light'. Oh yeah, I've heard all about his *conversion*," she dragged the word out, making it sound like something my cat barfed up. "I don't believe it for a second. And, if you ask me, hiring him was the worst thing TRC could have done."

We continued through the forest, more slowly this time.

"And Andres knows this?" I asked her after a few steps.

"Oh yes, though he likes to pretend it doesn't mean

anything. He actually had the nerve to suggest these poachers—uneducated, local men—had lied about Ernesto's involvement. Now, I ask you, if Ernesto wasn't involved, then why would these men say he was? How would they even know his name?"

I shook my head, puzzled and disturbed. "I don't know. It sounds pretty bad."

"Damn right it does!"

She plucked at my sleeve. I stopped and turned to face her.

"Look," she began, her expression pleading, "I know I'm not the easiest person to get along with. I know I get people's backs up. But this thing with Ernesto is *not* just me going off the deep end about something. I think he's still trafficking, and I'm very much afraid that we've found these macaws only to see them die in a suitcase somewhere."

I had to give her points for honesty. And her talents for persuasion were pretty impressive too. It was difficult to believe that TRC would have made such an error in judgment, but it wouldn't be the first time something like this had happened. Just a few years before, a world-renowned parrot expert had been arrested and charged with smuggling $1.4 million in endangered parrots. The man had been an outspoken conservationist, had written books and lectured tirelessly on the importance of preserving our disappearing birdlife. He was currently serving seven years in prison. Cynically, I wondered if he'd have a conversion too.

I scrubbed my forehead, more troubled than excited now about our find. "I don't know what to say, Liz," I told her. "We can keep a sharp eye on Ernesto, but apart from that . . . maybe we can push for a guard at the lick."

"A guard."

"In Brazil, they've got bodyguards for the last Lear's macaw. Why not here?" I warmed to the idea as I worked it through. "We can set up a permanent blind—we'll have to do that anyhow—and maybe we can get somebody living there. I'm sure we could find someone to fund it."

"Maybe." Liz looked doubtful.

"Have you got any other suggestions?"

She shook her head slowly. Reluctantly.

"Me either. So let's try it my way—at least at first. Ernesto doesn't have to know we're keeping an eye on him." It was my turn to plead with her.

Her gooseberry gaze held my eyes for a long moment. Then she nodded slowly.

"I'll keep my mouth in park," she agreed. "For now."

I nudged her shoulder. "C'mon. Let's go see some macaws. I want to run our guard idea past Andres."

News of the clay lick lit up the station that evening, and for a while, everybody seemed to be talking at once.

"A clay lick?"

"That's astonishing!"

"And how long were they there for?"

"What is a clay lick?"

This last was from Pepe, who was sitting beside me at one end of the dining room table.

"It's an exposed outcropping of clay," I explained to him. "For some reason, the macaws love it."

"They eat it?" He was doubtful. "Why?"

"Nobody knows. It could be they need the nutrients from it. Or they might be using it to detoxify some of the nastier defense compounds in their diet—they eat mostly seeds and unripe fruits. And clay is, after all, Mother Nature's version of Kaopectate."

"Kaopectate?" he asked.

Oscar explained to him in Spanish about Kaopectate. Then, "You have made a very valuable discovery," he congratulated me. "I can see how excited you are in your eyes. They are all sparkles and stars."

"Humm." I cleared my throat uncomfortably.

Macaws weren't the only thing putting the spring into my stride, but I didn't want to tell Oscar that. Andres had backed off a little bit—especially with Liz around—but while I'd spent the afternoon watching macaws, he'd spent a good deal of time making Mango Eyes at me. Flattering? Oh yes. But also unsettling.

"You will need to protect them, yes?" Oscar was asking. "Your new macaws."

"Yes," I agreed. "They must be very rare to go unseen for so long—even in such an isolated park."

"Very valuable for collectors," Oscar agreed.

I nodded reluctantly. "I know. We're going to see about getting a guard, but . . . ," I trailed off, not needing to explain about funding to Oscar. Over the past few weeks, he'd heard us gripe about the lack of it often enough.

Oscar gave my hand a comforting pat. "*Lo siento*. I did not mean to make you worried. I'm sure everything will be fine. I think maybe this threat of poaching is not as serious as you think."

Pepe wasn't paying attention to this. "How many parrots did you see?" he asked, tugging on my shirt sleeve.

"A lot. Mostly scarlet macaws. We only saw two of our new macaw."

"But how many?" he insisted. "How many altogether?"

I shrugged, perplexed by his intensity. "I don't know.

It's hard to tell if you're seeing new ones or the same birds coming back for more. I'm not sure yet how we're going to work that out."

"You will need lots of helpers, I think," Oscar rumbled.

"Probably," I agreed. "We really haven't gotten beyond celebrating the fact that we've actually found them."

"I would like to see this lick, if it is okay," Pepe said. "I have never seen this many macaws together before."

"What about your research project?" I asked.

He squirmed in his chair, and a decidedly uncomfortable look crossed his face. There was an outburst of laughter from the other end of the table, but I was curious now. This was the first time I'd really had a chance to sit down and talk with Pepe.

"What is your thesis project, anyhow?" I prodded.

"It . . . it will be about the changing climate, I think," he answered haltingly. "And how the birds will migrate to different elevations. This is what I am mostly interested in studying."

"Ah," I said. "I've read a bit about that. Wasn't it George . . . oh, what was his name?" I rubbed my eyes, trying to remember. "George Kricher!" I snapped my fingers. "Wasn't that the guy who first studied elevational migration in quetzals?"

"Yes," Pepe nodded happily. "Yes, George Kricher. That is right. He was studying the quetzals when they moved up into the habitat with the keel-billed toucans."

"Right," I said. But something didn't ring true.

"There are no quetzals here," Pepe continued. "But I can maybe study the scarlet macaws. There are still many things to learn about their migration. If I could see this clay lick—"

"Hey, Robyn!"

I glanced down the other end of the table. The rest of the macaw team was gathered there, their faces flushed with the news and the celebratory *cervezas*. Andres was motioning me closer. Patting an empty place on the bench beside him.

"Come," he called. "We are trying to think of a name for our macaw."

I slid down the bench towards them, but not without a last backwards glance at Pepe. Something wasn't right about that guy.

I jumped happily into the Name Game, but Pepe's words niggled away at me all evening. By the time I finally turned in for the night, we still hadn't come to a consensus about the name, though everything had been suggested, from Gray's macaw (which nobody really liked) to amethyst macaw (which worked for me) to the Barney macaw (proposed by Keith, and ridiculed by everybody else). The first thing I did when I got back to my cabin was haul out my *Birds of Costa Rica* field guide. But I wasn't looking for bird names.

I flipped first to one entry, then to a second. Then I snapped the book shut. Pepe, I realized, had gotten it wrong. Keel-billed toucans were low elevation birds. Quetzals lived higher up. It was the toucans who had invaded the quetzals' habitat, not the other way around.

"Who was that guy who studied the seasonal movements of quetzals?" I asked Viviana when she came in. "You know, the one who did all the radiotelemetry work."

"George Powell," she replied.

"Powell? Are you sure?"

She nodded. "Yes, of course. He adapted his techniques

for a study of great green macaws. It was very successful." She pulled on the large T-shirt she wore as a nightie and turned to look at me. "Why do you want to know about George Powell?" she asked.

I shook my head. "No reason."

"You believe we should be radio tagging our macaw?"

"Um, maybe. . . ."

We talked for a while about our study and how best to proceed. But after Viviana had turned out the kerosene lamp, I lay awake for a long time. Mulling over the puzzle of the PhD student who was so ignorant about the subject he was studying.

Chapter 19

"Janet! Janet! Take my picture!"

"What? What are you—oh my god! *Keith!*"

"C'mon. I can use it for my grad seminar."

"That's *disgusting!*"

"No, babe, it's cool."

Overwhelmed with curiosity, I closed my notebook and stepped outside. I didn't have much to add to the mud-spattered pages anyway. We'd been observing the lick for over a week now. Carefully detailing numbers and behavior and times of sightings. On each day except one, our amethyst macaws had made an appearance. But how to tell if they were new birds or repeats? We were still working that out.

I looked over toward Keith and Janet's dilapidated old cabin. They were standing off to one side of it. Keith had grabbed Janet's arm in excitement and she was struggling to put some distance between them. What the . . . ? I squinted at his face. There, stretched from nose to cheekbone, was a dark, glistening mass. A leech.

"Ewww!" I scrunched my face up and stuck my tongue out.

Keith saw me and grinned. "No, no. It's cool. It crawled up ten minutes ago, but I didn't have my camera with me. I had to run all the way back to the station."

"*You left that thing on your face for ten minutes?*" Janet was horrified.

I took a closer look at the creature. Inky black, two to three inches long, bloated and engorged now with Keith's blood. It was, I had to admit, pretty impressive.

"I just need Janet to snap a couple of shots for me."

"Ro-byn!" Janet wailed, pleading for understanding.

I shrugged, trying to hide a wide smile. "I dunno, Janet, it sort of works for me. Take his picture—he won't be happy until you do. His grad students will love it."

"But—"

"*I* liked seeing stuff like this when I was in school."

Keith turned back to his girlfriend. "See? I'm not the only one. C'mon," he urged her with a boyish grin. Then, "Hey, Nanook," he said to me, "maybe when I'm done with it, you could put it on your nose and get *your* picture taken."

A kind offer.

"Thanks anyway," I shook my head, silently thanking the gods that my academic days were over.

Janet was loading more film into her camera. "I feel like *I'm* hallucinating now," she complained. "I can't believe I'm doing this."

"Who's been hallucinating?" I asked.

"Keith had a few problems with the anti-malarials."

Concerned, I turned to Keith. "They gave you hallucinations? You didn't mention anything."

"No point," he answered carefully, trying not to dislodge his slimy hitchhiker. "They were just mild ones. Bugs crawling up the walls, that kind of thing. And one day the clouds looked pretty weird."

"Are you okay now?"

"Oh yeah."

"Except for the big leech on his face," Janet said.

Keith gave her a lopsided smile, then turned his attention back to me. "I stopped taking the pills last week," he told me, "and things seem to be settling down."

"And if you contract malaria?"

He shrugged. "I'll deal with that when it comes. Janet, are you almost done? I can feel my blood getting sucked out of me here."

"Bitch, bitch, bitch. *You're* the one who left that revolting thing on you in the first place."

"You don't like anything I like."

"That's not true. I like *me*."

Laughing, I left the two of them to deal with the leech. Of all the Berkeley crowd at Danta, I felt closest to these two. They were a lot of fun and, in many ways, the chemistry between them reminded me of my relationship with Kelt. An unsettling thought. With Andres smoldering at me every chance he got, I hadn't wanted to remember Kelt. But for some reason, I'd been thinking about him more and more lately.

I chewed a ragged nail thoughtfully, then shook my head. There were other things to contemplate besides my confused love life. The leech on Keith's face had given me an idea.

"Take pictures of the macaws?" Andres repeated, mystified.

Viviana and I nodded.

"But why?"

"Haven't you read about Charlie Munn's work in Peru?" Viviana asked, clearly incredulous at his ignorance.

It *was* surprising that he hadn't heard of it.

Andres frowned and shook his head, then he looked to me for explanation.

"He took black and white photographs of scarlet macaws at a clay lick," I told him. "Close-ups with big lenses."

"And they could identify individual birds from these?" Andres' interest was piqued.

"From the pattern of facial feathers," I explained.

"They *are* unique to the individual," Viviana added with just a hint of condescension.

"And then there're the marks and irregularities on the upper mandibles," I said quickly, with a stern look at Viviana. "Again, unique to the individual."

Viviana made a face at me, then turned back to Andres. "They took hundreds of photographs," she continued. Less sarcastic now. "Every few days for about a month. Then they could compare them to see who was new and who kept coming back."

Andres sat up straighter as she spoke. "This would be great!" he exclaimed. At least he was enthusiastic.

"As long as the amethyst macaws show the same characteristics," I cautioned.

"Have you talked to Janet?"

"Not yet." I shook my head.

"*You* are the team leader," Viviana said, resentment creeping into her tone.

Andres either didn't catch it, or he was ignoring it. "Well, let's find her." He rubbed his hands together. "I think this is a wonderful idea!"

So did Janet.

I finally tracked her down in the kitchen, helping Oscar and Liz with dinner. Ernesto, Pepe, and Keith were lounging along the length of the tall counter, making desultory conversation and outrageous culinary suggestions, and generally getting in the way. Keith, I was happy to note, had ditched his leech.

"I'd be delighted to do it," Janet told me after I broached the subject. "Hey!" This was aimed at Keith, who'd snitched a piece of pineapple from under her knife. "I'll cut it off next time," she warned him.

"We can borrow an old enlarger from Sirena," I said. "Apparently, they've even got the chemicals you need. Leftovers from some research project last year."

"I could set up a makeshift darkroom in the lab." Janet was running with the idea. "The generator's gas-powered?"

"Yeah. Oscar's still having trouble with it, but he thinks he can give you maybe an hour a night."

"I can work with that."

"We were thinking we could build a blind on the other side of the stream. So we don't stress out the birds or get them too accustomed to seeing people around. I don't know much about cameras, but you've got all the lenses and stuff?"

Janet nodded, her eyes bright with anticipation.

I hated to burst her bubble.

"We . . . uh . . . we can't pay you, though." I'd purposely saved that for the last. "At least not what you're worth. I'm sorry. Our funding just won't cover it. But Andres says we can spring for all the film and chemicals and maybe squeak out a bit more."

Janet shrugged it off. "I'm here anyway," she said, deftly slicing into another pineapple. The juice squirted across the counter.

"What are you making?" I asked, diverted for a moment.

"Pineapple custards," Janet told me. "With fingertips!" she yelled as Keith stole another tidbit.

Ernesto chuckled. "*Por favor*, no fingers for me," he said, shaking his head.

"Then sit on him for me, will you?" She turned back to me. "Look, Robyn, don't worry about the money. It's a fabulous opportunity for me. Right now, that's worth more than cash."

"Don't let Stephen hear you say that," Keith warned, referring to her sometime boss at an advertising agency.

"Oh, him," she dismissed the man with a wave of her knife. "That guy is so greedy, he'd sell his own granny if it meant making a buck—and he doesn't understand anybody who thinks differently."

"People will do many things for money." Pepe nodded his head sagely.

"Tell me about it," Keith agreed. "When my sister was a kid, she charged all her little girlfriends ten cents to kiss me."

"And I'm sure you loved every minute of it," Janet said as the rest of us laughed.

"Not even for a second," he told her with exaggerated sincerity. "I was saving myself for you."

I whistled. "Smooth, Keith. Very smooth."

Janet reached across the counter and ruffled his hair fondly.

"When *I* was young," Oscar said in his deep, rumbling voice, "I was not like this." He patted his ample stomach. "So to make money, I used to hang out at the Coca Cola Station, where the tourist buses arrived. I would tell the *gringos* that I was poor and had no parents. I would look at them with such big eyes. . . ." He demonstrated for us.

"Oscar!" I was torn between surprise and amusement.

He grinned at me. Unrepentant even now. "It worked very well for a while. I had so much money, I bought candies and toys for all my friends. Then *mi mamá*, she found out." He shook his head, wincing in remembrance. "I could not sit for many, many days."

"Well, when I was young," Pepe said, "I wanted to be an actor."

"An actor?" Janet stopped slicing pineapples and looked at him in surprise. "What's wrong with that?"

"Nothing," Pepe replied. "Not if that is what you want to do. But I discovered I did not really want to be an actor. I just wanted to be very rich and to kiss many beautiful women."

We all laughed.

"It was fun pretending to be somebody else," he continued after a moment, "but then I found out that most actors do not make much money. I am not Demi Moore. Nobody wanted to pay me twelve million dollars to take my shirt off."

"You know, *I've* had that same problem," Keith told him. "I don't understand it at all."

Janet sliced the top off another pineapple. "Well, even if someone offered me twelve million, I don't think I'd strip in front of the camera."

"Really?" Keith raised his eyebrows in surprise. "Huh. For that kind of money I'd run naked through a field with a carrot up my bum."

"Yeah, but who would pay to see it?" Janet smirked.

Keith was about to respond when Liz cut in.

"And would you sell a macaw for twenty thousand dollars?" she inquired crisply.

The smile fell off Keith's face. "What?"

"Um . . . we weren't really talking about that kind of thing," I ventured.

"It's a valid question," Liz shot back. "Pepe here says that people will do just about anything for money. Why not that?"

Pepe jumped at the sound of his name. "But I was not—"

"Ah, but some of us have done it, haven't they?" Liz tapped the side of her nose thoughtfully. She wasn't looking at Ernesto, but her meaning was clear.

"Liz," I warned.

She ignored me. "I wonder how you get into something like that," she mused aloud. "You'd have to have a real criminal streak. . . ."

"Give it a rest," I told her wearily.

She glanced over at me then and I caught her eye, trying without words to remind her of her earlier promise. She stared back at me with a look that said she knew full well what she was doing. I shook my head slightly and saw her nostrils flare.

"Well, I guess I'll be going to check my gear for tomorrow, then," she spat, tossing her knife and a half-peeled squash on the counter. And with that, she stalked out of the kitchen.

The rest of us squirmed in uncomfortable silence. It was Ernesto who finally broke it.

"When I was young," he began softly, "my uncle had many birds. Many parrots. He got them from poor people who captured them for money. They were so beautiful, those birds. One day when I was ten, my uncle had to leave town quickly. He told me to sell the birds for him and keep the money. I took those birds around on the streets and in one day, I had sold them all."

I sucked in my breath and Ernesto looked at me and nodded.

"It was so easy," he said. "And I made so much money. So I thought, why not do this? I bought a car when I was fifteen and by the time I was twenty, I was making thousands of American dollars a month."

Janet had stopped chopping as Ernesto spoke. It was so quiet, I could hear the faint gurgle of an oropendula in the distance.

"I sold more parrots than anyone else in Costa Rica," he said. There was an odd mixture of pride and shame in his voice. "But I always loved them. It was never just money to me, not like the poachers these days. They are criminals, these ones, only thinking about how many dollars they will make. Money is just money. But when the birds are all gone, that's it. These guys, they will be the end of the macaws."

A long silence followed this statement. Part of me wished now that Liz had stayed. That she could have heard the sincerity in Ernesto's voice.

I cleared my throat. "Not if we can help it," I told him. Then I turned to Oscar. "Have the rangers found out *anything* about those poachers?"

Oscar shook his head. "The radio is not working," he told me. "There has been too much rain, I think. Too much humidity. But Dan has not called on the satellite phone, either. I think—"

"*¡Hola!*" The greeting was shouted across the clearing. An unfamiliar voice.

Through the screened window, I saw two shifty-looking characters making tracks toward the dining hall. They were both long and bony with identical greasy hair. The rest of them didn't look too clean, either.

Oscar put down his stirring spoon. "*¡Hola! ¡Diay maes! ¿Cómo están?*" he boomed back. A flock of bananaquits fluttered up from the trees in surprise.

"My cousins! I told you they would return," Oscar declared to the rest of us. He rubbed his hands with delight as the men slouched into the hall. "Now we will have more *cabinas*. This is Ramón," he pulled one of the men forward, "and this is Juan."

Cousins, eh? I eyed them again. Ramón and Juan hadn't improved on closer inspection. They were youngish men but their faces were deeply incised with the lines of deprivation and self-abuse. They were not, in fact, clean. Ramón's once-white shirt was stained yellow under the arms and my nose detected a distinctly sour stench coming off Juan. I was astonished that they were in any way related to the well-fed and jolly Oscar.

"*¡Hola!*" Ramón greeted me with stale alcohol breath, his eyes sliding sideways, refusing to meet my own.

Juan held out a ropy hand, the fingernails black with filth.

I shook it, managing an uneasy smile. "*¡Hola!*" I said.

Oscar clapped them both on the shoulders. In the late day sunlight, I could see the clouds of dust puffing up from their clothing.

"They do not speak English," he told me. "But they will help with building. And don't worry, I will ask them to watch out for poachers, yes?" Oscar smiled and nodded. As if reassuring me there was nothing more to worry about.

Somehow, I didn't think my sleep would be any easier with Ramón and Juan on the job.

Chapter 20

The following day, Marco, Andres, and I set out after breakfast to build a blind. At the last minute, Pepe decided to tag along. He still hadn't seen an amethyst macaw. The one day he'd ventured out with us, the macaws hadn't shown their little purple faces.

"We must make certain we're not too close to the ant-acacia tree," Andres cautioned once we arrived at the lick. "It can really ruin things."

I pretended not to see the meaningful look he sloped my way. I was going to have to have a word with him about those Mango Eyes of his. Sooner or later, people were going to start noticing—either that, or I was going to start giving in to them. I liked to think the only thing that had saved me so far was my ironclad will. In actuality, it probably had more to do with the cold showers at Danta and the fact that I shared a cabin with Viviana.

"Yes," Marco was saying. "If we build the blind here, going to this spot over there, it should give us a lot of space and we will not be close to the ant-acacia."

"But we should really build there," Pepe pointed back the way we'd come in.

"We wouldn't see anything back there," Andres protested.

"Yes, I know. It's an old trick. If you build far away and move the blind each day closer and closer, then the birds will not get as nervous."

"So you don't stress them with a big structure all of a sudden," I said, nodding in understanding. "Good idea."

So Marco and Pepe began wielding their machetes to clear the undergrowth, while Andres and I went off in search of cecropia trees for the frame.

"I like this idea of Pepe's," Andres told me, "although our macaws do not seem very disturbed by us so far."

"No," I agreed. "But when Janet starts snapping pictures, they might feel differently. Look," I pointed to our left. "Aren't those cecropias over there?"

A couple of rabbit-like agoutis were foraging in the stand of trees, but they scuttled off as soon as we got close. We chopped down five smallish trees with our machetes and began lashing them together with the heavy twine we'd brought from the station. We had decided to build a rectangular frame, braced on both sides, with a covered roof, both to protect the watchers from rain and to hide them from any macaws flying overhead.

"You know," Andres said softly, "it has been quite a while since we were here together." His voice was low, pitched so Marco and Pepe wouldn't hear it. "You are so beautiful. I love you," he said. "I'm missing you."

The tree slipped out of the knot I'd made and I blew out my breath in frustration. I looked up at Andres. Mango Eyes again.

"You see me every day," I pointed out, obscurely irritated. Missing me? *Love me?* The guy didn't even *know* me. "I think you're exaggerating."

Andres flushed. "I think there are maybe not as many problems at Danta as you say."

"Forget it," I told him flatly. "If you can't see—"

"How is everything going?" Marco asked, joining us.

I bit off the rest of my words and Andres dropped his eyes. Marco stopped, sensing the tension in the air.

"Are you having troubles?" he floundered. "Pepe and I, we are finished clearing the bushes."

"No troubles," I managed to say. "Except with this miserable knot. If you could grab an end and hold it while I tie the sucker, I'll give you my dessert tonight."

Reassured by the joke (he knew me well enough to realize I'd do no such thing), Marco grinned and stepped up to help. As the four of us cobbled together the blind, there were no further opportunities for declarations of lust. I think Andres was frustrated by it. He was uncharacteristically quiet. Even when he laughed at Marco's jokes, his laughter had a bitter edge.

Well, what the hell did he expect? That I'd go skulking off into the woods with him? Yeah, right. What kind of woman did he think I was, anyhow? What made him think that—

"Um, Robyn, you are tying it to the wrong tree."

"Oh. Sorry."

"That's okay," Marco smirked. "Women, you know, they are not as good at building things as we men."

I bit back a sharp retort. Marco was only teasing me and there was no need to take out my irritation with Andres on him. "I think I should get *your* dessert tonight for that," I said instead.

But Marco wasn't paying attention to me anymore. His face was turned skyward. "Pepe!" he called out softly and pointed. There were two purple streaks winging overhead. "The amethyst macaws."

Pepe stopped what he was doing and gawked at them, his mouth hanging open. The birds flew right over us and dropped down to the clay lick. Pepe ran over to the pile of daypacks, grabbed his binoculars, and crept closer to the stream bank.

"They are at the lick!" he whispered back to us. His eyes were bright with excitement.

I put down the trees I'd been trying to lash together and went to join him. Shielding my eyes with one hand, I watched as another pair of amethysts joined the first one. There were seven scarlet macaws with them.

"Lovely, aren't they?" I murmured.

"They are beautiful," he whistled softly. "They would be worth a fortune."

I dropped my hand and gave him a sharp look.

"And look," he continued, oblivious to my scrutiny, "three, six . . . seven scarlet macaws. Three thousand dollars each in New York. And those amethyst macaws? Ten thousand American dollars—at least! Maybe more."

"Hopefully a lot less," I said pointedly. "As in 'nothing' because they won't be going to New York or Europe or anywhere else."

Pepe's cheeks colored. "Oh . . . of course," he said. "That is not what I meant."

"Of course not," I lied right back at him. "Come on. Let's go finish the blind." I was suddenly eager to get Pepe as far away from the lick as possible.

I stuck close to him for the rest of the day but he limited his conversation to normal subjects like natality rates and ranging behavior. If I hadn't caught the furtive looks he slipped my way, I'd have been tempted to write off his earlier remarks. His first sight of an amethyst macaw and his initial reaction was to calculate its worth on the black market. And Liz was worried about Ernesto?

One thing was for sure. Pepe had given me a lot more important things to think about than sex.

"You'll never find out anything meaningful if you limit yourself to the clay lick," Aleck insisted.

I inhaled slowly, trying to hold on to my temper.

"I'm aware of that," I said through clenched teeth. "That's why only one group works there at a time, and the others climb trees or go in the boat . . . *like I said.*"

The sarcasm was lost on him.

"Because if you spend all your time at the lick, how are you ever going to get information on the macaws' range?"

"We wouldn't, now, would we?"

"How are you going to find out about nesting activities? Why are the birds so rare? Is there a lack of nesting sites? Is there competition for the sites that are available? You'll never find that out just by studying a lick."

Did the man ever listen to anybody except himself?

"But they're not just working at the lick," Candi objected, walking up in the middle of the conversation. She arranged her breakfast plate and cutlery on the table. "Marco told me they'll be climbing trees to find out which areas are serviced by the lick and . . . ," she trailed off as Aleck turned a frosty glare on her.

"Maybe you should go with them, then," he suggested.

My ears pricked up at the oddly taunting note in his voice.

"You'd find a trip up to the canopy so fascinating. And I'm sure your project would benefit from it."

Candi blanched. "Um . . . I'm . . . not finished with the ground-level plants yet," her little-girl voice stumbled.

"Ah," Aleck replied, managing to impart a wealth of disbelief in a single syllable.

He was baiting Candi about something, that was clear. Was she afraid of heights in addition to everything else? There was an uncomfortable pause. Marco twitched toward Candi, but she sat down quickly and started toying with her fork, her eyes fixed on the plate in front of her. The color had come flooding back into her cheeks.

"We won't have time to help her with that," I said firmly. "Marco and I'll be up and down the tree with scopes and stopwatches. No offense, Candi," I paused and her eyes flew up to meet mine, "but you'd only be in our way. Maybe another day."

Candi's face flushed again, but with gratitude this time.

"Come on, Marco," I pushed away from the table, eager to put some distance between me and Aleck. "Oscar's already put out our gear. We've got a long day ahead of us."

"You are sure?" Marco asked again.

I waved him up. "Positive. Why am I always the one to go up first, anyhow?"

"Because you are always showing me how brave you are," he answered with a devilish grin.

Too perceptive by far.

"Well, now it's your turn," I told him crankily. "I already feel brave enough today."

Actually, I was still trying to blow off the irritation from my encounter with Aleck Tannahill. The man was an egotistical jerk. I squished down a lump of muddy clay with my boot, imagining it was Aleck. Nice of Candi to stick up for us, I reflected. Not terribly smart, though. She'd probably pay for it. And what was all that stuff about her climbing trees? Was she afraid of heights? And was Aleck really cruel enough to taunt her about it? Some advisor.

Marco had clipped his Jumars on the rope and started his ascent. I wasn't really paying attention. Too caught up in picturing Aleck Tannahill as a lump of mud. So I didn't see what happened next. But I heard it.

"AAAHHH!"

Marco's shriek of terror snapped me back to the present. Beside me, the ropes jerked.

I looked up. A confused image of Marco's body, bouncing against the tree trunk. Smashing into branches. Falling.

"*Marco!*" I screamed in horror.

And he fell to the ground at my feet.

I was on my knees in an instant, crouching beside him in the mud.

"Marco," I called again. Softly this time.

He didn't move.

Oh gods. Why hadn't I been paying attention?

He was lying on his back, eyes closed. Eyelids twitching spasmodically. His chest heaved once. Twice. Trying to suck in air.

"Come on, Marco," I urged. "Slow and easy. You can do it!" My own breath felt like it was stuck in my lungs. I rubbed his chest as if that would help the air return. "Just relax and breathe in."

Success came with a choked gasp. Another breath, easier this time. And a third. He opened his eyes and blinked.

I sent up a quick prayer of thanks to the gods.

Marco took another breath and moaned, tensing his muscles for movement.

"No! Don't move yet." I put my hands on his shoulders to stop him. "Try wiggling your feet. The left one . . . okay, now the right."

Marco hissed through his teeth.

"Okay, relax." I patted his leg. "Your foot moved, so that's good. You've hurt something, but I don't think it's your spine. Can you sit up?"

"In a minute," he wheezed.

"Take your time."

He gulped in some more air and muttered a few choice words.

I exhaled shakily. If he had enough breath to curse, then he was going to live.

"You scared the hell out of me," I told him. "What happened? Why wasn't the rope secured?"

Marco held his hand out and I helped him sit up. He shook his head at my question. "I do not know," he said. "I thought it was okay. It felt okay. Then the rope, it just decided to let go. It must have been rotting."

Not surprising in all this humidity. Even my pants were starting to mold.

"Do you feel all right? Sore ribs? Shoulders?"

"I think I am okay."

"You bounced all the way down, you know."

Marco grimaced and rubbed his right arm. "Next time, Robyn," he told me, "you can be the brave one."

I snorted. "Come on. I think we should get you back

to Danta. You're going to be feeling this before the day's over."

I helped him to his feet, brushing off the bits of dirt and moss that were streaked across his back. But as Marco took a first step, his right leg buckled and he tumbled to the ground with a cry of agony.

"My knee!" he hissed through clenched teeth.

I stood over him, hands on hips, mouth pulled to one side. "Alrightee. It looks like we'll be doing this the hard way."

I wrapped his knee with a tensor bandage from the first aid kit, and shook out a couple of aspirins for him. Then I settled him under the tree while I collected our gear. I clipped Marco's daypack to the front of me, and pulled on my own pack with our telescope and binoculars. Good thing he hadn't been carrying the scope. The climbing rope was clearly toast, but it might come in handy for drying laundry. I coiled it up quickly and slung it over my shoulder.

Marco had leaned back against the tree. Eyes closed. Forehead furrowed in pain.

"You need a drink?" I offered him my water bottle.

He opened his eyes and shook his head.

I slugged back a few gulps and clipped the bottle onto my belt. "Okay," I said, "let's get you back to the station."

It was a long hike back. Marco hobbled along as best he could with his arm slung around my neck. I staggered beneath the double weight of the gear and Marco.

"*Oof!* You did this on purpose, didn't you?" I grunted.

"Of course," he puffed back. "I wanted to see if you could carry all the ropes yourself."

"Not to mention your heavy carcass."

"I am . . . *ouch!* . . . not forgetting. You are very strong . . . for a woman."

"And you're pretty cheeky for a guy who needs a shoulder to lean on."

He yelped in pain as we stumbled on a root.

"Cheer up," I tried to jolly him on. "Maybe Candi will come and nurse you back to health."

"You . . . are imagining things," he told me.

"Am I?"

We stopped to catch our breath. I glanced at his face and felt my teasing smile fade. "You really like her, don't you?" I asked softly.

He looked up at me, his brown eyes filled with pain.

"I have never met anyone like her before," he began, his voice low. "She is so beautiful and so brave to be here even though she's scared. I try to teach her about the jungle, so she won't be so scared, but," he shook his head sadly, "I'm afraid she will leave and I'll never see her again."

I chewed on my lower lip. He had it bad.

"And even if . . . if she and I . . . uh," he faltered. "Well . . . I do not think her professor likes me."

I could, at least, reassure him on that account. "Hell, I wouldn't worry about that, Marco. A professor won't get in the way of . . . um, that sort of thing. He's just her professor."

Why I was encouraging him to pursue Candi, I didn't know. I liked my brash field partner. Did I really think Candi would be good for him? I shook off the thought. Marco was a big boy. He was old enough to figure out his own love life.

"Besides," I said briskly, "I don't think Aleck Tannahill likes anybody except himself. He's an ass—uh . . . a jerk."

"No. You had the word right the first time. I've heard

him talking to Candi. I have watched how he treats her."

I blinked at his tone.

"He is an *asshole.*"

I didn't know which was more disturbing. The fact that he swore in front of me. Or the cold, hard hatred in his voice.

X-Originating-IP: [199.137.52.16]

From: "Robyn Devara"
<macaw1@woodrowconsultants.com>
To: "Kelt Roberson" <batnerd@tnc.com>
Subject: Stuff
Date: Wed 15 May 23:10:08-1200

Hey, Kelt,

Sorry I haven't written in a while. I did get all your e-mails but things have been kind of weird here. Nothing wrong, exactly. And before you start to worrying again, no, we haven't seen hide nor hair of any illegal activities for quite some time now—and no more bodies in the forest, thank the gods. I think we might have scared the poachers off.

We've been observing the amethyst macaws for almost two weeks now. While the scarlet macaws still outnumber them, our amethysts may not be as rare as we thought (though 'rare' is a relative term here—they're ALL rare). I think we've got a small population though, and not just a few isolated individuals. Time will tell. So the study is going fairly smoothly—partly because we haven't seen any more evidence of trafficking, but mostly I think because Liz has gone off for a few days to attend a conference in Brazil. It's been a relief not to have her snarking around the station. I'm afraid we're not the most congenial of field teams.

I don't know what the problem is, but everything besides the study seems to be going wrong lately. The radio gave up the ghost a week ago, the satellite phone is fixing to do the same (I'll be lucky to get this e-mail off to you), and Marco wrenched his knee the other day when our climbing rope snapped and he fell out of a tree. Aleck Tannahill keeps pissing me off with his superior attitude, and Oscar's cousins (who are here to help with some building) give me the heebie-jeebies. Also, I think somebody was rummaging around in my bags last night. Viviana and I were out for a night hike with Keith and Janet (which, incidentally, you would've loved—here in the rainforest, the night really belongs to the bats). Anyhow, I could have sworn I left my dufflebag zipped up, but when we got back, it was open and my clothes were all jumbled around. Yeah, yeah, I know. The clothes were probably already untidy, it's just . . . I don't know. Maybe I'm the one who's hallucinating now.

Crap, I think my batteries are dying (not that this should surprise me). I'd better sign off. So much for not worrying you. I'm sorry. I didn't mean to e-dump all this on you. I guess I'm just feeling very far away from home tonight.

Give Guido a long hug from me and a good scratch behind the ears (and I'm sorry about your carpet. I hope the stain comes out).

Wish you were here,
Robyn

An ecosystem is a tapestry of species and relationships. Chop away a section, isolate that section, and there arises the problem of unraveling.

David Quammen
The Song of the Dodo

Chapter 21

"Oh, please," the voice oozed derision, "you can't be a *complete* idiot!"

Just another friendly consultation with an academic advisor.

"If you're sampling everything in a certain area, then you *sample everything*, don't you? If you want random samples, then you've got to set up a grid. You're just prancing around here and picking a plant there. It's scientifically meaningless. What kind of data set are you going to end up with? What will it say about species diversity at Danta? I can tell you what it'll say—*absolutely nothing!* What kind of scientific method is that?"

I hated to agree with him, but Aleck Tannahill had a point. Trouble was, he didn't seem capable of making it either briefly or constructively. I'd been listening to this for the past fifteen minutes.

I was in the solar dryer, hanging up shirts. Oscar had built the odd-looking structure a couple of weeks ago. It was a large, square, wooden frame—about ten square feet—completely covered with thick, clear plastic. An orange tarp served as a door, and five separate ropes had been strung from one side to the other as clotheslines. On a hot, sunny day, clothes could dry in a few hours. We had to share the space with a couple of four-inch poisonous centipedes, but a pair of rubber boots solved that problem. I figured it was a small price to pay for dry, mold-free clothing. If only the problem of Aleck Tannahill could be dealt with as easily.

"I'm telling you, Candace—and this is for your own good, honey—you're just not cut out for this line of work."

"But—"

"No," he cut her off. "You don't listen to my advice. . . ."

"That's not true—"

"You can't seem to develop a proper research project. . . ."

"I'm working—"

"You jump every time an insect flies by. . . ."

"Dr. Tannahill—"

"And you model your research on advice from people who don't even have *doctorates!*" His voice rose to an outraged crescendo.

Bingo, I thought to myself. The real reason Candi was getting chewed out.

"I mean, really, honey," Aleck's tone was amused now. Condescending. "Pepe? The man is an intellectual flea."

"I didn't—"

"Well, you did," he snapped. "And I think you'd better start revisiting your career. Clearly, you don't have what it takes to be a field scientist."

I heard a strangled sound. Then the door to Aleck's cabin smacked open and Candi came running out. I couldn't see her clearly through the plastic, but I could hear her gasping breath as she burst into tears.

I pushed past the tarp door with the thought of offering a shoulder to cry on. She'd headed in the direction of her cabin. But before I could follow her, I spied Oscar coming out of the storage shed. Glowering.

"You heard too," I said. It wasn't meant to be a question, and he didn't take it like one.

He snorted and muttered something under his breath. His disgust was plain.

"Excuse me?"

"That man is cruel," he flared. And without another word, he stalked off—aiming a murderous glare at Aleck's cabin.

"Have you guys seen Candi?" I asked Keith and Janet.

I'd found them in the cool shade of the lab. Pictures of bees buzzed back and forth across the table planks as Keith arranged them in some sort of order. Janet was keeping him company, perched on the edge of the table and swinging her legs like a child.

At my question, Keith looked up from his piles of photos. "Candi?"

"Why?" Janet stilled her legs, alerted by something in my tone. "What's wrong?"

"Ah," I threw up my arms in frustration. "She and Aleck had a big fight . . . well, he was the one doing all the shouting."

"Oh, now *there's* a surprise," Janet said sarcastically.

"Yeah, but the thing is, he pretty much told her she was washed up and he practically ordered her to leave."

Janet sucked in her breath.

I nodded. "I know. It was harsh. She went running off in tears. I've been trying to find her."

Keith was frowning, his lips thin with anger. "That prick!" he swore under his breath.

"He's not a sweetheart," I agreed.

"I knew he had a rep for this kind of shit. I just never

. . . ah, hell." He ran his fingers through his hair and blew out a heavy sigh.

"Why'd you guys pick him as your advisor, then?" I asked, seating myself on the bench beside him. I had a good view of the station's clearing through the screened window.

"No choice," Keith answered bitterly. "The other tropical guy's on sabbatical. And the woman at Harvard's fighting cancer."

"Aleck Tannahill was about the *last* person Keith would have chosen," Janet added. "The guy even took credit for a paper Keith wrote."

"You're kidding."

Keith scowled down at his bee pictures, then raised his eyes up to meet mine. "No. Janet's right. The bastard told me I'd get co-author credit. I barely made it into the acknowledgments."

I'd heard about this sort of thing before. "Couldn't you complain to your dean?" I asked.

Keith shrugged. "Not without pissing off Aleck. And by that time, I needed him for this. I had all my funding in place. I'd gotten all my permits. I figured I could put up with him for a little while longer. But now?" He paused and rubbed the back of his neck. "Now, I'm not so sure."

"You're a stronger person than me," I told him. "I already want to hurt the man."

Keith gave me a sour smile. "You wouldn't be the first."

I stared out the window, idly watching as Ramón and Juan strolled into the clearing. They were talking and gesticulating. Ramón had one of his trademark cigarettes dangling from the side of his mouth—tobacco so strong, you could use it as ratkiller. His teeth looked yellow even from this distance.

"He has a point about Candi, though," I said after a moment, "much as I hate to admit it."

Keith scrunched his brows together. "I know. She shouldn't be here. But believe it or not, she's a pretty decent botanist."

"Just not a jungle girl, eh?"

"No," Keith agreed reluctantly. "Janet and I have been hoping she'll settle down. Get used to the rainforest."

Ramón and Juan had dragged a wooden frame over to one of the freshly cleared areas. They dropped it with a muffled thump and went off again.

"It's been over a month," I pointed out.

Keith nodded. "I know. I just hate to see Aleck proved right about anything. He was against her coming here from the start, you know. Candi took it to the dean."

"Really." I was surprised she'd had the initiative.

Ramón and Juan were back in view again. They were shouting orders back and forth—each man equally loud, each equally deaf to the other's commands. Between them, they were dragging another wooden frame across the clearing, leaving deep scars in the soft, red earth. Once the frame was in place, Juan dropped his end of it and moseyed over to the first frame. He tried, failed, then tried again to raise it up. Ramón already had his frame half-standing.

"Did Aleck actually tell Candi to leave?" Janet asked.

I dragged my eyes away from the Ramón and Juan show and shook my head. "Not as such," I said.

"Well, then, hopefully—"

The rest of her words were lost in a booming crash and a spate of Spanish curses. We jumped up and dashed to the window. Both wooden frames were on the ground now, lying at an angle to each other. One of them appeared to have come apart. Ramón was berating Juan.

"What do you guys think of our construction workers?" I inquired.

Janet gave a mock shudder. "Let's just say I'm surprised Aleck moved into that cabin they built. Ours may be older and smaller—"

"Don't forget splintery," Keith reminded her.

Janet grimaced. "Yeah, and spidery too. But at least it's solid."

"Mmm," I agreed. "I'm beginning to wonder if Ramón and Juan could manage Lego."

"They give me the creeps," Janet said with a dark look. "Have you seen how they watch the women here?"

I shook my head.

"Well, it makes me wish for long overalls." Unconsciously, she folded her arms across her chest.

"I hadn't noticed."

"I spend more time around the station than you do," Janet explained. "I tell you one thing, though, they sure seem to like Candi."

Which brought me back to my first problem.

The three of us searched the station, but Candi didn't show up till dinnertime. She was uncharacteristically silent, answering Marco's questions in monosyllables and forgetting to tinkle with laughter at Pepe's anecdotes. As soon as the meal was over, she retreated to her cabin. Janet followed her out, only to return a few minutes later, answering Keith's murmured inquiry with a helpless shrug.

Candi, it appeared, did not want to talk.

Chapter 22

The scream split the night in two. I shot up out of bed. On my feet before being fully aware of consciousness.

"*What the hell?*"

Viviana and I tumbled out the door. There was a figure in the central compound. Silvered by the light. Shrieking. Leaping. Arms flailing.

Candi.

I paused to stuff my feet in boots, forgetting this once to check them for unwanted guests. Thankfully, nothing squirmed against my bare toes.

I ran towards the convulsing figure. "Candi! What's—?" I skidded to a stop, squinting intently at the ground.

The moon-bleached clearing seemed to buckle and heave. Moving. Scuttling. Pewter starlight glinting off chitinous armor. Ants.

Lots of 'em.

They were an inky river. Rippling and churning with the night's activities. Flowing with a sibilant hiss over rocks and bushes. Clambering over everything in their path. Unstoppable. I gaped for a second. Candi was right in the middle of them.

Recovering myself, I stepped up to the edge of the swarming mass and made a grab for her wildly swinging arm, intending to pull her to safety. She clouted me on the side of the head. The night exploded with stars and I fell back, clutching my cheekbone.

"Candi! Over here!" Viviana ordered. "Jump!"

Candi choked off another scream and, with a strangled gasp, she leapt over towards Viviana. Out of the river of ants.

Andres and Marco came pelting up.

"It's okay," I told them, still rubbing my face. "She's just stepped in ants."

"*¿Hormigas?*" Ernesto asked, joining us in the moonlit clearing. He was tucking his shirt into his pants.

"All this over a few *ants?*" Liz demanded from her cabin's steps. She did not sound impressed.

"More than a few," Janet snapped back.

The ants had, in fact, swarmed up Candi's legs. Scurrying and biting. Invading her clothing, her ears, her nostrils. Tangling her blond hair. Viviana and Janet were brushing them off as fast as they could. I started picking them out of her hair. I thought Liz would join us, that she'd at least want to help her cabinmate—until I heard the smack of the cabin door as she went back to bed. Obviously, the brief trip to Brazil hadn't improved her temper. What a bitch.

Fortunately, the ants wanted off Candi almost as much as she wanted rid of them. Between the three of us, we finally managed to sweep, crush, and flick them all away. By this time, Pepe, Oscar, and Keith had joined the crowd.

"There," Viviana said with a final, decisive brush. "I think they are all gone."

Candi had stopped gasping now. The only sound coming from her was the hailstone chattering of her teeth. I could see shining lines of tears coursing down her cheeks.

"I'm so sorry," she gulped. "I was going to the washroom and—" She swallowed audibly. "I'm sorry."

The men were still standing with us, watching the impressive river of ants march by, and admiring Candi's little sheer nightie when they thought nobody was looking. Pepe, especially, seemed more taken with the nightie than the ants. Marco, on the other hand, was more moved by Candi's obvious distress.

"Do not worry," he kept telling her. "It happens like this sometimes."

"I never even saw them!" she said tearfully.

"Well, of course you didn't," I interrupted her, hoping to head off the waterworks. "Not when you're half asleep."

The others were starting to break up now, heading back to their sleeping bags. Pepe and Marco lingered, each hoping for the opportunity to offer their comfort. But Viviana waved them away with a commanding flick of her fingers and they moved off reluctantly.

Before he left us, Marco reached out and touched Candi's arm. "It's okay now," he told her kindly. But she refused to meet his eyes and he turned away with a barely audible sigh.

"I'm sorry," she whispered again to the retreating shadows. A small voice in a vast wilderness. A lost, lonely sound.

"Come on," I nudged her shoulder. "We'll walk you back."

She hung her head and nodded, refusing to look at Viviana and me. The moon had bleached all color from her face, but I guessed that her cheeks were flushed with shame. Viviana put her arm around Candi and began walking back to the cabin. All her attention was focused on the miserable young woman, so I was the only one who saw Aleck Tannahill.

He was standing in the doorway of his cabin, backlit by a kerosene lamp. His arms were folded across his chest, and he slouched against the door frame. He hadn't come out to help. Hadn't even stepped off his porch. He watched us silently, offering no words of comfort, no gestures of encouragement. As he turned his head to track our progress across the clearing, the orange glow from the lamp lit his features. His mouth was twisted in a scornful smile.

The smirk infuriated me. So Aleck found this amusing, did he? I drew in a breath to reply, to say something to wipe that smug grin off his face, but before I could get a word out, he stepped back into his cabin and let the door swing shut.

Chapter 23

"Robyn! Viviana! Are you guys up?"

Viviana stirred and groaned. Or maybe that was me.

"Robyn! Hey, you guys!"

There was a noise too. A sharp, repetitive sound. Knocking.

"Wake up in there."

I dragged myself into consciousness. "Wha—?" I called out groggily.

"It's Janet. Can I come in?"

I made a noise, which Janet must have taken as a yes. By the time I cracked one eye open, she was standing in front of me, holding something. My nose identified it and forced my body to sit up. Coffee. I pried my other eye open.

"Wha's the matter?" I mumbled.

Viviana was still buried under her sleeping bag.

Janet passed me the coffee, steadying my hand under the mug. "I need your help. Candi's decided to leave."

I grunted and took a big gulp of the steaming beverage. Blearily, my brain tried to make sense of Janet's words. "Because of the ants?" I asked finally.

Janet sat down on the edge of my cot. "In part," she told me. "But mostly because of Aleck."

"That guy is an ass—" Viviana's muffled voice emerged from under her covers.

"—hole. Yes, I know," Janet said. She moved a second mug closer to Viviana. "Here, I brought you a coffee too."

A tousled head poked up out of the sleeping bag like a gopher. Her nose twitched at the rich aroma.

I was starting to wake up now. "What do you want us to do about it?" I asked Janet. "It's probably for the best. She really shouldn't be here. You said so yourself."

"That was Keith," Janet shot back. She paused and pulled on her bottom lip. "Look, I know she's a bit of a pain, but I just can't stand to see Aleck win this one. Maybe if he'd been a little more supportive, she wouldn't be having so many problems."

I grunted, unconvinced.

"Come on, Robyn. Don't let Aleck get away with this."

I yawned and scrubbed at my face. Considering her request. I glanced over at Viviana. She was nodding slightly.

"What the hell time is it, anyway?" I asked.

Janet's expression took on a guilty cast. "Um . . . early."

"I'd sort of figured that out for myself," I grumped. "With the dark sky and all." I yawned again, cracking my jaw in the process. "Is it today or tomorrow?"

Janet heard the capitulation in my voice. "It's tomorrow," she said, bouncing up from my bed, all smiles now. Way too perky for this hour of the morning—whatever the hour was. "Thanks, guys. Candi's just outside with Keith."

I grimaced at Viviana and tucked my sleeping bag around my legs. "Well, bring them in, then," I told Janet.

Our tiny cabin quickly took on the air of a council of war; the soft glow of the kerosene lamp illuminating the pre-dawn darkness, the cups of half-drunk coffee littering the small table, the haggard, sleep-deprived appearance of all present. Even Candi looked exhausted.

It had been coming on for some time now, but I was still surprised to find I felt genuinely sorry for our perfume bunny. She was pale, even in the warm glow of the lamp, and her face appeared to be completely devoid of makeup, which was a first. There was something else different about her this morning, but my sleep-fuddled brain couldn't pinpoint it.

"I don't see that I really have much choice," she was saying. "Obviously, I'm not cut out to be a field scientist." Her tone was one of bitter disillusion.

With a start, I realized what was different. Candi had dropped the little-girl voice.

"That's not true," Keith was shaking his head.

"Why would you think that?" I asked her. Curious.

Candi looked at me with red-rimmed eyes. "Because Aleck says my methodology sucks. Because my project isn't well thought out. Because—"

"Why?" I interrupted.

She blinked. "Why what?"

"Let's forget about Aleck for a second here. I heard some of the stuff he was saying to you yesterday."

Candi hung her head, ashamed.

"The only real criticism that didn't seem to involve his own ego was your sampling method. So what's the problem? Why *aren't* you sampling everything? Or at least doing proper random sampling? It's pretty basic stuff."

Candi nodded without lifting her head up.

"So what's the problem, then?" I asked again. Gently this time.

She was quiet for a long moment. "I'm afraid," she said, her voice so low I had to strain to hear it.

Afraid?

She raised her head and looked at me, her eyes bright with unshed tears. "I'm afraid to go into the clearings," she admitted. "Not here around Danta. The little ones, the ones in the forest. I'm afraid of getting shot, but mostly I'm afraid of snakes. I'm afraid of scorpions and centipedes and Aleck keeps telling me I have to sample all those spots that Dan said would have snakes and Pepe had an idea so I wouldn't have to but Aleck just—" She choked off a sob. Her hands were tight fists in her lap.

"Candi," Viviana began, her smoky voice low with sympathy. "It's okay to be afraid."

"Of course it is," I said. "Are you kidding? I almost crapped myself when I stepped on that fer-de-lance."

Viviana nodded. "Yes, and once when I put on my boot without checking, there was a big centipede in it."

Candi shuddered.

"And I think we were all a little afraid of getting shot after finding that guy's body," I said. "I know *I* kept looking over my shoulder every few minutes."

Candi shivered again.

Viviana patted her arm. "Candi, sometimes field biology is really about testing yourself. And testing is all about learning your limits. That's all. So you are not easy in the rainforest." Viviana shrugged. "It's no big deal. You tested yourself and found your limit. I am sure you are comfortable in North American forests."

"Oh yes!" Candi looked up. "I never felt like this back home."

"So don't be ashamed. You are not running away."

"And it doesn't mean that you're not cut out to be a field scientist," I chimed in.

"Don't let Aleck do that to you," Keith urged. "Listen

to these guys. You're a good botanist. You'll be a good field scientist in the States."

Candi stared at him, wanting to believe it. Her hands plucked at her shirt sleeve.

I took another sip of coffee and grimaced. It was stone cold. I set it aside and tapped Candi's hand to get her attention. "You know, I once read about a guy who climbed Everest," I said. "He went through all the months of training and acclimatizing and all the other stuff they have to go through. But when he finally made the big push to the summit, he stopped sixty yards from the top."

"He stopped?"

I nodded. "Yeah. He realized that he had enough energy to summit, but not enough to get back down. So he turned around—*sixty yards* from the summit—and walked back down. And nobody thought he was a coward or a quitter. On the contrary, he got a lot of respect for knowing his own limits."

It gave her something to think about.

By the time the sun began sparkling on the morning dew, everybody was up and preparing for the day and Candi had packed her gear. We hadn't convinced her to stay, but I think we managed to make her feel good about her decision to leave. And that was more important. Maybe she wouldn't give up the idea of working as a field scientist.

"You can have Scott Gray's old field notes, if you want," she said, pulling Janet aside and offering her a packet of papers. "I'm not going to need them now, and maybe you can use them for your article."

"Thanks, Candi," Janet smiled her appreciation. "I'm sure they'll come in handy."

"How are you getting back?" Andres asked, having

missed the details of her preparations. "Did you radio the ranger station?"

"The radio's still out. I called them on the satellite phone. One of the rangers is going to meet me with the boat. Marco said he'd walk with me to the mooring."

Pepe shot Marco an envious look.

"You sure you can make it?" I asked Marco with a significant glance at his right knee.

"I am good," he assured me.

I shrugged inwardly and decided not to mention the fact that he was still limping. Who was I to get in the way of love? Robyn Devara. Cupid, second class.

Candi hugged us all (a little tearfully) and thanked us (profusely) and promised to so keep in touch. And she managed to do it without a single giggle. The irritating little-girl voice didn't come back, either. There may be hope for her yet, I thought as she and Marco disappeared down the path.

Liz wasn't feeling well that morning, but she peered out her window to wave them off. Aleck did not even come out to say good-bye.

The rest of the day was colored by Candi's abrupt departure. The early morning sun had given way to gunmetal clouds, which hung ominously low, brushing the canopy with the promise of rain. The humidity was close to one hundred percent.

With Marco gone to the mooring, I decided to tag along with Viviana and Ernesto. They were going to the clay lick with Janet, in the hopes of photographing macaws. We had quite a collection of pictures tacked up in the dining hall now—though Janet had had to play around with different lenses to get the clear close-ups we needed.

But the ill omens of the morning dogged our working footsteps. Viviana dropped her binoculars, smashing one of the lenses. Ernesto discovered he'd forgotten the data sheets and his insect repellent. And Janet had trouble with her camera equipment because of the high humidity—which, as it turned out, didn't really matter because not a single amethyst macaw showed up for the photo op.

We were a tired, grumpy bunch when we arrived back at the station. We hit the dining hall hoping to find a spot of cheer, a reprieve from the general lousiness of the day. Instead we found Andres, Liz, and Marco, each silent and solemn, each seated just a little too far from the others. A psychic as well as physical distance.

"What's with you?" Janet asked Andres, who was nursing a beer. His expression was especially glum.

"I scratched my hand on a thorn," he said in disgust. "A monkey's comb tree. I was out by myself and I did not see it until it was too late."

"Oh."

"Is the beer helping?" This from me.

He shrugged and we waited for an answer. Nothing.

Okay, then. "Where's everybody else?" I asked instead.

His frown deepened. "Pepe burned dinner and Oscar has kicked him from the kitchen. Keith is in a bad mood about his bees. I think he's in his cabin. And Aleck," his mouth twisted in disgust, "he is—"

"Hey, Janet, give me five!" Aleck smarmed, stepping into the dining hall and holding his hand up high. Pepe and Keith trailed behind him.

Janet's expression could have sent several lifeforms the way of the dodo, but a quick glance at Keith and she held up her hand reluctantly. Aleck did the high five thing.

"So how was the day at the lick? Get a lot of photographs?"

"Not one," she replied coldly.

Aleck raised his eyebrows in surprise. "You're not working hard enough, then. You've got to get out there every day. Stay out till you've done a decent day's work. It's the only way you'll make *any* kind of progress."

"Our progress is just fine," I said, enunciating each word with icy clarity.

He turned to me and pretended to ward off my glare.

"What's the matter? You can't take a joke?" he blustered.

My nostrils flared at his proximity. His breath reeked of alcohol again.

"You've got to get a move on if you're going to start attracting those tourist *colones*."

"*What?*" Liz blazed. Her eyes flashed like a glint of sunlight on something very sharp.

Aleck didn't notice. "It's a natural," he said, warming up to his lecture. "Think about it. What do most tourists want to see in the rainforest?"

I drew in a breath to answer, but he didn't wait for one.

"Animals!" he exclaimed with a clap. "Birds, mammals, turtles, whatever. And what do they end up seeing? Plants!" He opened his arms wide to emphasize his point. "Lots and lots of plants."

I could see where he was going with this.

"Now, plants are all very well and good if that's your thing. But, let's face it, most people'd prefer animals. With this clay lick, you have the perfect tourist attraction right under your freckled little noses. Think of it—

guaranteed sightings! How many places can offer that? You could make a *fortune*. Build a hotel, improve the paths. You could even arrange to 'encounter' the odd dangerous creature. A snake or something. Attract the thrill-seekers—"

"And what about our project?" Viviana inquired.

Aleck shrugged. "Oh, you can keep on studying the birds," he said airily. "Maybe you could even use the tourist income to fund the station. Rename it Parrot Park. You know, make the wildlife pay for itself."

Individual protests were drowned out in the general uproar.

"What do you mean, 'pay for itself'?"

"That's the *stupidest* idea I've ever heard."

"*Parrot Park?*"

Oddly enough, it was Pepe's soft voice that made itself heard above the rest of us. "Wildlife should *not* be required to pay for itself," he stated firmly.

Fine sentiment for someone who'd tallied up the value of the macaws as soon as he'd seen them.

Aleck just sneered at him. "Hel-lo! This is the twenty-first century. Get with the program, Pepe. Like it or not, ecotourism is where it's at."

Which brought on another uproar.

I kept silent this time. Ecotourism might be where it's at, but it wasn't exactly a problem-free concept. For one thing, nobody had quite figured out how to bring tourists into fragile areas without degrading the very places they wanted to see. Aleck was an ecologist. He knew this. Which meant he was *trying* to be a shit disturber.

Andres shook his head as if puzzled by Aleck's suggestion. "It is a bad idea," he said finally. "How can we think about having tourists at this point in our work? We do not know how many amethyst macaws live here. We do not know how they will respond to human activities. We do not know their range, or which habitats they like best. Besides, Corcovado is more like a nature reserve than a national park. We're fixing up Danta for science, not tourists."

I waited for Liz to say something, but, although her eyes flicked from one speaker to the next, she remained quiet. Listening. Evaluating. An indecipherable expression on her face.

"Dinner is ready," Oscar announced into the charged silence that followed Andres' words.

I started at the sound of his voice. He hadn't said a word all through the argument, either. Probably too busy salvaging dinner.

It wasn't much of a save. Canned tuna and rice and a roomful of bad vibes. I wasn't on cleanup duty that night, so I bolted my food and left.

I felt better once I'd quit the poisonous atmosphere, but I wasn't thrilled about shutting myself up in the cabin for the evening. I considered a nighttime stroll in the jungle, but I didn't want to go alone and I figured if anyone else came along, we'd only bitch about Aleck. The man had ruined enough of my day without that.

In the end, I settled on assembling our gear for the following day. Marco and I were going to try climbing again and, after his little tumble, I wanted to check over our ropes myself. I snagged a kerosene lamp from the lab and headed over to the storage shed.

Several matches later, I gave up on the lamp and backtracked for a new one. The kerosene lamps never looked like anything was wrong with them, but they seemed to crap out at the least little bump. I left the first lamp in a growing pile of broken equipment.

The third lantern lit without a hiccup, its orange flame settling down into a steady glow. I lifted it into the darkness of the shed and realized that, in one area at least, Oscar had been falling down on the job. The shed was a disaster.

Climbing gear had been piled haphazardly on wooden crates. Blank data sheets, wrinkled with damp, had blown off the shelf and across the dirt floor. The three-inch nails that Ramón and Juan had used to build the cabins were scattered among them. The nails glinted orangely at me in the light of the lamp. I stared at the mess in dismay.

Each morning before anyone else was up, Oscar laid out our gear on the raised planks in front of the shed. I was never really clear on why he did this. I just assumed he had his own system for organizing the shed and didn't want us to screw around with it. But if there was a system here, I sure couldn't see it.

I hooked the lantern on a long nail and set about tidying the shed. I scooped up the spilled nails, re-stacked the data sheets, and hung the ropes and harnesses on various hooks. Then I collected the Jumars and descenders in an old coffee can. These really shouldn't have been left lying around. There was no way to tell if they'd been dropped or stepped on or simply placed on the ground. When you're climbing trees that are a hundred and thirty feet high, you don't want to be wondering if your ascenders have hairline fractures. Or if your ropes are starting to rot or fray because they've been stored improperly. I pursed my lips and made a mental note to have a long talk with Oscar about equipment safety.

I was still thinking about ropes when I spotted the yellow coils of a climbing rope beside one of the wooden crates. I'd tossed the rope into the shed the day Marco had fallen, assuming in the excitement that Oscar would deal with it. It didn't look as though anybody had touched it. I remembered my thought of using it as a clothesline.

I pulled it out, shook off a couple of cockroaches, and held it up to the lamp. It looked diseased, splotched all over with black mold. I wrinkled my nose at the musty smell. No wonder the thing had given out. I ran the length of it through my fingers. Might be long enough for a clothesline.

As my fingers met the end of the rope, I felt something odd. The rope slithered out of my hand and fell to the floor. I picked up the end of it again and held it close to the lamp. I was right. There was something funny here.

I bent down and fingered the other end. It seemed normal enough. I lifted the first end up to the light again, examining it closely. Yes. The fibers were stretched and broken unevenly on one side, but on the other, they were all exactly the same length.

This rope had been cut. Not all the way through. And not so you would notice, unless you were looking for it. Just a little bit on one side.

Just enough to weaken it.

Chapter 24

When the screaming started that night, I sprang out of my sleeping bag, half-expecting to rescue Candi again. Then I remembered. Candi had left.

And this time, the cries were deeper. Harsher. Desperate.

"*What?*" Viviana gasped awake in the darkness.

"I don't know," I said, already up and pulling on some clothes.

I could hear muffled thumps now, mixed in with the hoarse cries.

I snatched up my flashlight and yanked open the door, listening for an instant to pinpoint the source. Over to the right. Past Keith and Janet's cabin.

Andres burst out of his cabin. "What's going on?" he demanded.

I was already sprinting across the clearing. "It's Aleck!" I shouted back.

Viviana and Andres were behind me, Keith, Marco, and Oscar close on their heels. I hit Aleck's door running and burst in. The sour stench of alcohol and vomit smacked me full in the face, choking off my breath. But it was the sight of the room that stopped me dead. Somebody bumped into me, started to protest, and fell silent. The harsh, white beams of our flashlights illuminated the nightmare inside.

The desk and chair had been overturned, books and papers spilling across the floor, wet and glistening with blood and vomit. Shards of broken glass glinted in the light. And in the middle of this was Aleck.

He must have flung himself across the cabin in an attempt to reach the door. His limbs were tangled in twisted bedding. He was convulsing. Teeth clenched. Foaming bloody froth at the mouth.

"*Holy shit!*" Keith swore.

It broke our shocked stasis.

"Grab his hands!" Viviana took charge, snapping orders at the rest of us. "Get this desk out of the way. Watch out for that glass. Keep him still! Andres, take his arm—ouch! Hurry!"

"*Shit!* Okay, I've got him."

"Help—"

"I've got his legs!"

"*Son of a bitch!*" This from me. I'd tried to pin down Aleck's left leg. It was slippery with blood. Had he cut himself on the glass?

"He's been bitten!" I cried. "Look!" I pointed to the bloody leg where the two telltale puncture wounds were leaking blood and fluid. The bite wound was already badly swollen—angry red deepening to ominous purple.

"Okay, keep him down," Viviana said calmly. "Take off his sock and don't lift the leg above the heart. Somebody get some extractors."

Andres was back with them in seconds.

Viviana was sprawled across Aleck's heaving chest, fighting to keep him still. He was delirious with pain.

"*It burns!*" He shrieked over and over again.

"Don't just stand there," Viviana rapped out to Andres through clenched teeth. "Use them!"

"No!" Oscar shouted as Andres crouched down. "You have a cut. *Es fatal.* It's too dangerous." He snatched the extractors out of Andres' hand. "I will do it. Hold him still!"

Marco had clamped down hard on Aleck's injured leg. Keith was holding the other one. Oscar positioned a yellow extractor over one of the bite wounds and sunk the plunger down. Blood spurted up into the tube, tinged amber with venom. Another extractor over the other puncture. More blood and venom.

"Oh my god!" Janet hissed. "*Look at his eyes!*"

I raised my flashlight to his face. Aleck's jaw was rigid, his features twisted in agony. His eyeballs bulged out like glass marbles, stained red with broken blood vessels. Trickles of watery blood ran down the creases in his face.

I swore again.

"*Oh god! I can't see. Why can't I see?*" he sobbed, flinging his head from side to side. "*Help me!*"

"It must have been a fer-de-lance," Viviana gasped as Aleck spasmed again. "His blood vessels are collapsing."

"Can we give him antivenin?"

"No!" Liz barked from the doorway. "Not unless you know for sure what bit him. The antivenin will kill him if it's the wrong kind."

Aleck cried out again. A strangled, tormented sound.

"He's dying now, in case you hadn't noticed," Keith snapped.

"Search the room!" Viviana ordered. "Maybe the snake is still here. Robyn, call Sirena. We're going to have to get him out of here."

"Right." I spun around and was out the door before Aleck could cry out again.

I ran to the dining hall, my flashlight beam jumping in front of me. The satellite phone was on the shelf opposite the kitchen. I snatched it up and hit the power button. Nothing. Again. Still nothing. Swearing under my breath, I flung it back on the shelf and turned to the radio. I swept the stack of papers off it and flicked the switch. Not even a hum. *God damn it!* I smacked the box. Did nothing work properly at this station?

I jogged back to the cabin. Someone had lit a couple of kerosene lamps. Aleck was still squirming, his breath wheezing in and out of his body now like a bellows. He was whimpering in pain.

"The phone's dead," I said quietly.

Viviana looked up at me in disbelief.

"I tried the radio too. There's nothing."

"We must use the antivenin," Oscar said to Viviana. "He is dying. And all this bleeding? *Terciopelo.*" There was no doubt in his tone.

She stared at him, and for a moment all movement in the cabin ceased. Then Aleck cried out again.

"His heart is not beating evenly," Andres said, his hand on the man's chest, his voice straining with the effort of staying calm. "He is not going to make it."

Viviana bit her lip. "All right," she capitulated. "But we must check him for allergies first. Mix up the antivenin and put a drop in his eye. If everything is okay after fifteen minutes, we can—"

"*Fifteen minutes?*" Keith exploded. "Are you insane? We can't wait that long!"

"We have to!" She cut him off. "It's made with blood serum from horses. If he is allergic to it, he'll go into anaphylactic shock and—"

Aleck choked and convulsed again, his eyes almost

starting from his head. He tried to scream, but blood burbled out of his mouth, drowning the cry in a gush of bubbling crimson. A massive shudder rippled through his body and then, as we watched in helpless horror, he went suddenly, utterly still.

Chapter 25

Janet was crying quietly in the corner of the dining hall. From the look of her, Viviana was wishing she could do the same. Hell, if it came down to that, I might even join in.

Aleck Tannahill was dead.

He'd died right there in front of my eyes. Convulsing. Pleading for mercy. Crying tears of blood. It was the most horrifying thing I'd ever seen.

Viviana had tried to revive him, but I think we all knew it was hopeless. He'd started bleeding from his pores. His leg had turned blackish-purple and the tissue around the bite wound had begun to dissolve. Only a fer-de-lance could inflict such damage in so short a period of time. But even so. . . .

"Why did he die so fast?" I asked Viviana as the thought occurred to me.

Her eyes were pools of anguish in a pale face. She shook her head slowly. "I . . . I'm not certain," she said. "I think he was drinking before he was attacked."

"I think he was drinking pretty much all the time," I said.

"Yes, you are right," she agreed wearily.

Keith was sitting with his arm around Janet. "The alcohol made the venom act faster?"

Viviana nodded. "You should never consume alcohol if you have been bitten."

"Then Aleck's drinking problem. . . ."

"Perhaps killed him faster."

Keith sat with that for a moment. "Maybe that's a blessing."

Viviana nodded again and we fell silent.

After a while Janet lifted her head. "Did they find the snake yet?" she asked.

I straightened up to peer out the window at the bobbing flashlight beams around Aleck's cabin. "I don't think so. They're still searching."

"It's probably long gone," Liz said quietly. Her tone lacked its usual sarcastic edge.

"What are we going to do about—" Janet swallowed. An audible gulp. "About—"

"The body?" Liz suggested.

Janet nodded, huddling deeper under Keith's comforting arm.

"He must go to Sirena," Viviana answered, her voice sounding huskier than usual. "The phone is not working and neither is the radio. We have no way to call the ranger station to tell them to come. We'll have to take him ourselves." She looked at me. "What time is it?"

I glanced down at my watch. "Almost four-thirty."

She nodded once. "Soon it will be light enough to travel. I think—"

"*Terciopelo!*" The cry rang out across the compound.

Janet started visibly and we all looked up, peering through the window into the night.

"Be careful, Pepe!"

"It's a big one."

"Oscar, look out!"

"*Get it!*"

Liz jumped to her feet.

"Okay!" It was Marco's voice. "It is okay, I got her. *Está muerta*. She's dead. Ah, look, she's very big."

Liz sank back down on the bench and covered her face with trembling hands.

Ever since Marco had killed that other fer-de-lance, I'd wondered if its mate was still around. It appeared my question had been answered. I stood up, needing to do something. "I'll get some coffee on," I announced.

"Good idea," Viviana agreed, rising from the bench. "I think we'll feel better with something warm to drink. Let me give you a hand."

By the time the stove-top percolator began bubbling, the rosy blush of dawn was lightening the sky. A hush had fallen over the station. Even the early morning birdsong seemed muted. We were clustered in the dining hall, faces pale, nerves still raw from the night's events, reluctant to return to the isolation of our cabins.

Andres was seated beside me, waiting for Oscar to reappear. They'd be taking Aleck's body to Sirena, carrying their grim load on a stretcher that Oscar had rigged up. Keith and Ernesto were going to help them as far as the mooring.

"How did it get inside the cabin?" I finally asked. "I thought they'd all been snake-proofed."

Andres raised his head and regarded me with smudge-shadowed eyes. There was an oddly awkward silence.

I held his eyes, waiting, refusing to be put off.

After a heartbeat, he cleared his throat. "You cannot really snake-proof a cabin," he started out. "Not completely. But in Aleck's cabin there was a hole in the floor, I think."

"A hole."

"Pepe found a floorboard. It did not go all the way to the wall."

"I see."

"Oscar is asking Ramón and Juan to check all the others today," he said quickly, reading my mind. "But I think Aleck's cabin was the only one with this problem."

"Okay."

"It was only an accident," Andres said.

"An *accident?*" Viviana's low voice rose in anger.

Andres blinked at her in surprise. "Of course. What else?"

"How about incompetence?"

Andres scowled at her. "What are you talking about?" he demanded.

Viviana's eyes flashed right back at him. "I'm talking about the fact that Ramón and Juan built that cabin. I'm talking about Aleck's drinking problem."

"I did not know a *terciopelo* would go into his cabin," he protested.

"No, but you knew Oscar's cousins could not build an outhouse."

"Viviana." He tried to interrupt her with a weak smile. "They are not *that* bad."

Viviana wasn't having any of it. "Don't be so blind," she retorted angrily. "They are terrible! Just look at those new cabins they are building. You should know, you are living in one of them. *Muchas gracias,* but Robyn and I will check our own cabin. I do not trust those two."

"Have it your way," Andres answered quietly, still trying to keep it polite. Not understanding it was a lost cause. Viviana's frustration had been building for a long time.

"And what about Aleck?" she demanded.

"What? He is dead. What do you want me to—"

"You knew about his drinking," she accused. "You knew he drank too much and you didn't say anything about it."

"What did you want me to say, Viviana?" Andres finally snapped. "'Oh, Aleck, please do not be drinking your alcohol at Danta?'"

Viviana threw up her hands in disgust. "I don't know what you should have said. *You* are the station director! But it was dangerous to leave it, Andres. Perhaps if you had said something to him, he would not have been drinking quite so much. Yes, the snake bite was an accident, but it was one that maybe did not have to happen."

Andres' scowl deepened and his cheeks flushed red. In anger, I thought at first. Then I realized he was embarrassed.

"Andres! Keith! Are you ready?" Oscar's shout broke the uncomfortable tableau.

"We're coming," Andres called back, his eyes still locked with Viviana's. "We will talk more about this when I get back," he told her.

But by the time they got back from Sirena, there were other things to discuss.

Chapter 26

"Candi did not meet the ranger boat."

"*What?*" I dropped the squash I was cutting up for dinner and stared at Andres, waiting for his words to make sense.

"She was not there when Ricardo arrived. He thought he had mixed up the day, so he went back to Sirena."

"But . . . well . . . where is she?"

Lines of worry slashed his forehead. "I do not know," he told me. "Nobody knows."

"Nobody knows?" I echoed. "Has anyone looked for her?"

"Yes." Andres rubbed his eyes. They were puffy and rimmed with red, evidence of the sleepless night. "Yes, Oscar and I searched the riverbank. We found nothing."

"Nothing."

Andres shook his head slowly. "Not even a water bottle. I was hoping she came back here."

I didn't need to tell him she hadn't.

"Dan has given us a radio that works. We will organize searching teams." His expression told me he didn't have much hope of them finding anything—or, at least, anything alive. "At least those poachers seem to be gone." Andres' mouth twisted to one side. "But there are many other dangers besides poachers with guns. I do not have a good feeling about this, Robyn."

Just then, Pepe stepped up into the kitchen, ready to help with dinner. He froze when he saw our faces. "What has happened?" he demanded.

"Candi's missing," I told him. "She didn't meet the boat."

Pepe mouthed the words silently. Disbelief etched on his face. "Candi? But . . . where was Marco? Didn't he stay with her until the boat arrived?"

"I don't know," Andres said, "but I'm going right now to find him and ask." The chill of glaciers was in his voice.

"I swear to you I left her at the mooring!"

"Why didn't you wait with her?"

"You knew how much the jungle scared her."

"You knew that guy got shot a month ago. How could you just leave her?"

Marco's dark eyes were bewildered as he looked from one face to another. "I . . . she . . . she did not want me to stay."

"She wanted to be alone?" Pepe's disbelief was patent. "She hated the rainforest. Why would she want to be alone?"

Marco flushed. "I do not know."

"Marco," I broke in, trying to speak calmly. There were too many emotions flying around as it was. "Did you take her all the way to the mooring?"

Marco turned to me, his face reflecting his gratitude. "Yes, of course."

"So what happened after that?"

He took a deep breath. "She wanted to sit on that big rock by the boat."

I nodded, knowing the one he meant.

"I was going to stay with her, I had brought some empanadas because," he took another breath, "because she did not eat breakfast. But she said she was not hungry. And that she would be okay by herself. She was happy to be going home."

"It never occurred to you the boat might be delayed, or not show up at all?" Keith demanded, struggling to keep his tone even.

Marco shook his head. "I never thought about it."

"And clearly, neither did Candi," I added, coming to Marco's defense. "Or she wouldn't have sent him off."

Andres held up his hands. "We are not accomplishing anything with this."

Someone snorted.

"Candi had a daypack and a large red backpack," Andres said. "Did anyone see a sign of these yesterday? What about today? Keith, Ernesto, did you see anything on your way back from the mooring? Any clothes or equipment? No? Was anyone else out there?"

"Viviana, myself, and Liz," I said.

Andres turned to me in surprise. "You went to the clay lick?"

"Viviana and I did. We . . . needed the distraction. But we didn't see anything—nothing of Candi's, that is."

He frowned. "Where did Liz go?"

I shrugged.

"She went by herself?" He was not pleased.

I nodded again. "You and Ernesto were gone and Marco's knee was bothering him."

Viviana put her hands on her hips. "I told her to come with us. I said she should not go alone in the jungle. She told me I wasn't the project leader and that she would do what she wanted."

Andres' frown deepened.

"I think she just needed to be alone," I offered in Liz's defense, though I wasn't sure why I was making excuses for her. "You know, after last night."

"After last night, she should not have gone in the jungle by herself," he flared.

I closed my mouth.

Andres took a deep breath and let it out noisily. "I am sorry, Robyn," he apologized. "I am just very worried. Now we have had two accidents in two days . . . and before this we had Guillermo getting shot. What is going on here?"

I didn't know what to say to him.

Pepe was still glaring daggers at Marco. "You should have stayed with her," he muttered bitterly.

But Marco didn't need any help feeling guilty. His distress showed in the line of his shoulders, in the haunted look in his eyes.

Andres straightened up and rubbed the back of his neck. "I have already radioed Dan," he said with a heavy sigh. "We will start searching tomorrow morning, but"—his outflung arm took in the hundreds of miles of dense jungle around us—"I am not holding my breath."

Neither was I.

That night, despite our freshly snake-proofed cabin, I found myself eyeing the smallest shadows with suspicion. Even my time-sharing cockroach friend got shaken out of my sleeping bag with more force than usual. So when Keith came tapping at our door, it wasn't surprising that I nearly jumped out of my pajamas at the sound.

"What's wrong?" I demanded.

He hesitated in the doorway. "Someone's been going through Aleck's stuff."

"Um . . . what stuff?"

"His papers and notes."

"How can you tell?" I asked, remembering my last sight of Aleck's cabin. The crumpled papers strewn across the floor. The blood-soaked books. . . .

"I know." Keith read my expression. "I'm not talking about the stuff on the floor—or, at least, it wasn't on the floor last night."

"Perhaps you should come in and sit down," Viviana suggested.

Keith stepped into the cabin but instead of sitting down, he began pacing. "Last night," he said, "when we burst into Aleck's cabin, there were a lot of papers and stuff on the floor."

We nodded.

"But there's a shelf on the far wall of that cabin, the one opposite the door. And last night, all the books and papers that were on that shelf were still there. I saw them." He squeezed his eyes shut and rubbed them wearily. "I don't know why I noticed it. I guess the whole scene just imprinted on my brain. But I saw a bunch of Aleck's stuff still neatly piled on the shelf. The guy was totally AR. He was always fussing with papers on his desk."

"And now they're not neatly piled anymore?" I guessed.

Keith shook his head. "They're not even on the shelf anymore. They're all over the floor. Everything is on the floor."

"You went in the cabin?" Viviana asked, a grimace of distaste crossing her face.

Keith's expression mirrored hers and I saw his jaw twitch as he clamped his teeth together. Remembering the sight. "I was looking for emergency numbers," he explained after a brief pause. "I need to contact the university. I don't know if I should be staying or going or what." He laughed once. A bitter sound. "I mean, what are you supposed to do when your advisor is killed by a fer-de-lance and you're in the middle of goddamn nowhere?"

"But your funding. What will happen to it if you leave?"

Keith shook his head. "I have no idea. This isn't exactly covered in the grad seminars. That's why I was in Aleck's cabin tonight."

"Which brings us back to your original problem," I said. "Who went through Aleck's stuff, and why?"

Keith nodded, his eyes shadowed by more than the inadequate lighting. "This is giving me the creeps," he admitted. "Aleck dying like that, Candi missing, and now somebody going through Aleck's stuff. And what about that guy who died? You know, I was willing to go along with Andres about Aleck's death being an accident, but now I'm not so sure. It's one thing for me to be here, but I brought Janet too. If anything happened to her. . . ."

"Come on, Keith, listen to yourself." I tried to bolster him up. "Do you really think somebody put a snake—a fer-de-lance, no less!—in Aleck's room? Who would do that? Ye gods, you'd have to *pick up* the fer-de-lance to start with. Who would be stupid enough to handle a snake like that?"

"Robyn is correct," Viviana was nodding at my words. "And Candi's disappearance is . . . well, you know what she was like in the jungle." Her smoky voice grew strained. "I don't like to think about her out there, but if she was unwise enough to wander away, she easily could have been killed or injured. There are many dangers and Candi was—is—not good at avoiding them."

"And the papers?" Keith challenged.

"There could be many explanations for that," Viviana insisted.

But I couldn't think of one and, when pressed, neither could Viviana.

As I burrowed in my sleeping bag that night, I felt the first shiver of real uneasiness. Keith had had a point. Why would a fer-de-lance crawl into a cabin? They liked to hang around human habitation, but not usually *in* human habitations. And our cabins were built a couple of feet off the ground. A snake would have to try pretty hard to get in. Did someone put the snake in Aleck's cabin? A ludicrous thought. Or was it? Why had his cabin been searched?

And what had happened to Candi? The thought of her lost or hurt in the jungle was truly upsetting. But why would she have wandered away from the mooring? Over the past few weeks, she'd learned her limits and they didn't involve traipsing around deep jungle by her lonesome. It just didn't make sense.

These weren't the only mysteries, I realized, as my brain nudged another thought that had been lurking in the background. There was also the matter of the cut rope. I opened my eyes in the darkness. With the horrible manner of Aleck's death, I'd forgotten all about the climbing rope. Marco had been hurt because of it. If he'd been higher up, he could have been killed. Had the rope been damaged by a thorn or a sharp snag? Or had it been cut on purpose?

I found myself wishing I could talk to Kelt. He'd

always been a good sounding board. But with the satellite phone not working, I couldn't even e-mail him. When I finally drifted off to sleep, my last conscious thought was the hope that Candi would show up tomorrow at the station. I could almost picture it. Her Barbie doll smile, her hot pink fingernails, and that little-girl voice telling us there'd been so no need to worry about her.

Chapter 27

But it didn't happen. A day went by. Then another. And pretty soon it had been over a week since Aleck's death. There was no sign of Candi. Not even a daypack. I still couldn't get my mind around it. Every time I went out with the search teams, I expected to see her. And each time I came stumbling back to the station muddy, weary, and dejected.

After nine days, the search was scaled back. Andres spent a lot of time at Sirena, trying to explain to Candi's relatives what everybody suspected had happened. Her parents were devastated, and Andres' expression was more drawn every time he returned to the field station.

Slowly, painfully, the daily routines of living and working at Danta resumed. Keith and Janet were staying—at least for a while. Keith managed to contact his dean, who urged him to stay and finish his own research. Liz recovered her spirits enough to renew her antagonism towards Ernesto. Ramón and Juan moved on to other things, leaving behind an unfinished lab and two more rickety cabins, which nobody wanted to move into. Pepe was now helping Oscar finish the lab. He appeared to have abandoned his own research studies altogether. And as for Marco . . . I was worried about him.

A few days after Candi disappeared, he confided the real reason why he'd left her at the mooring.

"I thought I would never see her again," he told me quietly. "I didn't want her to go. I said I loved her."

I tightened my lips in sympathy. "But she didn't feel the same," I guessed.

He blinked a few times and shook his head. "No." A simple word. A wealth of emotion.

It took a while for the whole story to come out, but it boiled down to one simple sentence. Candi had firmly (and rather harshly) given Marco the heave-ho. I tried to reassure him. To tell him that she'd probably been confused and distracted by other events, unable to cope with any more emotional scenes. But Marco was tormented by the fact that, against his better judgment, he'd left her alone. And that she had now disappeared so completely.

"I am afraid we will find her like we found Guillermo," he said miserably.

"Guillermo was shot," I said. "He had a falling out with some of his buddies and he was shot. That's not going to happen to Candi."

"Guillermo was *not* a poacher," Marco flared. "And if someone could shoot him, then they could shoot Candi also. Why didn't I see this? Why did I leave her!"

I didn't know what else to say. As the days passed, the mischievous spark went out of my field partner. And though he continued to do his job competently, all too often our workdays felt like a slog.

We'd resumed our study, but the atmosphere at Danta remained heavy, lacking the light bantering of earlier times. Perhaps it was this that gave Andres the idea of bringing more people in.

"Tourists?" Liz was incredulous. "I thought we'd hashed that out with Aleck."

"Not just tourists," Andres explained. "Workers. Volunteers to help with the study. I've been thinking we could hang posters at the *pensiones* to advertise for volunteer researchers."

"Sort of like Earthwatch," I suggested.

Andres turned and smiled at me. "Yes! Exactly. Earthwatch has many projects where people pay to help the scientists. It gives them a taste of fieldwork and they provide very useful help. I do not see why we can't do this."

"You don't see—?" Liz snorted derisively. "That's *all* we need around here is a bunch of unskilled biologist wannabes."

"You were not skilled at one time," he pointed out. "Everybody has to start somewhere. And besides, we would not ask them to do anything complicated. They could help with observations and keep watch at the lick. That way, we could expand the study. We would have a better chance of tracking our macaws if we had more people working here. They have tourists at La Selva." He named another biological research station further north.

"But La Selva has been operating for many years," Ernesto said quietly. "It is very safe there."

"Andres," Viviana broke in. Her expression was one of disbelief. "Listen to yourself. Keep watch at the lick? For what? In case the poachers return? Do you *want* another accident to happen? Aleck and Candi were not bad enough for you? You are talking about sending *tourists* to stand guard against armed poachers. And what about Guillermo? He was a tourist as well. At least that is what he told you. Look where that ended up. This is a very stupid idea."

"Viviana!" Andres rapped out her name, his face dark with anger.

"I'm sorry," she conceded grudgingly, "but I do not agree with this idea at all."

Andres held onto his temper with visible effort. He turned to me and gave me a tight smile. "Robyn, what do you think?"

I paused, as if mulling it over. I already knew what I thought. "Not the greatest plan," I told him with an apologetic shrug.

He threw up his hands in frustration.

"It's too rushed," I said. "I like the idea in general—and the extra help would be useful—but you've got to admit there are a few safety issues and we don't know whether or not those poachers have left for good. Personally, I suspect not. I might be overly cautious, but I'm fairly sure your funding won't cover a lawsuit—"

"No, it will not," Viviana said darkly. "If anything happens . . . *pfft!* There goes the study."

"But it's a good idea in principle," I tried to cheer Andres up. "Maybe next field season."

The impromptu meeting broke up with Andres unwillingly convinced to put his idea on hold for the time being. I went off to wash some laundry in the tubs behind the kitchen. Janet was there, scrubbing out some socks on the washboard.

"Not the best idea," she commented when I told her about Andres' brainstorm.

"No," I agreed.

"I mean, unless Danta needs the money."

"I don't think he was going to charge them. It sounded to me like he'd provide them with room and board in exchange for free labor. But I don't know, maybe he is thinking more of an Earthwatch sort of thing."

Janet started to wring out her laundry. "Those aren't cheap."

"I know," I nodded. "I always wanted to go on one, but could never afford it." I dumped my dirty laundry into one of the tubs. "Maybe the station needs the money. I don't know what the finances are like, but it can't be cheap to run this place."

"Yeah, the last guy had trouble keeping it afloat. He was going to try bringing in tourists too."

"The last guy?"

"Scott Gray."

"Scott Gray? That was ten or fifteen years ago. How do you . . . oh, the notes that Candi left you?"

Janet nodded, then glanced around to make sure nobody was listening. "Did you know that Liz used to work here?" she asked in an undertone. "When Gray was running the show."

"Liz?" It came out louder than I'd intended.

Janet shushed me and nodded again. "She was a grad student under Gray."

I gaped at her, my arms up to the elbows in soapy water. "But she never mentioned anything—"

"I'm not surprised." Janet lowered her voice even further. "After Gray died, Liz and another student tried to keep the station running."

"Tried? What happened?"

Janet shook out another sock and shrugged. "They lost their funding, mostly."

"But that happens all the time."

"Ye-ess," Janet dragged the word out. "But she was the one who lost it."

I made a silent 'o' with my lips.

"Most of the stuff Candi gave me was Gray's field notes. But there're a few other documents. Funding applications, grant permits and . . . a handful of notes written by the other grad student. A guy named Jorge Montoya. According to him, Liz blew the whole funding gig."

"How?"

Janet gave me a pointed look. "You need to ask? Suffice it to say, she hasn't changed much in ten years."

"Ah. No wonder she never said anything."

"Mmm," Janet agreed as she gathered up her freshly washed socks. "Too bad. She would have been a great resource for me. But if she's touchy about it, then I'm sure as hell not going to be the one to bring it up."

I made a face. "Not if you want to live to a ripe old age."

"Robyn! Oscar! Help!"

"Viviana?" I called back, startled.

Oscar and I were just finishing up the dinner dishes. At the sound of Viviana's voice, Oscar ran to the door of the kitchen, his hands dripping soapy water on the floor. "What's wrong?" he demanded.

Viviana jogged up to the dining hall. "It's Andres," she said breathlessly. "He has been hit by a seed."

A seed?

"He is okay," she hastened to reassure us. "He's just knocked out. But I cannot lift him to bring him back."

"Where is he?"

"Down the north path. I'll show you."

We followed her past the station and part-way into the rainforest. We'd eaten an early supper that night, so it wasn't completely dark yet. There was just enough light to see Andres' prone figure propped up against a tree. As we got closer, I spied a large, roundish object lying on the ground a few feet away.

"Is this what hit him?" I asked, toeing the baseball-sized seed.

Oscar had crouched down beside Andres and was lifting his eyelids.

Viviana glanced over at the seed and nodded. "Yes, we were standing here talking and we heard a crash from the tree. Andres looked up and . . . *smack!* It hit him right here." She indicated her right temple.

I winced in sympathy. "Is he going to be all right?" I asked Oscar.

As if on cue, Andres stirred and groaned.

"He will be fine," Oscar told us. "You will be fine," he repeated to Andres.

"What . . . happened? Viviana?"

"I'm here," she said. Her husky voice was reassuring. "You were smacked by a seed."

"A seed?"

"A big one." I held it in front of his face so he could see it.

He gave it a slightly cross-eyed look and cursed under his breath.

"I think you have a concussion," Oscar told him. "Let's take you to the station."

"How did you . . . ?"

"Viviana came to get us. You are too *gordo*—too fat. She could not budge you."

"Me? I am *gordo?*" Andres laughed weakly. "Ha! If I am *gordo*, then we better hope *you* never get hit by a seed. I don't think all of us together could budge this stomach." He poked Oscar's ample belly.

Oscar shouted with laughter and hauled a wobbly Andres to his feet.

Back at the station, Andres' accident was the subject of much discussion—and hilarity. All in the interest of keeping him awake, of course.

"You'll be famous," Janet told him as she set the seed in a place of honor on the table.

Andres threw her a startled look. "You are going to write about this in your article, aren't you?" he accused.

"Hey, the public needs to be informed."

"Don't worry, Andres," Keith patted his shoulder. "It could have been worse."

"Yeah, you could have been bitten by a wiener dog," Janet said solemnly.

A wiener dog?

I looked at Janet, but she was watching Keith, her eyes dancing with merriment. Keith was blushing furiously. "A wiener dog?" I prompted, arching one eyebrow up.

Keith glared at Janet, though I could see the corners of his mouth twitching upwards. Then, "It was three years ago," he wailed. "And she's still laughing at me."

"What is a wiener dog?" Andres asked, mystified.

I explained in a few words and turned my attention back to Keith. "Sooo?" I drew out the word, making it a question.

"It was stupid," Keith groaned. "My friend had this wiener dog. It was always a friendly little thing. And then one night, I was visiting and when I left, I bent down to say good-bye to it."

Janet was chuckling in earnest now. Tears of laughter leaked from the corners of her eyes.

"The little bastard just reached up and tore right through my left nostril."

We were all laughing now.

"I had to get eight stitches in my nose! Do you have any idea how embarrassing that was? I had to tell the nurse what kind of dog attacked me. And then she told all the other nurses to come and look at the guy whose nose was almost torn off by a wiener dog." He shook his head. "It was humiliating!"

"You are right, Keith," Andres said finally, wiping the laugh tears from his cheeks. "A seed is much, much better than a wiener dog."

Which started another bout of laughter. It took a while for things to settle down, but when they did, it was Oscar who sounded a note of caution.

"These seeds are still dangerous," he rumbled. "It is funny now for us, but you could have been hurt much worse, Andres."

Andres fingered his temple carefully. "It feels bad enough," he said. "But I know what you're saying. We should tell everyone to maybe stay away from that spot in case there are more seeds." He paused and looked around. "Liz and Marco are not here?"

Viviana shrugged and patted his hand. "They did not come out to laugh at you. But don't worry. We will be certain to tell them all about your seed."

Andres made a face at her. "I'm sure you will," he said.

"What were you guys doing out there, anyhow?" I asked Viviana later as we prepared for bed.

She scrunched up her nose. "He wanted to discuss my *attitude*. He did not like being called stupid earlier today. I was not calling him stupid, I thought his idea for tourists was stupid. How can you make a mistake about that?"

"Why didn't he just talk to you at Danta?"

She picked up a brush and started running it through her hair. "Who knows?" she shrugged. "I was very angry with him."

"Maybe he thought you were going to yell at him in front of everybody."

"Robyn!" she chastised. "Would I do that?"

"Absolutely," I replied without hesitation.

Viviana gave me a crooked smile. "Well . . . ," she temporized, "perhaps you are right."

I laughed and shook my head at her. "You two certainly seem to bring out the worst in each other. But. . . ."

She stopped brushing her hair and turned to face me. "But what?"

I didn't quite know how to ask my question.

"What's the matter?"

I took a deep breath and plunged in. "You're sure it was an accident, right?"

She stared at me for a few heartbeats, then her expression darkened. "You do not think that *I*—"

"Gods, no!" I exclaimed. "That never even crossed my mind. It's just . . . we seem to have had more than our fair share of accidents lately and, well, I wondered—"

"Robyn." It was Viviana's turn to interrupt me. "Do you *really* think somebody threw a seed at Andres and knocked him out?"

I hesitated for a second, then pulled a face. "It sounds ridiculous, doesn't it?"

Viviana nodded and grinned. "*Sí*. I'm afraid it sounds very silly." She gave me a sidelong look. "Although he *was* making me very angry," she added. "*Gracias a Dios* for the seed. If it wasn't for that, I might have smacked him on the head myself."

I laughed and settled down for the night with an easier heart. It had been a stupid notion. After Viviana turned off the lamp, I lay with my arms folded behind my head, listening to the light rain drumming its melody on our metal roof.

It occurred to me that I might have been jealous of their little tête-à-tête in the jungle. Jealous of the sparks that flew off them when they butted heads. Any reader of romantic fiction could tell you this sort of thing usually meant the two were destined for one another. So. All this and I hadn't been jealous—still wasn't even now that I thought about it. Was it because Andres had backed off since the day we'd built the blind? Or was it because Janet and Keith's relationship reminded me more and more of the rapport I had back home with Kelt?

Andres was sexy as hell, but were we right for each other? No. Probably not. I plumped up my pillow again, remembering how close I'd come to munching mangos in the buff. What a fickle thing the human heart could be.

Thinking of love (both unrequited and otherwise) led to thoughts of other suffering souls at Danta—namely, Marco. I wished there was something I could say or do to make him feel better. But I couldn't think of anything apart from producing a healthy Candi—and the chances of that grew more remote with each passing day. I punched my pillow again and thought about her, as I did now every night. Wondering what had happened to her. Wondering if we'd ever find out. And knowing I wasn't the only one who lay awake at night, thinking about it.

The state of morale at Danta had been pretty bad lately. If Andres' giant seed did nothing else, it had certainly improved the atmosphere around the station. I was, of course, very glad that he hadn't been seriously injured (though Oscar had confined him to the station for a few days), but it had been a long time since Danta felt so relaxed.

I should have enjoyed it while I had the chance.

*In many cases, it is lack of observation that keeps
a creature a secret from science for so long.*

Gerald Durrell
Foreword from *The Lost Ark:*
New and Rediscovered Animals of the 20th Century

CHAPTER 28

"Listen!" I held up my hand to stop Marco and Ernesto.

They drew level with me and paused.

The sound came again. Faint, but unmistakable.

"There! Do you hear that?"

Ernesto's grim countenance lightened and he smiled at me. "A macaw."

I nodded happily. "It sounds like an amethyst."

Marco was swiveling his head back and forth, trying to triangulate the call. "This way," he decided, pointing to the northeast.

We unhooked our machetes and started chopping.

"We are not near the clay lick," Marco puffed as we made our way through the steaming jungle.

"No," I agreed, a little breathless myself. "But we've seen them fly off this way for the past couple of days."

"Perhaps we will find a nesting site," Ernesto said.

"Do we win *cervezas* for finding a nest?" Marco asked.

I grinned. "You'll have to take that up with Andres," I told him. I paused to wipe the sweat from my eyes. The call was much louder now. A harshly metallic-sounding squawk. I stayed still for a moment. Listening.

"It sounds upset," I said to the other two. "Listen to it."

They stopped and turned their heads in the direction of the sounds.

"It is not happy about something," Marco agreed after a moment.

I looked at Ernesto to see what he thought and was astonished to see his normally florid face drain of color.

"What's wrong?" I demanded.

He didn't answer me. Instead he pushed past us, heading closer to the macaw.

"Ernesto!" I called out.

"There is something wrong," he tossed back over his shoulder.

Marco and I looked at each other for a split second, then we were hard on Ernesto's heels.

"What's wrong?"

"How do you know?"

The hoarse squawks were getting louder now, echoing through the forest like they were being broadcast through a gigantic sound system. I resisted the impulse to cover my ears. There was no point in asking Ernesto what he thought was wrong. I wouldn't be able to hear his answer.

Then I knew. Even before we spotted the bird, I knew.

It was trapped.

We burst into the tiny clearing and my eyes took in the entire sight in a second. The large palm tree—a roosting tree—its bared branches scraped free of mosses and epiphytes. And high up on one of the branches, in a tiny, metal cage that had been knocked on its side, there was an amethyst macaw.

Even as I let loose an angry curse, I was moving toward the tree. Shedding my daypack and digging out the climbing harnesses. All without taking my eyes off the purple feathered form. With the cage tipped over like that, the bird could barely stand up. How long had it been trapped there?

The macaw screamed again.

The poachers had left their guide rope. It was Marco who went up the tree, climbing the ropes with the speed and agility of a monkey. He grabbed onto the branch and stopped, swearing under his breath.

"What is it?" I asked.

Ernesto was standing beside me. "Bird lime," he said.

"It's very sticky," Marco called down. "They have put a kind of glue on the branches."

I turned to Ernesto and raised one eyebrow. "Bird lime?"

He nodded, refusing to meet my eyes. "To trap them. They use a decoy to attract more birds. The others get stuck on the branches when they come to see what is wrong."

I pursed my lips, irrationally furious with Ernesto for knowing about bird lime, for probably having used it himself at one time.

"I see," I said coldly. "A trick of the trade, is it?"

He turned away without responding, but not before I saw the look of shame on his face.

"Robyn! I am going to lower him down to you," Marco called. "Just one moment . . . okay, I have got him untied from the branch . . . now I will put the rope onto the cage."

I could hear him crooning to the macaw. The bird had given one last shriek when Marco had righted the cage.

"Okay, here he comes. Be careful. He does not look so good."

Not so good, indeed. Seeing the amethyst macaw close up almost brought me to tears. Its feathers were greasy, plucked right out in some spots, broken and sticking out at odd angles in others. The bird was probably starving, definitely dehydrated, and it was bleeding. Trembling so badly it could barely stay on the perch. Or . . . I held up the cage to get a better look at its feet. And sucked in my breath.

"His feet!"

"It is the bird lime," Ernesto told me quietly. "When they pull the birds off the branch, sometimes the toes are left behind. *Lo siento.* I am sorry."

There was a remorseful note in his voice. Was he apologizing for telling me or for his past? At this moment, it didn't much matter. Anybody who could knowingly do this to a living creature was beyond my understanding—and forgiveness.

"Give me your water bottle," I ordered. "Let's see if we can get him to take some water. Marco!"

"*Sí.*"

"We've got to do something about that bird lime. Can you scrape it off?"

"No. I have already tried. It's very sticky."

"Did you try using a knife?"

"Cover it with moss," Ernesto called up to him. "Or some parts of plants."

I tore my attention away from the macaw and spared Ernesto a quick, piercing look.

"I *am* here to help," he reminded me as he handed over his water bottle.

If only I could believe that.

"All we can do now is wait," Viviana announced as she and I joined the others in the dining hall.

"How is it?" Janet asked.

Viviana's mouth tightened. "Not very good," she told

her. "He was very dehydrated. I gave him water, but I cannot get him to take any food."

"And the blood?" This from Marco.

"I think he beat himself against the sides of the cage. I tried to clean him up a bit, but he's very traumatized. I do not want to handle him too much."

"I have already radioed Sirena," Andres told her. "Dan is warning us to be careful. He doesn't want any more dead bodies."

"Still no sign of Candi?" Pepe asked.

Andres shook his head once and pursed his lips. Since Candi's disappearance, not a day passed when Pepe didn't ask about her. I wasn't sure why he persisted unless it was some sort of guilt trip aimed at Marco. Or perhaps at Andres, who, Pepe felt, had not done enough to find her.

"What about a wildlife rehab center?" Liz was saying. "I can take him to Sirena for transport."

"He's way too stressed for that," I said. "He'd never make it. And another thing. . . ." I hesitated, afraid of the reaction I was going to get. "It's one of ours."

Liz stared at me, her gooseberry eyes sharp. "One of the macaws Janet photographed?"

I nodded and heard several curses around the table.

"Do you think they caught him at the lick?" Keith asked.

"It's possible," I admitted. "More than possible. We've got a fairly well-defined path going there now." I grimaced a little and shrugged. "Can't be helped."

"So it's dangerous, then," Keith said flatly.

Janet, realizing where he was going with this, put her hand on his arm. "Keith. . . ."

He covered her hand with his own. "I know I'm being an alpha male," he told her, "but, c'mon, Janet . . . *armed* poachers?"

"We don't know they're armed."

"Tell that to the guy who got shot!"

"That was weeks and weeks ago! It's probably a different group and besides—"

"They are armed," Andres broke in.

Keith and Janet stopped and stared at him.

"They are armed," he said again. "Dan has just told me that Ricardo and Frielo heard gunfire."

"*What!*"

"South of Danta."

"How far south?" I asked.

"Not far enough to make me happy," he told us.

"What kind of gunfire?" Pepe wanted to know.

"I don't know." Andres sounded frustrated. "What does it matter? There was someone shooting. Who cares what kind of gun they had?"

"It makes a lot of difference," Pepe argued. "Perhaps it was someone out to catch some dinner. Perhaps it was something else. There is a lot of difference between a shotgun and a machine gun, Andres."

"I'm certain there are no machine guns around here," Andres blustered.

I suddenly remembered the unusual bullets I'd found under the desk at the TRC house in San José. I opened my mouth to say something about them, but as I did, I caught Ernesto's eye.

He was sitting quietly in the far corner, where he'd been ever since we got back with the injured bird. He was watching me. Not glaring exactly. You couldn't even call it threatening. He was just . . . watching. A tremor shivered down my spine and I snapped my mouth shut. Perhaps it might be wiser to tell Andres about the bullets in private.

Chapter 29

The amethyst macaw died just after lunch.

I looked down on its sad, bedraggled body, feeling angry and helpless. Like I wanted to hit somebody. This was the second dead amethyst macaw I'd seen now. Two too many.

I sat with Viviana while she stuffed and mounted the bird. I took a few samples for sequencing. At least something positive would come out of its death. A small consolation.

As I fiddled around with my field notes later that afternoon, I found myself thinking hard about a lot of different things. Top of the list was the continuing question of Ernesto's past. Namely, whether or not it was his present as well.

And Liz. After the macaw died, Liz hadn't said a word. Not a single one. She just turned around, went into her cabin, and shut the door firmly behind her. How could she stand to be in this line of work if she felt such things so keenly?

Then there was the problem of the bullets, Pepe, the cut rope, the fact that someone had searched Aleck's papers, and the increasing antagonism between Viviana and Andres. I closed my notebook and rested my chin in my hand. We were supposed to be here to study the amethyst macaws. To map their distribution, identify their habitat requirements, and to evaluate any threats to their population. So why did the threats seem to be coming from within Danta? What would Kelt make of all this?

RAAAAAAAHHRK KEEREEK

I lifted my head. A macaw!

I jumped up from the small table and threw open the cabin door. The bird called again. It sounded like an amethyst macaw. They'd never come this close to the station before! I paused only long enough to catch up my binoculars, then I strode off in pursuit.

On some level, I knew that I shouldn't really go off by myself. But if I was going to huddle in the station, afraid of my own shadow, then I might as well go back home to Canada. If a fer-de-lance hadn't scared me into leaving, then I was damned if I was going to let a few wildlife traffickers do the job. I pushed through a stand of cecropias and started down the path.

If I'd seen anyone on my way out of Danta, I would have told them where I was going, explained what I was following, invited them along. But I didn't.

And the jungle closed in around me.

I won't go far, I told myself. Just far enough to see if it was an amethyst macaw. If I was right, then it would be a first for the station. And it would give us a start on those ranging studies. I ducked under an elephant leaf and tried not to think about what Andres would say to me when I got back. The macaw croaked somewhere off to my left. I picked up the pace and sped down the path.

"I'm hardly a novice rainforest hiker anymore," I muttered under my breath. And the bird really did sound like an amethyst. Besides, the gunfire had been in the south. I was going north. Still, would Andres see it my way? Somehow, I doubted it.

I chased the sound for almost twenty minutes before it started moving off to the right, winging away faster than I could follow. If I wanted to stay with it, I'd have to leave the path. The thought of Candi made me hesitate. Nobody knew where I was—didn't even know I'd left the station. As I paused, the decision was made for me. The hoarse squawks suddenly ceased. I waited and listened.

Nothing.

I turned around slowly, trying to pick up the sound again. My ears rang with the effort. Still nothing.

"Crap," I muttered, disappointed.

But at least I hadn't left the path.

I turned and began to retrace my steps, working out the details of what I'd tell Andres when I got back. I hadn't gone very far when I came to a fork in the path.

A fork.

I pulled my mouth to one side and regarded the trail unhappily. I didn't remember a fork. I looked around, hoping to recognize a tree or the shape of a leaf. Anything that would tell me which path to take. But nothing looked familiar.

"Okeedokee," I said out loud, trying to jolly myself up. "Eenie meenie mynie mo, catch a viper by the toe. . . ."

The final 'mo' ended on the left path. So I took the right one just because.

I walked much more slowly now, stopping every few paces to peer behind me. If I had to come back this way, I wanted to be able to recognize the path. I walked until the jungle began to get darker. Until I started getting worried. Was I really lost? I should have reached the station by now. Why hadn't I brought a flashlight?

I began to consider the many benefits of yelling. And then I heard voices. Forgetting caution, I picked up the pace, almost running towards the sound of other people. Not that I was panicking or anything.

"Hey, you guys!" I called, but nobody answered.

I sucked in a breath to call again. But a few more strides and I was close enough to make out the voices.

"Tell me another one!"

"I am not lying to you."

"Bullshit!"

"I have not touched the birds. You cannot prove anything!"

"Maybe I don't have to!"

I was running in earnest by this time, trying to reach them before something happened. But I was too late.

Just as I reached the clearing, Liz backed Ernesto right over the edge of a stream bank. He cried out, more in surprise than anything else—it wasn't a steep bank. Then he shouted again. But not in surprise. In pain.

I saw him jerking around, slapping at himself, at the thumb-sized ants on his body.

Bullet ants.

"Shit!" I swore, dashing into the clearing.

Liz stood watching him. Just standing there as if it was all a dream.

I surged forward to help. "*What the hell do you think you're doing?*" I cried.

At the sound of my voice, she jumped in surprise. "I—"

She appeared to be at a loss for words. I didn't have time to help her find them. I held out my hand to Ernesto, but he was just out of reach. Where was a rope when you needed one? I whipped off my belt and tossed one end of it to him. He was cursing in pain, still slapping the ants, but he managed to catch it.

"I know you don't like the guy but . . . *ouch!*" A bullet ant stung me on the hand. "Goddamn it! What did you—*shit!*—think you were doing?"

I tried to haul Ernesto up the stream bank, but the mud was thick, slippery from this afternoon's rain. And the bullet ants—the most aggressive ants in Central America—had declared war.

Eep eep eep. Their high-pitched stridulations drowned out the cicadas. It sounded like an audition for *Them!*

They stung me on the arm, the neck, the ankle. "Help me!" I cried to Liz.

It seemed to shake her out of whatever fog she was in. With an inarticulate cry that might have been an apology, she sprang to my side and grabbed onto the belt. Together, we dragged Ernesto up out of the nest of enraged bullet ants.

Chapter 30

"I'm taking a tip from you," I told Andres slurrily.

"From me?"

I nodded my agreement, but the room started spinning so I stopped. "That's right," I told him. "When you cut your hand on that thorn, you drank a lotta beer to make it go away." I hiccuped and tried to cover it with a dignified cough.

Andres smiled, and for a second the deep furrows on his brow disappeared. But only for a second.

I didn't blame him for being worried. The Danta Biological Field Station was turning out to be more like Danta's Inferno. I hiccuped again, pondering the thought, impressed that I'd come up with something so clever. Danta's Inferno. Good one, Robyn, I congratulated myself. I considered telling Andres, but a quick look at his face told me he wouldn't appreciate the humor.

And really, there was nothing funny about what was happening. That was part of the reason why I'd sucked back so many beer. The other part had to do with killing the burning pain of bullet ant stings.

"You are not really supposed to drink alcohol when you have been bitten by a bullet ant."

"Really?" I blinked in surprise. "I thought that was only snakesss." It was a difficult word to say in my condition. I hoped nobody had noticed.

"Is it *dangerous* to drink after a bullet ant sting?" Janet asked quickly, gesturing towards my hand, which was cooling the burn in a basin of water.

Andres shook his head. "No, no. Don't worry. It will just hurt more. That's all."

"*That's all?*"

Andres winked at Janet.

"You're pulling my leg," I accused.

He grinned and the furrows receded again. "Yes," he agreed. "You are okay to drink a few *cervezas*."

I narrowed my eyes at him fuzzily and drained my glass.

"Nasty buggers, those bullet ants," Keith remarked.

Andres nodded his agreement.

"Didja know the sting from a bullet ant hurts thirty times more than a bee sting?" I informed them all. "Thirty times! And I got stung seven times. That's. . . ." I paused, trying to do the math.

"Two hundred and ten times more painful than a bee sting," Keith supplied.

"Two hundred an' ten!" I poked Andres on the chest to emphasize my point. "Hurts like hell! And poor Ernesto. He was stung all over. That's a lotta bee stings. How's he doing?"

The lines on Andres' forehead deepened. "I have given him some painkillers," he said.

"Does that help?" Janet asked.

"Not very much. And I am not joking this time."

She made an 'o' with her mouth.

Andres turned to me. "And now, Robyn, if you are

finished with your beer, perhaps you would like to come to my cabin and tell me what happened?"

Talk about an offer I couldn't refuse. I gave him what I hoped was a saucy wink and staggered up from the dining table. Keith reached out a hand to steady me.

"Careful there, Nanook."

"I'm fine," I assured him.

I might have sounded more convincing if the room didn't insist on tilting at such an odd angle. I hoped Andres' cabin wouldn't be so tricky.

The cabin was fine. Nice and even. But Andres only wanted to talk about what had happened between Liz and Ernesto. He'd be a lot happier if we just made out, I thought muzzily, forgetting that I'd decided we probably weren't right for each other.

"So Liz did not even try to help?"

"No," I told him. "It was like she was sleepwalking or something. She just stood there. Watching. It was kinda creepy."

"Did she push him?"

I chewed on my lower lip and thought about the question. "I don't think so," I answered after a moment. "I don't even know if either of them realized how close they were to the edge. From what I saw, she was yelling at him and . . . sorta backing him up. Y'know how people are when they're really pissed—I mean angry."

Andres didn't say anything, but his expression was serious.

"Ernesto's gonna be okay. Isn't he?" I asked, suddenly struck by the nature of Andres' questions. "I mean, they were big mean bastard ants, but they were just ants."

Andres caught my eyes and held them.

"They were just ants," I said again.

"Yes, but it seems Ernesto might be allergic to them."

"Oh, shit."

He nodded. "*Sí.* One of his legs is paralyzed. Only for a short while, I hope. Oscar gave him some steroids, but . . . well, we will have to cross our fingers."

"But he's not gonna die or anything." It seemed very important to confirm this.

Andres patted my hand (the one that hadn't been stung). "Don't worry," he told me. "He is not in danger of dying. But he will probably not feel well for a long time."

"That's a relief," I exclaimed. "I mean, not that he's gonna be sick. I meant, I'd feel terrible if he died—even if he is still trafficking."

Andres gave me a sharp look. "What makes you think he is still trafficking?"

I squirmed under the scrutiny. "Liz said—"

"Liz knows nothing!" he snapped, his temper fraying. "She has gotten this idea about Ernesto and nobody is going to change her mind. Do you really think TRC did not confirm this? This is an important study we are working on here. Do you think TRC would jeopardize it by not checking on Ernesto?"

"Well, what about the bullets?" I demanded, stung by his tone.

"Bullets?" He looked confused.

I told him about the bullets.

"That could be anything," he said after I'd finished. "They could have been under that desk for years. They could be hunting bullets, or—"

"Okay, okay," I said. "But if Ernesto's not trafficking, somebody is."

Andres' brows came together in a frown. "*Sí*, I know. So perhaps you would like to tell me why you were out by yourself in the forest when there are poachers out there who have already killed one person. And when you are finished, perhaps you can tell me why you didn't let anyone know you were going. And after you are done with that, perhaps you can tell me why you didn't mention these bullets before and if there is anything else you have forgotten to tell me."

I decided *I* would have been a lot happier if we'd just made out.

Andres reamed me out good. Not that I didn't deserve it, but it heralded the start of a very uncomfortable night, which, I felt, I really hadn't deserved at all. His lecture stung, but he had nothing on the bullet ants. The bites were excruciatingly painful, burning and throbbing with each beat of my heart. To make things worse, the beer I'd consumed insisted on going through me a trickle at a time. So every half-hour I had to crawl out of my sleeping bag and run to the outhouse. Each time, I checked the seat carefully for scorpions, fer-de-lances, and any other damn thing that might feel the need to add to my misery.

By my fifth trip, the station had fallen quiet. The lamps in the dining hall had been extinguished; even the cabins were dark. So when I heard a voice, I thought at first I was imagining things.

I turned slowly, trying to pinpoint the sound. It was coming from Aleck's cabin.

I forced my unwilling feet to move closer. Why would anybody be in Aleck's cabin? Oscar had cleaned the place thoroughly, but the building still seemed to retain a miasma of death and suffering. Despite the cramped arrangements in the lab, nobody had wanted to sleep there.

The voices were murmuring. The words indistinct. I moved closer.

No. Not two voices. One.

I crept to the side of the cabin and listened. The voice had fallen silent, but I was certain I'd heard only one person speaking. And that person had sounded like Pepe.

I leaned against the wooden wall, puzzling about it. Pepe wouldn't be the first person ever to talk to himself, but why was he doing it in Aleck's old cabin?

I heard movement inside. Footsteps! Moving towards the door. I darted back across the clearing and dove into our cabin. Viviana was sleeping, her breaths long and deep. I peeked out the screen window, but there were no shadowy figures crossing the compound. And no more voices in the night. I crawled back into my sleeping bag, uneasy for no reason that I could put my finger on.

By the time I woke up the next morning, Pepe was gone.

CHAPTER 31

"What do you mean, 'gone'?" I asked Viviana sleepily.

"He has left the station. All his stuff is gone too."

I stared at her. "Why?"

She threw up her hands. "Nobody knows. We don't know when he left, or how, or why. He is just gone."

"And he didn't say anything to Oscar?"

"No. Nothing to anyone."

I sat up and scrubbed at my sleep-wrinkled face. "You know," I said slowly. "I think I heard him last night."

Her gaze sharpened. "You heard him leave?"

"No, no," I shook my head. "I heard him talking. In Aleck's cabin."

"Aleck's cabin?" Vivian echoed. "Why would—?"

I was already shrugging. "I don't know. But I didn't hear anybody else in there. Maybe he was on the phone."

Viviana folded her arms across her chest and shook her head thoughtfully. "It's still not working," she told me. "Andres tried to call Sirena. It's dead. He had to use the radio."

"Have the rangers seen Pepe?"

"No."

"So he didn't head to Sirena . . . ," I trailed off,

uncomfortable with the thought that was formulating in my mind.

"What are you thinking?" Viviana asked.

"Well," I hesitated. "Do you think . . . what if Pepe is part of a trafficking organization?" The words came out in a rush.

Viviana started to answer, then snapped her mouth shut and stared at me.

"He's not a researcher," I said with some confidence. "I mean, the guy was supposed to be developing a thesis project and he's done nothing except hang around and shoot the breeze with Oscar."

I held up my fingers and started ticking off points. "He's supposed to be an ornithologist, and yet, he didn't know that quetzals are high-elevation birds. He didn't know that it was George Powell who did that study in elevational migration. He told Candi that she wouldn't have to go into the jungle to collect plants, which was in total opposition to her advisor's suggestions, not to mention pretty weak scientific methodology. And then, there are the amethyst macaws."

I took a deep breath and told her about Pepe's initial reaction to seeing the macaws. Viviana sank down onto her bed, still staring at me, concern carving a sharp crease in her forehead.

"We know that someone found the macaws before we did—the dead bird in Calgary proved that. But, Viviana, if they'd found this place before, then why weren't there more amethysts in that shipment? Granted we don't have the numbers of, say, the scarlet macaws, but the amethysts aren't exactly down to the last breeding pair. You know as well as I do that we've got six or seven pair out there—and it's probably breeding season, so they're not even congregating in flocks."

She nodded slowly.

"So, if traffickers had stumbled on this place before we got here, there should have been more than one amethyst macaw in the shipment. Which means, they've only recently found out about the population here. Which means—"

"We have an insider," Viviana concluded grimly.

"It's a distinct possibility," I agreed.

"Ernesto?" She was having trouble letting go of that idea.

I pulled my bottom lip. "Another possibility. Andres says not, though."

Viviana made a rude noise.

"I know," I told her. "But really, would TRC include him in our study if they had any doubts?"

She didn't respond but I could tell from her expression that she was troubled.

"Look, I hate what he's done," I said candidly. "I hate that he made a fortune from taking birds from the wild. I hate that he knows about resin-tipped arrows and using decoy birds and bird lime on branches. But. . . ." I paused, remembering Ernesto's reaction yesterday. "You should have seen him when we found that macaw in the cage. He was *furious*—we all were, I guess—but he really seemed to take it personally."

"You don't think he's still trafficking, do you?"

I gazed back at her for a long moment, then shook my head. "No. I don't." I said the words slowly, realizing the truth of them as they left my mouth. "Not anymore."

"And Pepe?"

"That's a different story. I don't know—not for sure—but you've got to admit, he's a suspicious character."

"*Sí,*" Viviana conceded.

I threw back my sleeping bag decisively and stood up. "One thing I do know," I told her, "there are poachers here. Now. And whether Pepe is involved or not, they're after our amethyst macaws. I'm going to the lick to make sure they don't trap any more of them."

And so, Viviana, Marco, Janet, Keith, and I all set out for the clay lick. Andres would have come too, but he was still grounded with a concussion. Ernesto was far too ill to go anywhere. And Liz declined to join us, claiming instead a painful migraine.

I had a bit of a headache myself that morning, but I figured it was my own damn fault, so I was ignoring it. I had to ignore the nauseated feeling in my stomach too. But when we arrived at the clay lick, pounding heads and rumbling tummies suddenly took a back seat to other, more unpleasant sensations.

"Is that a net?" Janet asked, squinting ahead at the small clearing across from the lick.

A net? My stomach clenched and I heard Viviana let loose a string of curses.

"Where?" I demanded.

Janet pointed and I saw the telltale shadow of woven fibers. We jogged down the rest of the trail to the edge of the stream bank. I could see it clearly now, across the stream. Three nets. The one Janet had spotted hung like a curtain, caught up on several trees. Two more were piled in a heap on the ground. There were no macaws at the lick.

I don't know what made me look off to the far right. Maybe a flicker of movement out of the corner of my eye.

Maybe the snap of a broken branch. But I turned around and saw two figures disappearing into the jungle.

I spat out an oath and before I really knew what I was doing, I was after them, splashing across the stream, pounding into the jungle in pursuit.

"Robyn!" I heard Viviana cry out behind me, but I could still see one of the men. If I stopped, I'd lose him.

I ignored her and kept crashing through the undergrowth.

I was gaining on them. I don't know how. I ran after them without thought of safety or caution or what I'd do if I caught them. I could almost hear the dead amethyst macaws urging me on.

One of the men glanced back over his shoulder. The look on his face was gratifying. Astonishment. Fright. It spurred me on to new speeds.

But just when I thought I'd win, my foot hit a large root and my legs went out from under me. By the time I got back on my feet, the poachers had vanished.

I bent over, trying to catch my breath. Swearing in between each lungful of air. I'd almost had them!

"*Robyn!*"

I lifted my head. It was Keith.

"I'm okay!" I shouted back. "They got away, though."

"Robyn! Come quickly!" Keith sounded panicked.

I straightened up. "What's wrong?" I called.

"It's Marco!"

Marco?

"He's been bitten by a coral snake!"

Chapter 32

Marco was lying on the forest floor. His dark eyes were wide with fear.

"I don't want to die," he kept saying over and over again.

Janet was holding his hand for reassurance. Keith had crouched down, applying pressure over the bite wound. Viviana was beside him. The contents of the first aid kit were spread around her.

"What happened?" I demanded.

"He went after you," Keith replied. "We all did. But Marco was first. I don't know . . . he just jumped over a log and there it was."

"I stepped on it," Marco told me with a trembling attempt at a smile. "Like you stepped on the fer-de-lance. Very silly."

I sank down to my knees beside him. "Very silly, indeed," I agreed. My heart was in my throat. "How do you know it was a coral snake?" This to Viviana.

She was mixing up the antivenin. "I saw the colors," she said without taking her eyes off the vials. "Red against yellow."

Kills a fellow, the rest of the old adage slithered through my brain.

"Did it envenomate?"

"I think so," Janet said when Viviana didn't answer. "It's turning red."

"We've got the antivenin?" I shook my head a little. "I'm sorry. Of course we do, that's why you're mixing it up." I was more upset than I wanted Marco to know. He'd been coming after *me*. Following *my* foolish chase. If anything happened to him. . . .

"Why aren't you using the extractors?" I asked suddenly, realizing what was wrong with this picture.

"They're gone."

"Gone!"

"They're not in the kit. I don't know why. There are no pressure bandages, either."

Marco started wheezing.

"What?"

"I don't know, Robyn," Viviana said again. "Marco says he checked the kit last night. Everything was there."

We'd brought my first aid kit that morning. Mine. The extractors *had* been in the kit last night. I'd checked too. And now they were gone. I couldn't think about what that meant right now. Not with Marco shaking and wheezing in front of me.

"You're going to be fine," I told him. I hoped I sounded more convinced than I felt. "Try to relax."

"Okay, Marco," Viviana approached him with the vial. "I am going to put a drop of this in your eye to test if you're allergic to the serum." She bent over and squirted a drop in his right eye. "Who has a watch?"

"I do," Keith said. "How long?"

"Ten minutes for coral snake serum. If the eye does not turn red, then everything is okay."

The ten minutes crept by. No red. No allergies. The rest should have been a cinch.

But it wasn't.

Shortly after Viviana injected the antivenin into Marco's buttock, things suddenly began spiraling out of control.

Viviana was preparing another shot of antivenin. The rest of us were talking to Marco, cracking jokes to take his mind off the danger. I don't even know what we said. But I knew when the antivenin hit his system. And I knew immediately that something was wrong.

His whole body stiffened, tendons popping as his jaw clenched tight. With an inarticulate cry, he started convulsing.

"I thought you said he wasn't allergic to it!" I shouted at Viviana as we jumped on his flailing limbs, trying to pin them down.

"He isn't!" she gasped. "I don't know what's wrong! I did everything right!"

"Well, goddamn it!" Keith swore. "Something's wrong! *Ouch!* Janet, sit on his arm if you have to!"

Marco screamed. A long, wailing, horrible sound. As if every nerve in his body had been sliced open. His voice cracked and broke from the pressure. The cry changed the very texture of the day.

"No!" The word was ripped from his throat. It tore at my soul.

And then, just like that, he died.

CHAPTER 33

Marco was dead.

Incontrovertibly. Unbelievably.

I couldn't get my mind around it. Not in all the time we spent trying to revive him. Not in the back-breaking hours it took us to carry his body back to Danta.

Marco was dead.

I huddled alone in the cabin. Shivering. Too weary to change out of my mud-soaked clothing. Too shocked to do more than just sit and stare at the wall.

Marco was dead. But why? It was a question I felt sure would haunt me for the rest of my days. He'd run carelessly through the jungle. And why? Because I'd stupidly gone tearing off myself. *I* was the reason he'd been sprinting through the forest. *I* was the reason he'd stepped on a coral snake.

But why had he died? We'd done everything right. Checking for allergies. Injecting the vials of antivenin. All the first aid books agreed that antivenin should be administered even if you're not sure the snake injected any venom. The symptoms from coral snake envenomation are often delayed and always difficult to reverse. So where had we gone wrong?

Had Viviana slipped up about the snake? Not likely.

Coral snakes were brightly striped, impossible to mistake for anything else. There were a few mimics—non-poisonous snakes that looked similar—but she'd described the correct pattern of rings. Red against yellow. And the bite wound hadn't displayed the twin punctures of a pit viper's fangs. Just a series of small, insignificant-looking scratches from where the snake had chewed on the flesh. Definitely a coral snake.

Which brought me full circle to the original question. Why had Marco died?

Trouble was, that led to a whole bunch of other questions. Why hadn't the extractors been in the kit? Or the compression bandage? Marco and I had both checked the kit last night. Which meant someone had taken them out. But who? And why?

Why. I was sick of the word. But the questions galvanized me into action. I stood up and quickly peeled off my damp clothes. I wanted to check that kit again. I pulled on some warm, dry things and left the cabin.

The first aid kit had been tossed into the storage shed with the rest of our gear. Nobody had bothered tidying or picking anything up. I spied the red bag buried under a daypack and jerked it free. The red kit was the one Marco and I always used. I popped the snaps open and the contents came spilling out. In the aftermath, Viviana had just crammed everything back in. I gathered it all up and turned towards the door to take the bag outside where the light was better. An inner caution stopped me in my tracks.

The light might be brighter outside, but anybody would be able to see me rooting around in the kit. If what I suspected was true, I didn't want anyone to know what I was doing. I put the bag down on top of a wooden crate, struck a match, and lit the kerosene lamp.

I searched all the little pockets. Aspirin. Band-Aids. Polysporin. Calamine lotion. Gauze pads. But no extractors and no compression bandage. I picked up the package with the pit-viper antivenin. It looked okay. The syringe. The tiny packet of sterilized water. The clear glass vial of antivenin granules nestled in its foam rubber bed. But . . . I held the vial closer to the light. The granules looked sort of weird. Not how I remembered them the day Andres showed me the kit.

I chewed my bottom lip for a minute. Then I turned to the shelf where we kept all the first aid kits and grabbed one of the others. They were color-coded so each group had their own. Yellow for Andres and Liz. Orange for Viviana and Ernesto. Red for Marco and myself.

I took the yellow one and yanked open the snaps, rummaging around until I found a vial of pit-viper antivenin. With hands that were trembling ever so slightly, I held it up to the flickering light.

It was different.

The grains were smaller. Less white-looking. I snatched up the first vial and compared the two. They were definitely different. Quickly I checked the vials in the orange kit. They matched the ones in the yellow kit. Same sized granules. Same color. I didn't need a lightbulb over my head to figure out what it meant.

If the pit-viper antivenin in my first aid kit was different, then it was a good bet the coral snake antivenin had been different too. I raised my eyes from the three vials and stared unseeing at the rough, wooden wall of the shed. I felt sick.

Why had Marco died?

Because there was something wrong with the antivenin.

I shoveled the first aid supplies back into the kits and tucked them away on the shelf. Did the orange kit go beside the can of Jumars, or had the yellow one been there? I couldn't remember. I left the orange kit beside the can and prayed to the gods that nobody would notice. Then I turned out the light and stepped out the door . . . right smack into a solid form.

"Oscar!" My heart gave a nasty leap.

"*Lo siento,*" he said. "I did not mean to scare you."

"Um . . . what are you . . . how . . . ?"

His eyes dropped down to the vials of antivenin in my hand.

"Is everything okay?" he asked.

With a nonchalance I didn't feel, I casually put my hand in my pocket.

"Uh . . . yeah. I guess," I answered. "I'm . . . still pretty shocked, actually."

He nodded his head in sympathy. "I cannot believe it, either. Poor Marco. His mother will miss him very much."

"His mum?"

He nodded again. "*Sí.* He is very close to her. Ever since his *padre* died. He is always writing letters to her at night. So she will not be so lonely, you see. He did not have brothers or sisters."

"I didn't know that," I said quietly. Sobered by how much I hadn't known about my field partner, by how much I would now never know.

Oscar's eyes flicked down at my pocket. As if he could see through the fabric to what I was holding.

I resisted the urge to clench my fist around the vials. "Did you . . . did you need something from the shed?" I asked, trying to distract him. "'Cause it's sort of a mess in there. I was just tidying up a bit. I . . . hope you don't mind." I managed to cut myself off before I started babbling.

He shook his head slowly, not taking his eyes off mine. "I do not need anything from the shed," he said. "*Por favor*, if you will excuse me, I am going to my room for a while." His shoulders slumped and he shook his head again. "It is very sad about Marco," he said softly.

My throat closed up. I nodded my agreement. Very sad, indeed.

But that wasn't all it was.

Chapter 34

Andres and Viviana stared at me.

"A . . . murderer?" Andres finally repeated the words, as if perhaps he hadn't heard correctly.

He had.

"It's the only thing that makes sense," I said. "Why are the antivenins different?" I gestured again to the three vials of granules that sat glinting on the table in front of us.

Viviana's eyes flickered down at them, then back up to me.

"I checked each kit," I told them. "The orange and yellow kits are fine. But the pit-viper antivenin in the red kit is different. Look at the size of the granules. The color of them. And all three have the same batch number on them. So it's not that."

"You believe someone has switched them?" Andres said, still looking bewildered.

"And probably the coral snake antivenin too," I said. "The stuff we gave to Marco."

"With what?"

I puffed out my cheeks and exhaled noisily. "I don't know." I shook my head. "And, quite frankly, I'm not about to touch it to my tongue to find out."

"You think it's poison, don't you?" Viviana spoke.

I held her eyes for a long moment, seeing disbelief waver into understanding. "I do," I said quietly. "You saw how Marco died. He wasn't reacting to coral snake venom. Not yet. We had plenty of time. The symptoms from a neurotoxin don't start to show up for hours. He died in a few minutes."

Viviana passed a hand over her eyes. She looked exhausted. "His symptoms were not consistent with a neurotoxin," she said haltingly. "I . . . I did not see that." She took a shaky breath. "Why didn't I realize this?"

Andres had picked up the vials and was examining them closely. At Viviana's question, he raised his eyes. "Because you were in shock," he said. "All of us have been shocked by this."

"Well, brace yourself," I said. "There's more." Briefly I told them about the severed climbing rope. "And those poachers I was chasing? I'm pretty sure one of them was Ramón."

"Oscar's cousin?" Viviana blurted. "Are you certain?"

I shook my head. "No. That's why I didn't say anything till now."

Andres was rubbing the side of his face. "Things have been going wrong from the beginning. First Aleck dies—"

"No," I corrected him. "First Guillermo disappeared."

Andres tried to wave that off. "Guillermo was a poacher," he said.

"Was he?"

Andres snapped his mouth shut and stared at me.

"How well did you know him?"

"I only met him twice."

"Well, Marco spent a lot of time with him and he

thinks Guillermo was just a tourist. A guy who was interested in biology."

"Then why was he shot?"

"I have no idea. But after everything that's happened, I don't think we can just write him off as a poacher."

Andres nodded slowly, conceding the point. "So, first Guillermo disappears. . . ."

"—and turns up dead. Then Candi disappeared. By accident? I don't think so. Not any more."

Andres stared at me again, revelation written in the lines of his face. Clearly, the idea had never occurred to him.

"But . . . who would do this?" Viviana asked the question that was nibbling away at my own peace of mind.

I threw up my hands in frustration. "Ramón, Juan, Ernesto, Oscar, Liz . . . if you don't include Guillermo, then it could be Pepe, Keith, Janet . . . hell, it could be one of us. Your guess is as good as mine."

"It doesn't really matter right now," Andres interrupted us. "We've got to get out of here."

"I know, but don't you think—"

"There will be time later for finding out. After we're all safe. Someone is not what they seem here. We know this. We're cut off and the radio is broken."

"Again?"

"*Sí*. But this time somebody smashed it."

A chill shivered up my spine.

"Marco is dead," Andres was saying. "Pepe is gone who knows where. Someone has changed the antivenin, cut your climbing rope, and now they have broken the radio. We need to get out before there are any more 'accidents'."

"It's too late for today," Viviana said.

I agreed. "We'll never make the boat before night."

"Then we will go right after breakfast tomorrow."

Viviana turned to me. "Does anyone else know about the antivenin?" she asked.

I shook my head. I was fairly sure Oscar hadn't identified the vials in my hand.

"Good," Viviana said. "Andres?" It sounded like a question.

He nodded once, signaling his understanding. "I will tell Oscar and Ernesto that we are leaving for Sirena first thing tomorrow."

"What will you tell them if they ask why?"

"I don't think the others should know," I said quickly. "Not the real reason. If the murderer knows we're suspicious, it might tip him over the edge."

Andres inclined his head. "You're right. Pepe is gone. Marco is dead. That is enough reason to leave."

Viviana considered that for a moment, then nodded decisively. "Yes, that should be good. Robyn and I will tell the others."

We all got to our feet. Primed for action. Relieved now that a decision had been made. That plans were being set in motion. And completely forgetting what the Scottish poet, Robbie Burns, once said about the best-laid plans of mice and men.

When you travel light, it doesn't take you long to pack up your things. I'd stuffed everything in my bags without regard to order or tidiness. Time for that later.

I would have liked to have gotten an e-mail off to Kelt. To let him know that I was okay, that we were leaving. That I was thinking about him. Why this would be so important to do right now, I wasn't sure I wanted to know. And without the satellite phone, it was a moot point anyhow.

I bounced off the walls for a few minutes, watching as Viviana began organizing her own stuff.

"Perhaps Ernesto needs some help," she suggested pointedly. "He is still suffering from the ant bites, you know."

"Good idea," I managed an apologetic smile. "I'll be over there if you need me."

She shooed me out with a flick of her hands. I crossed the compound and stepped up into the shadowy gloom of the lab.

Ernesto's tiny room was in the southwest corner. Right beside Marco's room. My jaw tightened and I had to avert my eyes as I walked past it. I couldn't face looking at Marco's things right now.

Ernesto was still in bed. As my eyes adjusted to the dim light, I could see that he was pale, his cheeks sunken. Still sick, then. But he was awake and struggling to sit up.

"*Hola*," I said.

He gave me a tight smile and nodded a greeting.

"Andres told you?"

His lips pressed together. "*Sí*. I am very sorry for you about Marco. *Me gusto*. He was a good man."

I tried to swallow the lump in my throat. "He was," I said simply. Then, "Do you need a hand packing things up? I can throw some stuff in a dufflebag for you if you want to have a shower or something."

Ernesto closed his eyes for a moment. When he opened them, they were bright with unshed tears. "*Gracias*," he said. "It is very kind of you."

I didn't quite know how to respond to his emotion. I turned my attention to a couple of old crates that were doubling as bookshelves. They contained several field guides and a dog-eared novel. I squinted to read the title. *Harry Potter y la piedra filosofal.* Ernesto was reading Harry Potter?

"Um . . . do you want me to pack this up?" I asked, indicating the shelf.

"*Gracias,*" he said again. "I do not want to leave my books behind."

"Which backpack is yours?"

"The blue one. It's in the closet beside . . . beside Marco's room. Robyn—"

I stopped on my way out the door and looked back.

"Robyn." He looked at a loss for words. "I . . . I wanted . . . I have been wanting to say . . . *muchas gracias.* Thank you. For pulling me from the *bala* ants. I did not know they would make me sick. I am very thankful you were there that day."

I gave him a lopsided smile. "Me too," I said. "And you're welcome. I know you would've done the same for me."

"But . . . I was . . . ," he fell silent, searching for the words. "I was a poacher once," he blurted out. "A trafficker. You have many reasons not to help me." There was a question in his eyes.

I hesitated, unsure how to answer it. "You *were* a poacher," I said finally, emphasizing the tense, "and, I admit, I despise that. But you're not anymore. And that's a very good reason to help you. Now I'm going to go find that backpack of yours, so why don't you try getting yourself out of bed."

He looked at me for a long moment, then his expression cleared. "*Gracias,*" he said again.

I knew what he meant.

"*De nada,*" I said.

The storage closet in the lab was about as tidy as the shed had been before I'd cleaned it up. The musty smell of mold tickled my nostrils and I looked in dismay at the pile of gear that had been tossed haphazardly into the corner. I didn't even know we *had* this much stuff at Danta.

I spied a dark-colored backpack in the middle of the pile. A few sharp tugs and it came free. I jumped and suppressed a shudder as a fat centipede plopped down at my feet and scurried off into the gloom. There was a kerosene lamp hanging from a rusted hook, so I fired it up and brought the pack closer to the light, intending to check for any other unwelcome hitchhikers.

Thunk!

The pack hit the wooden wall. Had Ernesto left a book inside? The second Harry Potter, perhaps? Without thinking, I unzipped the bag and held it open to the light. But what I found wasn't another installment in the adventures of prepubescent wizards. Wasn't even a book, for that matter. Inside Ernesto's bag, there was a gun.

I don't know much about guns, but I know a bit. This wasn't some little pistol. It wasn't a machine gun, either. It looked like something in between. Something that meant business.

I heard a step behind me.

"Robyn?" Ernesto was standing in the door frame. "Did you find my . . . oh, this is not my bag," he said, gesturing to the pack in my hands.

"It's not?"

"No. I think this was belonging to the man who was shot."

"Guillermo?" I stared at him stupidly.

"*Sí.* That is what Oscar told me. Nobody has asked for

his things so they stay here for now." He shrugged and took a shaky step into the room. I could see how unsteady he was on his feet.

"Hey, are you okay?" I asked, forgetting about the gun for a second.

"I have been better," he said with a wobbly smile. "*Aqui.* Here is my bag." He bent to pull another backpack out of the pile and staggered back against the door frame.

"Take it easy," I said sharply. "Here. I've got it."

Ernesto was breathing hard.

"Maybe you should go back to bed." I frowned.

But Ernesto shook his head. "No. I need to get up and move if I am wanting to leave tomorrow. But if you could pack my books and the other things on the shelves, I will be very happy."

"No problem. You going to hit the showers?"

He smiled at my phrasing. "I am going to hit them, yes."

"Okay, I'll see you at dinner, then."

Why would somebody have a gun at Danta? For safety? Safety from what? Jaguars? Peccaries? Poachers? If that was the case, then why was it hidden?

I strongly doubted the gun belonged to the late Guillermo. For one thing, the rest of the man's belongings hadn't been in the bag. I'd found them shoved underneath some broken equipment. Concealed from casual view. So why had someone gone to all that trouble to hide a gun? The obvious answer was because it was a murder weapon. And the only person who had been shot was Guillermo.

Guillermo. The man everybody seemed to think was a poacher. But what evidence did we have for this? Nothing really beyond the simple fact that he'd been shot. Why hadn't we questioned that a little more? We had all been so certain he was trafficking.

Except Marco, I thought. Marco never bought that story. Marco had stood firm in his belief that Guillermo was just what he'd appeared to be—a Costa Rican tourist with a penchant for biology. And now Marco was dead. Along with Guillermo. Along with Aleck and probably Candi. So many dead.

I packed up Ernesto's things, thinking about the people who had died. I decided to ask Andres and Viviana about the gun. To see if they could come up with another reason why a gun like this might be hidden in an old backpack. But by the time I tracked them down to the dining hall, everybody else was there too and the evening meal was underway. Hardly the time to bring it up. I'd have to wait until after dinner.

I sat down beside Viviana, noticing that Marco's usual place at the end of the table had been left vacant. The tears pricked at my eyes. I couldn't believe he was gone.

"Are you all packed for tomorrow?" Andres asked, passing me a bowl of beans.

"Yeah, I'm ready."

"And Ernesto?" Viviana asked from across the table. "He is ready too?"

I wasn't hungry, but I fumbled a tortilla off the plate. I was determined to maintain a semblance of normalcy, though nobody else seemed to have much of an appetite, either. I nodded in response to Viviana's question. "As ready as I could get him."

"You should really tell Ernesto to come and eat,"

Viviana said to Andres. "It will be hard for him to hike out tomorrow. He has not eaten properly since the ants."

"He said he'd be here for dinner," I assured her. "He went to have a shower. In fact," I looked at my watch and frowned, "he should be here by now."

Andres gave me a sharp look. "Was he okay?"

"Well, no. Not really. He was pretty shaky on his feet."

Viviana caught Andres' eyes. "Maybe you should check on him," she said softly.

"Good idea." Andres pushed away from the table and slipped outside.

"What's wrong?" Janet asked nervously.

Viviana patted her hand. "Nothing for worrying about. Ernesto has been very sick. He might have fainted, that's all."

But it wasn't.

Chapter 35

"Ernesto is dead," Andres announced. "In the shower."

His face was pale and splotchy-looking with shock. As I stared at him, I saw a tremor ripple through his body.

"*What?*" Viviana jumped to her feet. "What do you mean? Are you sure?"

Andres caught her arm before she could leave the hall. "I am certain," he said quietly.

She stopped and searched his eyes, not bothering to shake off his hand. "Ernesto is dead?" she repeated, the implications starting to sink in. "How?"

"*Escorpione,*" Andres told her.

I didn't need a Spanish-English dictionary to figure out what an *escorpione* was. I saw Janet's already pale complexion whiten. She covered her mouth with her hand. As if to prevent her own soul from escaping.

"It must have been in the shower," Andres was saying. "I found the stinger under his body. It looks like it was very quick."

"But. . . ." My mind had leaped ahead. "But, why didn't he call us?" I asked. "Why didn't he come out of the shower? I didn't think scorpion venom acted that quickly. I thought—"

"Could have been a combination of things," Liz

mused. She didn't sound particularly upset by the news. "The allergic reaction. All those bullet ant stings. Maybe it just overloaded his immune system."

I eyed her with distaste. If it hadn't been for her, Ernesto wouldn't have had all those bullet ant stings in the first place. She gazed back at me without expression.

Andres put a calming hand on my shoulder. "I do not know why he died," he said. "Perhaps it was, as Liz says, an overload. But for right now, Keith, Oscar, I'm sorry, but I need you to come and help me get him out of the shower. We'll put him in the spare cabin."

The one where Aleck had died. Where Marco's body now rested.

"What about tomorrow?" Viviana asked after a moment. "How are we going to—?"

"We'll have to leave them here," Andres interrupted her. "We cannot carry two bodies back with us. The rangers will come for them. Right now, it is more important for us all to get out safely."

"Maybe we should spend the night here in the dining hall," Janet suggested in a small voice.

"Don't worry," he told her kindly. "These are terrible accidents. Very shocking. But you must not react too much. We will all try to get rest for tomorrow. Tired people make mistakes and it will be a difficult day. If we are rested, then there is less chance of more accidents."

If I hadn't known better, I might have been reassured by his little speech. As it was, I found myself examining the faces around me. Wondering if I was the only one who found Andres' words a little too glib.

Viviana and I left the dining hall with everyone else, quietly, without discussion. We walked Janet and Liz to their respective cabins. Our solemn goodnights were like a bad joke. It was doubtful any of us would have a pleasant night. By the time Viviana and I reached our own cabin, I could hear the grunts of effort across the compound as Ernesto's body was extracted from the showers and carried to the spare cabin. I closed the door on the sounds.

And the rain began falling.

X-Originating-IP: [199.137.52.16]

From: "Robyn Devara"
<macaw1@woodrowconsultants.com>
To: "Kelt Roberson" <batnerd@tnc.com>
Subject:
Date: Mon 10 Jun 02:39:57-1100

Dear Kelt,

I'm not really sure why I'm writing to you. I have no way of sending this e-mail. But it's almost 3:00 am, it's still pouring rain, and I can't sleep. Talking to you—even like this—makes me feel a little better.

Marco and Ernesto died today. I still can't believe it, even after typing the words. I thought at first all these deaths were accidents, but I know now that Marco, at least, was murdered. I'm starting to worry about getting out of here alive.

Gods, I wish you were here, or rather, I wish I was there. I miss you. I miss talking to you and joking with you and even arguing with you. I miss watching bad sci-fi movies with you with Guido the cat snuggled in between us. I miss swapping mystery novels and going out for falafels. I miss watching you try not to make a face everytime you eat something I've cooked. I miss YOU.

As I sit here wide-awake on this horrible night, my one regret is that I never told you how much you mean to me. How much more I want you to mean to me. We always seem to miss each other's signals. But let me say for the record . . . you take my breath away. The first time we met, something inside me recognized you. I'm sorry it took me this long to realize what it meant. I'm sorry I didn't recognize your ambivalence as lack of self-confidence. You showed me how much you cared in so many ways and I was too clued-out to see it. So many missed opportunities. If I was there right now . . . well, no sense going down that road. I've got to stay focused for tomorrow. So I can get through this in one piece. So I can come back to you.

I doubt I'll ever be brave enough to send you this letter. But when I get back, there are a few things I'm going to say. Until then, I hope, on some level, you know that I'm thinking about you.

Robyn

To do science is to search for repeated patterns, not simply to accumulate facts. . . .

Robert MacArthur
Geographical Ecology: Patterns in the Distribution of Species

Chapter 36

It was still raining the next morning.

Rain. Even the word sounds gentle. Tripping off the tongue like spring showers misting sleeping gardens into flower. In the tropics, there should have been another name for it.

All through the previous night, rain had thundered down on the earth. Beating leaves, flowers, entire plants into the ground. Turning trails into swirling streams of muck, and washing rocks and debris down slippery slopes. By dawn, the field station was flooded, the ground unable to absorb the deluge. And even worse, it showed no sign of letting up with the break of day.

We gathered in the dining hall for breakfast. Faces pale, eyes smudged with shadows. Expressions lightening with relief to see everyone was well.

"I think we must wait until the rain stops," Andres said to us all. "I have checked the trail, I'm afraid it's not in good condition."

I nodded slightly, unsurprised by his decision. But Janet looked miserable and I saw Keith slip a comforting arm around her.

"Any idea when this'll stop?" Keith asked, jerking his head towards the window.

Andres threw his hands in the air. "I have no clues," he said. "It should not be raining like this at this time of year. Usually the heavy rains are in October or November."

"Well, can't we just hike out anyway?" Janet asked. "I mean, so what if we get wet? If we go slowly—"

Andres was already shaking his head. "It's not being wet that is a problem," he told her. "The trails are very slippery and they are probably washed out in some spots. The streams will be flooded and so will the river. They will be fast and full of branches and small trees. There is also a danger of flash floods."

It was sobering to hear how isolated we were now—and we were already a pretty sober bunch.

"So we're stuck here," Liz said sourly.

I raised a quizzical eyebrow at her tone. Yesterday she'd scoffed at Andres for closing down the station. Now she wanted to leave?

"Perhaps we can work around the station today," Viviana suggested. "We can put everything in order so it will be easier when we come back."

When we come back.

Under the circumstances, it seemed an overly optimistic statement. But maybe that's what we needed right now—a good dose of optimism. And besides, a task might help us take our mind off things.

Or not.

Aleck. Candi. Marco. Ernesto. Guillermo. I thought about them as we began crating up supplies and equipment. I crammed a field reference guide in a plastic baggie and stacked it in the wooden box. Worst-case scenario: they had all been murdered. Why? Well, Aleck hadn't been a pleasant individual. Ernesto had had a pretty shady past. But Candi? Marco? Guillermo? Who would want to kill them?

Who. Perhaps the most important question of all. I stuffed a few more books into the box. If I included Guillermo on the list, then that narrowed my choice of suspects substantially, eliminating Andres, Viviana, Ernesto, and all the Berkeley crowd. Or, I hesitated . . . did it? Thoughtfully, I stacked another reference book on top of the others. Andres had been here before. He said he'd met Guillermo. And hadn't Pepe come out for a few days as well? Yes. I remembered him saying something to Viviana about checking the place out before he came to study. Had he been here at the same time Guillermo went missing?

"A *colòn* for your thoughts," Liz said as she brought over a couple of smaller crates.

"Excuse me?"

"You looked pretty unhappy."

"Not much to be smiling about, it seems."

"Yeah." She shoved one of the crates on the shelf beside mine. "I keep thinking about Pepe."

She wasn't the only one.

"I just wonder why he left like that. So abruptly. Without saying a word to anyone. It makes you wonder what he was up to. Although," Liz paused to heave the second crate onto the shelf, "it seems like *he* got out just in time."

"What do you mean?"

"This rain," she gestured out the window. I could barely see the cabins thirty feet away. "It'll go for longer than a couple of days, take my word on it. We might be socked in here for weeks."

My throat suddenly felt tight.

"Why do you think he left?" I asked, trying to take my mind off the possibility.

"Trafficking, of course," Liz replied. "I suspect he was in it up to his greedy little eyeballs."

"Yeah," I said grimly, "Viviana and I came to the same conclusion." I went over to the dining table and started packing another crate.

If Pepe was trafficking, did that mean he was also our killer? His strange disappearance was certainly damning. All his gear gone with him. Nobody knowing when or how he'd left—or how far away he'd gone.

According to Ernesto, traffickers these days were violent men. Well-armed. But when it came right down to it, the only death I was certain was unnatural—besides Guillermo's—was Marco's. So why would well-armed wildlife traffickers resort to putting poison in an antivenin kit? It didn't fit the profile. Unless they were trying to frighten us away from Danta. Trying to clear the playing field so they could hunt the amethyst macaws without interruption.

I chewed my bottom lip. I didn't like that scenario one bit. Not that I cared much for any other explanation I could come up with. I kept hoping that somehow I was mistaken. That four people had died in the last month because of accidents.

Yeah, right.

The more I thought about poachers trying to scare us off, the more I kept thinking about that hidden gun. As in, how did it fit in? If Pepe was a murderer, why would he hide a gun in Guillermo's backpack? It didn't make sense. An unpleasant thought struck me. What kind of bullets went in a gun like that? I hadn't thought to check. But what if it took the same kind of bullets as the ones I'd found in the TRC house in San José? Would that mean one of my team members had put it there? As far as I knew, Pepe had never been in that house. But Andres had, along with Liz, Ernesto, and probably Oscar and Viviana.

I hoisted the full crate onto a shelf with a disgusted grunt. I hated this kind of speculation. I felt guilty for considering my friends and full of self-doubt for considering the others. Well, there was only one way to set my mind at rest about it.

"I'm going over to the lab to get a few more crates," I told Viviana.

She nodded. "Can you see if there is another lamp that works too? It's getting very dark in here."

"Sure."

I pulled my raincoat on and sloshed over to the lab. Once I was out of the rain, I didn't waste any time. Without even pausing to slide off my coat, I strode over to the storage closet and fumbled for the kerosene lamp. It was like night in there. The flame flickered once, then died. I cursed and tried again. It worked the second time.

By the wavering glow, I scanned the messy room. The backpack was just where I'd left it. Off to the right of the door. But as soon as I picked it up, I knew somebody had beaten me to it. Even before I unzipped the main compartment, I could feel the difference in weight. I held it up to the light to make sure. The gun was gone.

"Do you need some help?"

I jumped and whirled around.

Oscar was standing in the doorway. He looked at my face, then down at the backpack still clutched in my fingers.

"Are you looking for something?" he asked.

"I, uh . . . I was just trying to find some more crates," I managed to say. "I thought there might be some in here, but all I've found are backpacks." With a casualness belied by my thumping heart, I tossed the empty pack back onto the pile.

He gave me a funny look. "Why didn't you just take the crates from the lab?"

"The lab?"

"*Sí.* Look, there are many crates right here against the wall."

I turned to where he was pointing. A dozen crates were stacked neatly against the wall. In full view of the storage closet. "Oh," I laughed awkwardly. "I guess I didn't see them there."

Even to my ears, it sounded weak.

It was my turn to help Oscar with dinner that night. I can't say I was looking forward to the job. All afternoon, I'd been racking my brains, trying to think of a more plausible explanation for why I'd been rooting around in the lab's storage closet. So far, I hadn't come up with a single one. But as it turned out, it didn't matter.

"*¡Hola,* Oscar!" I greeted him when I stepped up into the kitchen. Determined to pretend there was nothing wrong.

Oscar was at the counter, chopping up vegetables. I could smell a pot of beans simmering on the stove. I thought at first he hadn't heard me. Hadn't caught my greeting over the sound of the rain. I tried again.

"*¡Hola,* Oscar!" A little louder this time.

He glanced up at me and nodded once. Curtly. And I

realized he'd heard me the first time. Heard me and ignored me.

I cleared my throat. "I'm here to help with dinner," I said.

"It is not needed."

"But you're chopping stuff. I could give you a hand with that."

He kept his eyes on the task. "I do not need help," he rumbled.

I watched him hack through another squash. "Is . . . is everything okay?" I asked.

"Everything is fine," he replied.

But he wouldn't meet my eyes.

I wandered out into the empty dining area, feeling uneasy and on edge. I sat down at the plank table and rested my chin in my hand, considering what I really knew about Oscar.

He was a beefy, generally good-humored character. Fun. Patient with my feeble attempts at cuisine. Interested in our study and fascinated with the amethyst macaws. He'd known that Marco had written to his mum. But what about those 'cousins' of his? Had I really seen Ramón running away from the clay lick? If so, then that put a whole new spin on our friendly station manager—and his interest in our macaws.

Before I could go any further with this line of thought, Viviana joined me at the table.

"You look like I feel," I told her, taking in her haggard appearance.

She was quite white, her freckles standing out like splatters of dark ink against her pale skin. There was an oddly greenish cast to her face and the dark circles under her eyes were like bruises.

"Hey, are you okay?" I asked, after a closer examination. "You really look bad."

"I am not feeling well," she admitted. "It has been a hard day."

I nodded my agreement.

"I have been trying not to think about . . . well, you know. But it is difficult."

I nodded again. "Tell me about it."

"It's. . . ." She looked around and lowered her voice. I had to bend closer to hear her over the rain. "I have been wondering who would want to hurt Marco. All day, I've been thinking of this. But Robyn, maybe it was not meant for Marco. That kit was for both of you."

I stared at her. I suppose on some level, I'd realized the same thing. And something on that level decided it didn't need to go any further up on the conscious thought-o-meter.

"*Lo siento,*" Viviana was saying. "I didn't want to worry you."

"That's okay."

"It seems better to be cautious."

"I know."

But my stomach twisted uneasily.

Viviana closed her eyes and rubbed her temples. "I really do not feel well," she told me. "I think I will maybe have a nap."

"Want me to wake you for dinner?"

She shook her head and winced at the movement. "No, *gracias*. I don't think I will be eating tonight."

"I'm not hungry, either. I don't think any of us have much of an appetite."

She stood up but before she left the dining hall, she turned back to me, a puzzled look furrowing her brow. "Aren't you supposed to be helping Oscar?" she asked.

I shrugged. “Apparently, he doesn’t need my help.”
She gave me a searching gaze. “I see,” she said finally.
I wished I did.

CHAPTER 37

The following morning, I had to slop through ankle-deep mud to get to the outhouse.

The rain still pounded down relentlessly, and Viviana was very ill, complaining of sore muscles and a stabbing headache. Two red fever spots were the only color on her face and she'd been coughing since dawn, a dry, rasping sound.

I didn't think things could get much worse, until Keith came knocking at our cabin door.

"Have you got any Kaopectate?" he asked urgently.

I shushed him and pointed to Viviana's sleeping form. Then I pulled the door behind me and joined him on the step.

"I think so. Are you sick?" I asked.

He shook his head. "No, it's Janet. She must have picked up a bug or something. She's been up all night. I'm afraid she's getting dehydrated. She can't even keep water down. She could barely make it to the outhouse last time. I don't know what—"

"Calm down," I ordered.

He stopped and I saw his chest heave as he drew in a deep breath.

"Viviana's sick too," I told him. "I was just going to wake Andres up."

"Is it the same thing Janet's got?"

I shook my head. "No, I don't know what's wrong with her. But she's worse than she was last night. Even if the rain stops, she'll never be able to hike out. And neither would Janet, from the sounds of it."

"We're going to have to get help," Keith said.

"I know. I've been thinking we might be able to get a helicopter in here."

Keith turned and looked out at the waterlogged station. "A helicopter?" he said doubtfully. "There's no room for one to land."

"I thought so too at first. But look, the whole area around the showers is relatively free of vegetation. If we pulled down the shower stalls and cut away the larger bushes, a helicopter should be able to land over there."

His expression had brightened as I pointed it out. I really hated to burst his bubble.

"But first," I said, "somebody's got to get to Sirena."

His face fell.

I knew exactly how he felt.

Keith and Andres left for Sirena an hour later. They were back five hours after that. Drenched, covered in mud, and shivering.

I hastened to pour them some coffee.

"How's Janet?" Keith asked, before he took a sip.

"Not great," I said. "But she's hanging in."

"You didn't get to Sirena, did you?" Liz asked intently.

Andres shook his head and answered her through chattering teeth. "No. The boat is gone."

"Gone!" I exclaimed.

"Washed away by the river, I think," Andres said.

"The river's completely flooded," Keith said. "The whole damn mooring's under water."

I frowned. "We've got to find a way to get to the ranger station. We can't leave Marco and Ernesto in that cabin for too much longer. And," I paused, reluctant to be the bearer of more bad news, "Viviana's really sick."

Andres looked up from his coffee cup.

"She still has a fever and her cough is worse. Very phlegmy." I hesitated again. "I think... I think she might have psittacosis."

Andres swore under his breath.

"What's that?" Keith asked. "Is it bad?"

"It's a disease carried by parrots," I explained. "You get it from handling them. Normally, it just makes you kind of fluey, but if it goes untreated, it can develop into pneumonia."

"And Viviana was handling that amethyst macaw before it died."

I nodded. "She was the only one who touched it."

"How bad is her breathing?" Andres asked, his voice a combination of concern and bone-deep weariness.

"Bad."

Silence followed.

"I'm going to check on Janet," Keith said, putting his cup down. "I'll be back. Maybe we can come up with another plan."

Andres stared at his own cup until long after Keith had left. Finally he raised his eyes and regarded Liz and me.

"Where is Oscar?" he asked.

"Staying in his cabin, I think," I replied.

Andres tensed. "But he is okay? Has anyone checked on him?"

Liz blinked at Andres, puzzled by his intensity. "I saw

him about an hour ago," she said. "He made himself something to eat and went back to his room."

Andres relaxed.

Liz looked from Andres to me.

"You want me to go get him?" I asked quickly, trying to deflect her interest.

"*Gracias,*" Andres said with a nod. "We need to find another plan and many heads are better than one."

I patted his hand and got to my feet.

"What's going on?" Liz demanded. "Why are you so worried about Oscar?"

Somehow, Andres managed a wobbly smile. "I am just tired," he lied. "Everything seems much worse when you are tired."

I glanced back at them as I left the building. Liz was staring at Andres, clearly unsatisfied with his answer. If I hadn't known the real reason for his concern, I wouldn't have been too happy with it myself.

CHAPTER 38

The rain pounded incessantly against the corrugated metal roof of our cabin, drowning out any other sound, obliterating all thought with its torrential roar. Viviana thrashed and turned in her bed. She'd kicked off the weight of her sleeping bag, but the liner was twisted tightly around her limbs. Her face was shiny in the dim light, her skin flushed and curiously translucent. The fever had a good hold on her.

"Hang in there," I said, more to hear the sound of something other than the damned rain. I could barely hear my voice.

To my surprise, she opened her eyes.

"Viviana!" I cried in surprise.

Her gaze was clouded and she stared at me for a moment without comprehension.

"Viviana." I called softly to her again, but her eyes fluttered shut without seeing me.

I did my best to straighten her sleeping bag liner before going back to my vigil by the lamp. My field notebook lay open on the table in front of me but I couldn't bring myself to write in it. What was I supposed to put down? I'm trapped in the middle of the jungle, someone is killing us, all hell has broken loose, and I'm afraid I won't get out of here alive. It might make for exciting reading back home, but it was hardly helpful now.

We'd spent the rest of the afternoon trying to come up with a plan to get out of here. Or at least to get help *in* here. But the discussion went round and round without any viable ideas spinning off. I'd finally left to be with Viviana in case she woke up.

I scrubbed my forehead with my fist. If only this rain would let up.

The dark gray of afternoon faded into the inky blackness of night, and a damp chill settled over the station. Viviana's feverish struggles seemed to ease, but I was afraid the cool temperatures might add to the problem. I stood up, my legs stiff from sitting in the same position for so long.

She was still sweating, her dark hair plastered across her face in seaweed-like clumps. I wrung out a cloth and sponged off her face and neck. She was burning up. Her temperature must have been well over a hundred. I knew it was dangerous for an adult to run a high fever, but right now there wasn't much I could do except maybe try to get some aspirin into her. I helped her sit up and coaxed her into swallowing the pills.

I had a spare sleeping bag liner so I rolled her gently off her own sweat-soaked one and replaced it with mine. At least it was dry—though in this humidity, "dry" was a relative term. I don't think she was aware of what I was doing, but her rest seemed easier after I'd finished.

And still the storm roared down.

I felt very alone. Cut off from the outside world by the failure or sabotage of our communications equipment, cut off from the other members of the team by the sheer magnitude of the deluge. I was feeling the chill now, goosebumps rising on my arms, my teeth beginning to chatter. I rummaged around in my dufflebag. There was a fleecy in here somewhere. Ah! There. I yanked on the fabric of it, an incongruously cheerful apple red. As I pulled, something fell to the floor. I didn't hear it fall—couldn't hear it with all that rain—but I saw a brief flash in the light. I crouched down and peered into the corner. A cassette tape?

I picked it up and tilted it towards the light. Rachmaninoff's *Etudes for Two Pianos.* It was the tape Kelt had made for me. I'd forgotten all about it. I squeezed my eyes shut and tried to ignore the way my throat closed up at the thought of Kelt.

I dug around in my bag and dragged out my Walkman, hearing his voice, like a distant dream, describing the music.

"It's very beautiful, very relaxing. Almost spiritual. I think you'll love it."

Well, if ever I needed to be relaxed and spiritually uplifted, it was now. I covered my ears with the headphones and pressed play.

One banana, two banana, three banana, four—

What the . . . ? My eyes flew open but before I could press the stop button, I heard Kelt's voice in my ears.

"Hey, Robyn! Who wants to listen to classical music when you can listen to Saturday morning cartoon themes? I hope you're having a great time. Don't forget to spare a thought for me up here in the frozen north once in a while. And remember, I *really* miss you!"

Four bananas make a bunch and so do many more.
Over hill and highway the banana buggies go
Coming on to bring you the Banana Splits show.

"You bastard!" I exclaimed aloud, but I was smiling.

Tra la la la la la la. . . .

It was just so quintessentially Kelt. Here I'd been expecting the soothing strains of Rachmaninoff and he'd given me The Banana Splits. It was exactly what I needed. With the rain thundering down outside, my field partner dead, Viviana sick and feverish beside me, and a killer on the loose, I listened to Spiderman and The Groovy Ghoulies and Magilla Gorilla and laughed until my sides were sore.

It was either that, or cry.

CHAPTER 39

Morning. The rain still pounded the forest, the clouds barely lightening with the onset of day. Viviana's temperature was still high. But even more disturbing was the blood-tinged sputum she'd started coughing up. I had to do something. I was very much afraid that she wasn't going to make it.

"Don't go anywhere on me," I told her as I straightened her sleeping bag. "I'm just going to have a word with Andres."

She didn't open her eyes.

I pulled a rain poncho over my head. A futile move. I was so damp that a little more moisture wouldn't make much difference. But I was running on autopilot now. I tipped a cockroach out of my boots, stamped into them, and ducked across the clearing to Andres' cabin.

"Andres," I called, rapping smartly on his door. The waterlogged wood absorbed my knock. It was possible he wasn't up yet. It *was* very early. I knocked again. "Andres, are you awake?"

I pressed my ear against the door. I couldn't hear anything in this gods-cursed rain.

"Andres! Wake—"

The door opened and I looked up into Andres' white face.

"Shit," I swore. "You're sick too?"

He staggered back to bed as I surged into the room. "Yes, all night. Keith is also not well."

"The same thing Janet has?"

He crawled back into his sleeping bag with a moan. "Yes, I think so. How is Viviana?"

"Much worse."

He cursed weakly.

"I'm worried," I told him, then hesitated. "Andres, I'm going to try to get to Sirena."

"*What?* Robyn, the boat is gone, the river is flooded—"

"I know. But I'm a good swimmer. I even won ribbons when I was a kid. Backstroke. Second place." I tried to smile, but it died on my lips.

"But Robyn, that river, it's not calm—"

"I know," I said again, then I took a deep breath. "Andres, she's got pneumonia and I can't keep her temperature down. If we don't get help soon . . . ," I trailed off.

Andres stared up at me, his black eyes shining with fever.

"Enough of us have died," I said.

"Robyn," he began, then stopped. He knew I was right. We needed help and we needed it now. "At least take Oscar with you. You know you shouldn't hike by yourself."

Take Oscar with me? Not likely.

I'd had a lot of time to think things over the previous night. And one name kept cropping up. Oscar. I was now certain that it had been Ramón and Juan setting nets at the clay lick. Poaching. I hadn't figured out where Pepe fit in all this yet, but Oscar fit all too well.

His cousins had built Aleck's cabin, complete with a handy hole in the floorboards just big enough for a fer-de-lance to slip through. And when I'd found that constrictor in the kitchen, Oscar had handled it like a pro—or like a trafficker who was used to handling snakes. I had a feeling he was probably a dab hand with fer-de-lances too. Oscar looked after all our gear, including the climbing ropes and the first aid kits. It would have been easy for him to slice a rope, to substitute poison for antivenin.

He kept popping up in unexpected places. I was certain that he'd known exactly which backpack I'd had in my hand the other day. And I had a feeling he knew why I'd been searching it. But apart from all this, he was the one—the only one!—who had cooked dinner the other night. A dinner that had left Janet, and now Andres and Keith, very sick. Thank gods I hadn't eaten that night. Taking Oscar along on this desperately stupid venture was the last thing I wanted to do.

Andres saw my hesitation. "Robyn!" He grabbed my arm, his fingers pressing painfully into the muscle. "Promise me! Take Oscar with you. *Es fatal.* It's too dangerous. Do not try to do this alone."

Gently, I disengaged his fingers. They left bright spots of red on my skin.

"I promise," I told him. "You stay here and rest. Check on Viviana if you're feeling better. I'll be back as soon as I can."

I ran back to the cabin and started gathering my things. Water bottle. Some granola bars that I'd kept for emergencies. My Swiss Army knife. A map. And what about a rope? It might come in handy if things got too slippery. I glanced outside. True dawn was just breaking.

Now that I'd made up my mind to go, I didn't want anyone seeing me. But I needed a rope.

There were ropes in the storage shed, but Oscar slept on the other side of that shed. I couldn't chance his hearing me. There was only one other place I could get a rope. I scanned the grounds. Nobody was stirring. I slipped out the door, making sure it didn't smack shut behind me. Then I dashed over to the dryer.

The plastic sheets bulged heavily with water. I had to duck low so I didn't dump them. A sheet in the corner had broken beneath the weight and the ground was slick with mud. Five ropes stretched from one side of the frame to the other. Quickly I began sawing the nearest one with my knife. The rope was swollen with water and splotchy with mold, but it would have to do.

Thump!

Even through the pounding rain, I heard the muffled noise. I spun around and crouched down, my eyes darting towards the other cabins. I held my breath and waited, but all I could hear was rain. Maybe a tree had fallen, or a branch. I waited another minute, then I stood cautiously and began coiling the severed rope over my shoulder. Another careful scan of the compound. Still deserted. I ducked past the orange tarp and scuttled back to the cabin.

Safely inside, I tied the rope to the side of my pack and settled the whole thing onto my shoulders. I noticed the machete by the door, hesitated for a moment, then picked it up and fastened it to my belt. Viviana hadn't moved.

I stood over her for a long moment. "I'll be back," I promised.

For whatever that was worth.

Then, before I could change my mind, I slipped out the door, closing it softly behind me.

Chapter 40

Soaked.

Miserable.

Afraid.

I was all these things.

I slid and squelched down the washed-out path, stubbing my toes on hidden rocks, sliding on slick roots.

A small clearing.

A faceful of water.

Choking. Coughing.

The realization that I might drown while walking through a forest.

The thought made me bark with laughter, but it sounded edgy and I could hear the note of panic in it. I choked it off.

It was still dark, though it was already mid-morning. As dark as night. As dark as a tomb, my overactive imagination chimed in. I ignored it with a grimace and stopped to catch my breath, hoping the deluge would let up soon, convinced it would not. Why should the gods take pity on me now?

Leaves, vines, clods of moss, and torn bits of epiphytes tumbled down along with the rain, which was falling, not in the sheets you always hear about, but more in duvets. Thick, heavy duvets of choking, cold water.

I was alone in the jungle.

Up until this point, the rainforest had seemed like a fairy wonderland of fascinating flora and fauna. Now it struck me by its very alienness. Mottled leaves pretending disease fought with each other for the meager light. Bulging spiders sat on their webs, bloated with the night's kill. Vines choked everything. Squeezing, strangling life in their quest for survival. The air was oppressive and heavy with the rotting smell of corruption and decay. I sensed rather than saw the fer-de-lance coiled in the leaf litter, the marching bullet ants bristling with aggression, the centipedes lurking in dark crevices. It was a goddamn war zone. What the hell was I doing here? I had never felt so out of place in my life.

Another faceful of rain. I coughed, overcome by a burning desire to breathe crisp, northern air, to hike through the sharply scented and oh-so-familiar forests of Canada. What were bears and cougars compared to the hidden dangers of a tropical jungle? In this predator-rich environment, every lifeform could be on *Survivor*.

I missed my life in Canada. I missed my apartment. I missed my cat.

"One of these things is not like the others," I sang softly to myself, trying to lighten my mood with humor. "One of these things doesn't belong. . . ." But the dense vegetation and pounding rain absorbed my voice easily, deadening the sound to an insignificant murmur. So much for the power of *Sesame Street.*

Lack of sleep was making me clumsy and the faint trail was almost impassable. I slid again, tripped up by the spreading buttress roots of a large tree. I grabbed at the trunk, caught it and clung to it. And with a cry of surprise, let go just as quickly.

"Shit!" I swore.

Something had stung me.

I held my palm up. There was a bright red splotch by my index finger. It hurt like a son-of-a-bitch. I peered through the rain at the tree trunk. I didn't see anything. No, wait! Was that movement? Between those bromeliads. I bent closer and carefully moved a leaf to one side. Yes.

There was a scorpion on the tree.

It was huge—at least four inches in length. The body and pincers were blackish-brown, the legs an evil sulphur yellow. I sucked in a breath of air. A scorpion! Ernesto had died from a scorpion.

Waves of pain radiated up my arm and I thought I could feel a tingling sensation on my tongue. Was this what Ernesto had felt in the moments before his death?

Relax, Robyn.

I closed my eyes and forced myself to breathe slowly. In and out, slow and calm.

Panicking isn't going to help anything.

In and out.

Don't worry.

In and out.

There aren't any deadly scorpions in Costa Rica.

In and. . . .

And then, the pain in my hand suddenly cleared the fogginess in my brain, and I listened to what I was telling myself.

There aren't any deadly scorpions in Costa Rica.

And I knew, like the flash of a starship going into warp, that Aleck, Candi, Marco, and Ernesto had been murdered. More importantly, I knew who the murderer was.

CHAPTER 41

It had taken a scorpion to sting me into recognizing repeated patterns. I'd been so busy accumulating facts that I'd forgotten to look for the patterns—the very basis of scientific inquiry. It had taken a scorpion to remind me of a scorpion. Ernesto had not been the only member of Danta who'd been killed by one of these arachnids.

It had happened over a decade ago. Danta had been shut down because of it. Ten years ago, Scott Gray had been killed by a scorpion. And the only similarity in the patterns beyond the location was one person. Lizabeth Brechtel.

When Danta had been closed all those years ago, the unique fauna of the area was protected by its very isolation. No roads. No trails for scientists to wander. No trails for poachers to use. And that was why Liz had turned killer. To protect Danta and its creatures.

It was all so obvious now. Aleck had wanted to open up Danta for tourism, so had Scott Gray, according to what Janet had read in his notes. Gray died from a scorpion sting and Aleck was attacked by a fer-de-lance *in his cabin.* That last fact had always sat uneasily with me. How had the snake gotten into the cabin if someone hadn't helped it? But who would want to handle a fer-de-lance? Only someone who had worked with snakes before.

"I worked at the Serpentario in San José for almost a year."

I remembered now the words Liz spat out to Andres after Marco had killed the first fer-de-lance. Serpentario. A collection of live snakes—including the deadly ones.

Was that why Marco had been murdered? Because he'd killed a snake—and not one, but two! He'd killed the snake that attacked me and the one that had gone after Aleck. And it had been *our* climbing rope that had been cut. *Our* first aid kit that had been sabotaged. I recalled the poisonous look Liz had given me after my encounter with the fer-de-lance. Viviana was right. She'd been after both of us.

So. Aleck had been killed because he wanted to open Danta to tourists. Marco had been killed because he'd had the bad taste to actually kill a dangerous snake. Ernesto? It didn't take much of a leap to figure out why Liz had killed him. But the method!

There aren't any deadly scorpions in Costa Rica. I remembered Kelt's words now. But there are some pretty nasty scorpions in Brazil. And Liz had gone to a conference there. It wouldn't have been difficult for her to tuck a small traveler in her luggage.

She'd forced Ernesto into a nest of bullet ants, counting on them to take him out. But when the ants fell down on the job, she'd just trotted out her little Brazilian friend. No big deal. She'd done it before. Ten years ago.

And Guillermo? Candi? Regardless of whether or not Guillermo had been trafficking, Liz had made her thoughts on the matter clear. She'd convicted and sentenced him without a trial. No doubt she'd shot him to make it look like a falling-out between poachers. And as for Candi, I could only imagine what had happened to her. Liz must have followed Marco and Candi to the mooring that morning, planning on taking them both out before Candi could leave. But Marco had told Candi he loved her. And he'd left her by herself after she turned him down. A proverbial sitting duck. Liz could wait on Marco, but Candi had to be eliminated right away. As far as Liz knew, Candi was the only one who could connect her to Scott Gray. Thank the gods Janet never told Liz that she'd inherited Candi's notes. Otherwise, a snake might have crawled into *her* cabin, or a foreign scorpion might have offered to scrub *her* back in the shower.

Apart from Guillermo's murder, all these deaths could have been accidents. That was the dark beauty of them. If I hadn't gone nosing around the antivenin vials, I might never have started making the connections. Now that I had, my mission to get to Sirena was more urgent than ever.

I picked up the pace as much as I could, which wasn't much at all. My bad leg throbbed with each stride and I was getting tired, stumbling over roots as I tried to step over them. I was on a decline. On the last stretch to the Rio Sirena. A small slip now would be possibly dangerous, definitely painful.

By the time I stood on the banks of the swollen river, gasping for breath and staring at the turbulent waters, it was dark and stormy, but it wasn't night yet. That almost made it worse.

In the daylight, I could see what was in the water.

Stained brown with sediment, the river swirled and churned with an angry growl. A thick clump of vegetation bumped by, covered with the sundry survivors of the flood. Fleshy, neon-colored spiders, silvery scorpions, and a solitary, miserable-looking agouti. On another clump, a tight knot of the ubiquitous leafcutter ants formed a mass at one end; the other was occupied by a poison arrow frog hunkered down in the waterlogged vegetation. They huddled on their unlikely ark, predator-prey relationships temporarily forgotten. Drawn together by their instinct for survival.

A large log sailed by. It too had its Noahs clinging precariously to the slick bark. In fact, every piece of debris, every branch, every leaf seemed to function as a life raft for some creature or another. It made me wonder what was going to hitch a ride on me.

"Just go," I urged myself on. "Don't even think about it."

But once I started, it was hard to stop. And until this moment, I'd forgotten all about the sharks.

Hammerhead sharks, I had discovered on this ill-fated trip, often swam up the Costa Rican rivers during the rainy season. When the waters were high and brackish. Well, technically it wasn't the rainy season, but the Rio Sirena looked pretty damn high to me right now. High enough for sharks? I shivered as another icy finger of water found the gap in my collar and trickled down my back. I could think of many more pleasant and much drier places to be. And things were about to get a lot less pleasant and a lot more wet. All I could do was hope I'd been a Jesus Christ lizard in a previous life.

I took a deep breath, choked, and coughed out some water. That's when I saw a figure moving towards me.

I froze. It wasn't tall enough to be Oscar. And none of the others at the station could have hiked this far in their condition. A poacher? The figure moved closer. Silvered by the mist and rain.

Oh gods.

Liz.

I didn't wait for her to get any closer. I could hear her angry cry as I spun around and jumped.

And then, the river took me.

CHAPTER 42

Spinning.

Choking.

Grasping for a tree. A branch. Anything to hang on to.

My backpack weighed me down, pulling me under. I felt the machete twist and tear away from my belt. I was stunned by the sheer force of the churning water. Powerless in its grip.

Something hit me on the cheek. Scraping across my skin. I went under for a second and fought furiously to get back to the surface. The pack was too heavy!

Whump!

My shoulder went numb from the impact. Instinctively, I grabbed. A tree! Broken and splintered on one end, but reassuringly solid in this watery maelstrom. My fingers slipped on the slick bark, and I cried out as it spun from my grasp. I clawed desperately at it. My sleeve caught on a snag and I managed to haul myself close to its dubious protection.

I should have taken my chances with Liz.

Liz.

Was she coming after me? I looked back, but my eyes were blinded by rain and river water and I couldn't see a thing.

The thought of her spurred me on. I had to get to Sirena. I clutched the tree and starting kicking. My legs were leaden, my breath rasping in and out as I kicked towards the far shore. The churning current sped me along. Was I even making a difference? It didn't seem like it. The riverbank blurred by me. I gritted my teeth and kept kicking.

At least there weren't any sharks. And as far as I could tell, nothing had hitched a ride. A golden orb spider washed up onto the tree. It lay there unmoving, probably drowned. I spat out another mouthful of water. Keep kicking, Robyn, I told myself. You won ribbons in swimming, remember?

My bad leg ached with the effort, but I kicked until my legs burned, kicked until they spasmed with cramps. Trying all the while to move diagonally across the current. And still there was no sign of the other side. The brief surge of adrenalin had burned off, leaving me spent and shaking. Stubbornly, I kept kicking.

If this was Hollywood, the passage of time would be shown in a more civilized fashion. With fade-outs and fade-ins. With makeup to achieve that properly exhausted look. With an army of assistants waiting just outside camera range to leap to the aid of the star. None of this unending journey and snot-soaked heroine crap.

I was beyond fatigue. Beyond thought.

Peering blindly through the deluge.

The spider swept away by the churning current.

Coughing.

Kicking.

Time seemed to have gone all tricky on me. I felt like I'd been in the water for hours. For all I know, I might have been. I couldn't feel my legs anymore. And still I kept kicking them.

When my feet finally touched the ground, it took a moment for the reality to sink in.

Solid ground.

The riverbank.

I'd made it.

I took another step. Then a few more. Until my body was half out of the water. I tried to let go of the tree and couldn't. My hands were locked in a cramping grip. With an effort that brought tears to my eyes, I managed to release it. Dully, I watched it bump down the river. I tried to gather enough strength to take another step.

Sirena. I've got to get to Sirena.

My feet stayed where they were.

Everybody's counting on you, I told them.

Still no movement.

Do you want Kelt to know you choked at the finish line?

My feet considered that. And, to my surprise, they moved. One step. Then another. Uphill through the muddy water. Past the slippery rocks. Another step. Staggering. Falling. Icy water filling my mouth, burning my throat. I struggled to regain my footing, came up gasping and coughing. The water at waist-level now. Another few steps. Thigh-level. Step. Step. Then knee-level. I was almost out!

And then, I was crawling through water-choked vegetation. Over the newly formed riverbank. But before I could stand, a sharp shock of pain streaked up my bad leg as a hand grabbed my ankle.

Liz!

The gods knew how she'd managed to follow me. I didn't even know how she was able to hang onto me. I was drenched and covered in slimy muck, but her grip didn't so much as slip. And I felt myself getting dragged inexorably back to the river.

I cried out, grabbing at anything that would give me leverage against her. Grasses sliced through my fingers. My leg was hot agony. Fingernails splintered and tore as I scrabbled at roots. And then, miraculously, I caught a vine. My hands were slick with blood, but I hung on to it and Liz's vise-like grip started to give.

I kicked back viciously and connected with something. I hoped it was Liz. I lashed out again and the hand slipped off my ankle. Without wasting a second, I threw myself up the bank, sliding in the mud, scraping the skin off my knees. When I got to the top, I spared a glance back. Big mistake.

Oof!

Liz slammed into me and all the air in my lungs came whooshing out. I fell back against a palm tree, gasping to recapture my breath, trying desperately to fend her off. She grabbed for me again, yanking my raincoat and wrenching me off my feet. I fell in the mud and before I could scramble up, she was on top of me. I squirmed and bucked, sucking in air with wheezing gasps. It was everything I could do to keep her cold fingers from my neck. We rolled and struggled in the rusty red goo, pulling hair and tearing clothes, each of us so damn slippery with mud that neither could get a purchase on the other.

There were men who paid a lot of money to see this kind of thing.

I rolled again and my foot hit something solid. A tree trunk. A massive one. Without hesitating, I braced my feet against it and shoved Lizabeth away from me. The tree gave me the purchase I needed and the savage push sent her skidding across the small clearing. With a roar, I jumped on her and slammed her head against the ground.

Her bulging eyes stared at me in disbelief before rolling up into the back of her head. And with a massive shudder, she went limp.

Chapter 43

I got to my feet, shaking and coughing. I choked, stumbled a few steps, then fell to my knees and threw up over and over again, dry-heaving when there was nothing left in my stomach.

It took a while for the cramps to subside, even longer for me to realize that I was, indeed, alive. But was Liz? I realized then that I didn't care if she'd died. Regret was not an option. I had never understood predator-prey relationships so vividly in my life. Kill or be killed. Nature was as simple as that. Humans were the only animals that complicated the issue.

I struggled back to my feet and made my way over to her. Now that I could see beyond my own survival instinct, I noticed the rock behind her head. But wait . . . my eyes sharpened. Yes, there it was again. A breath. Faint, but definitely present.

So. I'd only knocked her out. I hadn't killed her, after all.

A second wave of relief washed over me, unexpected this time. Tempered, of course, by what had happened, but still present. I closed my eyes and took a deep breath. I may not have cared if Liz was dead or alive, but I knew then, with a bright sense of deliverance, that I had no desire to be the instrument of her death. That if I had killed her—even under these circumstances—I would have regretted it for the rest of my days.

But just because I didn't want to kill her didn't mean I was going to wait for her to regain consciousness and have her own ethical dilemma. She had already demonstrated a distinct moral vacuity. There were five dead people to prove it.

I propped her against a tree and tied her up with the rope I'd brought from Danta. I honestly couldn't think of another way to deal with the situation. A snake might get her, or a peccary, or even a jaguar. But with any luck they were all too busy surviving the flood. I just couldn't take the chance of having her come after me again. I had no illusions about my victory over her. It had been a total fluke. The gods had taught me a thing or two over the years—like not to count on Lady Luck stopping by every time you needed her.

I marked the spot with a dozen fluorescent orange trail markers. Checked her breathing again. Strong and even. I tightened the knots for good measure. And then I set out for Sirena.

I had no idea where I was in relation to the ranger station. But I was pretty sure I was still upstream from the trail leading to it. Pretty sure. It was not a comfortable feeling.

The hike was a blur.

I was beyond exhaustion now, traveling on reserves I didn't even know I had. The sky seemed brighter somehow. I didn't know if I was imagining it or not, hallucinating from fatigue and shock. But I knew when the rain stopped. And I knew when a beam of sunlight suddenly burst through and lit up the orange ribbon that marked the trail to Sirena. I couldn't have asked for a cheesier cliché. I felt like Dorothy, except instead of finding myself in the Land of Oz, I'd ended up in Hollywood. Land of the happy endings.

By the time I limped into Sirena, the sun was starting to set. Dan and Ricardo had burst from the ranger station and were running towards me. I stopped and dropped my pack, unable to take another step.

Roll the credits, I thought, sinking down to my knees.

And fade to black.

Chapter 44

Phase 1 of the macaw project was essentially complete. We'd proved the macaws were there—and that there was a half-decent population of them. And we were confident that the DNA samples we'd sent for sequencing would prove the birds were a new species. Ahead would be years of study: demographic surveys, population monitoring, food and foraging studies, habitat and ranging behaviors research. Work on the project was only beginning, but my part was finished.

A lot of things had been made clear to me over the past few days. A lot of things explained. A lot of loose ends neatly laced up. Among the most surprising was the revelation that Pepe was a undercover wildlife enforcement officer.

I just stared at Dan when he told me.

"*Pepe?*" I said in disbelief.

Dan nodded. "That's right. Been working in that field for fifteen-odd years."

Fifteen years? The guy looked like an undergrad. "How old is he?" I asked.

Dan chuckled. "Older than you'd think," he said. "I knew what he was, of course, but nobody else did."

"Why?"

"Oscar," Dan said.

"Oscar?"

"Yeah. Seems he's part of a trafficking organization based in San José—same one that shipped those suitcases up to Canada. CITES has had their eye on him for quite some time. Once he wriggled his way onto your project, I guess they decided to send Pepe in."

Oscar. A wildlife trafficker.

It explained a lot of things, most of which I'd already guessed. His intense interest in the amethyst macaws, his suspicious behavior, his so-called cousins who couldn't, as Viviana had said, build an outhouse. And it explained why Pepe had spent so much time chatting up Oscar instead of working on his fictitious research project. Trying to insinuate himself into the organization. But. . . .

"Why did Pepe leave the station, then?" I asked Dan. "I mean, nobody had a clue what he was doing. Why leave? And why like that? In the middle of the night without telling anyone."

Dan's expression grew sober. "He thought Oscar knew," he told me. "The day you guys were finding that caged macaw, there was an explosion in San José. Pepe's partner and his wife were killed."

I sucked in my breath.

"Pepe had his own satellite phone out there and someone gave him the word."

"So he came to Sirena?"

Dan nodded. "Yeah, he called Ricardo, asking him to come first thing in the morning with the boat. I wish now we'd just come and hauled you all out of there."

So did I.

"So what's happening with Oscar now?"

Dan shrugged. "Not sure. I don't know if Pepe found enough evidence to charge him."

I grimaced at the thought of Oscar getting away. I'd told him all about the amethyst macaws. All about our study methods. All about how to find macaws. He'd used me and I'd played right along, mistaking his questions for interest. His kindness for friendship. It left a bitter taste in my mouth.

Dan gave my hand a comforting pat and his wife, Faviola, brought me a plate of beans and rice.

"Have some *gallo pinto* before your plane is arriving," she said kindly.

I smiled my thanks.

"Are you heading home right away?" Dan asked as I tucked in.

I shook my head. "Not for a few days," I told him. "I've got some odds and sods to tie up and the police want to interview me again."

"You'd think they would have asked you everything by now."

"You'd think."

Liz had been recovered where I'd left her. Still tied to the tree. Soaked, furious, and utterly insane. It wasn't like the police had to do much investigating. She had confessed all. Actually she hadn't so much confessed as bragged about it. Boasted of her clever idea to make Guillermo's death look like something it wasn't, of strangling Candi and disposing of her body in a deep ravine. Aleck, Marco, Ernesto, Candi, Guillermo. She'd killed them all. It was still difficult to comprehend. Still surprising that any of us managed to make it out alive.

According to the very polite policeman who had questioned me, Liz believed herself completely justified in her actions. Her predominant feeling was one of pride that she had struck such a blow for conservation. Nobody told her that Andres had started the wheels turning to get tourist volunteers the following season. There was no point. She wouldn't be back at Danta in this lifetime.

"You gonna visit Viviana while you're in the capital?" Dan asked, interrupting my thoughts.

I nodded. "Yeah. She's still in the hospital. But getting better every day."

"You give her my best, eh? Tell her I'll look forward to seeing her next year."

"I will," I promised.

"And what about you?" Dan asked. "Are we going to see you back here?"

"Some day," I said with a smile. "I don't think you could keep me away for long."

"I am glad to hear this," a voice behind me said.

I turned around and met with a pair of shining, dark eyes and a beaming smile that had knocked many the hiking boot askew.

"Come to see me off?" I asked him.

Andres nodded. "Of course! I could not let you go without saying goodbye." He paused and Dan took the unspoken hint.

"I've got some paperwork to finish up," Dan told me with a friendly clap on the back. "You have a good trip back—and don't forget to send me some syrup."

"I will," I promised with a grin. Dan had been reminiscing about Canadian maple syrup for days now. "Thanks for everything."

He winked and sauntered off into the back office.

"Would you like to go outside?" Andres asked. "There are some toucans in the tree by the airstrip."

Even though I'd seen toucans almost every day for the past four months, I had never tired of them. We strolled out to the airstrip and stopped in a patch of shade to watch the birds bounce around in the branches.

"I'm going to miss these guys," I said, as a wave of sadness swept over me.

"But Robyn," Andres said softly. "You don't have to miss them."

I turned and gazed at him. His dark eyes were serious.

"You could stay here," he suggested in that smoky tone. "We are just starting this study. There are many years of work here. And . . . and I would like you to stay."

He was standing very close to me now.

"Andres," I began.

His arms came up to encircle me.

"I'm sorry," I said quietly.

He froze.

"I'm very fond of you," I told him as gently as I could. "And I loved working in the rainforest, but I have work in Canada. I have a life in Canada. I need to go back."

I could see the hurt in his eyes, but he managed to pin a smile on his face and I hugged him for it.

"I will miss you," he said.

"I'll miss you too." My eyes were unaccountably wet.

I suppose I could've quit my job at Woodrow Consultants, found the funding to stay down here. But Viviana once told me that she looked around the rainforest and knew her life's work was here. When I looked around this forest, I saw a wildly beautiful jungle with delights, dangers, wonders, and puzzles to last uncountable lifetimes. Despite all that had happened here, it still touched my soul. It was still *pura vida*. But when I looked around, I knew my life's work was elsewhere. Among the pines and oaks and aspens of Canada. I'd be coming back to Costa Rica, I knew that. Probably even many times. But I *belonged* in Canada. And as I kissed Andres a fond goodbye, I knew I also belonged with a certain Canadian.

"Robyn!" Viviana's husky voice rang out, full of delighted surprise. If that didn't reassure me of her returning health, her bright eyes and pink complexion did.

"You look much better," I told her. "Like night and day."

"I am feeling very much better," she said. "And now you have finally come to visit me. Sit! Tell me everything that happened. I want to hear all the details."

It took all afternoon.

"And what about Keith and Janet?" Viviana asked after I'd finally run down. "Have you seen them? What are they planning to do?"

I leaned back in the chair and shrugged. "Stay at Danta—at least for a while. Keith still has to finish his bee study, but I think he'll be done in another week or so. They told me they'd come to visit you before they went back to the States."

"Good. I would like to see them again. They are nice people."

"They are," I agreed. "It was hard to say goodbye. But they've promised to come and visit me in Canada next year." I paused for a moment. "Viviana, I hope you'll come too. I don't want to lose touch with you."

She gave me a bright smile. "Of course I will come!" she exclaimed. "You have many birds that I have never seen before. I will only come if you promise to show me a blue jay and a snow owl."

I gave her a crooked grin. "I pretty sure I can manage that."

We were quiet then for a moment.

"There's still one thing that's bothering me," I said pensively.

Viviana waited.

"The night we went out with Keith and Janet, somebody searched my bags. Ever since Liz was arrested, I've been racking my brains, trying to figure out what she was looking for. It kind of freaked me out, you know, and I just can't imagine . . . what . . . what are you laughing at?"

"Your bag was unzipped?"

"Yeah."

"And the things inside all in a mess?"

"Well, yeah."

"*Pizote!*" She burbled with laughter. "It was a *pizote*—a coati."

A coati?

"I chased him out of the cabin when you were in the outhouse," she said. "They are terrible bandits—like your raccoons—always getting into things. They can open zippers, no problem. I didn't realize he had opened your bag."

A coati.

I shook my head and sighed ruefully. "Do you know how long that's been bothering me?"

"You should have just asked me."

"I should have," I agreed.

Viviana leaned back on her pillows and gave me a long look. "And so? Now I must ask you something. What about Andres?"

I squirmed a bit. "What about him?"

"I was certain he was going to ask you to stay."

"Well . . . who said he didn't?"

"Ah, I see." She nodded sagely. "This one you told me about before. Kelt? He is the reason you are going back?"

I shrugged uncomfortably. "Partly. I don't know if there's anything there but . . . I guess I need to find out." I gave her a small smile. "Who knows. Maybe I'll be back here sooner than I think."

"That would make Andres happy. And me too." Viviana reached out and patted my hand. "But I do not think you will be coming back alone."

I appreciated the vote of confidence.

I'd deleted the last e-mail I had written to Kelt from Danta, my courage deserting me before I could send it. Instead, I had sent him another one telling him all about Liz and the people she'd killed and a bit about the nightmarish trip to Sirena. I'd tried to be matter-of-fact about the whole thing but, judging from his reply, he had read between the lines. I felt bad for worrying him, but his concerned response had been gratifying. It gave me cause for hope.

"You will let me know how it works out, yes? I will be crossing my fingers for you."

"Thanks," I said with a smile. "I promise."

It was hard to leave Viviana. Life in the field tends to exaggerate things. Likes. Dislikes. Personality clashes. But it also brings you much closer to your colleagues—especially if you're lucky enough to run into a kindred spirit or two. I had close friends in Canada, but I was going to miss my Costa Rican *amiga*.

"You'd better go," she said finally. "Look at the time! You are going to miss your plane."

"I know." I leaned over and gave her a hug. "Take care," I said.

"You too."

I came out of the hospital into the bright, tropical sunshine.

"Taxi?"

A cab driver had spotted my pile of luggage.

"You go to airport?" he asked with a friendly smile.

I helped him load my gear in the back. "Not yet," I told him.

I still had one more thing to do before I went home.

"Senora Vasquez?"

"*Sí.*" The woman looked at me cautiously through the half-opened door.

Her black hair was heavily streaked with gray, pulled back into a tight bun. Her skin was the warm bronze of most Ticos, but her complexion seemed dull, like the dark eyes that regarded me so suspiciously.

"*Soy* Robyn . . . *una amiga* of—I mean *de* Marco," I stumbled.

"Robyn?" The door opened wider. "Robyn Devara?"

"Yes! I mean, *sí.*" I struggled for the words.

"You work with my son," she said haltingly. "With my Marco."

"Yes," I told her. "He was *muy bien* at his work. A very good worker."

She opened the door and motioned me inside. "Come," she invited.

She showed me into a tiny living room with worn furniture and a large painting of the Virgin Mary on the far wall. The other walls were bare except for two photographs, blown up and framed. One was of an older man, probably her husband. The other was Marco.

"You will drink *un café?*" she was asking.

"*Gracias,*" I nodded. "That would be very nice."

She must have had a pot brewing because she was back in a few minutes with a tray of coffee and a small pitcher of hot milk. She seated herself on the couch opposite me.

"I wanted to tell you how much I liked your son," I said slowly, hoping she would understand. "Marco was a very nice man. *Me gusto*. I liked him very much. He was my field partner, you know. He saved my life. Saved me from a *terciopelo*."

If only I could have repaid the favor.

She looked at me, her eyes bright with unshed tears.

"*Lo siento,*" I said. "I'm . . . I'm so very sorry. He was a good man."

Her silent grief was like a spike in my heart.

I broke eye contact and bent to rummage around in my pack. I knew what I was looking for was in the front pocket, but I pretended to search anyway. Finally I pulled out a white envelope.

"Here," I held it out to her.

Her eyes flicked to the envelope, then back up to me.

"Marco was writing you a letter before he died," I explained. "I found it in his room and I . . . I knew you would want it."

Her eyes widened but she didn't make a move to take it.

"It's from Marco," I told her again.

Slowly, without taking her eyes off me, she reached out and took the letter. She held it gently in her lap and, as I watched, the tears spilled over. Her sorrow streaming silently down her cheeks.

I had to swallow a few times before I could speak. "I'm sorry," I said again, my voice coming out gruffly. "I have to go to the airport now."

She nodded and rose, carefully placing the letter in the center of the table. To be treasured later in private. She walked me to the door, still not saying a word. But before I left, she turned and gave me a hug.

"*Gracias,*" she said as she clung to me. "*Muchas gracias.*"

I hugged her back. "*De nada,*" I said to her. It was nothing.

It was nothing and yet it was everything. Such a small thing to do. A brief moment out of my life. But for her, it meant reading the last words from a son who would never come home.

I waved to her before I climbed into the orange taxi and again as it started to pull away. She stood on the front porch and waved back at me. Smiling through her tears. As the cab turned onto the main road, I leaned back against the seat and closed my eyes.

Now I could go home.

Epilogue

My troubles ended when he *walked into the airport. He was a dark brunette, hair more black than brown, and he came in on a pair of legs that had never heard of quitting time. His peepers were green, big, and full of questions. The kind of eyes that could say their piece without tacking on a bunch of words. They were trying to hand me a line right now. And I was ready to listen to them.*

It wasn't the first time he'd sauntered my way, and I was willing to lay odds it wouldn't be the last. I didn't know what kind of scam he was running, but from the look of him, I had a hunch a Swedish massage might be in my future.

I sauntered over and smiled, a slow, sensuous kind of smile. "Going somewhere?" I asked.

Kelt was grinning at me like a fool.

"I couldn't wait to see you," he blurted out. "Thank God you're back. And safe! I . . . ah, screw it." Without further ado, he folded me in his arms and bent his head down to meet my lips.

I was expecting it to be sweet. With all the fantasizing I'd been doing lately, I was expecting it to be wonderful.

What I wasn't expecting was the jolt of electricity that coursed down through my body as my mouth touched his. I stumbled, dropping my backpack, and Kelt's arms came around me, pressing my body closer. It couldn't be close enough for me. His lips glued firmly on my own, Kelt bent my head back and I melted into the most exquisite kiss I'd ever experienced. I hoped he'd keep on holding me up because I was pretty sure my legs weren't up to the job.

When we finally emerged for air, Kelt looked down at me with a sweet smile. "Welcome home."

We hit every red light on the way home. On purpose. By the time Kelt pulled up to my apartment building, I was shaking with fatigue and unadulterated lust.

"You're probably exhausted—" he began half-heartedly.

More like quarter-heartedly.

"Kelt," I interrupted this impressive display of willpower. "Why don't you come upstairs?" I put my hand lightly on his thigh. He was burning up. Or maybe that was me.

He grinned briefly. His eyes were very bright. "I don't know if I can keep my hands off you that long," he admitted, his voice hoarse with need.

I snickered and pushed the car door open. "Race ya."

I was beyond exhausted, my body weak and shaky like warm jello. But happy. Very, very happy jello.

We lay on my bed in a tangle of blankets and sheets and pillows. I had no idea where my clothes had gotten to, but I had a vague memory of leaving most of them by the front door.

There had been a moment of anxiety when I noticed the waistband on Kelt's underwear. 'Mr. Brief,' it said in large, foreboding letters. Not exactly a selling point. But I needn't have worried.

I smiled and pressed the length of my body against

Kelt's. He was so warm. I buried my face against his chest and breathed in the scent of him. He groaned and slid his hand up the back of my neck and under the tangle of curls.

"You're going to be the death of me, Ms Devara," he said.

"Really?" I did something with my hand. "Huh. Look at that. You're not dead yet."

His eyes flew open at my touch. He smiled and took my hand away, kissing my fingertips lightly. "That's not what I meant, and you know it."

I snuggled closer to him. "I know."

"I thought the thing with the spotted owls was bad enough," he said. "But I think Costa Rica has taken years off my life. When I think about what could have happened to you," he broke off and gathered me into his arms. Overcome not by lust this time, but relief. I'd felt the echoes of his anxiety in our lovemaking.

"I'm sorry, Kelt," I said when I was finally able to breathe again. "I don't *try* to get into this kind of trouble, you know. It just seems to . . . I don't know, follow me around or something."

He stroked the curls back from my temples in a gesture so loving I had to close my eyes against its tenderness.

"I know," he told me softly. "I suppose you wouldn't be you if you weren't getting into one scrape or another. It makes me care about you all the more."

I reached up and tangled my fingers in his hair, bringing his head down so I could kiss him. "Remind me to keep getting into trouble, then," I murmured against his lips.

He pulled back, green eyes flashing. "I'll do no such

thing. Look!" He bent his head to one side. "A gray hair! Because of you!"

I laughed and ruffled the offending hair. "Vain," I told him.

"No," he said, serious now, "just very worried about you."

I thought about fer-de-lances and scorpions and Andres with his mangos (though Kelt didn't—and wouldn't—know about that). He'd certainly had cause for worry. I hugged him hard.

"I'll be more careful next time," I promised, forgetting in the heat of the moment what my mother always told me about not making promises I couldn't keep.

More Mysteries from

When it Rains
Laura Cuthbert

Reporter Cait Whyte covers the gruesome murder of a fif-teen-year-old girl and when her article is later found at the scene of another murder, Cait becomes convinced that the two deaths are connected and takes it upon herself to track down the killer.
0-88801-269-1/pb $14.95 Cdn./$12.95 U.S.

The Dead of Midnight
Catherine Hunter

Members of the book club at the Mystery au Lait Café are getting nervous as events from their favorite murder mysteries start to come true—right in their own quiet neighborhood.
0-88801-261-6/pb $14.95 Cdn./$12.95 U.S.

Polar Circus
D.A. Barry

An edge-of-your-seat thriller featuring bickering environ-mentalists, isolated in the Arctic wilderness, who find themselves surrounded by polar bears—and the bears look hungry . . .
0-88801-253-5/pb $14.95 Cdn./$12.95 U.S.

Chronicles of the Lost Years:
A Sherlock Holmes Mystery
Tracy Cooper-Posey

Cooper-Posey picks up where Sir Arthur Conan Doyle left off. *Chronicles of the Lost Years* is the "real" story of Holmes' adventures in the Middle East and Asia during the three years Watson believed him dead—commonly referred to as the Great Hiatus.
0-88801-241-1/pb $16.95 Cdn./$14.95 U.S.

The Case of the Reluctant Agent:
A Sherlock Holmes Mystery
Tracy Cooper-Posey

When Sherlock Holmes' brother, Mycroft, is shot and left for dead, Sherlock is forced to go to Constantinople to uncover the man behind the deed.
0-88801-263-2/pb $14.95 Cdn./$12.95 U.S.

Available at your local bookstore.
www.ravenstonebooks.com